THE THUNDERBIRD ACADEMY TRILOGY

VALIA LIND

Skazka Press

OF WATER AND MOONLIGHT

Thunderbird Academy - Book One

Valia Lind

It takes courage to grow up and become who you really are.

— E. E. CUMMINGS

Have enough courage to trust love one more time and always one more time.

— MAYA ANGELOU

There are no guarantees in life, but I'm pretty sure this day has been the most embarrassing day of my existence. Not only have I snagged my t-shirt on the door, ripping a hole at the seam, I have also managed to knock not one but two students into the wall. It's like I've suddenly forgotten how to be a regular human being. Granted, being a witch, I'll never be normal, but all these stares are driving me insane. I am not one for being the center of attention.

It's the first day of school of my second year at Thunderbird Academy and I, Maddie Hawthorne, feel like I'm a new student all over again. Year one was nice. It was quiet. I kept to myself and hung out with my best friend. I read books over the weekends while I practiced magic in my room. Cool. Fun. Under the radar. Just how I like it.

But then, the Ancient evil started waking up right on the outskirts of my hometown, and our whole magical community has been put on high alert. Now, my best friend is not coming back. The school is in uproar because of the dangers right outside our walls. And, oh yeah, I've apparently become a celebrity because my sisters and I performed an older-than-dirt ritual that cast a hedge of protection around my hometown of Hawthorne. I didn't even do that much, just allowed my water magic to be part of the elements of the spell. My sisters did most of the work. But that doesn't seem to matter. I was there, and therefore, I must've done some impressive magical things.

Now everyone knows about it, and it's like I have a target painted on my back. And front. And sides. They're expecting great things from me apparently.

That's what Headmaster Marković told me this morning while I was trying to hide the hole in my shirt.

"Maddie, we are very proud of you," Headmaster Marković said. "You did your coven a great honor by performing that ritual. There is great power in you, and I look forward to seeing where you go from here."

No pressure or anything.

"Watch it!" A shout snaps my mind back to present. I glance up in time to see a group of guys walk almost directly into a group of girls who are busy staring at something in front of them. There's giggling and hair flips, but I can't make out what has them so fascinated. The guys don't seem very happy to be inconvenienced and ignored. A few try to strike up a conversation when they see the girls, but it's a no go. I smile to myself, duck my head, and keep walking. I need to figure out my room situation. Typically, Kate and I would already have all this figured out, but her family has gone into hiding, pulling her out of school. This danger has set the whole world into panic.

When I get past the crowd of people, I see what all the fuss is about. Three guys are leaning against the wall in that nonchalant, cool way I've always found fascinating. I don't think I've ever been that cool even when I've tried. Which might be my very problem, but that's not the point here.

All three look to be around six feet, or taller. Dark haired and gorgeous, like a star-filled night. They could be on the cover of any magazine with their broad shoulders and messy hair. I can't see their faces, but I imagine them to be just as striking as their build.

I'm only a few feet away when one of them turns, his eyes snagging onto mine, and it's like my whole world shifts. Light blue, like the sky after a rainstorm, they pierce right through me. I think this is the moment I've read about in books where the heroine is swept into an insta-love situation. But instead of a romantic encounter, like maybe a smile, I get a grimace and a hard glare.

My own notions solidify as the guy continues to watch me, and I meet his glare with my own. A flash of something else comes over his eyes, but it's gone before I figure out what it is, and then he's turning back to his friends.

That's fine. It's not like I'm a girl who attracts guys anyway. I've always been a little "too intimidating" as they like to put it. Even though I grew up with two older sisters, I've always been my daddy's girl. While my sisters focused on growing herbs and studying spells, I was more of a feral creature, running wild in the woods.

Since dad doesn't have any elemental powers, he taught me how to live off the land and how to take care of myself. Those times in the woods are some of my favorite memories from my childhood.

My heart grows heavier the more I think about him, and it's difficult not to let the tears fall down my cheeks. He's been missing for four months, and we have no idea what happened to him. Only that he was taken.

That's what this year is about. Finding my dad. I don't care about being popular or well liked. All I care about is learning everything I can about the Ancient evil that has risen and figuring out if they had anything to do with my father's disappearance.

The Ancients were kept a secret from all of us and only those who have in-depth knowledge of our history knew of their existence. That all changed when suddenly my hometown was assaulted by shadow creatures and then struck with incurable sickness. I went home over the summer to try and help. Which I did. But that one small spell is only the beginning. There is so much more to learn.

An announcement alert sounds, and the hallway grows silent instantly.

"Please report to the grand hall for announcements. This is not a request."

The voice sounds almost robotic, and it repeats another three times before it shuts off. There's a moment of stillness right before the student body begins to move. I follow the crowd, trying to keep my head down as much as possible. It's not working.

Thunderbird Academy. A place where anyone can be themselves. Yet, right now, I wish I was anywhere but here.

THEY WON'T STOP STARING. IT'S LIKE I HAVE A NEON SIGN OVER MY head, and the moment I step into a room, it starts flashing. I keep to the back of the crowd, but it doesn't help. It's weird to be here by myself. I already miss Kate's spunky presence and her constant commentary on the Academy. I understand why her parents want to keep her close. A lot of students didn't return because of the dangers brought on by the Ancients.

I think back to the information I recently learned about the Ancients. They were the first to walk the earth. The creatures who created the magic within and around us today. But their selfishness and need for power drove them to evil ways, and they almost destroyed the world. Warring within themselves, they brought on apocalyptic events and nearly wiped this whole earth from existence. Such magic is draining, and eventually, they had to make a choice. They had to slumber to replenish their power, and we have been living without them for generations. Their story has become nothing more than a fairy tale told to little children to scare them into obedience. And then, the stories stopped completely. The only reason I even learned about them was because they were already awake.

A part of me wonders if they hadn't woken up, if I would even have any information about them. For some reason, their presence right under our feet was the biggest secret my parents kept from me. And even still, the only reason my mom knew about them is because of her position as the coven leader. No one else even had an inkling.

When they started waking up, the Elders thought it would only be near Hawthorne. They were wrong. That's not a mistake anyone will make again. *We* will never underestimate them again. Because whether my mom likes it or not, I am part of that solution now. It affects all of us, and that's not something we can hide from.

As I study the faces around me, I realize there are quite a few new ones. Just like with Kate, I know some didn't come back. Everyone is in the midst of this battle now. But there are a lot more people here than would consist of a freshman class. Faces I haven't seen before, both younger and older.

"Good morning, Thunderbird Academy." Headmaster Marković speaks up from the stage, his voice amplified by magic to be heard throughout the whole room. "Welcome back to another year. I know many of you have questions regarding the Ancients, among other things, and I will do my best to address all of them."

He walks across the stage, and it seems that his eyes meet each and every student before he speaks again.

"As you may have noticed, the school is over capacity. That is not a mistake. This school is one of the safest places in the world, and students have been sent here from other institutions for that exact reason." He pauses again, and I glance around. Everyone seems to be riveted. "Room assignments will be given out when you leave this room. You have each been assigned a roommate." There are a few murmurs at his words, but he's not deterred. "Yes, it will be a tight fit, but we will make do. Packets with your class information are already in your rooms. We will have mandatory weekly meetings to keep you updated. Please." He pauses, and I feel the heaviness of the moment fall across the whole room. "Follow the rules. Stay inside the grounds. We will keep you safe, but we will need your help to do so."

With those words, we're dismissed. The students begin trickling out of the room, but I stay pressed against the wall, mulling over Headmaster's words. For them to make a public announcement, it means the situation is much more dire than I thought. The one thing I know about grown-ups is they keep their mouth shut about dangers until the last possible moment. It's that whole trying-to-protect-us concept. Which I hate because I clearly can help, if only I was privy to a bit more information upfront.

I'll need to call my sisters and see if there are any developments. We performed the bonding spell over the town, but everyone knows it won't keep. Other towns have followed suit, and I'm sure the academy has their own sets of protective barriers. Headmaster wasn't kidding about that. This building and these grounds are hallowed, protected by generations of ancestors and their magic. But the one thing I've learned in the last few months is that assuming is the worst thing we can do. The Ancients are too powerful, and we're too unprepared.

I will not be unprepared again. That's a promise I make to myself right here and right now.

When I finally push from the wall and head toward the teachers handing out room assignments, I let that thought solidify within me. This school is a safe haven, but it's also a haven of knowledge. I may not be as strong as my sisters, or as experienced as my mother, but I will do my best to help. Whether they like it or not. After all, I have a few tricks up my sleeve, and I'm determined to use them.

🦋   2   🦋

When I open the door to my room, I have no idea what to expect. I've always thought I'd room with Kate, if the time ever came for that. Instead, a pretty blonde greets me with a tentative smile.

"Hi, I'm Jade," she says, standing in the middle of the room. We study each other in silence, assessing each other. She's about my height, with hair down to her collarbone. She has bright makeup on and a red cami and jeans. She looks colorful next to my dark t-shirt and dark jeans.

"Hi. I'm Maddie."

"Well, this is awkward," she says, after another pause.

"Glad you called it." I chuckle a little, shutting the door and walking to my side of the room. My name is on the packet lying on the bed. I rip it open and do a quick read through of the classes. I have independent study this year which means I'll have time to sneak over to the hidden library I found at the end of last year. That's a knowledge I have only been able to share with two people, both of whom are no longer here. Kate and Liam. While Kate is hidden who knows where, I know where Liam went. Back to Fae. That is one place more secure than the grounds of Thunderbird Academy. I shake away the melancholy of missing my friends and look up as my new roommate speaks up again.

"Look, I don't expect us to be best friends or anything," Jade continues, "but I hope we won't be enemies."

I smile at that because I understand. I've heard horror stories about being roomed with someone who makes your skin crawl. I never thought I'd have to worry about it at Thunderbird Academy because we've always had our own rooms.

"Well, at least there's not three of us in here. Because that might cause some friction," I reply, and that earns me a smile. I'm not picking up anything that would set off any internal alarms in me, but I also don't dive in headfirst into trusting people. It'll take time, but at least we've broken the ice.

"Are you a transfer too?" she asks as she turns back to her side of the room and begins unpacking her suitcase. My duffle waits for me at the side of the bed as well. Part of the service provided by the academy.

"No, this is my second year here. Where did you come from?" As I ask the question, I realize that maybe she has no idea who I am. It's possible if she's not from around these parts. My last name is pretty known in the witchy circles, but there's a possibility I'm not as talked about as I thought. It's a nice reprieve.

"A small town in southern California called Idyllwild."

"I don't think I've heard of it," I reply, turning to lean against the bed. She moves around the room, placing a few items on her desk, including a framed photograph of what looks like her parents.

"It's not super known, but it's a good community. We've always lived there. It's in the San Jacinto Mountains surrounded by pine trees, which is, like, my favorite part. I went to a secular prep school out there and then took classes within the coven. But with the Ancients coming around, my parents wanted me somewhere safer."

She glances at the photograph then, a tiny frown forming between her eyebrows that I can relate to all too well. I feel the same sadness anytime I think of my family.

"It's just the three of us," she continues, still looking at the picture. "I've never been away from home before."

"Don't worry, they'll be fine."

She looks up at me sharply, surprised by my nailing down her concern without even trying. I may not be a Reader witch, but I've picked up a few tricks from my sister's best friend, Krista. It's becoming easier to discern people's emotions the longer I do it.

"I'm worried about my family too. It's natural. It's not exactly safe out there."

And I don't think it's safe in here either. But I don't add that last part. I know Thunderbird Academy is more protected than most of the places around the world right now. Sure, there are other academies offering their campuses as protection. Magic schools have become sanctuaries. But a part of me is worried that by doing so, we've also become a bigger target.

"Well, maybe if you're not too busy later," Jade begins, shaking off the sadness like a pro, "you can show me around the academy?"

She looks hopeful and I get it. Last year, I was lucky to have Kate here with me. Jade doesn't have anyone. I think we can both use a friend right about now. So, I give her a warm smile before replying.

"Well, I'm claws sharp, and I have no problem with that."

Jade stares at me with confusion, and that's when I realize what I said. Shrugging a little, I explain.

"My dad and I have this running competition to see how many older phrases and slang we can discover and use in our everyday conversation. *Claws sharp* means having a lot of knowledge about various things."

Jade's laugh rings out, but it's not a mocking one. I can tell she finds it as amusing as I do.

"That's pretty great," she says, grinning. "You will have to translate though because I'm completely clueless in that area."

"Deal."

"Your dad and you must be close," she comments, as we turn back to our suitcases. My hands freeze, reaching for a shirt, a pang of hopelessness shattering my bravado.

"We are," is all I say, but she must hear something in my voice.

"Maddie?"

I can't exactly keep this a secret. I'm sure she'll hear all about me when we step outside these walls and into the rest of the academy. But for a second, it was nice to pretend everything in my life was fine. I turn to face her once more, resigned to the truth.

"My dad is missing. He's been missing for about four months now. We're not..." I stop, swallowing audibly. "We have no idea where he is or what happened. He was on a research trip for Ancient defenses and then he was gone."

"That must've been awful," she whispers, and her eyes flicker to her photograph before they're on me once more. She's clearly close to her family, so I don't have to explain how this hurts me.

"I'm going to find him though," I say, standing up straighter, determination fueling my words. "I will do whatever it takes to figure out what happened."

"I'll help anyway I can," she says, and I believe her. There's an air of kindness about her, and I decide to trust it.

Maybe having a roommate won't be such a bad thing after all.

WE FINISH UNPACKING, CHATTING ABOUT OUR LIVES AND COVENS, and while she's a lot more hyper than I am, I like her. I still haven't mentioned my last name. I know it'll come up eventually, but it's kind of nice having someone not know who or what I've done.

When a bell dings three times, I glance at the clock and see that it's dinner time. Jade offers me a confused look, and I motion her toward the door.

"Three dings means mealtime. They don't use the PA system very often, just to notify us of the beginning of the day, meals, and important announcements. If you hear continued rings, seek shelter. It means immediate danger."

"Good to know," she replies, nodding her head.

"Don't worry, they go over the rules in orientation. And I'll stick close to your side until you figure it all out. Plus, we have three classes together. That'll help."

"I have to say, I expected more magical classes," Jade comments as we leave the room and head toward the dining hall. A crowd of students is migrating that way as well, and it's really noticeable just how many more people are crammed within these walls.

"You'll have plenty of magical studies," I assure her, staying close as we make our way through the crowd. "Even regular classes like English and History always have magical applications. It's how the school works. Which I love, to be honest."

"I can understand that."

When I started here last year, I had the same thought. Why wouldn't I have potions or spell casting classes? But the headmaster, along with the teachers, want to make sure we have a proper knowledge of every subject in the world. After all, we live among the humans.

"It's a buffet style setup," I say, as we walk into the large rectangular room. There are floor to ceiling glass doors at one end which are typically open once the weather cools down a little more. Tables are set up throughout the space with the buffet at the opposite side of the room from the doors, near the entrance. It's a good setup, except when you have twice as many students present. It'll probably take a while to get food and find a seat.

I spy the headmaster standing next to Mr. Olsen, the history teacher. They're conversing, but their eyes continuously scan the room. I'm not sure if it makes me feel better or worse having them here.

"So, are we going to talk about the fact that everyone seems to be staring at you?" Jade asks, as we get to the back of the line. I groan aloud, receiving a few more looks thrown my way, and a part of me wants to glare in return.

"I probably should've mentioned..."

"That she's a Hawthorne."

The deeps voice comes from my left, and I turn in time to see the guy from earlier step up to the line. He reaches past a few people, grabbing an apple off the counter.

"Excuse you, there's a line," I say, annoyance dripping off every word.

"Yep, I see it," he replies, moving past us and grabbing a few more items off the counter. No one stops him, which makes me even madder.

"Hello! You are not the only person here," I say, taking a step toward him. He turns, his eyes flashing as he does a once over.

"Eyes on my face," I snap, and they instantly fly up to meet my own. A mask of indifference comes over his features before I can decipher any of his other emotions.

"Does Duchess have something to say?" he asks, and his voice burrows straight under my skin, irritating and exciting me at the same time. Why does he have to sound so good? That deep baritone is made for secrets.

"Don't call me that," I almost growl, taking a step closer to him. "In case you haven't noticed, there are people waiting. I don't know what kind of manner-less hole you crawled out of, but it's polite to let people in line be the first ones to get the food they've been waiting for."

"Wow, Duchess has some bite to her. Here I thought you were all bark." His friends step up then, and he hands over the food he grabbed before taking a step toward me.

"You're a jerk," I say, not backing down.

"Never said I wasn't."

We stare at each other for a second longer before he moves past me, making sure to keep a wide berth and then he is gone. I glare at his retreating back before I step back into line next to Jade.

"Wow, that was hot," she mumbles, keeping her voice as soft as possible. A school with all kinds of supernatural beings requires us to be a particular kind of careful. Shifters, for example, have amazing hearing.

"That was annoying," I reply, but she's still grinning at me. "What?"

"Nothing. I've just never heard of anyone standing up to shifters and live to tell about it."

"He's a shifter?" I ask, a little louder than I intended. Jade narrows her eyes at me for a second, contemplating.

"You have no idea who he is?"

"Only that when I first got here, he made sure to glare at me from across the room."

The line moves forward, and we finally reach the counter. Grabbing a plate, we begin piling on food. I'm so hungry, I'll have no problem finishing the salad and Mac and Cheese.

"Well, he was in the registration line with me, and I know his name is Aiden and he's a wolf shifter. And that he's hot. So are his friends. Is that a shifter thing?" The words tumble out of her, and I have to laugh.

"Maybe. The pack in our town consists of pretty good-looking men," I reply just as a table opens up, and we hurry to it. It's right by the glass doors, and the forest outside makes me think of Hawthorne and my family. The last time I walked through the woods, I was with them.

"I'm sorry I didn't tell you who I was," I feel inclined to say. I didn't mean to not tell her.

"I knew who you were, Maddie," Jade replies, shrugging, before she takes a bite of her sandwich.

"But you didn't say anything," I point out after a small pause.

"I didn't want you to feel awkward around me. What you guys did, it's pretty incredible. But it's a lot of pressure and responsibility to carry around with you. You clearly need a break from all the scrutiny."

I stare at her, completely in shock. It's kind of what Kate would say if she were here. A grin splits my lips.

"I think I love you," I say, and then we burst out laughing. It's much needed after the day I've had, and maybe it's not the most embarrassing day of my life after all. It was a pretty full one though. I managed to make a friend and an enemy. I wonder what comes next.

⚜ 3 ⚜

The first week of classes is pretty uneventful but busy. Every teacher has given us their course curriculum, freaking me out at how much work there is to be done. I've had no time for my own research. When Saturday morning comes around, that's all I want to do. Figuring out how to sneak over to the secret library, that's the real problem.

Jade is sitting at her desk, head bent over a history book. We have a few chapters to read, but she's actually pretty good at this, considering she went to a secular school. I know some other students are struggling because they've never been outside their coven or its teachings. But my roommate has adapted better than expected.

The whole secret library thing is a bit of a conundrum though. I have a feeling Headmaster Marković knows I've found something, but he hasn't really asked me about it. And the few times I tried telling him, or even my sisters, something always prevents me. I think there's a spell on the library, which would explain a lot. Except for why it was revealed to me. Liam and Kate have both been inside the room, and that is the only reason they know of its existence. Whatever the case with that place, I'm thankful I was the one to find it. If it wasn't for one of the books in that room, we never would've figured out that the ritual my sisters were trying to perform was missing an ingredient.

"I'm going to take a walk," I announce, getting off my bed. "I'll be back in a few."

Jade doesn't look up from her studies, just waves a goodbye in my direction. I really am starting to like this girl. It's not like I'm replacing Kate, who I still haven't spoken to since I've been here, but it feels nice having someone on my side. Especially since I have someone against me.

Actually, it feels like I have a lot of people against me. Jealously is a powerful emotion, and it seems like many students here have been displaying it towards me. Or resentment. Or something I can't even name. Aiden is on top of that list. Every time he's in the vicinity of me, I can feel his hot glare on my skin like a brand. Thankfully, we only have two classes together. So, I guess it could be worse.

Even now as I walk down the corridor, the few students who are out of their rooms give me a quick glance. I can't explain the reasoning behind it, but I won't be pushed into hibernating in my room. Even though it's one of my favorite activities. It will be my choice to hide away, and that's what I'm planning on when I reach the secret library.

The school has always fascinated me. It's housed in an old castle building, but it's far from ordinary. The layout, if looking overhead, is c-shaped. But every part of the building is unique. The central area near the front doors, which I'm passing at the moment, is of the old baroque style. It's very theatrical in its display with grand staircases on the outside and inside, on each side of the front door.

The rest of the castle can only be explained as eclectic. Dad and I actually did research on various styles used to make up the design of the building. The west wing, in which Jade and I room, is mirrored after the Neo-renaissance style. I had no idea that was a thing before I read up on it. Apparently, it was a mixture of gothic and French Renaissance. The east wing is more Neo-gothic, and there are spires everywhere. If I could describe exactly what all these styles mean I would say they are very extravagant. The creators of this place liked to be flashy, but I can't say I don't like it. It gives the school character and I love it.

The east wing is where I'm headed now, to the greenhouse built attached to it. Last year, I spent quite a lot of time among the different plants, researching potions and natural inspired spells to help my sisters. That's when I discovered an old cellar and the staircase that lead into the tunnels under the school. When I followed the pathways it took, I stumbled onto the greatest treasure. A library, much like the one we have back home, but filled with ancient texts.

The place looks like it could be inside the building with large windows and greenery on the other side of the glass. It's a circular room, filled to the brim with books. But when I tried finding a way to go outside, there isn't one. I'm not sure if it's glamour or what, but it's fascinating.

So lost am I in thought, that I don't even notice Aiden until I'm almost on top of him.

"Aren't you a little far from home?" he asks when we're only a few feet apart. I always have to prepare myself for the impact his eyes have on me. It's like he can look directly inside of me.

"Shouldn't you mind your own business, Aiden?" I don't think I've ever said his name before, and it jars me as much as it jars him. He stares at me for a second too long, and I feel it all the way down to my toes. Snapping myself out of our staring game, I move to walk around him when he steps in front of me.

"I *am* minding my own business, Duchess. You're in my hallway." It takes a lot of self-restraint not to comment on the nickname again, but I don't. Because I know he enjoys the fact that it gets under my skin. Instead, I meet him tit for tat.

"I don't see your name on it," I reply, placing my hands on my hips. We're back to our staring contest, and if there is one thing my sisters and I have in common it's that we don't back down from confrontation. Mom calls it stubborn. Dad calls it hard-headed. I take both as a compliment.

"Maybe you should look a little closer." He takes another step toward me. There's now only about three feet separating us, and the effect of his closeness is more unnerving than that hated nickname.

"No, thank you," I reply, looking him straight in the eye, "I have more important things to do. Like count how many lime trees are in the garden."

If I wasn't watching him so closely, I would've missed the way his mouth twitches at the corner. I think I almost got to him and that elevates me. I take a step, but he's not done. He moves with me, continuously blocking my way.

"Is there something else you need?" I finally ask, giving him one of my sweetest smiles. He blinks at me a few times. I expect another fight, but just as suddenly as he appeared, he takes a step back. "Carry on, then."

I move past him without a second look and half walk/half run toward the greenhouse. I know for a fact this isn't his hallway. He's two stories up in the southeastern corner of the building. I overheard some of his pack mates talking about it in the dining hall two days ago. He lives to annoy me, and if I'm to survive his torment, I need to add a few more items to my arsenal.

But right now, I push all thoughts of him away and head to the greenhouse. The secret library awaits.

⚜

THERE ARE A FEW STUDENTS IN THE GREENHOUSE ALREADY WORKING on their independent study projects. Since I'm a water witch, most of my independent study will be done by the pond on the east side of the property. A part of me is ridiculously excited, but another part of me is nervous. I'm only sixteen, and since my powers manifested when I was five, they've been unpredictable. What makes me nervous is the fact that since the ritual with my sisters, they've been pretty dormant. Still there, but it's as if they're taking a break.

Not that I would fault them, if that was a thing I could do. The ritual required the use of all five of the elements: Earth, Fire, Air, Water, and Spirit. The rest of the witches involved, my sisters included, had a powerful booster alongside them.

The soulmate bond.

As I walk around the different plants, waiting to sneak over to the cellar, my mind mulls over the legend. When I was younger, it was one of the bedtime stories my mother would read me.

Soulmates were a belief that there are two parts of a whole out there, and when one meets their other half, their hearts and magic are bonded to outrageous degrees. Up until seven months ago, this was just a myth. But then Connor returned to his pack and ran into my sister in the library. A witch and a shifter is not a union approved by many. Most of the time, it's looked down upon. But if I've ever met two individuals more perfect for each other, it would be them.

Then, of course, came Mark. A witch from another coven who swept my oldest sister off her feet. He and Bri are perfect for each other in every way, and it was their bond that awakened her active powers. I wouldn't say I'm jealous, I'm ridiculously happy for my sisters. But I am wishful. I can only ever dream about a connection such as theirs.

During the ritual, they had the soulmate bond on their sides. I didn't. Even weeks after, I can still feel the bit of drain on my magic, which I really hope will get replenished before I have to cast in public. I'm sure that'll go over well with the student body. A powerful witch with tiny magic.

With my mind going over everything, I don't notice the students moving out of the greenhouse until I'm alone. After another quick study, I walk over to the south corner of the room and move aside a few strategically placed palms. Then, I remove the wooden crate over the door, and I'm in.

The steps are pretty old, and the darkness is unnerving. But I've come prepared. After arranging the plants and the crate so it's not noticeable right away, I descend into the tunnel. People aren't usually in this part of the greenhouse anyway, but I try to stay as cautious as possible.

I've only brought Kate and Liam down here, and both times it was out of necessity. When I couldn't outright tell them about what I found, I could only show them. A part of me was sad, considering I loved having the place to myself. But I guess that resolved itself out, considering here I am again, all alone, descending into the darkness.

After about a six-minute walk, I timed it at one point, I'm in front of the doors. They look like any doors back in the academy. When I place my palm against the wood, it shudders, before opening up.

When I step inside, it's exactly as I left it.

The ceilings are incredibly high, and the bookshelves line every wall. It's a circular room with a few desks and chairs in the middle. And piles and piles of books. The view outside the window is just as comforting as the smell of books inside. The forest is strikingly green and full, and it makes me wish I could go outside and explore.

Instead, I make my way toward the desk closest to the window. The last time I was here, I had about four books on the table, and I see that they're all still there. Sitting down, I leaf through the pages, as if acquainting myself with an old friend.

For the first time since I stepped back into Thunderbird Academy, I am truly alone.

The thought makes me breathe easier for a moment, before the onslaught of emotions assault me.

The pang of missing my dad hits fast and hard, and I almost double over. There hasn't been even a clue to his whereabouts since he's gone missing. All that was found was his suitcase in the hotel he was staying in, but no information on what he was doing there.

He should be home. He should be reading books and trying to figure out how to fight the Ancients. But instead, he's gone, and for the first time in a week, I let myself feel it.

I miss my family. I miss my sisters. And I'm scared. All the time.

I can't let people see just how terrified I am, but I've experienced firsthand just how powerful the Ancients are. I can't pretend the fear away. But that's exactly what I've been doing. With everyone's eyes on me, I can't let myself breakdown. Even though I want to, basically at all hours of the day.

From the core of my being, I let it all go. So, when the tears start to fall, I don't wipe them. I let myself cry in this underground magical library as my heart misses my dad and breaks for the hole he's left in my life.

I cry for my family and the trials they continuously have to overcome to stay alive.

I cry for every person in this school and every family they represent.

Here, away from the prying eyes of the public, I let myself be a teenage girl and feel every emotion.

Because I know the moment I step back into the halls of the

4

"Do you think Mr. Olsen assumes he's the only one we have to do homework for?" I ask Jade as we head out of his class two days later.

"I feel like all the teachers assume they're the only ones giving us homework. But I can't deny I'm fascinated about this paper."

"You want to write about the infamous Salem witch trials?" I'm surprised. Most witches I know stay away from that subject, but Jade seems genuinely excited.

"I actually do!" she exclaims as we head to lunch. "It's such an interesting part of our history, and something that links us to the human world, even more so than they realize."

Of course she would be fascinated. She grew up in a mostly human community. And she's right about the connection. From what I know, most of those who lost their lives weren't even witches, but witches did their best to protect the humans from the stupid prejudice of the government. So many more lives would've been lost if the covens didn't step in. But I also know many still carry the heaviness of the knowledge that they couldn't save everyone. That's something I'm all too familiar with.

"Don't look now, but Aiden is staring again," Jade whispers as we grab our food and head to the table. I don't need her to tell me. I felt his gaze the moment we stepped into the room. It's like he's attuned to me, much like I am to him.

"I have no idea what his problem is," I say, before I raise my voice just a tad. "It seems like he needs a hobby. He must live a boring life."

I know for a fact that he heard me, even across several tables, because I swear, I can feel the air chill around me.

"You really shouldn't provoke him like that," Jade whispers with a smile. "But it's pretty entertaining to see you go at each other."

"Thanks," I reply dryly. "I'm glad someone is enjoying themselves at my expense."

Not that we've really "gone at each other". We've had three interactions total, and they went much like our first one. Or the current one. He glares, I poke fun, sometimes there's growling. But I'm not really mad at her. If anything, I'm mad at myself for letting him affect me the way he does. We've become these weird enemies, and I still have absolutely no idea what I've done to deserve it. One of these days, I will ask him. Until then, I will hold my ground.

I've only taken about two bites of my sandwich when the PA system sounds, and a robotic voice begins an announcement. But even before it can begin, it's cut off by the continuous alarm. There's a pause in the air while everyone tries to figure out what to do, and then everyone is on the move. Chairs are pushed back in panic as students begin to scramble for cover. Some begin to scream as bodies clash together, trying to climb over tables to get to the exits.

"Come on, this one means serious danger," I say, reaching for Jade's hand. Before I can take it, we're pulled apart by people trying to get out of the room. I have to shoulder my way through the throng, and then I'm grabbing her arm and tugging her behind me.

The moment we're in the hall, I realize we're never going to make it to our room on time. The larger number of students in the school makes it very difficult to move around, much less head to the opposite side of the building. I flatten us against the wall, trying to stay out of the way.

"We're never going to make it," Jade says, coming to the same conclusion. She looks at me with fear in her eyes, and I try to think. I need to find a place to hide. Somewhere we can protect ourselves. The rooms seal with magic once the residents are inside, and I can already see students pushing into rooms that are not their own.

"Come with me."

I twist around to find Aiden on the other side of Jade, his eyes hard. I open my mouth to protest, but he cuts me off.

"My room is closer. Come on."

He turns, heading toward the stairs, and now it's Jade who doesn't hesitate. She grips my arm and pulls me behind her as we weave through the bodies. With Aiden in front of us, it's much easier to make it up the stairs. Once on his floor, we race toward his room, stumbling inside just moments before the alarm shuts off. He closes the door, and the quiet slams into us. I can feel the magic of the school sealing us inside as we stare at each other, Jade and I breathing heavily.

"What's happening?" she asks, glancing between Aiden and me as the two of us continue staring at each other. He doesn't take his eyes off me when he answers.

"The school grounds have been breached."

❧

Jade has been pacing for ten minutes now while Aiden leans against the door, and I stand by the window. I've been trying to see if anything is going on out there, but the lawn has been completely deserted.

"How can the school have been breached?" Jade asks for the third time, and I can't blame her. This is supposed to be impossible, but here we are. Not even two weeks into the school year, and we're already in lockdown.

"Jade—"

"There's—"

Aiden and I speak at the same time, and I glance at him in time to see him nod. I accept it for what it is and reach for Jade to bring her toward me, sitting down on the bed.

"The truth is, we don't know what's going on. Maybe this was a test. Maybe something set it off without it getting inside the school's grounds. There's no telling the possibilities. We just need to stay calm until we can know for sure." My soothing voice and solid explanations seem to get through to her and she nods slowly. Then, she stands, walking over to the window and proceeds to stare outside.

I can understand her concern. I'm worried myself. But I know better than to display that kind of emotion, especially in front of a shifter. I'm not about to let a predator treat me as prey just because I'm feeling weak. Folding my hands on my lap, I do my best to keep them from trembling.

"Not bad, Duchess," Aiden comments, still leaning against the door. He's been guarding it as if he's afraid someone is going to get in if he leaves his post. I throw a glare his way, but I don't engage. Instead I turn my eyes to the rest of the room, studying it fully for the first time.

It's not much to look at. There are no decorations, or personal items. Just textbooks and notebooks along with a cup full of pens. The beds are made, and the rest of the area is as spotless as if no one actually lives here. I have questions, but I don't want to ask those either. I just need to keep it together until the doors unlock, and I can get out of here.

"Really? No response?" Aiden isn't deterred by my silence. "I thought you were all about confrontation."

"What is that supposed to mean?" He knows he's got me, and I silently curse myself for giving in.

"Nothing particular. Just that you seem to like the spotlight. Being a hero and all."

I see Jade glance over at us, but she's staying out it. He watches me for a moment, waiting to see what I'll say. Instead of the anger I expect to feel, all I feel is tired.

"Look, my sisters are the heroes. They're the ones who are eager to be on the front lines of this. I'm more of a background noise," I reply, almost sighing.

"Right. Because sneaking out of Thunderbird Academy and bringing vital information to them in Hawthorne, before you participated in one of the biggest rituals known to man, is totally staying in the background." Aiden folds his arms in front of him, staring me down. Both Jade and I look at him as if he's lost his mind. For a second there, he doesn't sound like he hates me. There's a hint of admiration in his tone, and it punches me straight in the gut.

"What? They had a class on my life where you're from?" I ask, meeting his eye.

"I like to know what I'm up against." He offers it up like a challenge, and I feel his look across my skin. Even though I'm trying hard not to let him see just how affected I am, a tiny shiver races up my spine.

"I did what I had to do to help my family. That's all there is to it."

He watches me with a newfound curiosity, his head cocked to the side. I wonder what he sees when he looks at me, what it is he finds in me that he has to hate.

Before we can take this any further, a single alarm sounds before the robotic voice comes over the PA system.

"All students and faculty, please report to the grand hall. Headmaster Marković will make an announcement."

The voice repeats the command three more times, but Aiden and I continue to watch each other. I can't even begin to guess what he's thinking, but then, he pushes off the door, yanking it open. Jade hooks her arm through my elbow, and we follow him out in silence.

I don't know what's going on in this school, but I can add Aiden to the list of frustrating puzzles. He's driving me bonkers.

⚜ 5 ⚜

The grand hall fills up fast. Jade and I find ourselves in the back of the room, around the same area I huddled on the first day of school. For some reason, I expected Aiden to stay by us, but the moment we're inside, he moves toward his friends without a backward glance. I want to talk to Jade about him and the confusing emotions currently warring inside of me, but then Headmaster Marković steps up to the stage, and a hush falls over the room. He looks more tired than I've ever seen him, and it makes me more nervous than I'd like.

"I wanted to take a moment and put your fears to rest," he begins without preamble. "The school's grounds have not been breached. I repeat, they have not been breached."

A murmur goes through the room, and I have a list of my own questions rising to the tip of my tongue. Jade and I exchange a look, but we don't speak.

"The alarm was not faulty, and there was danger right outside our borders. We decided to initiate the lockdown for two reasons. One, to see how fast we can get the school under lock and key. Two, we needed the freedom to check on the threat without worrying for your safety. Know that your safety is always the priority here."

He pauses again, but no one even makes a sound. The whole room seems to be holding its breath, waiting for him to go on. He does that slow study of each individual before he speaks up again.

"I do not want to keep secrets from you. I want you to always be prepared and to understand that there are many dangers out there. Not all of them come from the Ancients. I would like to be able to tell you that nothing can touch us here, but that is not true. While this is the safest place for you, it is a place that has a target on its back. The Ancients know of these schools, and they will not rest until they penetrate each and every one of them. However, they are not our only concern. There are still those radicals who wish us harm. We have always stood on the border line of our magical world and the human one. It has always been up to us to keep the world safe. We just have to work that much harder at it now."

He takes a deep breath before he continues. A feeling of dread washes over me, as if I know something is coming. And his next words solidify that thought, chilling me to the bone.

"While this is not something you have considered for yourself, we are instituting mandatory combat training for everyone," the headmaster announces, and this time it's not a murmur that comes over the room. Everyone seems to be talking at once. The headmaster doesn't shush us, letting the students get their feelings out of the way.

"But most of us are not preparing for Task Force or protection detail after graduation," one of the witches closer to the front points out, her voice quieting the rest of the students.

"You are correct," Headmaster Marković says, looking down at her. "And while you do have your battle magic, sometimes an enemy cannot be defeated by it. Or by manmade weapons. I want each of you to be able to pick up a dagger or a sword and hold your own."

Jade and I exchange another look, but I don't even know what I can say. She looks scared, and I'm sure I do as well. Combat training is not something everyone is cut out for. There is a reason only the select are involved in such intense training. There is a possibility our bodies won't even be able to handle the strain, although that depends on the intensity of the training. My mind catalogues all these facts as Headmaster Marković continues.

"You have all been paired with a trainer. The information will be in your rooms. Please report to your appointed place and time. While this is not something you chose for yourself, I do ask that you choose to excel at it. It may be the difference between life and death. Dismissed."

Jade turns to me, her eyes big and round. Most of the students have never used battle magic, and now, they're being trained for combat. There's a heaviness in the air as people begin trickling out of the room. No one seems to want to talk about it. As I study my fellow students, I see fear and apprehension mirrored in each one. So many thought this would be a safe place, and now, it's like we have nowhere to go. We're halfway to our room before my friend speaks up.

"They're making us into soldiers," Jade whispers, and I shake my head.

"We're already soldiers, Jade," I say, the reality of the situation clear in my mind. "They're just making sure we're competent ones."

⊗

"DO YOU HAVE ANY IDEA WHO THE TRAINERS ARE?" JADE ASKS A FEW hours later, as we sit on my bed with the envelopes on our lap. There's no name on the paper, just a room number and a time. I am to report to the building on the eastern side of the property tomorrow at three o'clock in the afternoon. Which makes me a bit curious, considering most of the classes are in the main castle. From what I've heard, special permission needs to be given in order to work in the areas around campus. I wonder the reasoning behind this.

The other paper that was left on my bed is a note from my sisters.
We're fine. Everyone is safe. We miss you.

Just three sentences to keep me updated. I hate this communication lockdown more than I can say. When Headmaster announced it, I really thought I could handle it. But now, I just want to be able to pick up a phone and talk to my family. Right now is definitely not the time to be thinking about that. I tear my eyes away from the paper and get back to the issue at hand.

"I would guess the students training for Task Force," I reply, focusing on Jade. The Task Force is basically our magical law enforcement. Many go on to serve in human equivalent positions, such as police or FBI. Some stay as personal protective detail within different cities or towns. These are the best of the best, men and women who have spent most of their lives training for this. I can always spot them from across the room. It's an upper level program that requires extra classes on top of the regular ones everyone else attends. There's an exam after your second year, and if you don't pass it, you get moved to a different group. Until you can retest again. They're the only ones I can think of who would be up to this task.

"It's so weird," Jade comments, bringing my attention back on her. "I've never imagined myself using any of the defensive arts I've learned."

"Have you ever used battle magic?" I ask, genuinely curious. Most witches our age haven't. I've heard that some covens don't even teach it until later in life.

"Once. And it wasn't even a huge deal." I nod but don't prod further. Battle magic is a tricky subject. I know from firsthand experience, some witches don't like talking about it. I'm not about to push Jade if she doesn't want to talk about it.

"It's just so strange," Jade bursts out, turning to me. Okay, I guess she does want to talk about it. "I mean, battle magic is all instinct. Regular spells have words and rules, but with battle magic, it all comes down to feeling. It seems uncontrollable."

"You're right, it's uncontrollable and a little scary." She glances at me sharply as if she didn't expect me to agree. "But it's part of us, just like anything else. I think it's important we learn how to use it now and not when it's too late. We shouldn't be afraid of our magic."

"I've never met anyone like you," Jade comments, cocking her head to the side.

"What do you mean?"

"I guess it's probably because I don't know that many witches our age, but you seem to be wise beyond your years."

Playfully, I push her shoulder and she laughs. It's not as if I had a choice about growing up. Everything that has happened in the past year has taught me I need to take every lesson and learn from every situation. There is so much more to discover about my magic and the magical community overall. I want to be ready.

"One of the witches who now lives in my hometown," I say, getting back to the original subject. "Is a boxer. For fun. I've never met anyone like her. But she can take care of herself in hand to hand combat like no one I've ever seen. I think it'll be interesting to learn such skills here."

"You would." Jade chuckles, before getting off my bed.

"What is that supposed to me?" I narrow my eyes at her.

"Just that no matter how much of an introvert you say you are, you are always up for trying something new and exciting."

I smile at her, letting her words warm me from the inside out. It's something my dad would say, and I appreciate it that much more hearing it now. He's the one who taught me how to love the learning process and how to explore the world around me. I need the reminder, because most of the time, I feel as inadequate as they come.

"You know, Aiden was right," Jade says, keeping her voice soft.

"I don't think I ever want to hear those words again," I reply, but not unkindly. She chuckles, sliding a notebook off the shelf by her bed before turning to face me.

"You are a hero. It's in you. Which is why I know you will find your dad. You'll do whatever it takes. I just know it."

She sounds so sincere that I do the only thing I can do. I jump off the bed and give her a tight hug, letting her know without words just how important her friendship is to me. She clings to me just as tightly, and I think we both need this. Regardless of whether I said it or not, today scared me. And I know from the pit of my stomach that it'll only get worse before it gets better.

❧ 6 ❧

All morning and afternoon, the only thing I can think of is the training. Classes seem to drag as my mind is full of possibilities. A few students already had their first lesson and so far, there are no issues. As soon as classes are over, I don't even bother with lunch. I rush over to my room and change into a pair of leggings and a loose t-shirt before I pull on my tennis shoes and head toward the building.

Most of the school is housed inside the huge castle, but there are a few buildings scattered on the grounds, used for various purposes. I've never been in this one, even though it's the closest structure to the main campus. It's three stories high, windows on every side. It looks like it was once a barn that was later converted.

Once inside, I head to the third floor. The room I'm training in is the farthest away in the corner. When I step inside, I see two walls covered in windows. However, even though it's sunnier than anywhere else I've been today, it's a nice, cool temperature. With this many windows, it should be a sauna in here, so I'm thankful for whatever magic is keeping me from dying in the heat.

There is no one else in the room, so I do a few stretches before I head to the window and proceed to study my surroundings. This is a good vantage point, and I can see over the tops of some trees closest to the structure. From where I'm standing, I can see the pond and the tiny island in the middle of the water. A bit of my magic flares up as I think about running my hands through the tiny waves created by the wind, and it makes me smile.

When I hear the door open behind me, I don't turn around right away. But then, before I even do, I feel him there. Slowly, I raise my eyes as I look over my shoulder and I find Aiden standing right by the entrance. He doesn't look happy finding me here, and I wonder if he also wasn't told who he'd be working with. I wouldn't put it past Headmaster Marković to be secretive.

We continue our stare down, and I'm trying very hard not to be the first to break. I need every victory I can get when it comes to the shifter. I don't seem to get many. Aiden seems to come to some kind of a decision then because he finally leaves the doors and walks to the center of the room. After a moment, I come to stand in front of him, neither one of us ready to speak. He continues to study me, and it takes a lot of self-control not to fidget under his imploring gaze.

After what seems like an eternity, he rolls his shoulders and finally speaks. I count this as a victory.

"Have you ever had any self-defense training?"

His voice still gives me goosebumps, but now it seems to be followed by a shiver up my spine. I hate how he affects me, and I hate it more that my body has become a traitor when he's near.

"My dad taught me some basic moves," I reply, keeping my voice as professional as possible. The room is large, it can probably house a hundred people easy, but it feels like the walls are closing in on me.

"Such as?" he asks in that same spine-tingling tone.

"Knee in the groin, the heel of the palm to the nose, kick to the side of the knee."

Aiden nods as I rattle off the list, his eyes as unreadable as always. What I wouldn't do to take a peek inside that stonewalled facade. I would love to know what ticks him off, purely for selfish reasons. If I knew what got to him, I would proceed to do exactly that.

"We'll start with some basics and go from there," he says, rolling his shoulders once again. I don't think it's a nervous tick, but I've seen him do it a few times.

"Why do you do that?" I find myself asking before I can stop the words, and his eyes flash as he looks at me. But now that I've asked, I refuse to back down. Maybe even a few months ago, I would've said never mind or sorry. But I'm not that girl anymore. I can't afford to apologize for my curiosity. When I don't flinch away from his hard glare, he does the shoulder roll again, but surprisingly he answers.

"My body is looking for a shift." His answer is gruff and to the point, but now that's he's given me this small gift, I'm hungry for more.

"Does it mean the wolf is dominant?"

"The wolf is always dominant," Aiden replies, no longer looking me in the eyes.

"So, how do you suppress him?"

"It's not really suppression," he replies as he begins to circle around me. "I am one hundred percent me, and I am one hundred percent wolf. But when my—" He stops abruptly as if he's about to tell me more than he wanted. "It's complicated," he finally says, "and not why we're here."

Then, before I can figure out what his intentions are, he moves toward me.

"Defend yourself."

❧

MY ARMS FLY UP TO HOVER IN FRONT OF MY CHEST, A WALL BETWEEN him and me. When he's close enough, I thrust both hands out, pushing him back as I take him by surprise. It doesn't take long, and he's on me once more. My knee flies up, but he's prepared for me and deflects it. Then, before I can think too much about it, his arms are around me, and he's holding me pressed against him, my back to his chest. He lifts me straight off the ground, and I dangle in his arms as I try to find a way to get at him.

"Let me go!"

"I don't think that's how this works," he growls right into my ear, and I'm too frustrated to keep my body's response hidden. A shudder goes through me and he pauses. I take advantage of his hesitation and stop struggling, making my body go completely dead weight. The move surprises him enough that he stumbles forward, and before either of us can know what's happening, we're falling.

But Aiden is faster than gravity, apparently. He twists in midair, landing solidly on his back, with me still pinned to his front. A gush of air leaves him, ruffling the hair at the back of my neck, and then I'm scrambling off him.

When I'm about two feet away, I turn to see him still on the floor. Alarmed, I rush toward him, but recognize my mistake the moment his arm snakes out and grabs my foot. He pulls me down, catching me with his other arm, and then he shifts us so that I'm under him, arms pinned overhead, legs captured by his own body.

"Not fair," I whisper, his face just inches from mine. The blue of his eyes drinks me in, as if he's just as fascinated by the closeness as I am.

"Sorry, Duchess. But there's nothing fair about war."

I bristle instantly, squirming beneath him, which puts our bodies even closer, now with the added effect of friction. He growls and I freeze instantly. That was a purely animalistic sound, and I felt it everywhere.

"One of the biggest lessons you can learn is never to trust anyone. Your friend can become your enemy. Don't be afraid to hurt them."

There's something behind his words that goes straight to my heart. For the first time, I think there's genuine emotion in his eyes, and it makes me stumble over my own breath. We stare at each other, neither one of us ready to burst this tiny bubble we have found ourselves in. I don't know what possesses me to speak up, but I do.

"That's a very sad way to live." My words are only a whisper, but the moment is gone, and he's moving off me while he pulls me to a standing position in the same motion.

"It's a way of life that will keep you safe. More so than what your dad taught you about self-defense."

"Please don't talk to me about my father."

I'm not sure why his words hurt me, but they do. I rearrange my clothing, giving myself a moment to reign in my emotions. I'm not about to cry in front of Aiden. He's the last person I will ever allow to see my weakness.

"And why not? He clearly fuels your actions at the moment. Tell me why."

"I don't owe you anything."

"Maybe not. But I was assigned to train you, and I need to know what I'm working with."

"You already have a perfectly fine notion of me in your head. I would hate to ruin it with the truth." I finally meet his eyes, delivering the words with a glare. But Aiden isn't deterred. For a second, I think he might smile. But I have yet to see one of those on his lips.

"I know he's missing."

"You don't know anything."

"You think the Ancients took him."

"Of course they took him! Why are we even talking about this?" I turn away, ready to leave all this behind, but he moves in front of me, blocking the way.

"We're talking about this because until you learn to control your emotions, you won't be able to control yourself."

"Oh trust me, if I had no control over my emotions, you and I would have an entirely different relationship."

His eyes flash, and the intensity in them burns me to a crisp. I realize too late how that sounds, but I'm not about to take any of it back. He stands his ground, and I have no idea who's winning or losing anymore. I can't seem to figure anything out where Aiden is involved.

"Are you so sure it was the Ancients that took him?" His question surprises me.

"They've been messing with my family for months. It's what makes sense. Why are you so determined to keep me from thinking they're the bad guys?"

"That is not what I said."

"Then, what are you saying?"

"Look, everyone knows the Ancients aren't the only ones hungry for power. There's plenty to fear out there even without them breathing down our necks. Some are using this as an opportunity to further their agendas. We have to stay on alert and consider all options."

"So what?" I snap, throwing my hands up in the air. "You think someone besides the Ancients took my dad?"

"Maybe." Aiden shrugs, completely unfazed by my outburst. "All I'm saying is you can't just automatically blame it on them. That seems like the easy way out."

That sets my blood to boil. I get right into his face, our bodies just a few inches apart.

"Nothing about this is easy!" I hiss, trying to control my anger and magic, which is finally showing its presence. "My dad is missing, and I have no clue what to do about it. Maybe you don't know what it means to feel so helpless, but I do. I don't need a lecture on my emotions. I'm holding it together just fine."

Something flashes in Aiden's eyes, and it's as if, for a second, he doesn't hate me anymore. I think he almost reaches out, and I notice just how close we're standing and how heated my body has become. But then I'm the one who moves away.

"I think we're done for the day," I announce before Aiden can come up with another biting remark. "I'll see you later."

Surprisingly, when I leave, he doesn't stop me.

7

When Jade and I go to dinner, we opt to sit with a group of our classmates instead of at a table by ourselves. I know she noticed I returned much earlier than I should've from my training, but she didn't press the issue. I can tell she's bursting at the seams to ask. I'm sure I'll be getting the third degree later. But for now, I hide in the crowd.

"Is it true that the Ancients are as big as a house?" Noel asks, and I zero in on him. He's watching me carefully, but there's definite excitement at the prospect of an answer.

"Noel," Jade hisses, and he ducks his head. It's been kind of an unspoken rule that my friends don't bombard me with questions. I met Noel last year, but we were never more than casual friends to each other before. Now he's part of my friend group, and as I glance around at the rest of the people at the table, I realize they're all curious. Apparently, it took someone over two weeks to be brave enough to ask, and I resign myself to my fate. After all, if I can't talk to my friends, who else am I going to talk to?

"I haven't seen one that big," I sigh, before turning back to my food

"What about those ones that can shift but into anything?" Vera asks in her calm manner. Her wavy shoulder length hair swings as she

40

ducks her head to take a bit of her sandwich, her light brown eyes focused on me. She's a second year like Noel and me, but she's a hawk shifter, so we didn't hang out last year either. But it explains her interest in shifters.

"It's possible."

"Have you see their minions? I heard they're like flying shadows." Christy pipes up, flipping her long black hair over her shoulder and leaning towards us. Christy is a transfer like Jade, but she comes from another academy school. It's smaller and only houses witches. They disbanded when the danger became too much for them to handle, but Christy is the only one who came here. The others went into hiding with their families, much like Kate's family did. Not that I can blame them. This isn't exactly the safe place we were promised it would be.

"I have." I take a bite of my lasagna, hoping the conversation is over. But no such luck. I answered one question, I've opened the gates.

"How was it to be there, in the midst of it all?" Noel asks, leaning close to me. He's sitting on my left while Jade is on my right, and I can feel her shooting daggers at him. I glance up to find his face very close to mine, completely enthralled. But before I can answer, a shadow falls over the two of us. Noel and I glance up to see Aiden standing by our table, a hard look in his eye.

"We need to talk," he snaps, as if I've offended him with my very existence. I give him an annoyed look before I turn back to my food.

"Can't. Busy."

"I see just how busy." I glance over at him and find his eyes on Noel. Not for the first time, I wish I was a Reader because I'd like to know what he's thinking. He half growls at my friend, and I've had enough. Pushing back my chair, I jump to my feet before grabbing his arm. There's a collective hush over the table at my manhandling a shifter, but I don't care. I'm too angry to care. I pull him behind me as I march out of the room and into the hallway, which is mostly deserted due to the fact that we're in the middle of dinner.

"What is your problem?" I ask, dropping his arm as if it burned me. It's true what they say, shifters run a little hotter than most beings. I can still feel the imprint of his skin against my fingers, sending tingling sparks up my arm, but I can't dwell on that at the moment.

"I don't have a problem." He shrugs, and it takes a lot out of me not to punch him in the gut.

"Oh really? You just enjoy growling at my friends for fun?" I place my hands on my hips, which is now my favorite pose when I'm around Aiden. He brings all kinds of responses out of me, ones that I'm not very used to.

"I wasn't growling."

"You were too! What has Noel ever done to you?" He seems taken back by my words for a moment, considering most people steer clear of confronting shifters. But if my sisters' significant others have taught me anything, it's that sometimes pushing a shifter's buttons is the best thing I can do. Even though it's dangerous. Aiden recovers quickly and is once again his stoic self.

"We need to talk," he repeats himself, bypassing my question. I roll my eyes as I fold my arms in front of me.

"So, talk."

He narrows his eyes for a moment, studying me in that intense way of his. But I don't back down. I've already decided that's the only way I will survive dealing with him. I have to give as good as he does.

"You ran out of training early today."

"That's not news to me," I comment when he doesn't continue right away.

"You're not making this easy."

"Did you want me to hold your hand through it? Whatever *it* is."

His eyes narrow again, glancing down at my hands, and I swear the temperature goes up a few notches. My mouth has a tendency to say things that can have a double meaning. At least when it comes to Aiden.

"I'm trying to say I didn't mean to make you feel as if what happened to your dad wasn't important. I just get frustrated sometimes by how easily everything is blamed on the Ancient evil, when there is plenty of regular evil out there."

His outburst takes me back a little, and I think it surprises him too. It's more than he wanted to share, that's for sure. He's apologizing, in his own weird way, and I can see this isn't easy for him.

"I get it," I say, meeting his eye as I shrug. "People can be very single-minded about all kinds of things. Magic is one of them."

We stand like that for a minute, each of us unsure of what to say or do next. We haven't reached a truce, far from it. But the fact that he would come and seek me out, it shows promise of... something. I just have no idea what.

"Practice tomorrow?" he asks, his voice softer than I've ever heard it before. It tugs at my defenses, and suddenly, I can't speak. So, all I do is nod. He looks at me for a moment longer, before he walks away. I stand frozen for a moment, waiting for my extremities to start working again.

The way he looked at me just then... I'll be thinking about that long and hard.

❧

"ARE WE GOING TO TALK ABOUT IT?" JADE ASKS THE MOMENT WE get back to our room. Once I could walk again, I made my way back to the dining hall and finished my dinner. My friends decided against bombarding me with any more Ancients questions, so instead we talked about school. But I knew Jade wouldn't let it rest, which was proved correct when we walk into our room.

"I don't know what you're talking about." I shrug, heading for my closet. As I pull out my pajamas, I can feel her eyes on me. When I turn, she's standing in front of her bed, waiting me out.

"Ugh, fine. What, Jade?" I sigh dramatically.

She giggles a little before running over pulling me toward my bed. She sits, turned toward me with an expectant look in her eyes.

"Yes?"

"Oh my gosh, Maddie! You're the worst. Tell me what happened with Aiden. And what happened earlier when you came back like thirty minutes before you were supposed to be done with training. And you were all flushed. "

"I was not flushed," I argue, but maybe I'm protesting too much. Knowing what will come next, I try to speak softly. Not that it helps.

"Aiden is my trainer." There's a pause, then Jade squeals and claps her hands. "Seriously, Jade. What is that reaction?"

"That reaction is you tumbling around on the mat, all hot and sweaty, with one of the hottest guys in school."

"Who hates me. Don't forget that part." But I can't help feeling slightly flushed right now at the mention of Aiden and me... tumbling on the mat.

"I don't know. There's a fine line between love and hate, no?" She wiggles her eyebrows, and I can't help but chuckle.

"You are a hopeless romantic," I say, which earns me another grin.

"And I'm proud of it. But seriously." She sits up a little straighter, a note of seriousness coming into her voice, "I've heard he's one of the best recruits they have. I'm not sure if he's doing Task Force after or what, but he's been trained from an early age. He's a great teacher to have."

"If only we didn't hate each other," I point out again, and it's her turn to roll her eyes.

"So, what was the dinner thing all about?"

I was kind of hoping she would bypass that, but no dice. I realize I'm about to add fuel to her theory with my reply, but I don't have a choice.

"We got into an argument at training. About my dad." She reaches over at my words and gives my hand a squeeze. "He came back to kind of apologize. To make sure I'll be in training tomorrow."

"Awe, that's so sweet."

"Jade." I give her my best glare, but she's not deterred. She's enjoying it way too much.

"He was very alpha in the way he nearly bit Noel's head off, did you see that?" I'm still not one hundred percent sure what that was about, but maybe shifters are just territorial in general. If I was to let my imagination run wild, I'd think it had something to do with me specifically. I'm sure that's what Jade is thinking, but I don't need any more help in that department. I think about him way too much already.

"Yes, I saw that. I made sure he knew I wasn't happy about it."

"Honestly, Maddie. I think you're the only witch I know who has no fear when it comes to shifters. The way you pulled him out of there? I nearly had a heart attack."

"I guess it's because of my family," I reply, shrugging a little. "I mean my sister is marrying a shifter, as soon as he asks her. Which I think may be soon. But they're adorable, and my sister's best friend Krista? She's marrying a shifter too. Although he's half Fae. And Mark's sister, the guy Bri is in love with, she's with a shifter too. So, I guess you can say they've changed my perspective on shifters."

"See? Romantic." Jade points her finger at me. "You're in perfect position to explore all this tension between Aiden and you."

"Get off my bed, weirdo." I laugh, and she jumps up to her feet. I don't want to think about Aiden in any way. When the heart gets involved, all reason goes out the window. I've seen that happen to my sisters, and even going back further, I've seen it with my parents. It's not like I don't want that kind of a relationship, to have someone in my corner twenty-four/seven. But I can't let myself get lost in the fantasy. Maybe I have a different outlook when it comes to shifters and witches, but this won't be that kind of a story. I have more important matters at hand.

For now, I pull out my history homework and dive into reading. After all, I'm at the academy to learn.

❧   8   ❧

"**Y**ou're not trying."

"I swear Aiden, if you tell me one more time that I'm not doing my best, I will blast you out of that window."

We've been at it for almost an hour, and I don't seem to be getting any better. I don't know if it's because of what Jade said earlier in the week or the way he looked at me, but I've been on edge even more than usual. We've had five lessons so far, and I'm still making no definite progress.

"Maybe that's your problem."

"Excuse me?" I round on him.

"When was the last time you released your magic?"

I freeze in my tracks, stopping whatever tirade I was about to unleash on him because I honestly cannot remember. My magic has been mostly dormant since the big spell a month ago, but I haven't even tried exercising it. I've been too afraid to see if I have any left.

"That's what I thought. It's been weeks since the ritual."

"So?"

"So, I think you need a release."

I'm pretty sure the images that assault me at that point have nothing to do with magic. Well... maybe just a different kind of magic.

I really need to get my head screwed on straight. I'm becoming unhinged.

"We haven't had any spell casting classes yet," I say slowly, realizing that he may be right. I haven't channeled my magic since I've been back. Being around him, I'm more hyperaware of every heartbeat and every creak of the floor. Maybe it's my magic that's making me so unbalanced.

"Okay, show me what you got." He steps back, folding his arms in front of him as he watches me.

"Right now?"

"No time like the present."

I want to argue, I want to refuse. But I do neither of those. Walking over to my water bottle I unscrew the top before placing it back on the floor. It's been way too long since I've practiced my magic. I take my time as I head back to the middle of the room, concentrating on my breathing and keeping my mind clear.

I can feel Aiden's eyes tracking my every move, but I don't look at him now. If I do, I'm not sure I'll be able to keep going. This needs to be between me and my magic.

When I'm in the middle of the room, I take a deep breath and reach out. I feel the magic rush through my blood, energizing every part of my skin. It races to my fingertips and it's like welcoming back a friend. Instantly, I feel better knowing it's still there, one with my being. I open my eyes, calling upon the water, and it lifts out of the bottle and races toward me as if it's been waiting for the freedom to fly.

With a flick of the wrist, I leave it hovering in front of me. Another flick, and it begins to shape. It spreads out like a flower blooming. The petals dance around the center as I move my hand left to right and back again. After a moment, I bring my hands together, and the water is once again an orb, hovering in front of me. With palms touching, I twist my hands in a circle, creating a cyclone. Then, just as it's picking up momentum, I send it flying into the air above me, and it bursts like a firework, leaving behind hundreds of stars in the ceiling above our heads.

"That's incredible." Aiden's voice is only a whisper, but it reaches deep inside me and makes itself a home there. I turn toward him, thinking he's watching the water and my magical stars, but his eyes are entirely on me.

"Just a little magic," I reply, and suddenly, I can't take my eyes off him. It's as if I'm seeing him for the first time, and there's no one in this world but Aiden. My gaze roams over him, hungry to take in every detail. His dark complexion, his messy hair, his intensely blue eyes. The t-shirt that clings to his chest in all the right places. I watch as his arms flex, a muscle jumping in his upper arm, and then my eyes are on his hands. They seem strong and capable, as someone who can hold me and chase all the demons away.

My magic flares up, and the water around us explodes, tinnier than the raindrops, but they don't fall on us. We're surrounded in a sparkling bubble of water lights, and it's more mesmerizing than anything I've ever experienced before.

Aiden inhales and the movement of his chest spurs me into action. Tearing my gaze away, I raise my arm in the air and motion the water back into a sphere. Then, I walk over to the water bottle, and pick it up. The water rushes back in, and I seal it with the cap.

A heavy quiet falls over the room and I find that I can't turn around and face Aiden. My display of magic was unexpected, and I don't know what to do with the feelings he evokes in me when he looks at me that way. But it's not like I can hide from him in this large room with just the two of us in it. So, I force myself to turn around.

He's standing exactly where I left him, his eyes still on me. I can't begin to guess what's going through his mind. But we need to get back to even ground because I feel like it keeps shifting under our feet. I'd never call myself brave, but I take the first step toward him now.

"Shall we?" I ask, jarring the silence with my words. He seems to recover as he nods, stepping up to me. Without a sound, he attacks.

I know he's holding himself back, slowing down his moves so I can figure out what to do, but I'm still so new to this it's difficult to keep up. Aiden reaches for my hand and I twist into it, wrapping it around my torso, as I slam into his front with my back, my elbow at his gut. He catches the blow, pinning me against his body, and the heat radiating off him momentarily fogs my senses.

Aiden picks me straight up off the ground, and I remember to relax my weight. He's ready for me, but I slip just enough, and I throw my head back into his face. The move is startling enough that he drops me back to my feet, and I twist in time to deliver the heel of my palm to his nose. At the last moment, he snags my hand, pulling it behind my back, which puts my chest directly against his.

We're both breathing heavily, our faces inches apart. Something is happening to me, and I can't put a name to it. He was right of course, I'm much more focused after the magic release. But I'm also much more focused on him.

"That's better," he says, releasing me suddenly and taking a few steps back. "I think we're done for the day."

Then, without another glance my way, he's gone, and I'm left standing in the middle of the room wondering what just happened.

❧

THAT NIGHT, I CAN'T SLEEP. JADE WAS GONE MOST OF THE EVENING with a study group, which was a blessing and a curse. I didn't want to answer any more questions about Aiden, but I also didn't want to be left alone with all my thoughts. Which is where I am now, tossing and turning at two in the morning, trying to shut off my mind.

After a few more attempts, I give up. The rule is that no one should be wandering the halls after dark, but I need to get to the library. Maybe putting myself into work will help.

Carefully, I slide out of bed and reach for my leggings and a hoodie. Both are black, like a lot of my clothing, and perfect for staying in the shadows. I don't put my shoes on until I'm out of the room and moving toward the greenhouse.

The toughest place to sneak through is right by the front doors. With the two staircases going up on each side, there's always a concern that someone is across the way. Since the Ancients started waking up, everyone has been on high alert, which means the school has extra patrols now. A lot of them are graduates who went into Task Force or protective agencies. Sometimes, the student who are in higher levels of training are assigned to participate.

I manage to get down from our floor and onto the main one without too many accidents. Luckily, I haven't ran into any shifters because they would be able to sniff me out, even if I am hiding. When I finally make it to the east wing, I have to wait a few patrols out, but then I sprint toward the greenhouse without a second glance.

Thankfully, no one ever patrols inside the greenhouse. I have to keep away from the floor to ceiling windows, since there are patrols outside. Other than that, I just need to make sure I don't make any noise moving the plants and the crate.

Before I make it too far into the greenhouse, I pause. With the moonlight bathing the plants in its glow, it looks magical in here. I've never noticed just how many of the plants thrive in this atmosphere. My oldest sister, Brianna, would know each of these by name. I just know there are flowers that bloom only at night.

When a small noise comes from behind me, I'm instantly on alert. My battle magic flares up, coming much easier now that I've exercised it a little, and I start moving carefully past the row of plants. When Aiden steps in front of me, I nearly have a heart attack.

"Chicks on a raft! Do you have to sneak up on me?"

"You're the one sneaking around," he replies, his eyes sparkling in the moonlight. It almost looks like he's going to smile, but no luck.

"I wanted to come see the night blooming flowers." I pull out the first excuse that comes to mind, a little proud of myself.

"Nice cover. Also, did you just say chicks on a raft?" This time there is definitely amusement in his tone, and I can't help it. I like it.

"It's similar to eggs on toast."

"Still not sure how that relates to your current situation."

I shrug, probably enjoying this a little too much. But his question does bring with it quite a few memories. A part of me wants to share all of it with him, but I have to remind myself that Aiden and I are not friends. This isn't show and tell.

"It's something my dad says when he's surprised," I reply, going for the truth but keeping the emotions out of it. I don't need to break down in front of Aiden. He watches me for a moment longer before he nods, as if coming to some sort of conclusion. Instead of replying, he begins to walk around the greenhouse, looking over the plants. I feel like we lost some of our footing again, but then he speaks up.

"So, are you going to tell me why you're really here?"

I bristle at that, his tone ruffling my feathers. There's that footing I've been missing.

"If you don't believe my explanation, that's on you."

"I just know you a little better than that," is all he says as he continues to move around. Now it's my turn to follow him, a little peeved at his words.

"I'm not sure you know me at all," I announce, stopping near one of the blooming plants. Instead of looking at him, I study the flowers. I have to admit, they are worth the price of admission.

"Don't kid yourself, Duchess. You're not that complex."

That... that makes me angrier than I thought he could. Spinning on my heels, I face him head on, not realizing how close he's standing. I have to look up into his face, cursing his tall physique.

"You know nothing about me. You should really get your head checked out. I think you're becoming delusional," I state, my hands once again on my hips. He doesn't seem affected by me at all, yet here I am, all tangled up in little knots.

"You're honestly telling me you would risk reprimand by sneaking out of your room after lights out to come look at some flowers?" he asks, his words washing over my skin. He's so close, I would only need to move forward a few inches, and I'll be pressed against him.

The moment the thought enters my mind, I shut it down. What is wrong with me? I'm like a lovesick puppy all of a sudden, and I have no idea where it came from. I can make up a hundred excuses here, or extravagant stories, but for some reason, I settle for the truth once more. Maybe a part of me does want him to know me a little.

"If you must know, I love flowers. Any and all. They bring me joy. So yes, I would risk reprimand to come see something as unique and beautiful as a flower blooming in darkness."

My honesty descends on us like a blanket. I expect him to contradict me, or make another biting remark, but he doesn't. He studies me for a long minute, in which I try to keep my breathing as even as possible. Finally, he speaks.

"I'll walk you back to your room."

❦ 9 ❦

"What is one of the most recognizable events in human history revolving around magic?" Mr. Olsen asks the next morning. I've gotten so little sleep, it's difficult to stay awake. Even though history is one of my favorite subjects, my mind is either drifting to mine and Aiden's walk back to the room last night or just plain zoning out completely. We didn't talk on the way back, and even though I didn't tell him the truth about why I was in the greenhouse, I offered him a bit of an insight about myself. That's not sitting too well with me right now. He keeps winning, and I don't like it.

He's in this class, of course, so there's no escaping the fact that I can feel his presence. Even though I refuse to look in his direction.

"Come on, I know it's not even eleven o'clock yet, but someone give me an answer."

"Salem witch trials," Vera answers from the front. Mr. Olsen claps three times, stopping in front of her desk.

"Thank you, Vera. The rest of you haven't even started on your papers, have you?" I vaguely remember Jade mentioning this, and when I glance at her, she shrugs. I really need to check over my course curriculum to make sure I'm not missing assignments. I'm usually so good at keeping ahead of the curve. I can't believe after three weeks, I'm falling behind.

"Your paper, for those of you who haven't began their research, is about the effects the Salem witch trials had on our community. Specifically, how it affected you personally." He looks each of us in the eye before continuing. "What is one misconception that is known about the trials?"

This one I know, so I raise my hand.

"Miss Hawthorne?"

"That any witches were killed."

"And why is that?"

I realize everyone is looking at me now. I'm not sure what possessed me to answer, since I've been trying to keep a low profile, but here we are. Even though I won't turn in his direction, I can feel Aiden's eyes on me.

"Because those who were put on trial were simply humans under the influence of a fungus."

"Do you know the name of the fungus?" I'm waiting for him to move on from me, but he continues to watch me, waiting for an answer.

"Ergot." Thank you, Bri for making sure I had that knowledge stored away. I remember my oldest sister going on and on about the way people, human and magical, have a tendency not to treat plants in the way they should be treated. After all, we are elemental witches and our connection to the earth is what makes us so strong. Bri has studied plants her whole life and runs an herbal shop now. I've heard her Salem witch trials story more than once, and now I'm super glad I paid attention.

"Very good, Miss Hawthorne."

He moves away then, heading back toward the front of the classroom.

"As Miss Hawthorne pointed out, yes. No actual witches were killed during the Salem trials. Those accused of witchcraft were found yelling and screaming and convulsing, spreading mass panic across the villages. Many of your ancestors were there and tried to help the best they could. It is a known fact that they healed and saved countless individuals who could've been dragged to court but were never even suspected. Sadly, they couldn't get to everyone.

Because of this one event in history, people outside these walls have an idea of witchcraft that is warped. With the rising of the Ancients, we're on the brink of another historical event. Some major events have already happened." Mr. Olsen looks straight at me as he says it, and I want to crawl under the desk. "Some are still in front of us. It is important that we don't allow outsiders to write our narrative. This is why I want you to do this paper. I want to hear your history and your family's history relating to one of the most well-known historical events. I think we can all learn something from it."

He dismisses the class then, and instead of jumping up and rushing out of the room, I take my time. Jade doesn't even question it, but matches my pace, as the rest of the class files out in front of us. I feel Aiden move past me, but I don't raise my eyes, and I don't react. After the room is clear, I finally glance up at Jade.

"We really need to talk about this, girl," she says, and I nod. I'm not getting out of this one.

❧

WE GRAB A COUPLE OF APPLES AND COOKIES BEFORE WE LEAVE THE dining hall behind. Neither one of us feels like being inside at the moment, and the weather is just cool enough that we don't need to go back to grab our jackets.

Heading east away from the school, we enter lime avenue. It's a literal road lined with lime trees. Once spring hits, it's one of my favorite places because it smells amazing. However, we don't linger here now, but move past the trees and toward the pond. Dropping our bags on the ground, we take a seat right next to the bank. Being this close to a large body of water makes me feel elated.

"Maddie, spill," Jade says, as she breaks off a piece of her chocolate chip cookie. I chuckle at her words.

"Wow, let's just dive right in then."

"There's no other way." Jade shrugs in response. "You've been avoiding me all week. And don't think I didn't notice you sneaking out last night."

"Well, that's definitely not true. The avoiding you part." I bite into my apple, chewing slowly to prolong the not talking, but Jade is smart. She continues to wait me out until I have no choice but to give in.

"Oh, fine," I mumble, turning to face her as I criss-cross my legs in front of me. "Here's the short version."

I give her a quick recap of my week of training, including the magic lesson and the run-in last night. When I'm done, Jade is wearing the biggest grin on her face.

"Please don't do that," I say, turning to stare out at the water. I didn't quite mention how he's been making me feel, but I think she knows.

"I can see why you've been so cagey lately," she says. "Doing magic with a boy, tsk tsk."

"That's dramatic," I roll my eyes, but I realize she's right. Aiden watched me perform something that is sacred to me. He saw my powers as a display in front of him. Usually, that's only done between two people who trust each other immensely. I don't think I've ever showed off like that with anyone outside my family.

"You know, he has to shift in front of you now. That's the only way you'll balance the scales." I glance at her sharply. I didn't even think of that. I'm way out of sorts when it comes to him. Apparently even more so than I thought.

"I don't even know why he hates me, Jade," I find myself saying, my eyes back on the water.

"Maybe he doesn't."

"He does. I can almost feel it coming off him like steam. Ever since I met him."

"Now who's being dramatic?" she replies, shaking her head. "You don't know if he does. You only think he does."

"Well, he hasn't exactly put out the welcome mat."

"Neither have you," she points out.

"Okay, whose side are you on?"

"I'm on the side of the truth!" Jade puffs out her chest, saying the words as if she's proclaiming them to the world. Very dramatic and very Jade. "But also, I'm always on your side," she continues, lowering her voice.

I believe her. I've only known her for a few weeks, but I already can't imagine the academy without her. I miss Kate terribly, but with her in hiding, there is a piece of my heart that yearns for a friend. And I have found one in Jade.

"Have you heard from your parents?" I ask, turning the conversation back to her. I know she's been worried since we've been on a pretty tight communication lockdown. I haven't spoken to my family once since I've been here. Headmaster has been relying messages.

"I got a 'we're okay and proud of you' two days ago but nothing else."

I reach over, squeezing her upper arm in comfort as the sadness coats her voice.

"They're safe. That's what's important."

If anyone can understand being close to their family, it's me. Truth be told, I think that's what bonded me to this girl right away. There's something special in a person who loves and appreciates their loved ones. It's the kind of bond that speaks to me on a very personal level.

"Thanks, Maddie," she says, taking a deep breath. "It's just hard not being there. What if something happens? What if I can help somehow, and I'm so far away?"

"Trust me, that's something I understand all too well," I reply, closing my eyes momentarily. The feeling of helplessness isn't so forgotten that it doesn't bother me. I was here while my family was fighting the Ancients. I nearly lost my sisters and mom in the process. And my dad is still missing. "But," I say, opening my eyes and looking over at her, "All you can do is trust that your family knows what they're doing and that they won't hesitate to ask for help if they need it. It's the hardest thing, trusting that they'll be okay. But it's what we have to do."

"You're right. I know you're right."

"But it's not easy. I get it."

We fall silent then, each of us lost in our own thoughts. That desire to do something, anything, is almost overwhelming. I've been back to school for about three weeks, and I'm still nowhere near figuring out what happened to my dad. Not that I expected answers right away, but I can't even get down to the library to research. My sisters have given me no updates besides the very generic check in. All I wanted from this year was a chance to prove myself, to find something to help my dad. But so far, I've become angsty about a boy, who may or may not hate me, while I'm falling behind in classes. I'm really winning over here.

"Do you think...," I begin, but my voice is drowned out by the sudden sirens. Jade and I exchange a quick look before we grab our stuff and run.

We race past the trees, the siren sounding as if it's in our heads instead of all around us. I stumble twice, scratching up my palm before I right myself. Jade glances over her shoulder to make sure I'm following, as I try to catch up.

"Head for the training building!" I shout, because the castle is too far. I can't believe this is the second time we're nowhere near our rooms when the alarm sounds. This one seems to be even louder and longer than before.

Jade hears me and turns toward the building that's much closer. The feeling of danger intensifies with each moment, and then she's inside. But just as I reach the doors, they slam, shutting her inside with me on the outside.

"No!" I hear her scream and bang on the door. "Maddie!"

I hear a few more voices inside and someone shouting something.

"Jade, I'll be fine!" I yell, even as panic fills my chest. "Stay away from the windows and doors."

There's no time to hesitate. I push away from the doors, trying to orient myself. It makes no sense to head toward the castle. Everything is sealed with magic. But the school has to have a way to protect those who didn't make it inside on time. There has to be a work around for this. Except, I can't think of any. I will definitely have a few words with the headmaster after this is over. They should have instructions for these types of situations. Okay, I'm hyperventilating a little bit, I need to keep my head on straight.

I need to hide.

If this is an actual attack, standing in the middle of the meadow, completely in the open, is the dumbest thing I could do. Quickly, I weigh my options. My eyes zero in on the forest that surrounds the school's grounds, and I don't hesitate. I run toward the trees, pumping my legs as fast as possible.

A noise comes from somewhere behind me, as if a plane descending from the sky. I don't slow down, and I don't turn. If there is something there, it'll be easier to lose it in the thick of the foliage.

When I break through the trees in the next moment, I still don't let up. The need to hide drives me forward as the trees and the bushes get denser. With my momentum, I grab for the branch of the tree in front of me, catching myself as I swing onto it. It doesn't work the first time, and my hand stings from where I scratched it earlier. Instead of crying out, I take a deep breath and try again. This time, I'm able to hook my legs around it. Pulling myself up, I continue climbing until I'm far enough that I can barely see the ground.

My heart rate slows downs just a tad, but my senses stay heightened. I can still hear the noise, but it's centered more over the school than the rest of the grounds. I lean my head back, breathing in fully for the first time since the alarm sounded. I wish there was some way for me to know if the danger is real or if they managed to keep the school on lockdown. I look toward the direction I came from, but I'm much farther than I thought because I can't even glimpse the school through the greenery.

With the exhaustion overwhelming my body, I get a bit more comfortable on the branch before I hook my arms and legs into adjacent branches for safety. I have no idea how far I am, or even what is in these woods. We are not permitted to venture out this far, which puts me at a disadvantage. The only thing I can do is wait it out. Even though I have no way to figure out if the danger has passed and if it's safe to return.

Time goes by slowly. But even so, I can't tell much because the trees are tall and thick enough to block most of the light anyway. My watch is in my bag, which I dropped somewhere on the way to the eastern structure. I have no way of knowing what's going on.

After a few more long moments, I decide I need to get back to the main campus. Being all the way out here may be safe, but it won't be once the sun goes down. The noise from the alarm has long since faded, and my limbs have become numb from holding onto the tree so tightly.

Taking my time, I half slide, half scoot down the tree, staying as quiet as possible. I'm sure there are predators in this area as well. At least that's what I've read. We're safe if we stay in the designated areas, but the woods have always been a place for special assignments. I've heard the fae come through the forest sometimes, and while I know Liam, most fae kind of terrify me. I don't need to attract any more attention to myself than I already have.

When I'm back on solid ground, I do a quick study of my surroundings. I'm completely turned around, but thankfully, my dad has made sure I will never be lost. Moss doesn't only grow on the north side of a tree, but it mostly does because of the lack of the sun. It likes shady spots, so as not to dry out. I run a hand over the tree trunk, finding the prickly green. The majority of it is on the opposite side which means north is that way.

I head in that direction, keeping my steps as light as possible. To be honest, I have no idea what I'm walking into when I get back to campus, and I won't lie to myself and pretend I'm not scared.

It's not even five minutes later that I realize two things. I am much farther than I thought I was. And I am not alone.

SLOWLY, I DO A THREE-SIXTY, SCANNING MY SURROUNDINGS FOR any type of danger, but I can't see anything through the trees. It's so dark in this part of the forest, it's as if the sun never shines, even though I know it's not late enough for it to set already. I'm being very dramatic, but I'm sure my nerves are making everything that much more intense. A part of me thinks I stepped right into the realm of the Ancients.

The heaviness hangs in the air, and every shift of the leaves and flutter of wings from a bird taking off, makes my skin crawl. Even back home, we don't venture into the woods. The Ancients are the original elementals, and their connection to the earth is much stronger than ours. A part of me wonders if they can connect to every aspect of it, like insects and animals, and will them to do their bidding. Now, I'm just freaking myself out. Pushing the thoughts to the back of my mind, I take another few steps forward.

That feeling of being watched doesn't go away, and the battle magic at my fingertips crackles a little as my heartbeat speeds up. I feel a presence and hear a ruffle of leaves as my body tenses, ready for action. All that time training is about to be put to the test. Even my magic is itching to be set free. But at the last moment, something stops me. It's as if a force reaches out to me, soothing my nerves and calming my spirit. I watch as the brush opens up and a gorgeous dark-haired wolf steps through the branches. My heart thuds in awareness, goosebumps traveling up my arms and over my whole body.

The animal is more beautiful than any I have seen before. His dark brown fur shines in the darkness, as if it carries its own glow. He's large, probably tall enough to come above my waist. He looks like he can rip me apart with just one leap. His eyes are trained directly on me, and that's when it hits me all at once.

"Aiden?" I breathe his name, half question, half awe, and it's like his body relaxes just a tad at hearing my voice. He steps toward me and then we're only a few feet apart. We stare at each other, and I'm as mesmerized by his wolf as he was by my magic display.

Something changes in the atmosphere around us, an electric charge that races over my skin. It takes a fair amount of self-control not to reach out and run my fingers over his fur. I want to know if it feels as silky as it looks. Touching a shifter in his or her magical form is ridiculously frowned upon. There have been times where those who risked it were hurt in the process. But for some reason, I'm not afraid. A part of me knows that if I reach out, he would let me. It's like he wants to know what my hands feel like against his fur.

But I don't move, and he doesn't either. Because we both understand that's a line we cannot cross. Who knows how long we would've stood there if a howl somewhere deeper in the forest didn't break our concentration.

"I was heading back." I feel inclined to speak, thankful my voice comes out normal. He watches me for a moment longer before he turns and leads the way. I follow carefully, still keeping alert even though I sort of have a bodyguard now. Okay, not sort of. I am made in the shade with him by my side.

Another ten or fifteen minutes of walking, and the trees begin to thin out. I can almost make out the outline of the castle from here. When we reach the edge of the woods, Aiden stops.

"Aren't you coming?" I ask, looking over at where he positions himself. He shakes his head briefly, and a million questions rush into my mind. Something is going on.

But it's not like I can ask him anything, so I give him another searching look.

"Thank you," I manage, and once again, there's nothing but his intense stare. As I walk away, I feel his eyes tracking my every move. And when I finally do look back, he's still at the edge of the woods, watching me.

"Maddie!" Jade exclaims, rushing out of the eastern building and throwing her arms around me. My eyes are still on Aiden and when he sees Jade, he turns and heads back into the woods. "I was so worried. What happened to you? Once the lockdown was over you were nowhere to be found," Jade continues, pulling back and giving me a quick once over. "When the doors shut, I was so scared. I didn't know where you went. I started banging on the walls, hoping something would give. I even tried my magic."

"It's okay, Jade," I say, soothing her with my tone. "I know you did all you could." I definitely don't blame my friend for being left out of the building. That's on the headmaster and his lack of instructions for this exact scenario. My eyes roam over the people coming out of the structure while they head toward the main castle.

"Aiden didn't even hesitate to race out of there the moment the lockdown was lifted."

"What?" Her words stop me in my tracks, focusing my attention back on her.

"Aiden. He was in the building with me and he raced down and out of the building as soon as he could. Did he find you?"

"He did." I glance back over to the wood, but he's already gone. "I was already on my way back."

"Of course you were." Jade grins because I've told her about my father/daughter escapades. "But he still found you."

"I guess we're even now," I say, my eyes still on the trees.

"What do you mean?"

"I saw his wolf."

The school is in uproar when we finally make it inside the building. Two lockdowns in three weeks is a lot to take in. This is supposed to be the safest place for us, yet here we are.

"They haven't made any announcements yet," Jade says, as we push our way in the direction of our room. I can understand the panic these students are experiencing, even as I remain surprisingly calm. Being in those woods, all alone, was terrifying. But it was also a reminder that I am resourceful. I have to step up my game. No matter what, I am determined to make it to the underground library tonight. That place has helped me once, I truly believe it can help me again.

"Come on, let's wait in here." I pull Jade into our History classroom and out of the mob of students in the hall. By the time we make it all the way back to our room, we might have to come back anyway. She seems just as tired as I feel as she plops down into a chair.

"Education is exhausting," she comments, and I can't help but grin. It's such a random comment, and she delivers it so dramatically she should be in theater. We look at each other and then burst out in laughter, doubling over with amusement. Our emotions are so high, we can't seem to get control of them as tension seeps out with every giggle.

"The school is in danger, and you're laughing," The voice comes from the doorway and at this point, I'm not even surprised. I turn slowly, my eyes flashing.

"Three hundred and sixty-five rooms in this place and you end up in the same one as me. You know, stalking is illegal in all fifty states. And then some," I say, reaching for the comfortable hatred Aiden and I established on the first day of school because I desperately need to regain my footing. And not think about how much I want him to shift so I can see his wolf again.

"You didn't even look in here to see if it was already occupied. I could've been here first."

"No, you really couldn't have."

I know this because I would've felt him. I'm not sure when I became so attuned to his presence, but here we are. It's why I didn't attack in the forest, why I knew to trust a wolf I've never seen before. Something is stringing us together, and if I had an explanation for it, I would offer one up. But I've got nothing.

"What does that mean?" he asks, stepping farther into the room. His heated gaze is on me, and it's like he's branding me with his eyes. All air leaves my lungs, but I refuse to let him see just how affected I am.

"Wouldn't you like to know." I smile sweetly, and his eyes flash again, this time with so much emotion I nearly stagger where I stand. His gaze zeroes in on my lips, and I swear I can feel that look down to my very soul.

The moment becomes too much and not enough at the same time. If I could freeze time, I think this would be the memory I would want to hold onto the most. It's as if I'm seeing and feeling every emotion for the first time, and I don't know which way is up or which way is down.

I have no idea how our staring contest would've ended if the PA system didn't crackle to life with its signature announcement ding.

"The student body, please report to the grand hall. Headmaster Marković has an announcement to make."

"We are spending way too much time in that room," Aiden comments, finally breaking eye contact. The moment he looks away, it's as if a weight has been lifted off my chest. I look over at Jade, who's still sitting in the chair, watching us like some reality show.

"Let's go," I tell her before I pull her up, and we head out the doors. I don't have to look back to know Aiden is keeping pace with us. When we all file into the grand hall, Headmaster doesn't wait for us to quiet down.

"Listen up," he begins, and I notice he looks even more rugged than last time. Normally, his suits are tailored to his very fit body. Even though he's got pepper in his hair, he looks strong and sure of himself, even at sixty years old. Now, he's wearing his age in a way that makes him look even older. Whatever is happening, it's more serious than I can guess. "I am sorry to say that someone is tampering with our protective wards. No one breached the boundary and no one will. But whoever is doing so is trying to instill panic into these walls and it's working."

"Is he saying what I think he's saying?" Jade murmurs beside me.

"There is a traitor amongst us." Aiden's voice comes over my shoulder, and those are my thoughts exactly. The headmaster promises they are doing everything they can to find out who the culprit is, but I'm not sure how this will play out.

Everyone within these walls is a suspect now.

❧

"KEEP YOUR FEET PLANTED," AIDEN COMMANDS, CIRCLING AROUND me. We've been at this for three days now, but I have no idea if I'm getting better. I've spent a few hours every night in the underground library since the last lockdown, still unable to find answers. There haven't been any more false alarms, but everyone is on high alert.

Aiden included.

He's running me harder than he has been, and I can't really decipher his mood today. He's angry at me for something, and I have no idea what.

"They are planted," I snap, as I bounce a little on the soles of my feet.

"Not planted enough."

He attacks, his arm aiming for my right side, but I shift quickly, bringing my elbow to block him. He goes for the left next, but I catch him there too. We continue the dance, moving left to right to left again, and I keep up with him at every turn.

"I'd say planted enough," I finally announce, grinning at him. He blinks a few times, as if he needs an extra minute to focus before he walks around me and toward where he left his water bottle.

"Really? Nothing? Not even a grunt of praise?"

"You want me to praise you?" He turns around quickly, getting right in my face. The outburst is so uncharacteristic of him, it stuns me for a second. But only a second, as frustration bubbles up inside of me.

"Yes. I'd like to be told I'm doing a good job when I clearly am," I snap, placing my hands on my hips and taking a step closer.

"I'm sure your attacker would be more than happy to mention your form while he's ripping your head off your shoulders." His words are dripping with sarcasm, but he's not the only one who has mastered that particular personality trait.

"Wow, don't have a cow. If it's such a bother to be nice for a second, you should invest in some etiquette lessons. Which I'm sure is too much for you to handle, so I'll show myself out." I grab for my own water bottle, taking a few sips before I turn toward the exit. We're done for the day anyway, and I'm not about to stand here accepting his foul mood.

"Don't have a cow? Who even talks like that?" He grumbles under his breath, but it's enough to have me spinning on my heels and marching right back up to him.

"I do. I talk like that. I also like phrases like peachy keen and tickety-boo. Do you have a problem with that?"

I'm right in his face, but I don't care. I don't appreciate being made fun of. And coming from Aiden, it feels ten times worse.

"No problem," he replies, raising his hands in front of him as if to ward off any more attacks. "You enjoy your random tickety whatever."

"I am enjoying it, and I would be very appreciative if you would stop making fun of me for it."

His eyes narrow at my words, and he drops his hands to his sides, suddenly deflated somehow.

"I'm not making fun of you."

"Really? So, what would you call it?" I stand as tall as I can make myself, not backing down. But I'm still not imposing enough, and I know it.

"I would never make fun of you for being who you are." He says it so softly, at first I don't think I heard him right. But the intensity of his gaze sends pleasant shivers up my arm, which I'm sure he notices with his shifter senses.

"Then what are you doing?" I ask after a small pause. He doesn't answer right away, as if struggling to find the right words. When he speaks, it changes something between us.

"I'm just trying to understand you."

We stare at each other, and it's as if all the oxygen has been vacuumed out of the room. A million questions race into my mind, the biggest of all is why? But I don't seem to be brave enough to utter that one word. My whole world has tilted with his truth and I don't think it'll ever be right again. The magic inside of me is just as restless as the heart beating in my chest. I know he can hear it, and I think his own matches my pace.

Then, just when I think I'm ready to move forward, Aiden rips his gaze from mine, taking two steps back. That's all I need to find my legs and head for the door, leaving him behind. Whatever just happened, I don't think either one of us was ready for it. But just like always, I leave feeling confused and unbalanced. But now, I add wishful to that list.

❦ 12 ❧

We're in the dining hall a few days later, sitting around the table, talking about our English project, when Headmaster Marković walks in. The whole room grows quiet immediately, all eyes on him.

"Good afternoon, students," he greets us, his voice carrying across the large room, clearly amplified by magic. "In light of recent events, morale has been incredibly low. To help combat some of the sadness that has descended upon this institution, I would like to announce that next Friday we are having a dance. Think of it as welcome back to school event."

Before he's even done, everyone starts talking at once. Headmaster Marković smiles at the room before he turns and leaves the way he came in. The energy has definitely gone up since before the announcement, it was fairly quiet in here.

"A dance! That sounds like so much fun," Jade exclaims from beside me. Christy is already nodding her head with more enthusiasm than should be able to live in that small body of hers.

Typically, I would be excited as well. It's not as if we have dances very often. Kate would definitely be the one jumping up and down if she was here. But lately, I've just been tired. I muster up a smile, but I don't really join in on the discussion as everyone begins making plans.

"Hey, I'm going to head back to the room and lay down for a minute," I say as I lean over to Jade when there's a small lull in the conversation. She gives my face a quick study and nods.

"Do you need me to come with you?"

"No, thanks." I smile. "I just need a little bit of rest."

I say goodbye to our friends and head toward the rooms, determined to sleep. Since I know I'll be sneaking over to the library tonight, I'm way too drained for anything right now. My classes are done for the day, and the training with Aiden isn't until four. I have a good four-and-a-half hour window that I am going to use to catch up on some rest.

But the moment I lay down on my bed, my mind begins working overtime. Shutting my eyes, I push all thought of my family, the Ancients, and especially Aiden, far from my mind, but it doesn't seem to be working. I toss and turn a few times, refusing to open my eyes. If nothing else, Mr. Sandman, if you're listening, bring me a dream.

Except, he doesn't seem to be listening.

I focus on keeping my breathing even, my eyes still shut, and my mind as blank as possible. But it doesn't seem to be helping. It's like my thoughts are being pulled toward one inevitable subject: Aiden. He's definitely winning the topic of obsession in my mind right now.

We've been in such a standstill for days now. Since his mini confession about trying to understand me, I've been even more unbalanced around him than usual.

I've never had anyone wanting to understand me before. At least no one who said the words out loud. There was something behind them too, some kind of an emotion I can't identify. But then, I can't identify anything when it comes to Aiden. He's so hot and cold around me, it drives me insane.

Forcing all thoughts of him out of my mind I move onto the next issue at hand. My father.

Bri sent a message yesterday letting me know Nolan and Krista are traveling to Nolan's home to see if the Fae have any information they'd be willing to share. Even though the message was delayed before it got to me, I can hear the underlying worry in her words. The Fae aren't exactly known for their hospitality, and Krista and Nolan are like family. At least Nolan is Fae, and pretty high up on the royalty ladder. That should offer him a little bit of protection now that he's back in their good graces.

I've learned that prejudice runs deep within magical communities. And not only with shifters and witches. Nolan, for example, is part fox shifter, part Fae. That earned him a banishment for a long while. The only reason I know all this is because his half-brother, Liam, and I became friends last year. Still, it doesn't sit right with me that Krista and Nolan are crossing into Fae lands. It's a huge risk to take, but I guess that's what happens when there is a war going on and your loved ones are in danger.

Now that I'm thinking about my hometown, my mind is once again with my family. I miss my father something fierce.

I would do anything to see his gigglemug right about now. The word brings a smile to my face as I think about the first time he told me about it. He was grinning so hard I thought his face would split in two. When he told me the word, I couldn't help but laugh.

"That right there is the exact definition of the word. A perpetual smiler."

There's no telling how much of it is true or how many definitions he's made up just to see me laugh. I squeeze the blankets close to my chest as the tears sting behind my eyelids. Something's got to give soon, and I'm scared it might be me. How many more sleepless nights can I manage? How many times can I sneak over to the library before I'm discovered? I'm not doing nearly enough to help find my dad, and the guilt is about eating me alive.

I'm not sure how, but with that thought, I finally drift off to sleep.

A CONSISTENT KNOCKING IS WHAT WAKES ME. AT FIRST, I THINK IT'S part of my dream. But then it fades before I can remember it, and the knocking continues.

"What?" I grumble, getting off the bed and yanking the door open. Aiden stands on the other side, his hand raised to knock again. "Are you lost?"

"Love the look," he comments giving me a quick up and down. I realize I'm wearing my Superman pajama bottoms and Batman t-shirt. "You know they're not friends."

"Neither are we. What are you doing here?"

That earns me a glare before he pushes past me and into the room. He heads straight for my bed, sitting down on it, arms crossed across his chest. I roll my eyes before I shut the door and turn to face him.

"By all means, make yourself at home."

"Thank you for your hospitality."

The fact that he can dish out as good as he gets is an admirable trait. And a very annoying one. I try not to fidget under his scrutiny. I'm sure my hair is a bird's nest. I never have learned how to sleep without waking up looking like I just fought off a sleuth of bears.

"You didn't show up to practice. I am merely doing my civic duty and making sure you're not dead."

I glance over at the clock, shocked to find it's almost seven in the evening.

"I guess I must've really needed the rest," I shrug, hoping he'll leave it at that. Of course, I should know better by now. He scoots farther up my bed, placing his back against the wall, his long legs stretched out in front of him.

"You really did. You looked like you were about to fall over this morning."

"Oh, Aiden. Haven't we talked about stalking and how bad it is for you? And most definitely me?"

I'm trying to keep calm about the fact that he's on my bed. His body is long and large, and it makes my bed look like it's child sized.

"It's only stalking if you don't like it, Duchess."

"Well, it's stalking when it's stalking. But if this is the reasoning you are employing, I am happy to announce that I don't like it."

If I wasn't watching him so closely, I might've missed the tiny spark of amusement in his eyes. It's so strange to me, but I have yet to see him smile. I wonder if he'll look like I've imagined him in my mind. Not that I'm fantasizing about him or anything. I'm just curious, that's all.

"You know, you wouldn't be so tired if you stayed in your room at night," he says, nonchalantly bypassing my comment and surprising me all at the same time.

"I have no idea what you're talking about," I reply, really wishing I could find a mirror and figure out what's happening on my head.

"Come on, Duchess. Do you really want to play this game with me?" He leans forward just a little, and my mind conjures up all kinds of games we could be playing. When have I become this person and when has Aiden taken permanent residence in my head?

"I don't want to play any games with you," I reply, keeping my voice steady. Reaching for my hair, I collect it into my hands before I start braiding it. He watches as my fingers make fast work of the strands, the look somehow intimate. He doesn't speak until I put an elastic at the end of it.

"You don't even believe your own words," he says, raising his eyes to mine once more. I bristle at that, because I'm not about to let him get away with telling me what I think or believe.

"Just because you don't want to accept defeat, doesn't mean I don't know my own mind," I snap, tired and frustrated and ready to have him out of my space. He's making my skin tingle, and I'm afraid I'll do something I can't come back from if he stays any longer. Like blast him with some battle magic. Or other things I don't want to put a name to.

"I would never dare to tell you what you think," Aiden says, scooting to the edge of my bed. "But I think you lie to yourself more often than you realize."

He stands then, and without waiting for a response, walks out of the room. I lean against Jade's desk, unsure of what exactly just happened. Anytime I'm around him, I lose all ground I've gained. He comes in like a hurricane, disturbing everything in his path, and I'm left holding the pieces.

When I walk back over to my bed, I realize I can still feel him on the sheets. There's a lingering smell in my personal space that's entirely his. I stare at the bed, torn between laying down and ripping the fabric off the mattress. Angry at myself for even thinking these thoughts, I grab my English homework and march to my desk.

I will study, and I will force myself to forget about the fact that Aiden was just lying on my bed.

❧ 13 ❦

The whole week is a blur of preparations. Everyone is asking everyone to the dance like it's homecoming or something. We typically only have three dances. The winter ball, the new year celebration, and the end of the year send off. Now, I feel like we're about to have a party every month, just to keep the morale up.

"You are never going to believe what happened," Jade announces, walking into the room late in the afternoon. It's Wednesday, which means we end the day in different classes, so I haven't seen her since lunch.

"Someone asked you to the dance?" I ask, barely looking up from my reading.

"How do you always know everything?"

"I wish I knew everything," I mumble, before placing a bookmark on the page and focusing completely on my friend. "Tell me *everything*."

"Well, I was on my way to my last class and none other than Caleb steps into my path. But not in a weird way that made me run into him, just in a way that made me recognize he was in front of me. He then proceeded to ask me how I was doing and if I have a date and if I would be so kind as to go with him."

"And you said yes."

"And I said yes! How fun is that?"

"That's awesome, Jade. But I thought you'd be going with Noel."

"Umm," she turns away at my words, and I narrow my eyes.

"Jade. What are you not telling me?"

"Nothing."

"You are a terrible liar."

"Fine. Noel was going to ask you. Tonight, after dinner. You have to be surprised, and you have to say yes."

"Jade! Noel and I are just friends."

"Yes, which means you'll have fun together and can come with Caleb and me. It'll be great."

"Did you put him up to this?"

"I would never. He wanted to ask you, and I told him it's a great idea."

"Jade."

"Maddie. Come on. You cannot not go to the dance."

"I mean, I *could*." I was actually thinking about it because it would give me a good excuse to sneak over to the library. But now, I think I'll be scratching that plan off my to-do list.

"Madison Hawthorne, you wouldn't. It's our first dance together. We both have to go for that to be true." The pout she gives me is one powerful sort of magic because I can feel myself giving in. Plus, I know Noel and I would have fun. My mind drifts over to another boy in my life, but I scrap that before it can take root.

"Fine, fine, fine. I'll suck it up and dance the night away." I tumble back onto the bed, throwing a hand over my forehead.

"You are so dramatic," Jade laughs, and I know I just made her very happy. I guess it won't hurt to have a little fun once in a while. Just then, a knock sounds on the door before a letter is pushed under it. Since Jade is standing up, she grabs for it first.

"So, do we actually know how the whole note thing works?" my roommate asks, glancing down at the paper. "Is the knock attached to the magic that makes the paper appear under our door?"

"You're asking me this like I know the answer." I laugh, as she hands me the note.

"Well, this is your school." I shrug at that, glancing at my name written on the paper.

"It's a magical delivery system. That's all I've got," I reply, opening the envelope and pulling out the note. A huge part of me is hoping it's from my sisters, or Mama, telling me dad has been found, and I can breathe easier. But no dice. The note is short and to the point.

> *No training for the rest of the week.*
> *See you next Monday. - Aiden*

"What is it?" Jade snatches the note in alarm, reading it quickly. She glances up at me, a bit of confusion clouding her eyes.

"You looked like something was wrong," she says slowly, keeping her gaze on me. I try to shrug it off. "Maddie?"

"It's just weird is all. He's been so adamant about training. It's weird that he would cancel."

"Aha."

"Stop that." I point at Jade, taking the note back and dropping it on my desk.

"Whatever you say," she continues, before clapping her hands together. "But this is perfect because we can now pick out dresses together!"

"Dresses?"

"Yes! Since we can't leave campus to shop, they're bringing the shop to us. Today at four. I thought I would have to sneak a dress for you, but now I don't have to."

She's very excited and I can't exactly fault her for it. The faculty knew what they were doing when they announced the dance. Students have been in a state of elation for days. But as Jade settles down for her own studies before shopping and dinner, my mind drifts over to Aiden as my eyes find the note on the desk. It's odd for him to cancel. Something must be going on.

❧

When it's twenty minutes until four, Jade basically drags me out the room and down the stairs. Her excitement is contagious, and I find myself getting into it. I've never been one for fluffy dresses or high heels, but that's because I spent most of my childhood in the woods with my dad. There have been a few times where I've dolled up, but all the major celebrations are reserved for after we've come of age. Since I'm away at school, I miss out on the summer Litha or the moon cleansing ritual. Thunderbird Academy has one of their own, but it's not until I've reached the upperclassman level.

"How exactly are we paying for these?" I ask, as Jade and I line up behind a group of girls. I see Christy and Vera closer to the front, and the shorter girl waves, while Vera throws a nod our way.

"We're not. They announced this in one of my classes. The faculty is supplying the dresses and dress shirts. They're even setting up a flower stand."

"How very teen movie-esque of them," I say, but not unkindly. It's nice to know that those who run this school are taking a personal interest in our lives. It would be so easy for them to just focus on the academics. But not only are they putting themselves in danger to protect us when the time comes, they're making sure we have a full high school experience.

"I think it's pretty amazing of them." Jade smiles, and I answer in kind. We move forward slowly, staying in line. It's a little surprising how organized this whole process is. I mean, they are dealing with a bunch of teenagers. But I love the fact that everyone seems to be on the same page. Maybe it's true what they say, and difficult times do bring people together.

When we reach the front of the line, we step through the doors to one of the classrooms which has been revamped to look like a clothing store. There are hanging rods set up all around with dresses, shirts, skirts, and even a few suits. On one side, they've also set up dressing rooms, with a few full-length mirrors. Currently, one of the mirrors is occupied by a pretty girl in a dark purple pantsuit. Her long blonde hair spills over her shoulders, and she looks powerful and ready for anything while the color complements her complexion.

"Wow," Jade breathes out next to me, and I glance to see her watching the girl. "She looks amazing. I could never pull that off."

"Me neither. I think she's one of the fourth-year students."

"Come on." Jade tugs on my arm, pulling me toward the racks filled with clothes. There are so many colors and material options, everything swims in front of my eyes for a moment. Jade begins pulling items out, happily holding them in front of her body for inspection. I take my time, walking down the aisles, hoping something will jump out at me. I'm almost at the end of the row when something does.

A tiny sliver of green material is sticking out between the reds, so I walk toward it, pulling it out more fully. The color reminds me of the forest around my hometown of Hawthorne, the fresh leaves mixed with evergreens. It's a floor length, off the shoulder, emerald satin beauty, and I'm instantly in love.

"You have to try it on." I'm so mesmerized, I don't hear Jade come up to me. I glance over my shoulder and she tugs my elbow toward the dressing rooms as I grab the dress. She's carrying three with her, purple, pink, and red. I have to say, I see her in the red.

I let her go first, and after she tries the others, red is the winner I thought it would be.

"What do you think?"

"I honestly love it," I reply, as she twirls in front of the mirror. From my sisters, I know it's a tea length strapless sweetheart cut. Harper wore one to her homecoming. The red reminds me of the apples we picked in the Autumn, and I squish the melancholy threatening to overwhelm me.

"I do too! Now you. I want to see that number on you." She wiggles her eyebrows up and down, and I can't help but laugh. She brings the kind of lightheartedness to my life that I need right now. It would be too easy for me to get bogged down by my own mind.

When I step into the dressing room, I undress quickly. Once I pull the dress over my body, I know it's the one. It settles over my skin as if it was made for me. The length is perfect, touching the floor enough that when I rise to my tiptoes, it barely grazes the ground. The off the shoulder cut shows off more skin than I'm used to, but it also makes me feel as powerful as that girl looked in her suit. When I run my hands over the full skirt, I discover that the dress has pockets.

"Holy moly, Maddie," Jade says, when I step out to look at myself in the mirror. "You look incredible."

I do my own little twirl in front of the mirror, completely in love with the dress.

"Wait, does it have pockets?"

"It sure does!"

"Amazing!"

The fact that we're this excited about pockets just shows me I have no choice but to get this dress. It feels heavenly against my skin and makes me feel empowered somehow. I notice the line still out the door and quickly rush to the dressing room to change back. I think I could've stood in front of that mirror forever, and that's something new for me.

I've never been one to dress up because I never understood the importance behind it. I love what I wear, but it has always been more about comfort than fashion. That dress definitely showed me what a good outfit can do for my confidence.

"I can't believe we both found dresses," Jade says, linking her arm through mine as we carry our purchases toward our room. I'm about to answer when someone calls my name. I turn to see Noel heading toward us, and I know exactly what's about to happen.

"I'll just take that," Jade says, reaching for my dress before taking a step away.

"Don't leave me," I plead.

"Be nice," she replies, before rushing up the stairs. I turn in time to see Noel watching Jade retreat before he gives me a warm smile.

"Hey, Maddie."

"Noel. How's it going?"

"It's going. Do you think I could borrow your time for a minute?"

I want to say no, but I also don't want to hurt his feelings. I give him a nod and he leads me toward the front doors. Once we're outside, we head to one side of the staircase, away from the busybody onlookers. There always seems to be someone around.

"So, what's up?" I ask, ready to get this over with.

"I was wondering if you would like to go to the dance with me?"

His direct question takes me by surprise. I really thought he'd have to work up to it, but he just dives right in. I kind of appreciate it, to be honest. I already told Jade I'd say yes, but this makes me actually want to do so.

"I'd like that," I reply, and I can see him visibly relax. "But can I ask you a question?"

"Sure."

"I thought you'd ask Jade." That's not really a question, but I see his eyes cloud for a second, and I know I guessed it right.

"Maddie..."

"It's okay. I would still love to go with you, I just wanted to know if my suspicions were right. And I want to make sure you're going with the right person."

He laughs at that, which makes him look even cuter than usual. I can definitely see the appeal, even though I've never paid much attention before.

"Jade is going with Caleb."

"I know that." I watch him steadily, and he shifts from foot to foot.

"I was going to ask her, but he beat me to it."

"Why ask me?" I'm not upset, just genuinely curious.

"Because I consider you one of my closest friends, and I think we will have a blast together."

And just like that, my heart swells, and I realize how special he is to me. Somewhere when I wasn't looking, he's become one of my closest friends too. Without hesitation, I throw my arms around him, and he catches me easily. It's the kind of a hug that chases all the clouds away and fills the heart to the brim. I needed it more than I could've imagined.

14

The rest of the week flies by at the speed of light. The only noticeable drag is my lack of combat training. I'm trying not to let it affect me, but the fact that Aiden has gone MIA is keeping me a bit distracted. It also makes me search every hallway and classroom, waiting for him to show up. I'm annoyed with myself, to say the least.

"Earth to Maddie." Jade waves her hand in front of my face as Christy and Vera giggle in the background. The four of us are in our room, getting pampered for the dance tonight. The girls and I have all put on face masks, and Christy is currently painting Vera's nails dark blue. The shifter's dress looks like a galaxy and suits her perfectly. Christy chose a hot pink number, and I have to say, it's made for her. It's just as bubbly as she is.

"Sorry, sorry," I mumble, concentrating on the task at hand. Which at this moment involves picking out the perfect shade of lipstick for both Jade and myself.

"This one," I announce grabbing the tube out of the stack. "I don't think you can go wrong with a color called 'Firemen's Kiss'." Another round of giggles as Jade takes the lipstick and swipes it across her lips as a test run. Not to brag, but I can tell it's the perfect shade.

"You are a genius!"

I laugh, taking a little bow, as my heart squeezes in awareness at the scene in front of me. While I've never been much on makeup and spa days, my sisters, plus Krista, have done girl's night rituals much like these for years. They've always included me, even though I'm so much younger than them. Looking around, I feel that pang of homesickness that I usually keep at bay. I haven't heard from them all week, and on top of Aiden going missing, my emotions are at an all-time high.

"We should probably start getting ready with a bit more speed to our movements," Vera says, blowing air on her fingernails. "We're running out of time."

The rest of us glance over at the clock on the wall as Christy gasps.

"Vera! Why didn't you mention it sooner?" The other girl just shrugs, which is so like her. I don't think I've ever seen her lose her cool. Christy scrambles to her feet, rushing to the bathroom to wash up. There isn't much room to fit all four of us in, so we take turns.

Once my face is nice and scrubbed, I let Jade do my makeup. I could do it myself; I'm not a complete novice. Harper made sure her status as the second oldest sister was intact by teaching me all about eyeliner and mascara. But now that we're here, I want something more special. I could never achieve the perfect smokey eye, and I want to do the dress justice.

It doesn't take long for Jade to doll me up. She's a master, that much is clear by her every day striking looks. But when I finally turn and look at myself in the mirror, even I'm surprised by her skill.

My eyes look bigger, outlined perfectly in golds and silvers, making the green pop. The lashes are fuller than I've ever seen them, part- nered with a subtle cat eye. There is a tiny amount of highlighter on my cheeks, just enough to make my skin glow. I realize we didn't decide on a lipstick when she moves in front of me once more.

"I think a subtle pink, almost nude color, will be best." She raises the tub at my eye-level, and I have to agree. The color reminds me of rose quartz, one of my favorite crystals. I'll be wearing a bracelet with the stone around my wrist.

"Now who's a genius?" I reply, letting her apply the lipstick as well.

The hair is next, and I do my best to curl it halfway down my back, before I pin it to one side. It's a look I've seen Bri do for one of her dances, and I've always wanted to try it with the right dress. When it's time to finally pull the material over my body, it almost seems surreal.

Each part of the process, from the cleansing mask to the smoothing of the skirt over my hips, made me feel empowered. I didn't do this for anyone but myself, and I tuck the feeling closely to my heart to carry with me forever. I just learned a valuable lesson, and I hope I never forget it.

When the knock sounds on the door, there's no hesitation as I pull it open.

Noel stands on the other side, black suit, white shirt, a green tie the color of my dress. I'm not sure how he found the exact shade, but he looks great in it.

"Wow, you look amazing," he says, grinning at me.

"You clean up pretty good yourself," I reply, answering in kind.

"Did they manage to talk you into heels?" Noel asks, a glimmer of amusement in his eyes. We had a whole lunch discussion about how I was not about to wear any sort of heels to this shindig. I would break my neck, and probably something else in the process.

"We compromised," I reply now, raising the bottom of my dress so he can see the black booties I have on. They have a small, two-inch heel on them, but they're wedges. If I needed to run, I'd be all good to go.

"Love it. It's totally you."

And with those words Noel chases away any reservations I may have had about the evening. He gets me, and I don't have to pretend or hide around him. That's what friendship is, being yourself with someone who understands you. I give him the biggest smile and he loops his arm to offer me his elbow. After a quick bye to the girls, I shut the door behind me. Without hesitation I place my arm through the opening and together we walk toward the ballroom.

I'M NOT GOING TO PRETEND AND SAY IT'S NOT WEIRD THAT MY school has a ballroom. Sometimes I feel like this place is right out of the late 18th century. I can almost envision Mr. Darcy and Elizabeth

Bennett dancing right alongside us. The only thing missing is the candles as the only means of lighting.

When Noel and I reach the double doors, we line up behind all the other couples waiting to go in. I can hear music coming from inside and people talking and laughing.

"Is it me or is there a lot of pink?" Noel asks, as we study the people around us.

"It's not you." I reply, because girls and guys alike are sporting all kinds of pinkish shades. I've never been a huge fan of the color for myself, especially since it looks weird with my complexion. But some of them are really pulling it off.

"Oh, there's Jade," I say, just as my friend and her date finish descending the stairs. She looks incredible in the little red number, her hair swept up into an elaborate updo. The red lipstick is a perfect accessory to her dramatic cat eye. She looks like one of those Hollywood bombshells, minus the platinum hair, her shade is a little lighter. But it doesn't take away from her beauty. I'm not the only one who thinks so.

"Wow." Noel's barely whispered admiration is not missed on me, and I give his arm a little squeeze. He tears his gaze away from my friend and gives me a sheepish smile.

"Don't worry, I agree," I tell him in a conspiratorial whisper. He visibly relaxes, but his eyes dart toward Jade once more. The boy really has it bad. But I honestly don't mind. Jade could do much worse.

"Come on," I say, pulling him toward the doors as the line moves. "You owe me a dance."

He grins down at me and then we're inside the ballroom. The place has been decorated with glowing lights all around. It's like standing inside of a gazebo on a Christmas night. It's magical and incredibly perfect for the atmosphere. I see quite a few Fae moving around the room, making sure everyone is having a good time. While we don't have many at the school, everyone knows they're good for throwing a party. Which is why all of them are on the party committee.

There are already people dancing. The music is a mixture of current and older songs, and I would be lying if I said I'm not getting swept up in all of it.

"Ah, there you are!" Jade comes up to us, pulling Caleb along the way. We're not friends, but he is in one of my classes. I've seen him hang out with Ben and Owen, two of Aiden's closest companions. Not that I've spoken to any of them before. Caleb greets us warmly, and I do have to say, he looks pretty good in his dark blue suit. What is it about shifters that they can wear anything and look like models?

Speaking of shifters, my eyes do a once over of the room, but I don't see him. It's foolish to even be looking for him. But I seem to have no control over that part. I could ask Caleb about him, even though I know they're not super close. But I resist. For now.

"Are we dancing or what?" I ask instead, and the group nods as one. We move toward the middle of the room, and it isn't long before Christy and Vera, with their dates, find us.

The base turns up and everyone around me cheers. Grinning, I begin to move, losing myself in the sound.

I have a secret. I love to dance. My sisters and I used to throw dance parties in Bri's shop, just to let loose. I remember it even as a six or seven-year-old. Harper would make the wind dance with us, making the chimes play us a sweet melody.

The energy is high, everyone jumping and dancing, and I feel like, for the first time, I'm just a teenage girl, enjoying her high school experience. There is no missing dad. No Ancient evil. No traitor within our midst. Just a bunch of friends, having a blast. My eyes jump from person to person, and I see firsthand the happiness radiating off them. I've found my tribe, and even though I still think of Kate, and even Liam, I'm thankful I have people around me I can trust and have fun with.

It seems like forever before the music slows and the lights dim, leaving only the twinkling stars all around us.

"May I?" Noel offers me his hand and I take it instantly. He pulls me toward him, settling one hand around my waist, the other still holding my hand. My body molds against him, and I rest my head on his shoulder, pulling him closer. He feels safe and stable. I could use more of that in my life right now.

After a few moments I raise my head to look at him and find him already looking at me. Maybe I'm getting swept away by the moment, but even so, I don't stop myself from speaking.

"I'm glad you asked me to come with you," I say, my eyes on his.

"I'm glad you said yes."

I look away then, because I'm not sure if I'm feeling something or not, but I don't want this to just be an in-the-moment reaction. Noel and I are friends, and I trust that over anything else. When my gaze lands on the crowd around us I find another pair of eyes on me. Aiden stands against the back wall, his eyes hard. He's wearing a dark button up shirt, with his sleeves rolled up and looks nonchalant and gorgeous at the same time. Then, Noel turns us and he's out of sight. When I look back, Aiden is gone. Maybe he wasn't there to begin with. I don't get the chance to find out because just then, the sirens start going off, and the rest of the lights go out.

❧ 15 ❧

There's a collective hush in the room, as if people are holding their breaths as one, waiting to see the legitimacy of the alarm. When the room shakes from some kind of an impact, everyone snaps into action. There are a few screams as some push others out of the way. The dark is making it difficult to see, and it's the shifters who have the upper hand. They begin shouting instructions while the older students move to the exits to direct people out of the room.

I can feel the fear in the room, especially from the younger students. A few of the teachers create an illumination orb to help dispel the darkness, but for some reason, it's not having as strong of an effect as it should. Something must be blocking the magic.

"Come on, we need to get out of here," Caleb calls out, and I feel Noel's hand wrap around my own. I glance over at him, but I can barely see him, even this close up. We call out to each other, linking hands, with Vera and Caleb leading the way. The doors seem to be a mile away, and the bodies continue to bump into us. Before we can reach the doors, another shock ripples through the ballroom, sending glasses flying, raining glass over all over us. A few cut my skin, and then another magical shockwave rushes through the room, bursting the ceiling fixtures and the rest of the glass in the room. My water magic flairs up on instinct, and I throw my hand in the air, pulling on the liquid and weaving it into a protective shield right as the shards reach us. Everyone screams, but the water protects the immediate group around me. I can't tell how far it extends, but I know it's not that large. Students are crying out, and even though I don't have shifter sense of smell, I know blood has been spilled.

"Neat trick," Jade comments as my friends huddle around me. I concentrate on the shield, and the shards that are caught in the liquid, before pushing it away. Without having light to guide me, I'm really hoping I'm not about to spill a bunch of glass and water on anyone. That's when I realize the outside doors are closer and to my right. Some of the moonlight can be seen through the blanket of darkness. I can push the water that way, but without being able to clearly see, I might make things worse.

"I need to get this out of here," I say before I drop Noel's hand and move with my magic.

"Maddie!" Jade and Noel both call out, but with just a few steps, they're lost to the darkness.

"I'll be fine," I call back, trying to reassure them. "I'll catch up with you in a minute."

It's taking most of my concentration to keep the shield high above everyone's heads. I can't see it, but I can feel how full of glass debris it is, and if I don't get it out now, I might be causing more problems. When I reach the outside doors, I open them with one hand, keeping the other outstretched above my head. The magic morphs and shifts as I walk through the opening, staying with me. A few shards of glass drop, but they're small enough that they don't cut me.

Once outside, I raise my other hand and then push the water and glass as far as I can before dropping it. I can't see much outside either, but it doesn't sound like anyone's out there. I'll have to remember to let the headmaster know what I did so some poor student doesn't end up walking all over it.

With that thought in mind I turn back toward the ballroom and realize just how quiet it has gotten. Glancing around, I try to see through the dark, but the clouds must be obscuring the moon now, because any sliver of light there might've been has completely gone out. My eyes work to adjust as I look back and try to see into the ballroom, but there's just a wall of darkness. I take a few steps back, reaching for the handle, but it doesn't budge. I bang on the door a few times but hear no one.

"Great, just great," I mumble to myself, looking back out into the field and forest surrounding me. Without any landmarks to guide me, I already feel turned around. This darkness doesn't feel natural, and I wonder if this is another thing the Ancients can do. They can't penetrate the protective shield to come into the Academy themselves, but apparently whoever is on their payroll, so to speak, has been learning some new tricks.

Since the door is at my back, the front of the school must be on my left. Thankful that I opted out for my booties instead of the heels, I don't sink into the grass as I start to make my way there. As much as possible, I try to listen for any noises that might alert me to danger, but the silence is not disturbed. I leave my hand against the wall to help guide me, but that becomes problematic when I come to the bushes planted under the windows on one side of the building.

Taking a step away from the plants, I continue to walk straight, barely seeing few feet in front of me. I think I'm almost to where the building turns to the left, when I hear it. Something is out here with me.

I freeze in my tracks, my battle magic flaring up at my fingertips. The rush of it sizzles under my skin, making me that much more aware of my surroundings. Even though I've been taught these skills, I never thought I'd be using them so soon. As Jade and I discussed, battle magic is all instinct. We don't have to say words to cast spells, it's literal electricity that runs through our veins. Some carry copious amounts with them and have learned how to unleash parts of their magic I can't even imagine. I can't deny how powerful my magic seems when I put a bit of emphasis behind it.

The noise comes again, but I still can't pinpoint it, or figure out exactly what I'm hearing. It's like a movement, just beyond my line of vision. A ruffle of cloth against skin? Maybe I'm feeling the eyes on me, more than I hear anything.

Then, when I think it's nothing but my imagination, a low growl sounds somewhere in the darkness, making my blood run cold. I'm not without defenses, but I can't fight something I can't see. I wouldn't stand a chance.

Slowly, and as quietly as I can, I move backwards. I'm trying to think strategically. With the building at my back, at least I won't have to try and keep that covered. Something glitters in the space in front of me, sending fear up my spine. I'm being stalked, there's no doubt about it and whatever it is, it can see me. Without a second of hesitation, I abandon my plan of trying to be inconspicuous. I bolt.

Whatever has been stalking me gives chase.

I GRAB FOR THE BOTTOM OF MY DRESS, PULLING IT UP SO I CAN RUN more freely. My legs pump as I sprint blindly into the darkness, one hand outstretched in front of me in case I run into something.

Glancing behind, I still can't see anything, but I can feel the danger. It's as if whatever is out there is playing a game of cat and mouse. I have a feeling I won't be as lucky as Jerry on this one. I've got no tricks up my sleeve, except for one. I can stop running and face this head on. But once again, I think of how much I am at a disadvantage. My dad would be disappointed if I didn't think this through first. He taught me to be smarter than this recklessness. I have to think. I have to.

I yelp as an arm reaches out to grab me, but instead of the attack I expect, I get pulled against a solid chest as the other hand lands over my mouth.

"Don't," a voice says as I struggle against the hold.

The whispered word is all I need to hear to know who it is.

Aiden.

I stop struggling immediately as his arm tightens even more over my stomach before he removes the one covering my mouth. I'm tucked completely against him as he picks me up enough to spin us, tucking us into the space between the wall at the outer structure. Swiveling my head to the side, my cheek ends up pressed against his chest as I try to see into the darkness. But just like before, I see nothing. However, I feel safer than I've ever felt, in this moment, pressed against my sort of nemesis.

His breathing seems to match my own, his chest solid against my back. He's hotter than me, his body temperature raising mine. Or maybe it's his proximity. Even dancing pressed against Noel didn't feel this intimate. It's like Aiden and I are one, two beings in two different bodies, but breathing and feeling the same.

I think he feels it too, maybe realizes it at the same moment I do because he goes completely still. His hand on my stomach twitches, and I fight the sudden urge to place my own against it. Maybe it's the adrenaline, or the situation, but I want to hold onto him and never let go.

"Come on." His voice shatters our little cocoon of silence as he moves us out of our hiding spot. "We need to get inside."

But even as he says so, he doesn't move away from me. For some reason, I don't either. I turn my head slightly, glancing up at him, and find him staring down at me. My movement spurs him into action because he hastily takes a step away.

"We should...," he begins, his hand reaching toward me, but before he touches me, he stops. I'm not sure what's going through his mind, but I do the only thing I can think of. I close the rest of the distance and take his hand. There's a spark of electricity that races through me at the touch of his skin against mine, and I suppress a shudder. But just barely.

"Lead the way," I say, offering him a smile, which I know he can see with his shifter eyesight. He gives my hand a tiny squeeze before he starts moving.

We don't go too fast. He's taking his time to make sure nothing awaits us in the darkness. His grip on my arm is all the reassurance I need to keep my own heart rate down. I trust him to keep me safe, and that's saying a lot for someone who doesn't trust easily. Not where it truly matters.

After a few minutes, I realize we're not moving toward the academy but away from it.

"Aiden." I tug on his arm, ready to ask him the question.

"Not now," he replies before I can. Then, just as suddenly as he saved me the first time, he stops, making me run right into his back. My free hand lands on his waist, and it's his turn to inhale sharply.

"We need to move fast. Get ready."

I wish I could see what he sees, but even as I glance around, I'm completely useless out here.

"Now."

I don't hesitate. As he takes off, I keep up with him the best I can, trusting him to lead me blindly. When a structure materializes in front of us, I don't have breath left inside of me to ask questions. Aiden gets us inside before he shuts the door.

He drops my hand, and I can feel him moving around, as if he's making sure we're safe, before he comes to stand in front of me again.

"We're safe here for now."

"Where is here exactly?"

"One of the storage barns on the west side of the school."

"I didn't even know these were here."

"They're behind some of the trees planted along the walkway. Unless you come out here, you wouldn't know they're here."

Aiden heads toward one of the walls, leaving me in the middle of the room, unsure of what to do. The adrenaline is still pumping through my veins, but it's leaving quickly. I can already feel the onset of the panic I was repressing earlier. This whole ordeal, everything that has happened in the last few hours, it has left my emotions at an all-time high. I'm afraid I might burst into tears and not the pretty, delicate ones.

"Hey." Aiden moves so quietly that I don't notice him at my left shoulder until he's there, making me jump. "Sorry, come here."

He takes my hands tentatively, leading me away from the middle of the room and toward the wall. Slowly, as if he's keeping his movements to a minimum, he sits down, tugging at my hand. Without hesitation I follow suit, leaning my back against the cool wood, Aiden at my side. Instantly, I feel better not being on my feet.

We sit in silence as I try to hear what's going on outside, but I have too many questions buzzing around in my mind. I start with the most pressing one.

"Are we really safe here?" I whisper, afraid to raise my voice any louder. But I know Aiden hears me, and I feel him move as he looks over at me.

"For the time being. Headmaster Marković placed additional charms around all the buildings on the property. Just in case."

"What's out there, Aiden?" I don't even bother masking the tremble in my voice. I don't think I've ever been more scared in my life. I always thought I'd be braver when the time came. But maybe I'm not as brave as I think.

"I don't know, Maddie," he replies, shifting again, and I can feel the brush of his shoulder against mine. The air around us is cooling rapidly, and my naked shoulders are covered with goosebumps.

"Are you cold?" Aiden asks because I'm sure I'm not radiating warmth right now.

"No."

"Maddie."

He really needs to stop saying my name because I can feel it at the pit of my stomach, like the butterflies all those books describe. I don't want to become a cliché, but he's making me feel things, and it's messing with my mind. I've come to know myself as Duchess in his mind. The sound of my name on his lips breaks down all my defenses.

"Fine. A little cold," I finally say, before I feel him move once more.

"May I?" I turn towards his voice at the question and watch as he raises his arms, opening them up to me. I stare at him for a long moment before I scoot over and allow him to pull me close. The moment my back hits his chest I feel the warmth spread through me. His arms land around my shoulders, lacing over my stomach, and I'm cocooned in the safety of him.

For this one moment in time, we're not enemies or rivals. He holds me close, chasing away the fear and the worry. And for the time being, I let that be enough.

❧ 16 ☙

We sit in comfortable silence for a little while before the curiosity gets the best of me.

"What did you see out there?" I whisper, turning my head a little to look up at Aiden. He glances down at me, and I realize just how close our faces are. There's an intimacy to our embrace that makes my head spin, but I try to keep as still as possible.

"Nothing."

"What?" I jerk at that, sitting up a bit more fully so I can turn and look at him straight on.

"That's the thing, I didn't see what was chasing us. It was more like my shifter senses picked up on the being that was there, the danger it was broadcasting, but I couldn't find it. Even with my eyesight."

His words fill my mind with possibilities. My hometown of Hawthorne was attacked by shadow creatures sent from the Ancients, so I know they have a way of creating monsters no one has heard about. But this invisible attacker is something new. Something else occurs to me.

"But you know there's no one in here with us right now, right?"

"Yes, I still sense the creature the same way I would any danger, but I just can't *see* it."

I hear the frustration in his voice, and if I could see in the darkness, I'm sure it'd be written all over his face. He's allowing me this glimpse into his psyche, and I can't help but feel something toward his vulnerability. I don't think he'd ever give even this much of himself if the lights were on. Or maybe he would. Maybe he would for me.

"Where were you this week?" I find myself asking, and I can feel his body tense beside me. I almost wish I could take the words back because we were working toward something here, and I shattered it with my curiosity.

"I was on an assignment."

The tone of his voice shuts down any further questions, and I miss the small moment of camaraderie we shared. I want to lean back into his arms fully and find that peace again, but I'm too charged up now. And maybe, so is he.

"We should—" he begins, before he stops abruptly. I glance over at him and find his face in profile, staring at something I can't even imagine seeing.

"A—" I begin, but he places a finger to my lips, stopping the word in its tracks. Then, before I can figure out what's going on, he leans in, his mouth at my ear, sending a whole new batch of goosebumps up my arm.

"It's here."

My own body goes on high alert right before something slams into the structure. I yelp involuntarily, sliding back against Aiden as his arms come around me once more. He stands, lifting me in the process since I'm still pressed against him. He sets me on my feet but doesn't let go. Something slams against the opposite wall, but this time, I don't yell. I'm getting those sea legs back, as dad likes to say. I wanted to be brave, well it's about time I start acting like it.

"Can it get in?"

"I don't know, Maddie," he replies, right against my ear. "None of this is exactly playing by the rules."

I nod against him, placing my hand over where his is resting on my stomach. He tilts his hand, trapping mine under his when the building around us shudders. Twisting around, I try to pinpoint where the attack is coming from, but it seems to be coming from everywhere.

When the hit comes again, the walls around us shudder, and I realize we are no longer safe.

"Aiden."

"I know."

"I don't know any protection spells," I mumble, feeling completely useless.

"It's okay. We need to move."

He reaches for my hand, giving it a firm squeeze as he glances down at me. I can't make out his look completely, but I can feel the determination rushing through his body and my own rises up to match his. Maybe this is the moment when we put all our bickering in the past and become something other than frenemies, but there's no time to get into it. I give him a firm nod before I let my battle magic unfurl within me. It seems to light me up from inside, the electricity zinging my fingertips. It might not be much, but this is one thing I can do.

"Ready," I say, and I swear he grins, right before he turns and sprints for the door. There's a slight pause, a moment of silence, and then he yanks it open. We race outside into the darkness, my dress tangling around my legs. I almost faceplant on the ground before he catches me, pulling me up. I reach for the dress, yanking the hem up, but that second of hesitation on our part cost us. Something slams right into Aiden, ripping him away from me.

"Aiden!" I scream, fear gripping me and making my blood run ice cold. My magic rises up as I search for moisture all around me. When I find it, I raise my hands, and with them the water, before I blast it in all directions. The moment it makes impact with something, I race toward the sound. There's a grunt as I get closer, and I realize Aiden is fighting something. I can't blast the attacker with any kind of battle magic without putting Aiden at risk, so I do the only thing I can. I throw my body completely at them. My shoulder slams into something solid, and I kick out the way Aiden taught me. The impact sends both their bodies in different directions, and I land hard, wind knocked out of me. The sense of danger doesn't go away but becomes heavier by the second. I sit up, trying to orient myself, but there's nothing but a sheet of black all around me. Aiden grunts again, and I twist around, zeroing on the sound before I blast my battle magic in the opposite direction, away from him. There's another yelp and then Aiden's arms are under my armpits, pulling me up.

Battle magic is tricky for someone with water magic. In theory, the stronger I get, the more likely I will be to summon whole rivers of water to protect myself with, along with the standard attacks. Right now, I do nothing more than push the attacker a few feet back. But it gives us enough time. Aiden is once again pulling me behind him, and I do my best to keep up. My body is exhausted from the running and the fear, but I can't give up now. The huge building towers over us in the next minute, the stairs just yards away. Aiden doesn't slow down.

When we finally race through the front doors, they open with surprising ease before we fall inside and shut them behind us. Just as the sound of the slamming fades, the lights flicker on.

◈

I'M ON MY HANDS AND KNEES, BREATHING HEAVILY, WHEN AIDEN'S hand lands on my face, raising it to his.

"Are you okay?" he asks as his eyes roam over every inch of me. He looks like he's been through a battle. His clothes are torn up, exposing one of his shoulders, and his skin is marred by dirt. He's still the handsomest guy I've ever seen, and at first, I can't find the words. There's an intensity in his gaze that makes my eyes swim with unshed tears, and I don't even know what I'm trying not to cry about. But he sees the change in me, and so he does a very peculiar thing. He pulls me right into his arms, holding me close against his chest.

I don't hesitate to wrap my arms around his middle, burying myself in him. What we just went through, the almost certain death we almost came face to face with, I wouldn't have made it without Aiden. Without a second thought to how embarrassing I'm acting, I cling to him and he seems to hold onto me just as hard.

The noise of the academy coming to live around us is what finally pulls us apart. He seems to realize our position, letting go and getting to his feet in one swift motion. He reaches down to help me up, and when I place my hand in his, my whole body seems to sparkle. I drop it quickly, taking a step back as I try to smooth my dress out.

When I finally look up, his eyes are on me as he drinks me in. I have no idea what I look like, but I know my hair is a mess, and my dress is ripped in a few places. I wonder what he sees when he looks at me. There's heat in his gaze that warms me from the inside out. I'm almost afraid to breathe, if only to hold onto this moment for a little while longer.

A few shouts come from somewhere in the building before an announcement blares across the empty foyer.

"The academy is once again secure. Please return to your rooms and wait for further instructions."

It repeats another two times, but Aiden hasn't taken his eyes off me. It's like we're in our own little bubble, and a huge part of me just wants to get right back into his arms again. Maybe I move toward him, or maybe he sees my thoughts written all over my face, but suddenly a shudder comes over him, and he's back to the cocky shifter I've come to know.

"We should really go over your self-defense moves," he says out of nowhere. "You've got some work to do."

For a moment, I'm speechless. But then that familiar anger at being treated like I'm on a different level than him returns, and I'm ready for battle.

"Is now really the time to get into this?" I ask, my hands on my hips. I'm not sure what I'm expecting, but I feel incredibly exposed standing in the middle of an empty room with only this flimsy green dress as the armor between us. I thought maybe we reached some new understanding, but it's like he's back to the detached instructor versus the caring... whatever he was outside of these walls.

"Sure, why not? Or are you so eager to get back to your date?" The way he says date is almost like he's spitting the word out. I'm having a difficult time following his train of thought.

"Do you have a problem with my date?" I ask, not backing down. That's something I'm never going to do when it comes to Aiden. I may be terrified of whatever monsters are hunting us, but I will not allow myself to be afraid of Aiden. If he wants to fight, then I will give as good as I get. I think I proved tonight that I'm not as fragile as I thought I was.

"No, if you like those kinds of guys."

"And what kind is that?"

"Soft."

"What you mean to say is nice and kind and who treat me with respect," I snap, not even bothering to hide my annoyance. Who is he to say what kind of guys I like? And who does he think he is to make Noel seem less than he is?

"I see you've got a real attachment to that one." He smirks, and I fight the urge to use some of those combat lessons on him.

"He's my friend, Aiden. Something you wouldn't know anything about."

I spin on my heels, ready to be done with this conversation. I need to make sure my friends are safe, and that I don't end up in trouble either. I've already wasted too much time.

"Whatever you say, Duchess."

"What is your problem?" I spin to face him, not realizing he followed me. I almost collide with his body but catch myself at the last moment. The memory of him pressed against me just a few moments ago is imprinted on me forever, and I try to keep my body from responding to his proximity. "Why do you treat me like I'm some plague of your existence? I'm not some doll to play around with. I deserve respect, not this strange hatred you seem to be carrying for me."

"Is that what you think I'm doing?" He seems genuinely taken back by my outburst. "I could never..."

I wait for him to continue, and it's as if he's struggling with something within himself. I see the battle in his eyes, and I almost reach out. But he doesn't speak, and it seems to bring him almost physical pain.

"Can't we be friends?" I whisper, my heart in my throat. His eyes flash with heat, before they're cold once more.

"We can never be friends," he says, his voice low and those five words hit me straight in my gut. I think I would double over if I was alone, but instead, I hold onto whatever is left of my pride.

"Well, now that we've settled that," I say, and this time when I turn to leave, he doesn't stop me.

❧ 17 ❧

When I reach my hallway, everyone is out of their rooms, completely ignoring the instructions. I hear my name being called before Jade pushes through the crowd, throwing her arms around me. She holds me tighter than ever, and I hug her back just as hard. My emotions are all over the place and while I didn't cry when I left Aiden, I still want to.

"Where did you go? We were so worried. I was terrified actually. What happened?" She pulls back, giving me a quick study as she gasps. "Seriously, what happened?"

Over her shoulder, I see the rest of our friend group move toward, and I give them a reassuring smile.

"I got stuck outside. Had to fight some invisible monster."

"By yourself?" Christy exclaims.

"Aiden was there." I shake my head, and I feel Jade's hand tighten on my arm. Before anyone can say anything else, the booming announcement sounds once again, this time ordering us to our rooms for the night.

"*The initial lockdown is initiated for the night. Return to your rooms now.*"

It makes sense they're taking extra precautions now, but it doesn't make me feel any better. Everyone starts dispersing as Noel takes a step toward me.

"I'm so sorry. I never should've left you."

"You didn't," I remind him, giving his arm a quick squeeze. "I left to get the water and glass out of the room. That's on me."

He looks so contrite; I have the sudden urge to hug him. But something stops me. Maybe it's the memory of another boy holding me close just a little while ago.

"I'm okay, I promise."

He nods, and then he and Caleb leave for their side of the academy. Jade and I give the girls a quick goodbye wave, and then hand in hand, we hurry to our own room. The moment the door shuts behind us, Jade is pulling me toward the bathroom.

"Here, you can clean up while you tell me everything."

I glance at myself in the mirror, almost not recognizing the image staring back at me. My hair is matted and dirty, the bobby pins all but fallen out, just a few still holding on to dear life in my locks. My skin is marred by sweat and dirt, and my dress is completely ruined by the stains. One sleeve is barely there, ripped in half and falling halfway down my arm.

"Wow, I do look a little rough around the edges." I smile, but instead of playing along, Jade grabs my arm, squeezing it tightly.

"I was so scared, Maddie. We had no idea where you went and then they had to basically barricade us in some of the classrooms. There was this awful screeching noise that wouldn't let up for like ten minutes straight and some kind of thing kept banging into the building, making it shake. What is happening to this school?"

Tears are falling freely down Jade's face, and it's my turn to reach out to her, folding her into my arms. She may be one of the strongest people I've met, but tonight really got to her. And I can't fault her for that. Tonight really got to me too.

"It'll be okay, Jade. Somehow, someway it'll be okay. We have to believe that."

She clings to me for a little while longer, and I realize this is what my sisters would do. They'd hold me and tell me everything will be alright. Just then and there, I miss them so terribly it hurts. I miss my whole family, and I wish they were here to help me figure this out.

"Okay." Jade pulls back, wiping at her eyes. "Please tell me what happened."

And just like that, she's back to her curious self, and so I do what she asks. But first, I take a shower.

When I'm finally finished with my recap, we're sitting on our beds, in our pajamas, facing each other. My hair is still damp, so I braid it down my back.

"That must've been scary," Jade finally comments as I finish my braid and we both get under the covers. I reach for the light, turning it off, and the room is plunged into darkness.

"It was," I say, because it's easier to admit my weaknesses when she can't see me. "I thought I'd be better at conflict. But I guess all those rumors about me being a hero are exaggerated."

"Don't say that, Maddie," Jade replies, and even though I can't see her, I know she must be giving me one of her stern looks. "You came out on top tonight. You fought when it counted."

"Aiden helped," I admit grudgingly. "He more than helped."

"I think you give yourself less credit than you deserve."

"I just don't understand him, Jade," I huff, my thoughts once more on the strange way we left things, on how he did a complete one-eighty once we were inside these walls.

"He's a boy, I can't say I can help you on that one."

"He just gets under my skin so much," I say, my hands over my face. "I can't seem to find my footing when I'm around him."

Jade doesn't reply right away, and I wonder what she's thinking. When she finally does speak up, she takes me by surprise.

"Do you think maybe you have feelings for Aiden?" Jade asks, tentatively.

"Pfft. Yes. Feelings of annoyance and frustration and..."

"Maddie, I'm serious." I hear her sheets ruffle, and glance over in time to see her flicker on her bedside lamp. She's laying on her side, her eyes intently on mine. "You and him, you're more attuned to each other than anyone I've ever met. I know you have this rivalry going."

"Yes, he likes to push my buttons." I turn on my side, resigned to this conversation.

"He likes to push you. To be better. To be stronger. You'd have to be blind not to see it."

"Jade, you'd have to be a lot of things to think he cares about me at all." But even *I'm* not sure about that anymore. I remember the way he looked at me in my dress, the way his touch seared me right through. How he protected me without a second of hesitation. How he held me after we were safe. And how quickly all of that went away.

"He said we can never be friends, Jade. I think that sums up our relationship nicely."

I try not to show how much that still stings me, but it's difficult to push away the hurt. I thought we reached a new level in our partnership. I can't even call it a relationship, because that suggests a level of intimacy between two people. Yes, tonight we were on that level. But he shattered my every notion about us when he told me we could never be friends.

"Maybe he has his reasons," Jade draws my attention back to her. "We can't know what he's thinking. Or feeling. But I can tell you one thing, he's feeling something. And it's not hatred."

She lays back down then, turning the lamp back off, and I let her words settle over me as I stare up at the ceiling. I try not to let the hope blossom, but a big part of me wants to believe that Aiden and I are more than two people who were assigned to each other.

Jade might be right in her assessment of me. But I'm not quite ready to admit it to myself.

❧❦☙

THE NEXT TWO DAYS ARE SPENT IN OUR ROOMS. WE ARE ONLY allowed out for meals before we're sent back to the rooms. It's a long and boring weekend, but at least Jade and I catch up on our homework.

When Monday morning comes, it's as if nothing happened. Everyone gets up, gets dressed, and goes to breakfast. There is an undertone of hushed whispers, but no one is saying anything outright. The whole school has been cleaned up as if the dance never happened. That includes all the broken glass. The dining room is in pristine condition as well, and for a second, I wonder if I made the whole thing up. Maybe it was just a crazy dream. But then I glance down at my left hand and find the few scratches I discovered yesterday, which brings up the memory of Aiden pressed against my body. I know I didn't make that up.

"Good morning!" Christy calls out as chipper as ever. Today she has on a bright pink polo shirt and a kilted skirt, completing her preppy schoolgirl persona. I've wondered before why Thunderbird Academy doesn't require uniforms, but I'm not about to ask and stir the pot. I like the fact that I can wear my dark t-shirts and jeans year-round.

"How are you doing?" Noel asks as I take a seat beside him. His eyes are intensely on mine, and I can see that he still feels guilty about Friday night.

"I'm peachy keen." I reply, giving him a bright smile. Well, as bright as I can muster. My attention roams over the room, and I realize I'm looking for Aiden. Forcing myself to focus on my friends, I catch Jade's knowing smile, and I shake my head at her.

"I know no one is talking about it, but can we talk about it," Christy mock whispers, leaning in. Vera nods her head beside her. Today the shifter has on a long, dark blue dress that has pockets in the front, with a scarf wrapped elegantly around her shoulders. She always looks so put together. I take a swig of my orange juice before I notice that they're all staring at me.

"I don't know what you want me to say."

"We heard you came face to face with one of them monsters," Christy comments, her voice sounding more southern than I've heard before. It's true that the accent comes out more fully when the person gets excited.

"I can't tell you much about that because I didn't actually see anything."

"Well I heard that—"

"Miss Ferguson." Mrs. Lee is suddenly beside our table, looking each of us in the face before turning her full attention to Christy. "The administration would like the students to keep from speculating. I would suggest you get back to your breakfast."

Then after another quick glance, the science teacher moves on. We don't say anything for a second, and I see that Mrs. Lee isn't the only faculty present. There are quite a few teachers roaming around the tables.

"Big Brother is watching," Vera says under her breath, in that dry humor of hers, and the rest of us giggle. It's not that this is a funny situation, but I think we're all wound a little too tightly.

"Makes sense why we haven't been hearing much talk," Noel says before he dives into his food.

I agree, the presence of the teachers is a little unnerving, and I'm sure people don't want to be whispering with them so close by. But I also know it won't last. We're teenagers after all. We have our ways.

When breakfast is over, Noel surprises me by falling into step beside us.

"Can I walk you to your class?"

He's never offered before. I know for a fact that his class is on the opposite side of campus. Jade and I have English this hour, while he has it third period.

"If you'd like," I reply, because I'm not sure what to say. It seems like he needs this. Jade gives me a puzzled look, but I just shrug my shoulders, and the three of us say goodbye to Vera and Christy before we head toward our class. We walk in silence, and I'm a little confused by Noel's behavior. Maybe what happened Friday night is getting to him more than I thought. When we reach the classroom, Jade slips right in, leaving me with Noel.

"Thanks for walking us," I say, giving him a small smile. He seems a little unsure of himself, as if he's trying to say something, but not sure how to bring it up. After a moment's hesitation, he returns my smile. But before he can say a word, Aiden is there, brushing up behind him.

"Sorry, mate," he says, giving Noel a tight nod. "But you are blocking the doorway."

Aiden barely glances at me as he says the words. Noel looks over and nods before taking my elbow and leading me away from the door. Aiden pauses at the threshold, but still doesn't turn toward me, even though it seems like he wants to, and I'm feeling uncertain once again. What is his problem?

"He seems in a mood today," Noel comments, bringing my attention to him.

"He's always in a mood," I say, not bothering to even lower my volume. I'm sure the shifter hears me. "Anyway, was there something you wanted to talk about?" I decide to face it head on.

"Yes." Noel seems to shake himself to refocus. "Could we talk after class?"

"Of course."

He gives me another quick smile and then he's gone. I walk into the classroom, heading toward Jade. As I do, I pass by Aiden's desk, and the boy has his legs completely sprawled out across the walkway.

"Do you mind?" I ask, annoyed, when he doesn't move his feet from my path. I glance over at his friends, Ben and Owen, but neither comment. I don't even know if I've ever heard Owen speak. Ben gives me a half smile but that's it.

"I sure don't," Aiden replies, shrugging. I roll my eyes and step over his legs, trying to keep my anger from showing. "You're making after school plans with your boy toy already? That was fast."

I glance over my shoulder and find Aiden's eyes on me. He seems completely at ease, but I've learned a little more about him in the past few weeks, and I can almost see the underlying tension in him. Narrowing my eyes, I surprise even myself when I take a step back and lean over, getting right in his face. My hand rests on the back of his chair, barely grazing his shirt as my hair, wavy from being in a braid, falls forward over my shoulder. His eyes track the movement, before they rest on mine.

"What I do is none of your business," I say, my voice low. His eyes flash, but I don't give him a moment to respond. Instead, I straighten, walking over to Jade and take my seat. The teacher walks in then, as I try to get my breathing under control again. A tap on the desk brings my eyes to Jade as she points to her notebook.

That was hot.

I grin at her hurried handwriting. I have to say, I'm a little proud of myself. When I face the front, I feel a few sets of eyes on me but none of them belong to Aiden. Owen however gives me a long look, and I

❧ 18 ❧

The rest of the day passes uneventfully. I keep expecting something to happen, but nothing does. It's like Friday night was just a normal part of the academy experience. But it doesn't mean I haven't been on alert the whole time. I think everyone is a little jumpy, especially since this is the first time we've been allowed to congregate again after the ordeal. When classes have finally ended for the day, Jade and I head toward our room, ready for a break. At least I am. The stares I weathered when I first came to school have returned. It's most frustrating.

"Maddie!" Jade and I stop as I hear my name called, and that's when I see Noel walking toward us.

"You know," Jade comments. "You probably should not be meeting in a public place. We wouldn't want Aiden accidentally mauling him." I glance at her sharply, and notice she's wearing a tiny smile.

"What are you even talking about?"

She nods her head to the right, and I follow the direction to find Aiden, Ben, and Owen talking on the other side of the hall. For some reason, even this far away, I feel like his attention is on me.

"That boy is jealous," Jade whispers just as Noel reaches us. "Hi Noel. Bye Noel." And just like that, I'm left looking after her.

"What was that about?" Noel asks as he watches Jade retreat.

"Just some girl stuff."

"That's kind of what I wanted to talk to you about."

That captures my attention, and I swing my eyes back to him. He's wearing that a little unsure expression of his, and I narrow my eyes.

"You wanted to talk about girl stuff?"

"Yes. No. Could we go somewhere?"

The moment he asks, my eyes dart to Aiden, who stands facing us, but his eyes are on the person in front of him. Yet, I have no doubt his attention is on me, if only by the rigid set of his shoulders. He usually only looks that frustrated when I'm involved. So, I decide to test Jade's theory.

"Sure!" I reply brightly before I tuck my arm through Noel's elbow. Out of the corner of my eye, I see Aiden's eyes dart toward us, and I suppress a smile. Maybe there is something to Jade's knowledge of boys. I don't read into it too much though, because I know just how territorial shifters can be. Sometimes it has nothing to do with the person in question. Just an alpha being an alpha. But pushing Aiden's buttons? That's something I do seem to enjoy.

"So, what's up?" I ask as soon as Noel and I are outside. There are a few benches set up, covered by the trees, but we don't head there. We walk down the tree path for a few minutes before Noel finally speaks up.

"I wanted to talk to you about the dance."

"Okay?"

"We're friends, right?"

"Of course."

"And I can talk to you about anything?"

"Yes." I'm not sure where this is going, but I really hope it has something to do with Jade and not him suddenly developing feelings for me. I've heard of stuff like that happening. Not that it would actually ever happen to me, but I like Noel, and I don't want things to be awkward between us.

"Well—" he stops again, and the suspense is killing me.

"Noel, just tell me."

"I like Jade," he blurts out before getting that embarrassed look all over his face. "I know you know. And I asked you to the dance, and I wouldn't have wanted to go with anyone else, but I don't want things to be weird between us because we got... I don't know... while dancing and I wanted to tell you because I like her and maybe nothing will happen between us, but I can't bear the thought of you and me not being friends either and..."

"Noel, take a breath!" I take him by the arms, giving him a little squeeze. "It's okay."

"You're not mad? Or... disappointed?"

"You mean heartbroken?" I give him a quick smile as he shifts uncomfortably from side to side. "No. We kind of had this conversation already, remember? Nothing changed. Even though you're an incredible dancer. And honestly, I like you for her. Not that I would push the issue," I hurry on to add, because I'm not about to start playing matchmaker. "But there're no hard feelings between us."

"Oh good," he says right before he grabs me in a hug. I give it back to him because I feel like I need it too. He really has become one of my closest friends, and I'm glad we are both on the same page.

"You've made me very happy, Maddie Hawthorne," Noel says, looking down at me. Before I can reply, someone clears his throat, and we turn to find Aiden standing a few feet away. I have no idea how long he's been there, but he for sure saw our hug and heard Noel just now. If the hard look in his eyes is any indication.

"Sorry to interrupt, but Headmaster Marković has sent me to fetch you. He would like a word." Then without a word, he turns on his heels and walks away.

"What is with Aiden lately?" Noel asks, looking at his retreating figure. I shake my head, unsure of which answer I'd like to offer, settling on none.

"I better go," I say instead, and Noel nods.

"You're a great friend, Maddie."

"Right back at ya, Noel."

And just like that, we've cleared the air, and I honestly feel better. A part of me wondered if something would come from our little date and that moment on the dance floor, but after the dust settled, I couldn't see it. I'm glad Noel feels the same. I hurry toward the school and see that Aiden is waiting at the entrance. When I reach him, he doesn't speak but leads the way inside and toward the headmaster's office. I want to say something, but I can't figure out if this is a mood I can deal with right now. He's becoming more closed off and that's difficult to get past.

We reach the office and he knocks once before receiving an invitation. He pulls the door open, and I step inside. Then, before I can thank him, the door shuts and I'm all alone.

WELL, NOT ENTIRELY ALONE, SINCE HEADMASTER MARKOVIĆ IS sitting at his desk. He stands when I enter, giving me a comforting smile.

"Come on in, Miss Hawthorne. Take a seat."

I do as I'm told, taking the chair on the left of the desk. Once I'm situated, headmaster resumes his place as well, always the gentlemen. It's honestly something my dad still does, and it makes me smile every time. He always waits for Mama and the rest of us to be seated at the dinner table before he takes his turn. The pain is sharp and quick, but this time I welcome it with the sweet memory.

"I'm sure you know why you're here," Headmaster Marković begins, and I shake my head.

"I have no idea, sir," I reply honestly, because at this point it could be all kinds of things.

"What happened Friday was a very unfortunate incident," he says, and of course. I should've expected them to get to me eventually. "Mr. Lawson told me what happened, but I would like to hear your side of the story. It may yield a clue."

"I'm not sure how helpful I can be, but I can tell you what I know."

He motions for me to go ahead, listening carefully. It doesn't take long to go over the details, and he nods his head throughout, as if this is much of what he heard from Aiden. Obviously, I leave out my own confusing feelings when it comes to the shifter, but I don't downplay his role in keeping me safe. I wouldn't have made it without him.

"Aiden is a capable young man," the headmaster comments when I tell him as much. "He will be a great leader one day."

"Leader?" I ask, a little desperate to know more about the boy who's been haunting my every thought for days. "Isn't the term usually alpha?"

"You are correct, but Mr. Lawson's situation is a bit unconventional."

"What does that mean?"

"I am not at liberty to discuss, I'm afraid." Just like that, that discussion is over, but I am left with so many more questions. "Let us focus back on the events of Friday night. I understand that you and your sisters had quite a run in with the Ancients two months ago."

"I don't see how that's relevant," I say before I can stop myself.

"It is because I do not want you to put yourself in any unnecessary danger just because you have... experience with battle magic."

Ah, I see. He thinks I'm out here looking for trouble. I can understand the misconception, to a point. The whole school thinks I'm some kind of a super witch or an adrenaline junkie. Not that anyone would actually say anything to my face, but I'm not blind to the looks I'm still the recipient of when no one thinks I'm paying attention. It's only natural the rumors would get to the headmaster eventually.

"Sir, all I did on Friday was try and help. It backfired a little, considering I got stuck outside and had to come face to face with whatever that thing was. But I don't do this on purpose."

The tone in my voice must get to him because after a long pause, he finally nods. I'm not sure if he truly believes me, but he's giving it consideration. That much I can tell.

"Sir." I decide to push my luck a little and ask the hard questions. "Did the Ancients send in their minions? Did they actually get through the protective wards?"

At first, I think he's not going to answer me. Headmaster Marković is wearing that contemplative expression my dad sometimes gets. He is trying to decide if he's going to be honest or if he's going to try and protect me from the truth. In the end, he surprises me.

"They did not. The spell came from within the grounds, just like the last time. It was a very advanced glamour, coupled with a few offensive spells. A fascinating combination." Headmaster leans over his desk, looking me right in the eye. "I ask that you do not spread that around, as we are doing everything we can to insure your safety. But if you can think of anything from your dealings with the Ancients and their magic, please come to me directly."

And that is why he told me anything. He thinks I have an insight, just like my sisters do, about the Ancients. But at this point, I'm afraid I've already exhausted that particular avenue. What I need to do is get to the secret library. It's been days since I've been there, and the amount of knowledge that place holds can be of tremendous help. I think maybe now is the time to tell the headmaster about it, but when I open my mouth, no words come out. Whatever magic spell is keeping the library secret, it's a powerful one.

"I have one more question. What happens to the students who are outside the lockdown protocol?"

"You mean the time you ended up in the forest?"

"Yes, sir."

"The reason we have rooms as the place to go in case of the emergency is because the building itself is enchanted from generations past. The rest of the campus is too, but the enchantments are not as strong. It is unfortunate that you and a few others were unable to find shelter, and we are actively looking for ways to change that. One of the teachers found a protective amulet spell that we are trying to amplify now."

I understand all that, but the truth is, even the teachers can't protect us if this place overrun.

"What I ask, is that you do your best to follow the rules and stay close to areas which serve as a fortress against these types of situations."

There is so much I could say, but it would do me no use. I'm still just a student, and even though the headmaster gave me a lot more information than I assumed he would, he's not going to tell me everything. So, I give him my word and I'm dismissed. When I leave the office, I half expect Aiden to be waiting for me, but he's not. Miss Cindy, the headmaster's assistant, gives me a soft smile before getting back to the task on her desk.

I walk to my room alone, my mind mulling over what I learned and what to do next. I will definitely need to try to get to the library tonight. I've been putting it off for way too long. It doesn't help that the students have been under an incredible amount of scrutiny. We're watched more than usual, and I'm not exactly complaining in the grand scheme of thing. If it helps weed out the bad seeds, I'm all for it.

But another part of me is frustrated because I have no way of figuring out how to get to the library unseen. I think back to the way the door appeared to me when I touched it, when my blood seeped into the wood. There are secrets within those walls that are mine alone. I have no idea what it will take to finally unravel them, but I need to at least try. My whole existence may depend on it.

❦ 19 ❦

Once the lights out announcement is made, Jade and I are
under our covers almost immediately. Both of us, as I'm sure
is the case with the rest of the school, haven't been sleeping
well. Plus, she has an early study date with her group, since they're
presenting in our Elemental Magic class. I haven't been given a group
yet because Mrs. Roberts likes to only have one group present every
month.

It's about twenty minutes before Jade is fast asleep. I can always
tell when she's zonked out. She kind of unclenches her whole body and
spreads out. Especially lately, with everything going on, we've been
going to bed all wound up. Careful not to disturb her too much, I grab
the leggings and hoodie I stuffed under my comforter earlier in the day
and get dressed under the covers. After grabbing my boots, I head for
the door.

Before I exit, I take out two necklaces, wrapping my hand around
the three crystals and the tiny bottle at the same time. Malachite,
smoky quartz, and black tourmaline are attached to one of the necklaces as a charm. All three of the crystals are powerful protection talis-
mans, and I can really use some invisibility right now. The little plastic
bottle on the other necklace is filled with cinnamon, and a tiny
seashell, for hard protection. I close my eyes, concentrating on

reaching my center, before I push the intention through my hand and into the charms. The magic flares up, tingling my skin before it settles over me. This isn't going to make me invisible to the eye, but it will help guide me, so that I can stay off everyone's radar. And it'll mask me from the shifters. At least that's the plan.

That is another area of expertise I'd like to add to my list, protection wards and spells. I'm hoping the library can help me glean some information on that as well. I don't ever want to feel as helpless as I was in that barn structure with Aiden. I couldn't do anything with my magic, and that makes me a very useless witch.

The school has been implementing nightly security check ups, but they're not locking us in our rooms, in case we need to get out. I've been studying the security patterns since they upped the amount of patrols, and I'm about to put into test just how well I have it figured out.

It's not exactly ideal that the greenhouse and the entrance to the library are on the opposite side of the school. The helpful aspect of this adventure is that the school has plenty of nooks and crannies for me to hide in. The moment I see a shadow move, I dart into one of the indents in the hall or behind a pillar. It's slow going, but I manage to stay off anyone's radar.

When I finally reach the greenhouse, I'm surprised no one is stationed outside. It would make sense to be on rotation everywhere else, but this seems like a vulnerable entry point. Although, we've already discovered that we've got a wolf in sheep's clothing amongst us. Maybe it's pointless to try to keep someone from getting in when they're already here.

Once I'm inside the greenhouse, I do a quick scan but see and hear nothing. Satisfied that I'm alone, I move toward the far corner and the crates stacked there. A part of me is nervous at how easy it was to come down here, across the whole school. And how easy it would be for someone to hide right under our noses. They only need to know a little bit about their magic to create spells and charms. Nothing huge though because the school monitors magic activity. But something little, like the magic I created, it's mostly about intention. It can go unnoticed pretty easily. Not to mention, if the Ancients are supplying any of the spells or the magic, it would be nearly untraceable since it's not a signature the school has seen before.

Great, I just proved to myself that it can literally be anyone in this school. I'm not sure how that makes me feel. However, as I move the crates aside and the familiar rug greets me, I smile. This place, the library, it makes me feel like I'm not useless. Like I can do something. I haven't talked to my family all week, and I try very hard not to think just how much I wish I could. But I understand the precautions needed to keep the communication to a minimum. Still, I'm doing nothing to help find my father, and I'm doing nothing to help this school. All that is about to change.

I move the rug aside, pulling at the door in the next motion. The stale air of the underground greets me, but it doesn't take away from the excitement I'm feeling. I need this. I'm about to step down when a noise reaches my ears. I spin around, searching through the darkness and the plants, when I see a glow behind the row of greenery. My heart leaps into my throat, and my battle magic awakens. But even so, I don't run. Something keeps me rooted to that spot.

When the wolf walks out of the aisle, I realize it's because some crazy part of me knew it was Aiden. I can't tell if it's the feel of him in the air around me, or the look in his eyes. Even in wolf form, he's so purely Aiden.

The wolf walks toward me, stopping just a few feet away as we study each other. I've seen him before, when he came to get me in the woods, but this seems different. It seems more intimate somehow. As if he comes to some conclusion, he steps behind a row of plants, and then he's Aiden again. His eyes find me in the darkness once more, his bare chest a sight to behold. He reaches behind the plants and pulls out a pair of pants before he puts them on. A sweater comes next, but I just stand there, mesmerized as I watch him dress. I have no desire to run and hide. We're about to have a conversation, and I'm going to have to trust him completely. Something I'm really not good at.

When he finally steps out from behind the bushes that so strategically hid most of him from me, he's dressed. And his eyes are once again on me.

"Well, Duchess. You just can't keep yourself away from trouble."

"I AM ABSOLUTELY NOT GETTING INTO TROUBLE," I FEEL INCLINED to point out when he's standing just two feet away from me. He glances down at the open hole in the ground, before meeting my eyes once again. "This is not trouble."

"Really? Sneaking out of your room in the middle of the night and then unearthing some walkway into the underground is not trouble?"

"Nope. I'm just minding my Ps and Qs." I shrug, and surprisingly, that earns me a tiny grunt that almost sounds like a chuckle. I resist the urge to smile. Sometimes it's very easy to forget that Aiden and I are not friends.

"You are the only girl I know who's got the idiom collection of an elderly man."

"Why thank you, Aiden Lawson. You really know how to compliment a girl." I cross my arms in front of me, giving him the sweetest look I can manage. He smirks at me, but I still count this as a victory. If I can get under his skin even a fraction of how he gets under mine, it's points on my board. But all this back and forth is only stalling. We both know we have to talk about the entryway behind me.

At that moment, a noise reaches us, and Aiden steps forward, taking my arm and pulling me down beside him. My skin tingles under his hold, and I try not to let that become a visibly physical reaction. He looks over at me, our faces just a few inches apart, and for a moment, we're suspended in time. Just the two of us, breathing in the same air. Then, the sound of footsteps reaches us, and Aiden narrows his eyes, as if telling me to stay put. I nod, and then the pressure on my arm is gone and he's standing up.

"Hey, Pete," Aiden calls out as he disappears from view. "What's up?"

"Nothing much. Just thought I'd get some fresh air."

"Sorry man, but Headmaster said to keep the doors locked," Aiden replies, moving farther away from where I'm crouching down.

"Ugh, these patrols are killing me. I need to be in those woods," Pete replies. I can't see him, but for some reason I think he's the blonde guy Aiden hangs out with. He's not in any of my classes, so I can't be sure, but I believe he's a year ahead of us.

"I get it, trust me I do. I'll see if I can arrange something soon, alright?"

A few more words are exchanged, but they moved farther away, and I can't quite make them out. I think they're inside the school now, but I still don't move. Aiden is doing me a serious solid by keeping my secret. He's going to want answers in return. A part of me wants to climb down into the catacombs and hide away, but he would just come after me. Aiden isn't exactly one to give up.

After what seems like an hour, he finally comes back. I've settled right down on the floor, since my legs have gone to sleep crouching. He gives me an amused look, before he offers me his hand. I look at it like it's a snake that might bite me, but for some reason, I still accept it and let him pull me up to standing position.

"Are you going to take me on an excursion now?" he asks, his lips curling up at the corners. I roll my eyes, but I really have no choice.

"Look, where I'm going, it's a secret. But not because it's something bad," I hurry on to add. "It's something I..." There it goes not letting me finish explaining. I huff, before I continue. "If I show you, you have to promise not to say anything." Not that he will have much chance, but I feel like I need this from him before we can go any farther.

"I don't—"

"Promise," I interrupt, looking into his eyes intently. I'm never sure what he sees when he looks at me, but right now, it feels like we're on the same wavelength. The intensity behind his gaze always makes me a bit unbalanced, but right now, it almost adds fuel to my fire. After a moment he seems to realize just how important this is to me, and he nods.

"Out loud." I don't even think when I say the words, but it's something dad used to always say. It means more if the promise is spoken out loud. As if a verbal contract has been made. The emotion almost chokes me, but I push it down. I think Aiden sees it anyway but doesn't comment. He seems to be able to understand my moods better than I do at times.

"I promise."

Just two words, but they mean the world to me. There is no doubt he means them, if the way he's looking at me is any indication. We've taken a few more steps forward. I hope he doesn't take twice as many back.

"We have to cover this up, so no one finds it while we're gone." I point to the plants I usually stack in front of the entrance. "You go first, and I'll follow."

He doesn't question, trusting me, which is surprising all on its own. I wait for him to descend, as I move the plants in their designated spots. Then, I place the rug over the door and pull both over me as I close it. Even though we're in complete darkness, I know my way well enough. Aiden's arms reach for me when I'm close to the bottom, wrapping around my waist. I don't need his help, but I appreciate the gesture. Even so, I don't pull away. I allow him to guide me to the ground before I kneel and grab the flashlights I left here previously.

"Ready?" I ask, as I click on the light. He's standing right in front of me, his eyes doing a quick study of the tunnel. I push the other flashlight at him and move past before I do something stupid and ask if I can have a hug. The desire is sudden and nearly overwhelming, and I squash it down.

I'm becoming mush around him, and that is not allowed.

20

When we reach the spot where the door should be, it's not. I can tell Aiden is skeptical, but this is just part of what makes this library so special. It only reveals itself to me.

I step forward, placing my hand against the dark wall. At first, nothing happens. But then, the dirt ripples under my skin, and the door slowly appears, as if floating up to the top. Aiden inhales sharply, and I grin without turning around. I can't exactly credit this awesome magic to only myself, but the fact that it answers to me is pretty incredible. A part of me is excited to share this with someone. And yes, excited that the someone is Aiden. Even though I'm trying very hard not to let that become a thing.

When we step inside, I let Aiden through, watching his face for a reaction. His eyes scan over every surface, taking it all in at once. I close the door and follow him deeper into the library as the little hallway ends and the space opens up into the large high-ceilinged circular room.

"What is this place?" Aiden asks, his voice full of awe. It gives me a twinge of pride, seeing him amazed at this space just like I was. Like I still am.

"A library like no other. There are volumes upon volumes of

ancient texts I've never even heard of. It's how I found the spell that helped my sisters."

He turns at that, his eyes on me. "You've known about this place that long? Why haven't you said anything?"

"Honestly, I'm not sure. I tried to tell the headmaster a few times last year, but I think there's a spell that prevents me to do so. The place opened up to me that first time when I touched it with some of my blood. It's like it's only meant for me. I can't explain it. It's just a feeling I have."

I think he'll try to play it off or tell me how stupid that feeling is since this could be a huge help if it truly holds all these treasures, but he does neither. He turns back to the room and does another scan before he nods.

"I understand," he says before he walks toward the large window. My heart fills with just those two words, and I'm glad he's not looking at me. I'm sure my face will betray everything I'm feeling.

Seeing him here, a place that's so uniquely mine I think it holds a piece of me within it, I can't seem to keep my emotions in check. He continues to walk around, mesmerized by the sheer volume of this place. The wonder in his eyes is the same one I felt when I stepped inside the first time, and he's not hiding it from me. For this one moment, he's letting me see a real emotion in him, and I hold onto that. I have a feeling I'll be cherishing it down the line, long after this is all over.

"How many of these books have you studied?" Aiden's voice reaches out to me, and I realize I've been gawking at him. Shaking myself a little, I head for the table I've been using as my base of operation, a few dozen books piled on its surface.

"Not very many. It's difficult to sneak over here, as you can imagine." As I take a seat, Aiden comes around, taking the one next to me.

"You really haven't told anyone of this place?"

"Last year, when I first stumbled upon it, my best friend Kate was here. I brought her in, and she helped a lot. Also, Liam. He's a Fae. He didn't come back this semester, but he helped me decipher the spell that helped my sisters. Some of the books here are in different languages and from different realms."

"That's fascinating." Aiden turns, staring out the window at the evergreen forest. The light is just right, as always, making it seem like it's late afternoon and not the middle of the night. "And what's out there?"

"I've never been able to discover that," I say, looking out the window myself. "It always looks the same, the forest and the time of the day. There are no doors leading out that way and honestly, a part of me likes the mystery. I'm afraid it would be something disappointing."

I'm not sure what possesses me to add that last part, it's a little too intimate for us, but once again, Aiden doesn't make fun of me. He nods, as if he understands, and we share a look that sears me to my very core. Time seems to stop as we watch each other, and I think something shifts again, putting us into a new category. Too bad I have no idea what that means for us.

Tearing my gaze away, I grab for the first book on the table and pull it toward me. I need to concentrate. This is why I'm here. To check for protection spells, and to see if there's anything here to help us find the traitor.

"What can I do to help?"

"Grab a book and see what you can find," I reply, barely sparing him a glance. I can't let myself get distracted again. "There's no index or an organized system. Sometimes books appear where I didn't leave them, but that's very rare. One day, I think I want to spend time in here just to create some kind of organization to the chaos. But for now, I just read. And take notes."

When I glance up, Aiden is watching me once more. He grabs the first book in front of him and flashes me the tiniest of smiles,

"Read I can do."

I think my whole world shifts with that one look. I don't ever remember seeing him smile, and even though it's not a full one, it's the closest I've gotten, and it makes all the difference. There's a lightness in Aiden I haven't seen before, and I have no idea if it's this place or my sharing it with him, but I hold onto this moment and the memory it's creating.

It's a bit of simple peace in a world gone completely crazy.

THE NEXT MORNING, I CAN HARDLY CONCENTRATE. I HAVE A million thoughts in my mind and none of them are anything I can share with Jade or any of my other friends. And even though Aiden is in the know about the library, part of what I want to discuss has to do with him. All I want is to talk to my sisters.

"What has gotten into you today? Jade asks, as we head toward the dining room later in the day.

"I just asked her this," Vera comments, coming up to the other side of me. She had to repeat the question too because I was so lost in thought I didn't even realize she was talking to me.

"Sorry." I give both of them a quick smile as we reach the dining room and get in line. "I just have a lot to think about."

"Like what?" Christy jumps in, materializing beside us. I resist the urge to roll my eyes, but her nosiness is not appreciated right now.

"Just missing my family," I decide on a half-truth, but it seems to be enough. The girls all get a faraway look in their eyes, their own home-sickness making an appearance. If they can relate to anything, it's missing our families. The lockdown hasn't been easy on anyone. I saw a few students coming out of the headmaster's office just yesterday, wiping tears from their eyes.

"I know what we should do!" Christy exclaims, clapping her hands with excitement effectively breaking the silence. "We should have a slumber party."

Not that she would know this, but her words bring a bigger bout of sadness. I've only ever had a slumber party with my sisters. Even Kate and I never had a designated slumber party. That ping of awareness resonates in my chest, and I blink away unwanted tears. I'm not about to become a blabbering crying mess in the middle of the dining hall.

When I'm busy, it's so easy to forget how far away I am from family. But in times like these, I feel it in my very being.

"We can have it in Jade and Maddie's room. We can get a bunch of snacks and talk and braid hair..."

Christy's enthusiasm may be little over the top for my grumpy heart at times, but it can also be contagious. Even though the idea is appealing, it would put a damper on my plans. There is no way I'd be able to sneak away to the library. And as I keep reminding myself, that's my priority at the moment. But it's not like I can tell them that part.

"Yes! Let's do it, Maddie!" Jade chimes in, and now I'm between a rock and a hard place. I turn to the last girl in our group, hoping Vera's antisocial nature will save me from this impromptu party but no dice.

"Let's," is all she says, shrugging, as she reaches for an apple. This counts as her stamp of approval, and now I'm really stuck.

"Yes, yes!" Christy squeaks, earning a few looks thrown her way, but she doesn't care. "I will absolutely organize everything and get permission, and this will be great!"

"What will?" Noel asks, coming up to the group and reaching past me to grab a carton of orange juice. He flashes me a warm smile, stopping beside me.

"Is that all you're getting?" I ask, nodding toward his juice.

"I already grabbed food." He motions toward the table, and a few of his friends sitting beside a tray full of food. "I'm a growing boy. There is no way I'd be able to function on this little juice box."

I chuckle, which earns me another smile, before we all head toward the said table. Noel and I have really reached a new level in our friendship after our talk. There's a comfortable camaraderie between us that's almost thrilling.

When I went home in the summer to help my sisters, my whole town had a different kind of a dynamic. Shifters and witches were working together like they've been doing it all their lives. And more so, my sisters had guys in the house. For dinner. And movie night. Normal stuff.

It was new and fascinating.

I grew up in a community that is consciously female, and I've never thought anything of it. I love my coven and wouldn't trade it for anything. But besides Nolan's brother, I've never had many guy friends. When Liam stayed in Faery with his family instead of coming back this semester, I was once again minus guy friendships.

But here is Noel, someone I'm starting to trust. It's a new experience for me, and not one I'm complaining about. Maybe one of these days I'll be comfortable enough to ask him about Aiden. But not yet.

Christy is still chattering about the party, and while Jade and I have already exchanged a few looks, it's too late to bail now. I watch the petite brunette, amazed at her energy and go-get-them attitude. I think even if we resisted, she would've gotten her way. Maybe I need a little more of that in my life.

As I sit there, and let the conversation flow around me, a tingle starts up at the back of my spine, and I raise my eyes to scan my surroundings. Almost immediately my gaze lands on Aiden who has just walked into the room. He finds me right away, as if drawn to me, but doesn't approach. Talk about a new experience. What's happening between Aiden and me is even more unlike anything in my life before.

I find myself falling deeper and deeper under his spell. Noel bumps me with his shoulder, and I look over to see him pointing to the pepper he can't reach. I pass it on and when I look back at Aiden he is already lost in the crowd.

Glancing back at Noel, I wonder why can't I be attracted to someone like him? I know he's crushing on Jade, but he's got plenty of nice friends I'm sure he would be happy to set me up with. But no. Instead I'm getting all twisted up inside over tall, dark, and broody. I'm not sure how I'm supposed to spend my nights in the library with him.

Which brings me back to my initial dilemma. I look over at Christy one more time. I need to take a page out of her book and light some fires. Maybe if I'm even half as persistent as Christy, the headmaster will let me talk to my family.

~ 21 ~

After lunch, I wave goodbye to my friends and head straight toward the headmaster's office. I'm done with classes for the day, and I don't have training with Aiden for another couple of hours. I'm prepared to sit outside and wait Headmaster Marković out if need be. But when I reach the office, he's talking to Miss Cindy, and when I ask if I can speak to him, he makes time for me right away.

"What can I help you with, Miss Hawthorne?" he asks, motioning to the chair in front of his desk I occupied last time.

Deciding that diving right in is my best bet, I sit up straighter, leaning my shoulders back and meeting the headmaster's gaze head on.

"I need to speak with my sisters."

His eyes flash with something that is gone before I can identify it. He leans back in his chair, studying me carefully.

"Now, Miss Hawthorne, you know we are under strict rules at the moment."

"I understand that, Headmaster." I dare to interrupt, growing bolder by the minute. This is family, and that fuels me like nothing else. "But I ask you to give me this one leeway. It's been too long since I've heard from them and with my father still missing... I'm sure you can understand how unsettling that can be."

Even though we both know what I'm doing is manipulative, I think

Headmaster is a little proud of me for speaking up. I'm typically the one to keep to the background. I've always found it easier, since I have such powerful sisters. I don't have to be the one in the spotlight. It's why I hate it so much. But even if he's not proud of me, I am. It seems I'm finally finding my footing, and I'm not about to back down now.

"This is not to become a habit." The headmaster surprises me. "If I allow direct communication, it cannot be more than fifteen minutes."

"Understood," I reply, trying to keep the excitement at bay. But my whole body is buzzing with the prospect of hearing my sister's voices. If I get extra lucky, my mom might be there too. But I know that's less likely at the moment, so I will take what I can get.

Headmaster Marković pulls out a drawer before producing an older rotary phone. All of our cell phones were confiscated when the school went on lockdown, so even this piece of communication technology makes me happy. He proceeds to wave his hand over the device, and I can feel the magic stir in the air before he mumbles a few words under his breath.

"You have fifteen minutes, Miss Hawthorne." Headmaster Marković motions toward the phone before standing and walking out of the room. I don't waste a second to grab the receiver, dialing my house number. As the last rotation falls into place, I listen to the ringing in my ear, hoping my sisters are home by now. Unless something happened, at least one of them should be home.

After what seems like a hundred rings, no one answers. I push the hook down on the phone and dial Bri's shop next. If they're not at home, at least Bri should be at the store.

"Herbs & Trinkets, how can I help you?" Harper's voice sounds on the line, and I breathe a sigh of relief.

"Finally! Why aren't you home?"

"Maddie?!" Harper exclaims, and then I hear some commotion in the background, and Bri's voice comes on the line.

"Maddie, is something wrong?"

I realize after weeks of very strict communication rules, I probably just freaked them out.

"I'm okay, I promise. I managed to talk Headmaster Marković into letting me speak with you," I hurry on to say, and I can almost hear my sisters' shoulders relax.

"If you called, then you're not entirely okay," Harper comments gently, and I grin despite myself. They know me too well.

"I just miss you is all. Are there any news of dad?"

The silence on the other end of the line is heavy, and I know the answer before they even say it.

"No. Mama is with the council, trying to see if we can find another tracing spell," Harper replies, and I nod, even though they can't see me. It makes sense, but I wish Mom was there so I could hear her voice as well.

"What is it, Maddie?" Bri ask, her older sister senses tingling.

"There's just a lot going on," I begin, unsure of exactly to approach the subject. Even though Headmaster is giving me privacy, I doubt he's going to be too keen on me sharing sensitive information. Even though I know he enchanted the phone before he let me use it.

"I'm trying to find more information in that... place I told you about." This secrecy spell is really getting in the way of my communication. I have got to find a way around it.

"The... place." Bri stops, clearly confused. "Why can't I name it?"

"I think it's an enchantment. To keep it extra safe. I can't say it either, and when I've tried telling Headmaster about it, my mouth just won't work."

"That's curious," Harper comments, and I understand what she means. "I would be interested to know the reason behind it, if you ever do figure it out."

"I will," I can't believe after all this time I'm finally talking to my sisters. "But how is everything? Is everyone okay?"

"We are, Mads," Harper says. "The spell is holding strong for now, and it's been a very quiet month. If we stay inside the barrier."

"And the outside?"

"We try not to worry about that for now," Bri hurries to say, and that tells me what I need to know. A lot more is going on than they want to tell me. We're still protecting each other, even across miles and miles of distance. "But what about you? How are you? We miss you."

"I'm okay," I reply, wondering how much to tell them and how much they may already know. "This place has had its share of adventures, that's for sure. But I'm holding my own."

"Of course you are."

"There's also a boy," I say before I can stop myself. My sisters inhale simultaneously, making me laugh. "It's not unheard of."

"Tell us about him."

I think of how best to describe Aiden, and after a moment, all I can come up with is, "He's frustrating."

"Ah, those are the best kind," Bri replies, and I smile at the dreamy tone of her voice. From what she told me, she and Mark didn't exactly see eye to eye in the beginning.

"It's not like that. Well, I actually don't know. He's been training me in combat. And he knows about the place. He seems to be everywhere, and I just don't know what to do about it." The words rush out of me at once, as if I've been holding them in this whole time.

"Maddie, boys have a tendency to mess with our minds. And they don't even have to do much. It's kind of part of their DNA makeup."

"So, I'm supposed to be confused?"

"It's part of the process, I'm afraid," Harper comments and tears come to my eyes unbidden. I wish they were here. I wish I could sit and talk to them face to face.

"You'll figure out how you feel, Maddie," Bri says. "You are a smart girl. Even when he's driving you crazy, don't forget that. It's easy to let feelings cloud our judgement. But also, don't run from them. It's okay to embrace them and use them as tools to help guide you. We're emotional creatures by nature. But just because we are, doesn't mean we're not strong and resilient. You're a Hawthorne. That boy better watch out."

But running from my feelings is what I'm good at apparently. I've been denying it for weeks now, the pull I feel toward him. And a part of me has no idea what to do with this information.

"Thanks," I say, instead of getting into the details. I feel like I'm almost out of time. "I'll keep digging on my end, and please keep me updated. I feel so disconnected being this far away."

"We miss you, Mads. But you're always in our thoughts," Bri says warmly, and I tuck her words deep inside of me.

Just then, the door opens, and Headmaster Marković steps back into the room. My time is up.

"I love you," I add hurriedly.

"Love you too," my sisters echo, and then the line dies.

❧

INSTEAD OF HEADING BACK TO MY ROOM AFTER MY TALK, I GO outside. The weather has been turning cooler by the day, but I don't grab a jacket.

I follow the avenue of limes as it curves around the fountain and toward the pond. But rather than moving toward the little island, I keep going.

Kate and I explored some of the grounds last year, but we weren't as brave as I'm feeling right now. When everything started happening with the Ancients, everyone got paranoid. We were pretty confined to the main building for half of the year. Kate hated it. Her family is way stricter than mine, and she longed for the school to be her freedom. But now she's back home, and I have no idea how she's dealing. Not that her family is terrible or anything. They just put a lot of pressure on her. Which I can now understand firsthand.

My parents have always allowed me to be my own self. Yes, they want me to be successful, but it has never been about putting unrealistic expectations on me. I mostly do that to myself. But since the battle in Hawthorne, since I returned for my third semester, it's like everyone around me is holding me to that unreachable standard. Even the headmaster succumbed to it by letting me use the phone when no one else can. They're all expecting me to be something great. I'm not sure I'm cut out for that kind of greatness.

I'm good at magic, and I'm good at research. I always envisioned myself more as a Watcher, like my dad, than a leader like my mom and sisters. But now I'm being put in all kinds of situations that require me to be the one at the front. Like the library. Why can't I tell the headmaster about it? Why is knowledge of the place so guarded? It feels like I'm being given this responsibly over all this information, and I have no idea what to do about it.

When the trees around me get thicker, I realize I've walked farther than I planned. I'm on the opposite side of the pond, as far away from the school as I've ever been, while still within the grounds. From where I am, the island in the "middle" of the pond seems to actually be much farther away. I see that it's not directly halfway between the two ends. This side of the pond is much wider, almost like its pear shaped. I'm not sure why it's even called a pond. It's large enough to be a lake. But then again, what do I know.

Walking up to the water, I squat down to let my hand run over the silky waves. The breeze is just strong enough to make the sparkling liquid dance. When my finger dips into the pond, my magic shudders within me, as if shaking itself awake.

Maybe this isn't the greatest idea, but the call is too loud to ignore. I glance around quickly, but the coast is clear. The chill of autumn has been creeping in for days now, and the water is going to be even colder, but I can't help myself.

Stripping down, I'm in my undergarments and a tank. The air moves around me, prickling my skin with goosebumps. Before I can think too much of it, I step right up to the bank and dive in headfirst. The shock almost makes me come back up, but then the water engulfs me entirely, and I feel safe. I swim for a few seconds, then finally break the surface. A few months ago, I met Skylar, the newest addition to my hometown. She's half mermaid shifter, half witch, so her body temperature regulates in water, unlike mine. But even so, I enjoy the chill of the liquid against me.

The feel of the drops racing down my skin sooth me like a familiar caress. Sure, I take showers every day and am surrounded by water, but this feels different. There's something freeing about the natural water around, water that's connected directly to the earth. My magic is going haywire inside of me, bursting to be set free, and after a few seconds, I let it.

Surprisingly though, it builds slowly, like an oncoming storm. First, the waves move around me as if barely touched by the wind. But then, the turbulence starts, and the small pond becomes an angry ocean. The wind dances around me, sending some of the water into a whirlpool right in front of my eyes. If I was anyone else, I might be terrified at this display of power. Storms can be unpredictable, but I don't fear this one. I embrace it.

Lying back onto my back, I allow myself to float as I spread my arms out, and with it my magic. I'm being taken on a ride, and all I want to do is get lost in it. I close my eyes, and feel the magic pulse through me while the waves beat at my skin.

Suddenly, a pair of arms wrap around my waist, yanking me upright. Instead of screaming in surprise, I react. My leg comes up hard, my knee connecting with my attacker. My magic almost solidifies the water beneath me, and instead of trying to retreat, I'm suspended in place as I unleash my magic. I push both of my palms out, slamming them directly into the hard chest. The move and my magic blasts into the attacker, sending him skidding across the top of the water. At the last moment, before I plunge him into the depths beneath, I realize it's Aiden.

"Are you out of your freaking mind?" I scream dropping my hands and retracting my magic. Aiden drops below the surface of the water but comes up for air in the next moment.

"Are you trying to get yourself killed?" he yells in response, pushing the hair out of his face. With water dripping down his skin and his hair in disarray, he looks ridiculously attractive. But also very mad.

"Excuse me? I should be asking you that!" Now that my magic knows I'm not in danger, it settles, but barely, still just under my skin. He swims a few feet over, his eyes on me as the storm continues to dance around us. It quiets enough that it's not a danger to us but doesn't dissipate completely.

"I thought you were in trouble," Aiden says, not taking his eyes off me. Whatever I am about to say dies on my lips. There's genuine concern in his voice and it pierces me right through. Just then, he must hear how he sounds because his eyes dart away from my face, and to the water around us. I tread it to move closer to him, and now we're only a few feet apart.

"We're in water, Aiden. That's kind of my thing. My magic, it needed some exercise." I shrug, and his eyes come back to my face. A huge part of me wants to close the distance between us and reach out.

I'm not sure what I'm feeling yet, but I'm feeling it so intensely and entirely about Aiden.

"So, what you showed me in training, that wasn't even half of it?"

"No. Ever since the ritual I performed with my sisters, my magic has been unpredictable. For a while there, I thought it went dormant. But now I know it's been growing. Slowly."

"And you have been repressing it." He says it like a statement, but I still feel inclined to answer it like a question.

"Repressing it is easier than trying to explain it to the headmaster. I'm already too visible for my liking."

"You don't have to hide around me," he says it so quietly, but since it's just the two of us, I hear him. Not only that, I feel every word deep inside. My eyes catch onto his and suddenly, I want to show him what I can do.

"If I use too much magic, they'll be able to tell," I say, still watching him as I swim a little closer. "You need to be closer."

His eyes flash at my words, but then he swims toward me, so there's nothing but a sliver of water and my tank between us. If I breathe too deeply, our chests will brush against each other.

"I have to touch you." I realize how it sounds the moment I say it, but Aiden doesn't blink, just nods, giving me permission. One of my hands falls to my side, as my magic trickles down beneath our feet, while my other arm traces up Aiden's shoulder. It comes to rest right at the nape of his neck, and suddenly, we're breathing the same air.

The feel of him under my fingertips warms me from the inside, and the water doesn't feel so cold anymore. Aiden jerks, glancing down, trying to see through the water as the liquid solidifies to let us stand in one place. His hands drop to my waist, since he no longer has to tread water, and now I'm flush against him.

"Did you freeze it?" he whispers, rearranging our bodies a little.

"No. Kind of just packed the water molecules into something more solid than not." It's the best explanation I can come up with but it's enough. He looks fascinated. "If it gets too much, hold tight."

It's the only warning I give him as I raise the hand I've had in the water straight over our heads. The water rises all around us, creating a wall way over ten feet tall. Instead of keeping them straight, I pull at the points at the top and begin twisting them together. The waves and the wind dance, creating a beautiful picture, with us smack dab in the middle of it.

"It's like a Hershey's kiss," Aiden whispers in awe, staring straight up to where the funnel is twisting. I grin at his description, because I can see it. The waves move around us restlessly, and we're pushed even closer together. Our noses bump and everything inside of me stills. Aiden's hands flex on my hips, his whole body rigid, and it's like he's holding himself frozen to the spot. The storm around us is the same storm I see in his eyes. My breathing shallows as I try to swallow, but even with all this water, I'm ridiculously thirsty. His eyes flash again, and it's like he can see right into my head. All I have to do is move half an inch and his lips would be on mine. I've never been kissed, and I want him to be the first.

A gust of wind comes out of nowhere, pushing the water over us, and I tear my eyes away from Aiden to watch my magic spin completely out of control. Just for a moment, it's ruled by my emotions, and it's become unstable. The delicate way it was twining together has now become completely unbalanced. I try to pull it in, and I know what will happen when I do.

"Take a deep breath," I command, before it all comes crashing down on us.

$$\approx \quad 2\,2 \quad \approx$$

"Are you okay?" Aiden asks as we pull ourselves out of the water and onto the bank. We're both breathing heavily, soaking wet, and I have no idea how to answer that question. I nod, before I collapse onto my back, staring up at the sky.

Was I really just thinking about kissing Aiden? Did I really let my magic get out of control because I allowed myself to focus on him? This pull, this need I feel towards him, it's terrifying and exhilarating at the same time.

But the logical part of me understands that if he felt anything toward me, he would've taken the opening. Wouldn't he? Maybe that's something I need to talk to Jade about. She's at least has had a boyfriend before. While she might be clueless at times, she definitely knows more than I do. But for now, I'll just lay here, feeling embarrassed. Which is when I realize I'm still near naked, and he's only a few feet away.

"Maddie—" Aiden begins, but I can't meet his eye. Almost blindly, I reach for my shirt, pulling it over my head. I contemplate hiding behind the material, but I don't need to look any dumber than I already do.

"Maddie." This time his voice is a lot closer, and when my head pops out of the collar, I realize he's moved to stand beside me. I'm still sitting down, so I have to look way up to see his face. Which I don't. I reach for my pants next, pulling them over my legs in the most awkward way possible. My clothes soak through, and I shake my head at myself. Closing my eyes for a second, I pull on the water covering my body, flickering it away. Just like that, I'm dry again.

"Neat trick," Aiden comments as I stand. He's still shirtless, but I see that he didn't take his jeans off before jumping in. He was clearly worried about me, and I try to keep my heart from reacting to that.

"Stay still," I say, before I focus on the water clinging to him. It's hard not to stare at his magnificent chest, but I manage, just barely. "All done."

"Thanks."

I move away, as he pulls his sweater over his head, giving me a second to collect my thoughts. I need to stop letting my emotions rule my actions. Aiden and I are not friends. He's told me we would never be friends. I don't know why I would assume or hope we could ever be anything more.

"Do you want to train right now?" he surprises me by asking. I expected him to leave right away. He seems like he wants to.

"Sure," I reply, dropping my sweater before I can put it back on. Aiden takes his stance in front of me, and I follow suit. We've never trained outside before, and the feel of nature all around us exhilarates me. At my core, I am an elemental witch, after all. The more connected I am to the elements, the stronger I feel. And being this close to the water, with the droplets still clinging to the grass under our feet, I feel almost invincible.

Yet, when I raise my head and meet Aiden's steady gaze, all kinds of other emotions rush in. The magic didn't completely dry off his hair, and the water glimmers, clinging to his dark locks. I fight the sudden urge to reach over and send them into disarray with my fingers.

Now that I know what his skin feels like under my fingertips, it's difficult to focus on anything else. He's wearing a shirt once again, but it's almost as if I can see right through it.

"You ready?" Aiden's voice snaps me out of my thoughts. My face heats up, and I duck my head as I nod.

Aiden doesn't hesitate to attack. He moves toward me in one fluid motion, his right arm swinging at my neck. I block automatically, now so attuned to his movements, it's like a dance. My mind goes blank, focusing entirely on the way his body shifts with mine. Somewhere in the last month, we may not have become friends, but we have become partners.

I notice his move just a fraction before he sweeps his leg around. But it's enough for me to throw my body on him instead of falling down to my side like he intended. I wrap my legs around his middle, allowing my whole body to lean into the motion and then we're falling. At the last moment, he cradles me against him, and I unwrap my legs, so as not to get squished. He ends up beneath me, with me straddling his stomach, my head in the crook of his neck. For just a second we lay like this, breathing heavily as we both try to find stability in a world gone mad.

When I finally pull back, my hair falls over my shoulder, barely grazing his neck. His arm comes up, pushing the locks behind my ear and the movement is so tender, it brings tears to my eyes. Once more, we're in this moment of indecision. I want to lean down, and I want him to lean forward and neither one of us moves. His eyes grow dark, and his body tenses beneath mine, and then in one move, he's on his feet and he's setting me on mine.

"You're getting better," Aiden says, before he grabs his discarded shoes and leaves me standing beside the water. The compliment is so unusual that I don't get a chance to reply.

What is happening? I watch his retreating back, until he disappears. That's when I realize he didn't head toward the school. He went into the forest. A part of me wants to race after him, but I know that would be foolish. I've done enough foolish things for one day.

I sit back down on the grass, pulling on my own shoes. My body feels recharged after being in the water, and even that small spar didn't exhaust me like it usually does. Or maybe I really am getting better.

It seems that no matter what I do, I end up with more questions. Talking to my family helped, but it also made me miss them that much more. I can't think about my father without a part of me shriveling up inside. And now, Aiden is a puzzle I can't seem to solve. I'm not sure I'm cut out for all this, but it's not as if I have a choice.

Yet for this one moment, I stay by the water, and watch it dance in the tiny breeze in front of me, soothing my aching heart with its magic.

◈

THE NEXT DAY, AIDEN IS GONE. WHEN I FINALLY GOT BACK TO MY room, I went straight for homework, deciding to keep my weird feelings to myself. At least for now. Even though Jade and I haven't known each other for long, I trust her enough to talk to her about this. Just not yet.

I have to sort myself out before I can articulate what I'm feeling.

"Good news!" Christy runs up to me as I'm heading to potions class. "I got permission, and we're on for tonight!" She does her signature squeal, clapping her hands together and my heart drops a little. Apparently, a part of me was really hoping the faculty would advise her against this.

"We're on?" Jade asks, coming up to us. All four of us are in the class, and I'm sure Vera is already there. She doesn't dilly dally, but usually heads straight for her next class. I kind of like that about her. She's dependable. Whereas Christy is very... loud.

"We are absolutely on!" Another squeal. "I so cannot wait. It's going to be perfect. I'll grab snacks after lunch, since I don't have class. And after Jade's training, I can meet in your room and set it all up. I got a projector from the lab. Oh, and extra blankets."

We reach our class, and I'm thankful. My mood is definitely heavy on the grumpy because I have no excitement in me to be bothered with this sleepover. My eyes scan the hallway outside the room, and I internally berate myself because I'm looking for Aiden. He has a class across the way, but I don't see him.

"You okay?" Vera asks as I take a seat beside her. Even though Vera is a shifter, she has some witch blood in her, so she's been wanting to learn about our ways. I give her a quick nod, and she takes it at face value. Christy is still talking about the party, turned so she can face us. She and Jade are at the table in front of us.

Just when I'm about to put my head down in hopes of Christy

taking it as a sign to lower her volume, the teacher walks in. Mrs. Housely always looks like she's ready to walk down a runaway. Today she has on a yellow skirt that hugs her hips and flares at the bottom, with a black and white blouse tucked into the waistline. A large belt sits across her stomach, matching her heels. She's got 50s chic style down, and I'm a little envious. I'd love to be able to pull something like that off. All in all, Mrs. Housely definitely breaks the mold when it comes to what one would expect from potion teachers. From what I've heard they're usually a lot more scattered, and garden oriented. I can't really picture Mrs. Housely as a get down in the dirt kind of a witch.

"Please take out your notebooks," she says before Ben steps into the classroom. "Mr. Light, you aren't part of this class."

"I'm sorry Mrs. Housely, but I have a message for Maddie. It's in regard to her training."

"Very well." She sweeps her arm in my direction, and Ben makes his way toward me. He's got one of his signature tiny smiles as his eye meets mine.

"Maddie." The boy greets me, stopping at my desk.

"Ben," I reply, raising my eyebrows as I wait for him to continue. We've never actually spoken before, so this is new.

"Aiden has been called away for the weekend, so no sessions today or tomorrow." He watches me for a moment, and I expect him to continue, but no. That's all I get. He nods, turning to go, and I surprise myself by reaching out. His arm is hot to the touch, and I drop it almost as fast as I grab it.

But my bravado is gone, and I can't find the words to ask him about Aiden. However, Ben surprises me once more. He steps close to my desk, his eyes intensely on mine.

"If you need anything, just yell."

It's such an odd thing to say, and that's when I realize all eyes are on us. I nod quickly, and Ben seems satisfied with my answer. He gives a parting wave to Mrs. Housley and then leaves. The rest of the class is looking at me, and instead of ducking my head, I meet their eye. The few close by avert their eyes, and I sit back a little satisfied with myself.

"What was that about?" Jade asks, as Mrs. Housely begins talking.

"I have no idea," I reply, opening up my notebook.

For the rest of the class, I take notes, but it's like I'm two different people. My mind is constantly drifting to Aiden. Where could he have gone? We're on lockdown and this is the second time he just disappeared. And what's the deal with sending Ben to tell me about it? He could've sent a note like last time. But no, he's being all weird about it. Which Ben was kind of weird about it too, and what is up with boys? Are they always this confusing, or did I just get a special batch?

All day I've been trying to figure out a way to sneak over to the library before the slumber party. Something has been bugging me, and I can't figure out if it may be a passage I read or a book I saw. It's like it's on the tip of my tongue, but I can't find the words to express myself. It's a frustrating feeling, on top of the frustration I feel at myself for caring about Aiden. Or the grumpiness I'm experiencing at the thought of the party. My emotions are definitely heightened, and I'm not sure I know what to do about it. Maybe I should see if I can go out to the pond again and release some of this magic brewing inside me.

"Are you ready for all the fun?" Jade asks as I walk into our room. She's sprawled out on her bed, a book in front of her, but she sits up as I head for my bed.

"Yes, I'm so excited," I say over my shoulder. My roommate doesn't reply, and I turn to see her watching me carefully.

"You don't want to do this?"

I sigh, because of course she can see that. I haven't been all that good at hiding my emotions lately. Must be because of the imbalance I'm feeling. I take a seat on my bed, facing my friend.

"Honestly, I'm not feeling up to anything right now. Also, I've never had a slumber party without my sisters, and I'm feeling a bit emotional about it."

"Is that all you're feeling emotional about?"

At that, I almost smile. Jade deserves much more credit than I've been giving her because she's been paying attention. I still haven't talked to her about my last encounter with Aiden, only because I don't even know what I would say. But maybe this is the opening I need.

"It's weird that Aiden has been gone," I begin, scooting backward to rest against the wall. "But maybe it's been for the best."

"How do you mean?"

"Last time we were together." I swallow audibly, fidgeting a little. "I almost kissed him."

"What?" Jade catapults off her bed and onto mine in one swift motion, which takes me completely by surprise. She tumbles into me and I laugh, trying to push her off.

"Jade!"

"Tell me everything!" She's not to be denied, so I rehash what that happened by the water. Jade listens completely enthralled, her arms wrapped around my pillow. When I'm finished speaking, Jade watches me for a long, quiet moment. Then, she pulls a Christy, squealing loudly and jumping in her seat.

"Oh, Maddie. I've been waiting for this to happen."

"Wait, what?"

"You've been circling each other for weeks. And all that tension and repressed... everything. I mean, ah!"

"Okay, slow your roll. It's not like we're getting together. It's me being all emotional and nearly ruining everything."

"Why would you ruin anything?" Jade seems genuinely confused, and I pause to collect my thoughts.

"It's not like he feels anything for me," I finally say. "And I have to keep training with him, which will make things super awkward. Plus, we're..." My words freeze before I can mention the library. "It would be weird. That's all."

Once again, Jade doesn't speak up right away, and when I glance over at her, she's got that contemplative look about her.

"What?"

"Nothing. You just seem to have made up your mind about the way he feels without actually talking to him."

I stare at my friend for a moment before I shake it off. There's absolutely no way I would tell Aiden what I've been thinking. That's just not something I'm ready to do. Or will ever be ready to do.

"No, thank you," is all I say, as I scoot off the bed. I head toward my dresser, pulling out my comfy and matching pajamas. Now, I'm even more unexcited about the girls coming over. I think hiding under the covers sounds like a much better use of my time.

"Okay, okay." Jade gives in, but I think that's only because she knows the girls are almost here, and I'm shutting down. It's not as if I'm ever really open with my feelings, and Jade knows not to push it.

What she said dances around in my mind as I change. I was planning on asking Jade her opinion after all, it doesn't matter if I don't like it. But she's right. I have already made up my mind about this because I know how things go. Yet, at the same time, people assuming anything about me is one of my greatest pet peeves. So, how do I talk to Aiden about this without revealing my feelings? Is there a way that conversation can be had without me showing all my cards?

"I don't think I'm brave enough to have that discussion," I say not turning around, but I know Jade can hear me. She stops doing whatever she's doing and waits for me to continue. After I pull my shirt over my head, I face her and she's watching me with support shining in her eyes.

"I can't even imagine being the first to share my feelings. I just can't," I say, shrugging.

"I get it, Maddie," Jade replies. "Honestly, I talk full of bravado, but I'm the same way. It's even scarier when it's someone you really care about."

"Is that where I am?" I ask honestly, because I have no idea about anything anymore. Most of all this.

"Only you can decide that for yourself," Jade replies, getting off the bed. "But while you do, we're going to watch a movie and eat a bunch of snacks and do our nails and not talk about it. And you're going to feel much better in the morning."

Reaching for my roommate, I give her a big hug and some of the tension seeps out of me as she returns it. Maybe having girl time won't be such a hassle after all. It'll be nice to keep my mind busy with something other than worries.

THE GIRLS SHOW UP ABOUT TWENTY MINUTES LATER, ARMED WITH extra blankets and snacks. Christy is over-the-top hyper, which I'm used to. But even Vera seems to be enjoying herself as we make a pillow and blanket fort on the floor.

"Okay, so here is the list of activities." Christy pulls out a piece of paper as the rest of us exchange a look. This girl is really serious about her slumber partying. "Here are some snacks for consumption. We've got face masks and foot scrubs while we watch the first movie. Followed by manis and pedis, both or either, while we watch the second movie. Of course, it's important to hydrate, so there is plenty of water, and I was able to talk a certain lunch lady, who shall remain unnamed, into sneaking over some Coke as well."

Christy sweeps her hand over each item, the ultimate gameshow host, and I grin. This girl really does know how to party it up. Also, I haven't had soda in a very long time, so I don't even hesitate to reach for it.

"Ah, I knew that would be a winner! Let the festivities begin!"

The projector Christy was able to get is an old one, since the school doesn't really employ TV for education very often. Most of the teachers can conjure up whatever images we may need to see. But there are a few movies saved up for movie nights, and I grin as I look over at the selection.

"So, our options are a kid left behind at his house on Christmas, fighting aliens while looking for a way to protect earth from an oncoming evil, or sister witches?" I muse out loud. "That's quite some diversity."

"You really grabbed a witches movie for us to watch?" Vera comments, looking over my shoulder. Christy shrugs, already pulling out the face masks.

"I kind of really love their family." She goes back to unpacking all the essentials, some of which I've never even seen before. But then, I have one face wash that I'm loyal too and being a water witch, my complexion is fantastic.

"I vote for the alien movie," I say, and Vera nods.

"Me too!" Jade calls out as she heads to the bathroom. With the majority decided, we settle back as Christy explains the cleansing wipes she brought and the exfoliating brushes.

"This is intense," I mumble, receiving a very serious look from Christy.

"It's important to take care of your skin. That's how you become your own best friend."

I don't contradict the girl or comment any further. Clearly this is a big deal to her, and I'm never going to be the person that makes fun of other people's passions. That's one of the top lessons my parents taught me. It's amazing how I don't even think about these areas of life, but my family and my upbringing guides me in more ways than not.

My mind drifts back to the library and the nagging feeling I've had about it. Something jumped out at me last time I was there. I have to get back to those books tonight. Somehow.

We get our skin exfoliated and our masks on in the first thirty minutes of the movie. I've seen this one with my sisters, and it's always been a favorite. It doesn't help with the nostalgia I'm feeling, or how much I miss them, but that's okay. I'm learning, very slowly, how to own up to my own emotions. There's nothing wrong with what I'm feeling, I just need to use that to fuel me to move forward. And not get stuck in one spot.

As I glance around the room, I find that I'm truly enjoying myself, despite the sadness. These girls have become part of my school family, and I truly am lucky. It's so easy to concentrate on all the bad going on around me that I don't stop to appreciate the good. My dad has always taught me to remember the little details of life, and I've been missing out on that. Even though I didn't want the slumber party, I'm glad it happened.

"So, we should totally do a rating system," Christy announces much later. We've moved on to the witches movie and are working on our toe nails now.

"Rating for what?"

"The hotness in this school, of course!" Jade and I exchange a look at that, but Christy is already having too much fun. "I'll start. *Obvi* the shifters are on top of that list. I mean, Aiden? He's one hot alpha!" She giggles, and I grin. Even when he's not here, he's in everything I do.

"Vera, you go next!"

"I vote for Owen." The quiet girl surprises me. "I like the broody type." That actually makes sense.

"Oh, what about Mona?" Christy says, and I think back to the upperclassman Jade and I saw trying on a suit for the dance.

"That girl is gorgeous and fierce," Jade comments, and I nod.

"She's a shifter too," Vera says, and we burst out laughing.

"Of course they're all shifters," I say, when we've settled a little. "Vera, you're on that list too. There's something about shifters. The pack in my hometown? They're all beautiful creatures."

Vera blushes, but doesn't comment. I realize I put her on the spot, but I can clearly see she's pleased.

"I wouldn't mind me a shifter," Christy comments, wiggling her eyebrows up and down, and we're laughing once again.

When our nails are painted, and the whole place smells like Autumn morning at home, I snuggle down into my side of the blanket fort, eyes glued to the screen. We talked, we laughed, and it finally felt like I was just a girl, hanging out with friends. Now, I just need to wait for them to fall asleep, so I can get down to the library. No matter how relaxed I am, I won't be able to sleep until I figure out what's been bugging me.

$\mathscr{H}$ 24 $\mathscr{H}$

"Should you be sneaking around out here?"

I'm very proud of myself for not jumping at the quiet voice, but truth be told, I was expecting this. Just a little. Turning slowly, I narrow my eyes as a figure steps from the shadows.

"Ben, are you a creepy stalker?"

"Well, not creepy." He flashes me a grin, and I fight the urge to return it. I had a feeling I'd be seeing more of him while Aiden is away, so there's another pat on the back for me.

"Shouldn't you be on the opposite side of the castle, I don't know, sleeping?"

"I could be asking you the same thing." Ben takes a step closer. "Aren't you in the midst of an all-girl slumber party?"

"How do you—" I stop as he grins at me again. This shifter has no problem wearing his smile for all to see, and I have to fight the urge to return it. But if I don't get a move on, I'll either get caught or... actually, just get caught.

That's bad enough.

"Well, I'll be going now," I say, waving a hand in his general direction. But after I've taken barely three steps, Ben is beside me. "Can I help you with something?"

"Sure. You can pretend you won't argue with me when I tell you I'm to escort you to wherever you're going."

"I can pretend, but not for long." I snort, very un-lady like. Ben chuckles at the sound and despite how weird this situation is to me, I can feel a comradeship forming between us.

"Why are you here, Ben?" I decide to not beat around the bush. Ben gives me a long look, as if contemplating whether or not he'll tell me the truth.

"Aiden asked me."

For some reason, I'm not surprised. But Ben's words still bring a pang to my chest, and a sense of awareness I try so hard to suppress.

It's difficult to ignore my feelings when Aiden keeps doing these little things. In his own way, he keeps taking care of me, and I'm not particularly sure what to do with that.

"There's absolutely no chance in you letting me be?" I ask, looking Ben in the eye. He shakes his head in response, and I don't waste another minute. We need to move before the patrol comes by. It was hard enough sneaking away from the girls. The charms of protection I made last time are still in my pocket, but I didn't have time to replenish the magic. A part of me was nervous that if I did, the headmaster would notice. I have to use what I can and can't waste any opportunities I get.

I rush down the hall, Ben close on my heels. He stays true to his word and doesn't question where we're going. But I can tell he wants to. I mean, who wouldn't?

Suddenly, he grabs my hand, pulling me behind one of the columns. I'm smart enough not to make a sound as we squeeze in between the wall and the marble. A few moments later, one of the patrol guys rounds the corner. My vision isn't as great as a shifter's, but I can see him glance down the hall, before moving on. Ben puts a finger to his lips, and I nod. We have to wait for him to get farther away.

When Ben deems it safe again, he steps out into the hall, pulling me with him. He does another quick study before motioning me to move.

"Thanks," I say, and he smiles in return. It really is nifty having a shifter around. We continue creeping down the hall before we arrive at the back staircase. This is riskier, but it'll put us right near the greenhouse.

"Can you go first?"

Ben takes the lead without question, and I follow closely behind. I'm still not sure what I'm going to do with him when we get to the greenhouse. It's not as if I want more people to know about the library. I'm constantly contemplating what to do with the knowledge and how it's protecting itself. Maybe I should trust that the spell wouldn't allow anyone who's a danger to the place to know about it. It had no problem with Kate or Liam or even Aiden. So, I can't say I tested out that theory fully. I have a feeling the library won't have a problem with Ben either.

We reach the greenhouse with no problems, and I know it's only because of Ben. The security has been heightened, and I might not have made it this far alone.

"What now?" Ben asks once we're inside, and I stand looking around at the plants.

"Now you leave?" I reply, hopefully.

"No chance of that. I'm not about to go against my alpha's orders."

Of course not. I mull over my next move, but I really just have the one. Ben is about to find out about my secret.

"Okay, I assume since your alpha told you to protect me that means in all areas of my life?" Ben gives me a puzzling look as I continue. "What I'm about to show you is a secret. A secret that only four people know about, and it has to stay that way."

"Maddie, don't worry. Your secret is safe with me."

The way he says it, and the way he looks at me, I believe it. Having no other choice left, I head toward the corner of the greenhouse and unmask my little hideaway door. Ben stays quiet throughout the whole process, but I can read the surprise in his eyes. He definitely didn't expect this. Which means Aiden didn't prepare him and has kept my secret. I'm thankful for that because I'm almost positive, even with protective charms, an alpha would have a way around witch's magic if it came down to it.

When we reach the door to the library, I place my hand against it, and it glows i's welcoming light. Once inside, Ben is just as enamored with the place as I've been, but he still doesn't ask any questions. Deciding I'm stuck with him, I give him a quick summary of the place.

"This is incredible, Maddie. And no one knows?"

"I can't even talk about it outside of here. One day I'll figure out what that means, but right now I need to find the book I was looking at last time. Something has been bothering me for days."

Leaving Ben to explore on his own, I head toward the table Aiden and I sat at last time. My mind brings up an image of us there, but I push it away. I really have no business thinking about a boy right now.

Picking up book after book I try to pinpoint the feeling I've been carrying around. If it was something I read, I'd have to go through every page. But if it was something else, maybe I can rely on my intuition. Ben has moved closer and is watching me now but doesn't speak. I appreciate that, and I realize I kind of like having him around. He reminds me of Liam a bit. I find his presence sort of comforting.

"It's not working!" I finally snap, dropping the last book on the table.

"What is it you're looking for?"

"I'm not sure and that's the problem. The last time," I take a deep breath, "it was as if something reached out to me through the pages. And now I can't find that feeling."

"Maybe you're here with the wrong guy."

My eyes fly up to meet his, and I see him shrug.

"It's not like that," I hurry on to say.

"I just mean you and Aiden have a certain... magic about you. You're a Hawthorne. He's the next alpha. Maybe that's the energy that's needed."

It does make sense, but I also think Ben is talking about something else. I try not to read too much into it, but the magic aspect does give me an idea.

"Let me try something."

I spread out the books on the table in front of me, before climbing on a chair. Standing over the array of hardcovers, I close my eyes and hover my arms over the table. There isn't a specific spell I can try, but maybe I can just ask for the answer. I've seen Bri do this once or twice but have never tried it myself.

The magic inside of me begins to tingle, spreading slowly at first, then building faster and faster. My whole body feels like it's on fire as I push the magic to do my bidding. I ask it nicely, to show me what I'm searching for, keeping my intention as pure as possible.

"Maddie." After what seems like hours, Ben calls my name softly. I open my eyes and glance down to see one book glowing just slightly.

A grin blossoms onto my face as I reign my magic in and jump down.

"Okay, let's see what all the fuss is about."

❧

IT'S ANOTHER HOUR BEFORE I FINALLY FIND SOMETHING.

Ben has been sitting quietly, browsing through one of the books. But the moment my eye lands on the right page, it's like he can sense it. I feel him move closer, yet I don't take my eyes off the page.

It's a list of families, witch families, going back hundreds and hundreds of years. The page unfolds, a tree growing right there on paper. So many names, so much history.

"What is it?" I didn't realize he moved to the table and is now sitting beside me.

"It's a family tree. Of magic. These names go back hundreds of years."

"On this one spread of paper?"

"It's magic," I reply, smiling. I see the names change and move as I go further and further back.

"This is what you were looking for?"

"Yes. I didn't see the actual tree last time, but this page," I turn two pages back, "it speaks of a dark history of witches, and that's what has been on my mind."

"What do you mean?"

"My dad is a Watcher," I begin, turning my attention to the boy in front of me. "He's been a keeper of magical knowledge his whole life, and he's shared a lot of it with me. Not everything, obviously. I didn't know the Ancients were anything but a bedtime story until they started rising right outside of my home town."

"But isn't that the case with everyone? Even my pack assumed the Ancients weren't real."

"It's part of their plan. To be so forgotten that we're not ready to defend ourselves. But they've made waves in our lives before."

"When?"

"Well, I can tell you that thirty-five years ago, in Hawthorne, they sent a plague that nearly wiped out the town."

"I didn't know that."

"I didn't either. But my parents did. They were both there." He's silent for a bit as I continue to study the names.

"How does that help you now?"

"It helps because every family keeps a grimoire. It holds their individual spells, history of their time, charms that pertain only to them. If I can find some of the older families maybe they have information on the Ancients. The further back we go, the more chance we have of finding something new we can use. If my parents had dealings with the Ancients thirty-five years ago, can you imagine someone from three hundred years ago?"

"But wouldn't that information be readily available?"

"You'd think so, but no. Remember the Salem witch trials? Just one of the many times humans made it difficult for us to be part of the world. Families kept their secret and their grimoires under lock and key. There are so many covens out there that we have no idea about. This may be what helps us uncover those secrets."

I grab one of the notebooks I left here last semester and a pen and begin jotting down the names as they come up on the page. Ben lets me be, and we stay like that for a while. My mind races with possibilities and everything we can learn from this. I'll have to find a way to get the information to my sisters since they'll have a much better chance at figuring this out.

When I think I've copied down enough names, I take a piece of paper and bookmark the page. Then I stand.

"Ready to get back?" Ben asks, also standing. I nod, folding the paper and tucking it into my jeans. With one last look at the library, I lead the way out.

Once we're back in the greenhouse, a sense of dread reaches out to me. I can't pinpoint the feeling, but it's there, and I turn to Ben automatically.

"Do you feel—"

But I never get to finish. The whole school begins to shake, the ground unsteady under my feet.

"Ben?"

He grabs my hand, pulling me away from the falling shelves and into the hallway. I'm having a difficult time staying upright as the school trembles a few more times.

"What's happening?"

"Come on. We need to get out of here." Ben pulls me behind him as one of the pictures hanging on the wall shatters at our backs. The case displaying various potions topples over, making us jump back. The alarm begins to sound, shrieking commands at us.

"Can we get outside?" I yell over the noise and Ben shakes his head. The whole school is on its nightly lock down. I focus on the alarm long enough to hear the instructions. We need to be in a room, protected. And we're not.

"Where is the patrol?" I ask, thinking of the other people who would be out of their protective rooms.

"There are designated rooms for them," Ben shouts back, because of course there are. They wouldn't let students patrol if there wasn't a backup plan. The school shudders again, this one stronger than the last, knocking us off our feet. I land hard, on all fours, my palms and knees stinging from the impact.

"Come on." Ben reaches for me, picking me up and setting me on my feet, before we take off deeper into the school. Having no other choice, I rush after him as the school continues to shake around us. Glass shatters and the next thing I know, Ben is wrapping himself around me, tucking my face into his chest.

"You okay?" he asks, glancing down, and I manage a nod. This is definitely not how I imagined my night going. Ben grabs my hand once more, and we're moving. Another minute and he stops abruptly in front of a door.

Yanking it open, he pulls us in, shutting it behind. I stumble over my own feet and whatever is in the room, but even in near darkness, Ben manages to catch me.

"Can you work some light magic?" he asks and I nod, even though he probably can't see me. Illumination spell is one of the first ones I learned as a kid. Two waves of a hand and a few words, "Light the way, please."

An orb appears in my hand, and I glance around to find us in a storage closet. I look at the shelves full of items, but nothing is moving.

"How are we protected?"

"I'm thinking, even though it's a closet, it's still a room. The protective spell is in place." He shrugs, but he's a smart one, that's for sure.

We each take a seat on the floor, exhausted from the night. My mind keeps wandering back to what's going on outside this room, but we won't be going out there any time soon.

"What do you think is happening to the school?" Ben finally asks. I don't answer right away, trying to push away the panic.

"I think someone is doing their best to destroy it."

＊ 25 ＊

"Thank you for getting me out of there," I say, breaking the silence. We've been trying to listen to the sounds of the school, but it's as if we've been sealed inside of a cocoon. Every now and then a noise will reach us, but it sounds too far away to distinguish it.

"Anytime," Ben replies, sliding around to get more comfortable. We're sitting with our backs against the storage shelf, my legs criss-crossed in front of me, his pulled up at the knees. "What do you think is going on out there?"

"I think the faculty is doing a sweep, making sure no one pene-trated the school's grounds," I reply automatically. "It's standard proto-col. If someone did get in, I think we would've heard something by now."

Ben nods but doesn't comment and we fall back into silence. My mind is working overtime. These breeches are getting more frequent. Every single time the alarm goes off, I'm scared it will be it. That the evil will invade and this place will fall down around us. I can't imagine Thunderbird Academy not standing tall, but it's such a possibility now, it makes my chest hurt.

"Can I ask you about what happened in Hawthorne?"

A part of me expected this. It's a question everyone has been wanting to ask since the moment I returned. But besides my close friend group, no one else has approached me.

"It's okay if you don't want to talk about it," Ben hurries on to add, but I wave it off.

"There's not much to tell," I begin, resigned to talking about it. I do kind of owe Ben for tonight. This is the least I can do. "I found some information. Much like I found it today." Once again, I can't quite mention the library, and it's a bit annoying. "My sisters already had all the pieces. They just needed the missing part. I think they would've figured it out without me. It just would've taken them longer."

"And might've cost them more." I glance up at him at his words. "I don't think you should minimize your part in this."

"It's not like I'm trying to." I sigh, wondering how much to tell him. For some reason, I feel comfortable with him. And I'm not sure if it's because he's Aiden's friend or because I'm being a little more open to relationships now. But maybe it's simply because I don't know him, and I need to talk to someone.

"It's just that people expect more from me because I was part of this great spell. But truth be told, I didn't even do much. My magic may have grown recently, but I'm still nowhere near where people expect me to be."

"That's understandable. But Maddie." He leans forward, intensity written all over his face. "Aiden has told me just how skillful you are. You're smart and powerful. Selling yourself short won't help anyone. Most of all you."

He leans back as if he hasn't just delivered one of the most amazing encouragements. Of course, he wouldn't know how much those words mean to me, or how I'm soaking them up like a flower who hasn't been watered in a while.

The interesting part is that it's not as if I need a confidence boost, per se. I know my own power. I know there is a lot I can handle. I'm growing stronger with every test sent my way, every challenge. I'm not the same girl I was when I started here a year ago. Sometimes I forget that year even existed. Everything is so different now. But the doubts reach even the most confident of individuals and having Aiden's faith in me so blatantly spoken of makes me feel all warm and fuzzy inside.

Everyone can use a little of faith in them now and then. Apparently, I have that support in Aiden. Even though he won't tell me so himself.

"Thanks, Ben," I finally say, just as the door clicks before being pulled open.

"Madison Hawthorne. Why am I not even surprised?" Headmaster Marković asks, stepping into the doorway, the light at his back.

I stand, shrugging.

"I'm just lucky, I guess."

"Would you like to explain to me what you were doing, hiding in the storage room?" Headmaster Marković asks me a little later, as I sit in his office. The school is awake, students being interviewed as the faculty continues to comb through the grounds.

"It was the first place that was available after the alarm went off?" I reply, receiving a very unamused look from the headmaster.

"Maddie."

"I couldn't sleep," I say, going back to my prepared excuse. "My magic was a little restless, and I needed it calmed before it went haywire."

"So, you went to..."

"The greenhouse. The plants there helped."

Even though I know he's still suspicious, he can't deny the logic. As an elemental witch, the best place I can be is near nature. Since I can't go outside at night, the greenhouse would be the most plausible solution.

"How did Mr. Light end up in the same place as you?"

"We ran into each other when he was on patrol." I really hope he's actually scheduled to patrol and wasn't out of his room just because of me. I guess right because headmaster doesn't question me further.

"Where is he?" I ask, still afraid I got the shifter in trouble.

"He's been called away by his alpha."

My heart jumps in my chest, a dozen questions on the tip of my tongue. But I doubt Headmaster is in a sharing mood, so I don't ask.

"Am I free to go?" I ask instead and receive a go ahead. When I leave the headmaster's office, I'm met by groups of students huddled in the hallways wearing their pajamas. Miss Cindy is handing out cups of tea, trying to soothe them as best as she can. Without meeting anyone's eye, I hurry to my side of the castle, my mind on the shifter. For Ben to be pulled away, something had to have happened.

"Oh my word, Maddie!" Jade throws her arms around me the moment I reach our room. The girls are sitting with blankets wrapped around them on the floor, a worried look on their faces. "Where have you been?"

"In the headmaster's office," I reply, returning her hug. I don't really want to get into it with Vera and Christy here, and I give Jade an extra squeeze to keep her quiet. She seems to read my mind and doesn't press.

"What is going on, Maddie?" Christy asks, her eyes big and round.

"I'm not sure. They didn't say anything, but they're interviewing a bunch of people."

"They did come by and check on us, but we were all sleeping when the alert sounded. So, we didn't have anything to add," Jade explains as I settle back on my bed.

Exhausted from the events of tonight, I lay down, still fully dressed, as the girls continue talking. My body goes numb, but my mind won't stop working. So many possibilities rush through, none of them with good outcomes. It scares me to think that someone in this school wishes it harm.

Mentally, I try to put together a list of suspects, but I have no idea where to start. It's not like there are any stereotypical signs I can follow. With magic, anything is possible. The sweetest person can be the darkest witch. I could never put anyone into a box. It's with these thoughts that I let myself drift off into sleep.

THE NEXT MORNING, THE WHOLE SCHOOL IS IN UPROAR. THERE'S A

shadow hanging over the school, a heaviness that's finally descended upon us. When I woke up this morning, clouds made everything look gloomy.

"This weather is weird, right?" Jade asks on the way to our second class. The first hour was skipped and replaced with an assembly, but Headmaster Marković had nothing new to add. The school is still on lockdown. Magic is still being monitored closely. We can't wander off. This place no longer feels like a sanctuary. It's more of a prison.

"Typically, the weather is regulated by the upperclassmen elementals," I reply, my eyes scanning over every person we pass. I told myself I'd be more on alert, but it's hard. These are my fellow classmates. I can't get over the fact that one of them may be a traitor.

"So, why isn't it?"

"Maybe it is," I shrug, glancing at my friend. "We need gloomy days to balance the sunny ones, right?"

Jade takes that at face value, but I know she's not reassured. I'm not either. Something is happening, and the weather is just one aspect of that. It's not like the elementals watch it continuously, but they do help out when it gets too bad. It looks like an apocalypse is coming, so I would assume they'd do something. Unless they can't.

The rest of the day isn't much better. There are whispers and looks, and no one is trusting anyone. Aiden is still gone, and Ben has followed him apparently. I wonder what could be so important that the academy would break their rules and let them out.

"You doing okay?" Noel asks, coming up to stand beside me. I've been nestled between the wall and the bookcase, watching students rush by. I'm in observation mode, trying to piece together all the clues that have been showing up. At least, I think there are clues. Watching people's behaviors is a little exhausting, but necessary. I haven't been paying as much attention as I should've been. But I'm paying attention now.

"Sure. How about you?"

"Honestly, a little freaked out. They almost got in." That gets my attention. I turn fully to Noel.

"What?"

"I overheard one of the upperclassmen talking. The attack almost pierced through the protective shield. They almost got in."

That's news to me, but I'm not that surprised. It was going to happen eventually. There is a sense of foreboding that we've been living with, waiting for that other shoe to drop. The Ancients will never give up, and this school is of interest to them. Maybe this is happening with every academy. Maybe the plan here is to infiltrate the young minds. If I was masterminding a world domination, that's where I would start.

"What else did you hear?" I lean my shoulder against the wall so I can watch Noel and the crowd in front of us.

"The headmaster is putting together a plan of action. I'm not sure what he's thinking he can do at this point that they haven't already been doing, but it's something. That's all I know."

"It does make sense. They have to try everything. Especially since whatever they are doing is not working."

We fall silent as another few students rush by us, two of the girls giving me a quick once-over.

"Does that get tiring?" Noel nods toward the girls.

"You have no idea."

I push away from the wall, and Noel follows close beside me. We're heading away from the lunchroom, and I know I told the girls I'd meet them there, but I have no desire to be subjected to that many people at the same time.

"I'm going to head outside," I tell Noel, and at first, he seems like he's going to stop me. Instead, he gives me a long searching look, before inclining his head.

"Be careful, okay?"

"You too."

I leave him behind, and when I'm at the end of the hallway, I turn to see him disappearing into the crowd. With everything that's been going on, I haven't really taken the time to appreciate my friends lately. But I have been given some pretty good ones, and I make a mental note to focus on that a little more. If we survive this.

When the fresh air hits my cheeks, I breathe in fully. There are students and faculty on the stairs in front of the school building as well, but I walk past them without a second look. The paper with names is still burning a hole in my pants, and I need to find a way to relay the information to my sisters. I would go to the headmaster, but I'm not sure if there is a way to explain to him where I got the information without breaking the library's rules. I still have to figure out how to get around that.

I head straight down to the avenue of limes without any definite destination in mind. What I wouldn't give to speak to my dad right now. He would be able to make sense of all of this. I just know it. Even his presence is calming, and he has that air of knowledge about him that I've always found endearing. But these thoughts don't bring comfort, only pain. Even after months, I still have no idea how to find him, and there are no clues left to follow. I wanted to come back to Thunderbird Academy so I could help search for him the best way he taught me, and I've done absolutely nothing to reach that goal.

Not only am I failing as a friend, I have failed as a daughter.

Today is apparently a day for a pity party. If I was going to be mature about the situation, I could tell myself that it's not my fault. That I'm not responsible for what happened to him. But I feel the weight of his absence on me like a heaviness I cannot shake off. It's like everything around me is falling apart, and I am completely helpless.

But I'm not helpless. I can't let myself fall so far down this hole that I never claw my way out. My dad would say I have to pang-wangle, and he would be correct. In spite of everything that's going on, I have no choice but to fight.

This school is no longer the safe haven I so desperately searched for, and I can't sit by and do nothing about it. Just like that, the pity party is over. I'm pulling myself together, even if that's only because it's the one thing I have left to do. If everyone is going to think I'm this great witch, I better start acting like it.

⚜   26   ⚜

It's been close to a week and everything has been quiet. I've spent as much time as I can at the library, but I've found nothing helpful about the attacks. I have been able to find a few protective spells I can try, and I've been working on memorizing and practicing them. At this point, I may need to use them sooner than I anticipate.

The only other piece of information I could decipher are the ancient trials. Apparently, the Ancients held competitions with each other, trying to one up each other in various ways. If they're targeting schools now, maybe it's about the number. Or the individuals who go there. It's not exactly helpful, but at least it provides more of a motive for recruitment and these attacks.

This morning I felt unsettled, and when I step into the dining room, the feeling doesn't go away. It intensifies. It's as if my whole body has just broken out in goosebumps, but I can't pinpoint the source.

"What's up?" Noel asks, sensing my hesitation.

"I'm not sure. It's like there's a disturbance in the force." His smile is quick at my reference, but I'm not trying to be funny. Something is coming, but I don't know what. I scan the room but find nothing out of sorts. My friends move through the line, and I follow them automatically.

It seems that everyone is taking lunch at the same time today because the place is full. All the tables are taken, so we resign ourselves to going outside.

"Are we sure? It's kind of chilly out there," Christy whines, but follows us anyway. Truth be told, I'm happy to be out here. I needed to get out of that room. Not sure I could eat in there when I'm feeling so unbalanced.

The air has turned cool in the last week, as if Autumn finally decided to make her appearance. This time of the year is Bri's favorite, and I wonder if she had time to plant her herbs with all the craziness that's been going on.

"Oh, come on, Christy," I hear Jade say, "It'll be freezing before we know it, and then we'll wish we were out here."

I have to agree with my friend on that one. Even though the upperclassmen weather witches regulate much of the seasons here, they stay true to the rest of the world. After all, there is a reason why everything goes through seasons. Kind of like we do. Being at Thunderbird Academy is a season now. We find one of the unoccupied tables outside, taking a seat. The air is refreshing on my flushed skin, and I close my eyes for a second to enjoy the gentle breeze.

"Umm, Maddie." Jade's voice breaks through my moment of peace, and I turn to find her smiling at me. "Why don't we go get more juice?"

I glance down at the two bottles in front of us, confused by Jade's sudden behavior. She's still smiling at me, but I can tell it's a little strained.

"I think I'm good, thanks."

"You sure you don't want anything else?" This comes from Noel, who's sitting on my other side. I glance between my two friends, wondering what has gotten into them, when a shadow falls across my plate. I turn to look up and find Ben grinning down at me.

"Hey, Maddie!"

"Ben, you're back." I point out the obvious, as the boy rocks back on his heels. "Everything okay?"

"Somewhat." He shrugs.

"Maddie." Jade calls my name again as she places her hand on my arm. "I think we should go get some fruit."

"Jade, I'm fine, really. Ben," I say to the boy behind me. "Would you like..."

The question dies on my lips as he drifts to the side, opening up my view past his back. There's a group right by the doors we walked out of earlier. I recognize all the faces but one.

A gorgeous, dark-haired girl has her arms around Aiden's waist, gazing up at him like he's the love of her life. His eyes are on me.

I feel that look inside me, igniting and destroying parts of me all at once. The intensity steals my breath and shatters my thoughts, and I can't look away no matter how much I want to.

Ben steps back in front of me cutting off my view, and a gust of air rushes into my lungs.

"Maddie?"

"I guess Aiden is back too," I manage, knowing full well the shifter can hear everything we're saying.

"Who's the girl?" Christy asks, and I turn around to find my friends' eyes on me. Jade and Noel's behavior is understandable now. They were trying to protect me. Christy isn't paying attention to me though, she's looking over my shoulder.

"That's Natalie. She's Aiden's... betrothed."

For a moment, I don't think I heard Ben right. The wood on the table becomes crystal clear, as if all my senses are now completely focused on the spot in front of me. I feel a movement at my back, and then Ben takes a seat on the other side of Noel. Christy laughs, but the sound is hollow and far away.

"Betrothed? Is that a thing?"

"It is in our world." Ben shrugs, grabbing a piece of bread off my plate. I can feel his eyes on me, but I'm too stunned to organize my thoughts. I still can't seem to raise my head or articulate any of the words forming in my mind.

"How so?" I hear Vera ask softly. Or maybe I just can't hear well over the hum in my ears.

"Nat is going to be the Alpha of her pack. Aiden is the Alpha of his. It's a business arrangement."

"That's a little..." Jade begins but stops herself.

"Dated?" Ben finishes for her, and I can almost hear the shrug in his voice. "It's all we know. Oh hey, guys."

I'm trying really hard to find my footing, but even though I'm sitting down, I feel like the whole world is tilting under my feet. It's like I'm back inside the school during the earthquake. The group has moved toward us, and I can still feel Aiden's eyes on me, burning a mark into my back. Noel scoots just a tad closer, placing his hand on mine under the table, and I barely feel it. Then, a soft growl reaches my ears and that one sound is what finally snaps me back to reality.

Raising my head, I turn, meeting Aiden's eyes. I don't have to look to know that growl came from him because he doesn't miss Noel's move to comfort me.

"Everyone meet Natalie," Ben says while Aiden and I continue our stare down. I think I'm moving past shocked and straight into sad, so I need to escape somewhere before I make a scene.

"Welcome to Thunderbird Academy," Christy pipes up, grinning.

"Yeah, thanks." Natalie's voice is just as gorgeous as she is. When I finally look at her, I realize that she's the kind of girl countries go to war over. Smooth, tanned skin, large brown eyes, and lips as plump and red as a cherry. Everyone introduces themselves and when it's my turn, I'm not sure what to do.

My heart crumbles like a piece of paper in a clutched hand. Suddenly, I can't breathe and everything in me wants to flee, but I stay put. And I put on a smile.

"I'm Maddie," I find myself saying, "It's nice to meet you, Natalie."

THE TABLE STAYS SILENT AS I FINISH MY INTRODUCTION, AND THE girl in front of me gives me a quick study before turning to Aiden.

"We should really get going. Not to be rude," she hurries to add. Her smile is full and blinding, and I think I'm going to burst into tears any minute.

"I'll see you later," I hear Ben say, and I force myself to look at him and nod. Apparently, our little adventure has bonded us, and I'm glad. I like the guy. But right now, I want to hide from every shifter I know and never allow myself to feel anything ever again.

They move away without a word, and I realize the others didn't even speak up. Owen has always been silent and watchful, and I wonder how much he truly sees. There's a moment of silence as we're left on our own.

"Gosh, she's gorgeous," Christy breaths out, and I lose it. Standing quickly, I push past Noel and Jade, racing into the opposite direction the group went. I hear my name called, but I can't be there right now. Blindly, I run toward the pond, the need to scream almost overwhelming me.

I let myself be in this situation. I allowed myself to develop feelings for a guy who was never going to be mine, and now that he's not, I'm broken inside. And I don't know how to put myself together.

With the whole world falling apart around me, what a stupid thing it is to fall for a guy.

When I reach the pond, I'm out of breath. But it doesn't stop the magic building up inside me. I stumble right into the dirt at the bank and then I let it all out. The scream rips out of me as I thrust my arms into the water. The magic ignites, blinding me for a second, before the whole pond lifts up, hovering in the sky. The anger at myself, the sadness at the situation, the frustration, all pour out through my body as it shakes with power. The water begins to disperse, flying with the speed of a bullet in different directions. A second before it becomes too late, I realize what I'm doing, and I pull it all back.

The water snaps back into the pond, splashing over the side. A wave comes over me, soaking me to the core, but I don't care to protect myself from it. I fall onto my back, looking up at the sky while I force myself to breath normally. My body feels numb, as if I've just spent hours training, but somehow, exhilarated at the same time.

Slowly, I sit up, glancing at the water now resting calmly in its original space. How can I be so dumb as to fall for a guy I knew could never like me the same way? My sisters' fairytale love stories have blinded me to reality. Not that I would ever fault them for that. I love that they found happiness. I just hope one day I can have someone look at me the way Connor looks at Harper or Mark looks at Bri. Like they're their whole world and nothing can tear them apart.

I give myself another few moments as my magic completely calms inside of me. That was quite the outburst, and since the school is under even more monitoring than usual, I probably set off some alarms. Which means I really need to go tell the headmaster I'm the one causing the waves and not the Ancients.

Pulling the water out of my clothes, I'm dry once more. I square my shoulders and put on a brave face. I can't allow anyone to see just how much this situation is bothering me. Jade and Noel already know because I'm a lot more transparent around them. But I don't need Ben to know. I definitely don't need Aiden to figure it out.

When I'm back inside the building, I head straight to the headmaster's office. The hallways are still full of students, even though most of the classes are finished for the day. No one wants to separate themselves from the herd. There is strength in numbers, after all. Miss Cindy doesn't hesitate to buzz me in, as if she's been waiting for me. Which I wouldn't be surprised if she was. She's an elemental witch as well, and she's connected to the school. I'm sure she felt my magic release just like headmaster did.

"Miss Hawthorne." He greets me as I step into his office. "How lovely to see you again."

"I'm sorry," I blurt out, stopping right in front of his desk. "I didn't mean to set off any alarms. I just really needed to let it go, my magic has been building and it's been difficult..."

"Miss Hawthorne," he interrupts motioning to the chair. "Please take a seat."

I sit immediately, worried and confused. I didn't exactly expect him to be so calm about the whole thing. I know how on edge everyone has been, especially the staff. It's not easy to be responsible for so many students and their safety.

"You're not mad?" I finally ask, when Headmaster doesn't automatically get into it.

"To tell you the truth, I am surprised it has taken you this long to practice your magic to this extent."

"What?"

"Miss Hawthorne, we both know you come from a very powerful family and are a powerful witch yourself." Headmaster Marković leans forward, linking his fingers in front of him. "The need to allow your magic to run free will grow, just as your powers will. We have been monitoring your magical signature since the day you returned to school. And every time we have met since then, I have watched and encouraged you. Maybe not as well as I hoped."

"Oh." Well, that answers a lot of the questions I had. This is how they're watching for traitors too, I'm almost positive. But this means they also know when I'm in the library.

"You've watched me this *whole* time?" I ask, putting emphasis on the word. Headmaster Marković gives me one of his rare smiles, before replying.

"Yes. But your magic is not always discernible. Care to tell me about it?"

"I would," I reply honestly. "But I also can't. I found something that may be of help, but it seems to have a protection spell over it, which causes me to keep it a secret." Even those words are difficult to utter, but Headmaster doesn't seem surprised.

"There are places within these grounds that are unknown even to me. Magic has a way of choosing us, and when it does, we do not ask questions. We follow where it leads. If this... whatever it may be... has chosen you, you are accountable to it, and I hope you use it wisely."

His words calm my fears and make me braver at the same time. If he believes in me enough to let me have this secret, I can't let him down. I can't let the school down. Which is what inspires my next words.

"I need you to send my sisters a bit of information, and I need permission to be out of my room after dark."

❦ 27 ❦

The next few days, I do my best to avoid Aiden. And the rest of his pack. It's not as easy as it sounds considering our paths cross a lot more throughout the day than I originally anticipated. It's like they're everywhere. After receiving special permission from the headmaster to be out of my room at night, I've been spending a lot of time at the library. My sisters haven't gotten back to me about the ancestry, but they did praise my thinking. Bri mentioned there have been times when a witch can call on her ancestors at a time of need. It's a practiced skill, and an old one that hasn't been used for generations. But they're doing their research while I continue mine.

The more I learn about the Ancients, the more worried I become. There's no way of tracking them, no way to predict their next move. If they were truly the ones who took my dad, I have no way of finding them.

At least I get a little break when I'm in my witch classes. No shifters here, unless they share witch's blood. And there are only a few in the school like that. None of them is Natalie.

"Maddie, wait up!" My luck runs out when I step out of my potions class and hear Ben calling my name. I turn to watch him jog up to me, a grin on his face. Since I'm not actually mad at him, I can't keep myself from responding.

"What's up?"

"I just wanted to make sure you knew there was training today." He looks very uncomfortable delivering the news, and I can't blame him. Aiden has deemed him the one to make these announcements to me, and Ben would have to be blind not to see how unsettling it has become between his alpha and me.

"Sure. I thought so." I try on a smile, before turning to go. I have no intention of going, but I figured someone would tell me eventually.

"I'm sorry." Ben's words stop me, and I glance over my shoulder. Jade moves away with the girls, leaving Ben and I by ourselves.

"What do you have to be sorry about?"

"Making this awkward for you." he rubs the back of his neck, stealing small glances at me, as if he's not sure of his reception. And I guess maybe this is awkward for him. We're new friends, and he's been put into a situation where he's literally the bearer of bad news.

"Hey," I begin, placing a hand on his arm to stop his fidgeting. For big-bad-wolves, these boys really are just teenagers. I forget that sometimes. We're not that different after all. "You and me? We're solid. That's not going to change."

He gives me a blinding smile, and I answer in kind. But just as quickly as it comes, it dies away when I hear a growl behind me. Ben hastily takes a step away, his eyes over my shoulder, and I don't need to turn to know who's behind me.

"Ben." I address the guy once more and his eyes drop down to mine. "I'll see you later, okay?" Then, without another word, I pivot and leave them behind. I can't make myself look at Aiden, and so I don't. Technically, it's not his fault I had feelings he didn't reciprocate. But then again, I thought he did. And that makes me angry at myself. Angry enough not to be around him.

"Are you going to keep ignoring me?" Aiden's voice reaches me as I step outside the school's front doors. I've been spending a lot of time outside lately, when I'm not in the library. Not that Aiden needs to know my routine to find me. He's never had any trouble with that.

"I'm not ignoring you," I reply, moving down the stairs. "I'm busy."

"Busy ignoring me." It's a statement not a question, so I don't bother replying. Of course, he follows me down the steps and onto the pathway.

"What do you want?" I finally break the silence stopping to face him, because I know he'll just follow me around if I don't.

"You haven't come to training." He's right. I've avoided training for two days now and was about to do it again.

"And you've come to fetch me yourself? I thought you had people for that." I don't even bother to mask my annoyance as I glare at Aiden. He's not deterred though. I don't think I'll ever see him unsettled. At least, not in the way he makes me every time he's around.

"I won't apologize for telling Ben to keep an eye on you, Duchess."

"No, of course not. But it's okay. Ben and I are... friends now." I smile big as Aiden's eyes flash. Maybe I do get under his skin a little. "But I don't need a babysitter," I finish, folding my arms in front of me.

"That wasn't—"

"Don't you have your girlfriend to take care of?" I interrupt and watch his eyes narrow, but I'm not backing down.

"Maddie..." He starts again after a small pause, but I can't deal with him anymore. I especially can't deal with him when he uses my name like that.

"I need a break." I cut him off once more. There is absolutely no desire in me to know more about Natalie or his responsibility to her.

He watches me for a long moment, and it's hard not to fidget under that gaze. I feel like he sees right into me. But I keep my expression as neutral as possible.

"Okay, rest. We'll start again—"

"When I'm ready."

I walk away, leaving him standing behind, the distance between us more tangible than ever.

I can't deny this anymore. I've already come to terms with the fact that I like him. But I also can't pretend I'm not angry at myself. How did I let myself get here?

A part of me wants to turn and see him standing there, but I don't. Even so, I can feel his eyes on me as I continue moving past the trees and out of sight. When I know he's gone, I lean against the tree, taking a few deep breaths. For a moment, I think I'll cry. But I surprise myself when I don't. Instead, I give myself permission to feel everything. One of the greatest lessons my mom and sisters taught me is not to run from my emotions. Even though he doesn't feel the same, my feelings are still valid. I'm allowed to feel whatever I need to feel.

However, the knowledge doesn't take the pain away. It doesn't make this any easier. It doesn't soothe the burn or help me breathe easier. Maybe one day I will be able to look at him and not feel hollowed out inside. But today is not that day. So, I square my shoulders and march down the avenue of limes. At least the water will be happy to see me.

❧

MAYBE I'VE PUT TOO MUCH PRESSURE ON MYSELF, OR MAYBE I'M NOT putting enough. But a week later, I finally seem to find a break. I've barely slept and it's starting to show, but my friends are letting me deal with this in my own way, and I'm thankful. Both Jade and Noel have been a little extra clingy, but I forgive them. It's not like it's a bad thing to be surrounded by people who have your back.

Ben has become one of those people as well. Even Owen, although very stoic and one to keep to the background, has been watching out for me. Aiden must've realized just how badly I needed my space. Or maybe Natalie is keeping him so busy he doesn't have time to think about me. Either way, I'm trying to deal, so library and research have become my friend. Because without those books I wouldn't be able to survive. It's too easy to get lost in my head. I excel at overthinking.

When I think it's another night of nothingness, I stumble onto a story. Since starting my research, I have learned the best place to find information about the Ancients is in human stories. It's as if the Ancients were so unconcerned with the mundane population, they didn't bother covering their tracks. Which helps me.

The cover is old-timey, brown leather with intricate vine designs spreading out across the front and back. When I open the front page, the title is written in old English, an artwork all on its own. The letters are elaborate and fill up most of the space, *Stories of Olde*. The table of contents is full of story titles, most I've never heard of. As I browse through them, one catches my attention.

Orcnéas fram se Niht.

The words seem familiar, so I grab one of the many dictionaries on the table and start leafing through it. When that one doesn't yield results, I move to the next one. It's the third one that is finally old enough to give me a good translation.

"Monsters of the Night," I mumble out loud, breaking the silence. My eyes fly up to glance around, as if my disturbing the peace may offend someone. But I've been coming here by myself for days. I have nothing to fear. Instead of dwelling on that fact or the feelings of loneliness it brings, I grab the old book once again and turn to the story.

My heart squeezes in awareness as I try to make out the words. Dad taught me some of them, but he can read old English fluently and the pang grows more painful as I think of him.

I wish he was here.

I wish I could talk to him.

I will never not miss him.

Pushing the thoughts and emotions away, I focus back on the page in front of me. Grabbing one of my notebooks and the oldest dictionary, I get to work. It seems like hours before the words begin to take shape. My excitement reignites the more I translate and soon, I can't even sit still. This story is everything I've been looking for. A part of me wonders if others in this book may provide even more information. But for now, this may be enough.

Because what is does is spark an idea. Something I may have learned from my sisters.

There are plenty of spells in these books, more than enough information to create something greater still. With my family working on the ancestry aspect, I can work on perfecting my spell work.

I've never been great at it. Harper is much better at words than I am. But what if I was able to create a spell like a story? What if I was able to pull the Ancients into the pages of a book?

The story in front of me tells of the monsters that came in the night. They were feral creatures who roamed the forests and stole into the houses through the shadows. They preyed on human spirit and human flesh. Nothing could keep them out, not when they set their sights on their prey. Yet, some fought back. The humans found ways to protect themselves. They sang songs and they told stories and the creatures left, driven away by the imagination and the love in each spoken word.

Sitting back, I let that information sink in. Harper has always loved books, just like our father. It's something they shared and some of that has been passed on to me. But I've never been the one for beautiful prose. Or even regular spell casting. I use what is already written or what I have already been told.

But as I mull over these stories and the people who lived centuries ago, I feel inspiration knocking on the doors of my mind. It's like all of a sudden, I have to try, or I will go insane.

Grabbing my notebook once more, I jot down a few words that rush into my mind. I don't stop to second guess myself but allow the words to flow, if only to help me understand this magic. It's as if I'm telling myself this story now, for the very first time.

When I'm finished, I've only written a few sentences, but they speak to me on a higher level, and I wonder if there is magic on the page the way it used to be. There's no way I could story cast, but I did write something important. Of that I have no doubt. It's more than a feeling. It's a certainty deep within my veins. I know exactly what I need to do next.

$\approx$ 28 $\approx$

The next morning I'm at the headmaster's office before the sun even rises. Even Miss Cindy isn't at her desk yet.

"Miss Hawthorne, to what do I owe this pleasure?" Headmaster Marković greets me as he walks up to his office doors.

"What do you know about story spell casting?"

The man in front of me has never shown even one glimpse of surprise in the almost two years I've known him. Until now. His eyebrow twitches just enough that I know I said something he wasn't expecting to hear. I've barely registered his surprise before he masks it.

"I am not sure..."

"Please, with all due respect," I interrupt, before he can deliver whatever practiced excuse he has up his sleeve. "Don't hide the truth. I think this can really help us. I even wrote out the opening lines."

That stops him cold. This time, he doesn't even try to hide his surprise.

"You wrote out the beginning of a story spell?"

"Yes. It just came to me."

There's a tense pause, and it's like everything around us has gone completely still. I'm afraid to breathe too loudly as I wait for Headmaster Marković to speak. He studies me for another moment before he reaches for his door and unlocks it, motioning me inside.

The lights come on automatically, magic or modern amenities, I'm not sure. He heads for the drink cart on the other side of the office, pouring himself a cup of tea. Even from the distance, I can see the water is steaming hot, and once again I'm amazed at the magic of this place.

"May I ask how you found out about story spell casting?" Headmaster Marković asks after taking a tentative sip of his tea. He turns to me, watching me as he waits for an answer. Then, as if remembering my presence, he motions to the cart, and I shake my head.

"I'm okay, thank you."

He heads back to his desk as I try to find a way to explain to him my discovery. Already the magic of the library is preventing me from uttering any of yesterday's events. But headmaster doesn't push me, as if he knows I'm struggling.

"I have come across some information," I say, and the words taste true on my tongue. "When I decided to put the information to practice, there was no hesitation in my magic. It just happened."

He stays silent for a moment longer, taking a few sips of his tea, mulling over my words. I didn't exactly provide much to work with but maybe it's enough. Finally, he places the cup on a saucer and leans back in his chair.

"Story spell casting is an old practice, older than you can imagine," he begins, his eyes on something in the distance, as if he's remembering that very time as a firsthand participant. "Not everyone is gifted with the power of storytelling that is required of such spells. Many feared the intensity of the magic that came with those castings. Since it was so unique, it was just as feared as the Ancients. Back then, people spoke of the Ancient evil. Not as much as they could have, considering the protective spells were already in place. But more so than they do now. Story spell casting was one of the ancient arts, and those who did not understand it, feared it so."

"What happened?"

"Story casting was banned. Those who practiced it were dubbed evil worshipers, those who possessed dark magic. Chaos ensued and so, story casting became obsolete. At least, in the magic world."

"What do you mean?"

"The non-magical society has kept records of magic for as long as we have been on this earth. Some may have no knowledge of such things. But others have created their own societies to help us keep the records straight. To us, these are treasured texts."

I don't interrupt again, letting the headmaster find his own pace and his own words. I'm getting slightly impatient, when he speaks up again.

"Have you ever read the story of Beowulf?"

"Of course. We studied it in English class."

"What you studied was an ancient story spell, one that tells a tale of a mighty warrior, but also teaches the ways of casting."

"He was magical?"

"He was. Many of those whom you have read about were magical. Or had magical help. At one time, the world knew of supernaturals and lived in peace with them."

Headmaster's words stop whatever questions have sprung to mind. Living side by side with humans with nothing to hide? It's a concept I cannot wrap my mind around. Even though I come from a town that is very understanding and has broken through a lot of the prejudice within our magical community, it still doesn't seem possible.

"But how?"

"I wish I could give you a plausible explanation. But in all honesty, that kind of a unity is foreign even to me." He takes another swig of his tea, his eyes focused on something over my head. "For as long as I have been the headmaster here, and even when I myself was a student, magical and non-magical communities have warred. They have warred within themselves, and they have warred with each other. When the Ancients roamed the earth, it was not always so."

"Are you saying the Ancients have been awake since their original slumber?" I sit forward, leaning my hands on the desk. This is a completely new piece of information to me as I have been led to believe this is the first time they have risen up.

"They have. Not to this extent." Headmaster focuses on me once more. "I am telling you this, Miss Hawthorne, because I believe you have the drive to find the answers we so desperately seek. You have also clearly been granted access to areas of this school I myself am not privy too. But I ask you, please, keep this knowledge to yourself. It will only lead to mass panic."

He watches me steadily, waiting for me to agree, and I do so because I understand panic all too well. We still have no idea who they have on the inside, or how to protect this school from a full assault from the Ancients. There is no doubt in my mind it is coming. It's not like we can tell them to go away.

The idea sparks before I can fully form it, and I sit up straighter. Headmaster Marković notices my sudden intensity but doesn't ask, waiting on me to share.

"What if I wrote a story casting spell for the school?" I ask, not sure where exactly I'm going with this, but I know it's right the moment I speak the words. As I meet Headmaster's eye, I realize he's waiting for me to continue. "There has to be a way to protect this campus once and for all. What if a story casting spell is the spell you've been looking for? It could work, right?"

"It could," Headmaster replies slowly, mulling over his next words, "But it is incredibly risky. Story casting has not been practiced for generations. There are rules upon rules."

"But I think it's worth the risk. Don't you?" He meets my eye again and I'm ready for it. Something in me is refusing to back down. "If the lives of all these students are on the line, shouldn't you do whatever it takes to protect them? And I'm not saying you haven't," I hurry on to add when his eyes flash for a second. I don't want to make him mad, but I truly believe in what I'm saying. I have no idea where this is coming from, but I trust it. I trust myself. "This could be our shot."

"You make a valid point, Miss Hawthorne," Headmaster Marković finally says, and I feel like I'm out of breath just from waiting for him to speak. "I will bring it before the council, and we will go from there."

"That is all I ask." I smile, feeling better for it. A part of me feels like I've finally done something to help. I can't seem to save my dad, but maybe I can do something for the school. For my friends and those I care about. Standing to go, Headmaster Marković stops me when he calls my name.

"Story casting is no joke," he says, looking me straight in the eye as he stands behind his desk. "Your ancestors carry the magic within them, and so it seems, do you. That is the only reason I can see the truth has been revealed to you. But Miss Hawthorne, beware. It is not something that is to be taken lightly."

"Understood," I reply, reaching for the doorknob. "Thank you."

I don't wait for him to say anything else or offer any other warnings. It's not like I think I've suddenly developed some superpowers that will solve all our problems. But it also doesn't mean I'm just going to sit on this knowledge. Like he said, those books told me the truth for a reason. I can't let my ancestors down.

❧

THE WHOLE DAY HAS GONE BY AS A BLUR. I'M ITCHING TO GET BACK to the library, but I promised Jade that we would have a picnic in the meadow before the weather turns completely to winter. My friends need this shred of normalcy, and I'm not about to deny them that.

"Do you think things will ever go back to normal?" Jade asks, leaning over Noel to grab a bag of chips. It's the usual crew out here, Vera and Christy are present too. But we're not the only ones who are desperate for normalcy because there are a few other groups out and about around us. While the weather is still dark and gloomy, it's a little lighter than it's been.

"I don't know, Jade," I reply honestly, watching two girls and two guys throw a football around. "This may be our new normal for a while."

It's not what they want to hear, but it is the truth. We can't pretend our lives haven't been flipped upside down and the place that was supposed to be our salvation has become a target.

"Can you please stop being depressing?" Christy whines from the other side of the blanket. She's just as dramatic and over the top as usual, and I chuckle. "Let's play a game! I know Noel brought cards."

"That I did." He pulls out a few decks without hesitation, and I smile. It's crazy how you may know someone for such a short time and yet claim them as your own. Unwillingly, my mind drifts to Aiden. A part of me has begun thinking of him as exactly that, and while it wasn't smart, it's not something I could've controlled. Or maybe I should've. It would help to have my sisters here to navigate the madness of boys, but at least I have my girls. And Noel. I do feel like I can talk to him about this as well. Even though I think our next conversation should be about him finally making his move on Jade. He'll be pining forever if he doesn't step up.

I'm still thinking about my two best friends when I feel a prickle at the back of my neck. The rest of the group begins to argue about what game they want to play, but I'm no longer listening. Something is coming, or maybe it's already here. I can feel it like a rumbling under my feet. As I study those around me, I realize the shifters are out and about as well. I didn't notice them earlier, besides the regular patrols, but now I see they're everywhere. My eyes land on Owen first before I find Ben. There's no happy go lucky expression on his face. He's all business, and that makes me that much more worried.

A sudden shriek pierces the near silence, and I twist around to try and find the source of it. Rain drops from the sky as if being spilled from buckets, soaking us in mere seconds.

"What's happening?" Vera shouts, and even this close to her, it's difficult to make out the words as a full-blown storm descends on us in seconds. Jumping to my feet, I squint through the sheet of water, calling on my magic at the same time. But nothing happens. It's like my magic is being blocked.

"I can't stop it!"

"What?"

People are running in every direction, but the main building is too far, and the storm is becoming stronger by the second.

"We have to go!" I scream, trying to be heard over the pouring rain. The storm continues to rage, making it difficult to see five feet ahead. I wave my arms, trying to get everyone's attention. There's only one place we can go.

"Come on!"

With Jade close on my heels, I race toward the building I spent most of my afternoons in. Others seem to pick up on our intention, and they turn toward the building as well.

Chaos bombards us on every side, but I don't slow down. When Jade slips beside me, I grab her before she can faceplant, pulling her after me. Ben and Owen are suddenly by our side and then Aiden is there as well. The wind howls, nearly sweeping me off my feet and trying to push me in the opposite direction. I grip Jade's hand and beg for my magic to do something, but it merely reaches a foot in front of me before I feel resistance.

The house outline can be seen through the rain but barely. Others are rushing in, stumbling over each other as they try to get out of the storm. We burst through the doors as one, pushing past all the people. Aiden, Ben, and Owen are the last ones inside, barricading the door behind them.

"Stand back!" I command, and the boys move as one. I focus on my magic, trying to find my center. Whatever is blocking me outside is not about to win in here. Now that I have a second to concentrate, I let my magic reach out, pushing past the resistance. Already, I can tell my magic alone won't be enough, but there is one other thing I can try. Taking a deep breath, I call on my ancestors to help and guide me, hoping I'm doing the right thing. It's not like my sisters got back to me with a manual. Even so, I feel my magic grow a tad stronger, and I hold onto that.

"Protect, protect, protect," I whisper right as I thrust my hands forward, sending the magic flying. It smacks into the doors and spreads out around us, sealing us inside. The spell drains me instantly, and I stagger on my feet. Aiden moves towards me but stops himself as Ben reaches me first.

"I'm okay." I smile at the shifter, but I think it comes out more like a grimace because he doesn't seem reassured. A growl reaches my ears, and I glance up just in time to watch Aiden march toward me with a determined look on his face. He pushes past everyone, sweeping me off my feet and into his arms. I gasp, wrapping my arms around his neck automatically.

It takes my brain a second to catch up to what's happening, as everyone stands a little shocked around us.

"Umm, put me down," I finally say, finding my words.

"You're dead on your feet, Duchess," he replies, stepping around my friends as he carries me to one of the couches in the next room.

"Aiden."

"Maddie."

He doesn't let go until he's standing over the furniture. But even then, he hesitates. I try not to think about the way he cradles me against his chest or the gentle way he's supporting my body. When I meet his eye, a touch of concern can be found there. It moves straight into my heart and grows as he gently sets me down. His face hovers over mine, his gaze intense. If I move even a fraction of an inch, our noses will brush. It takes all my self-control not to pull him toward me. I think he can see the desire in my eyes and his own flash in response.

Just then, the building shakes from an impact, jarring both of us out of our staring contest. My gaze falls over his shoulder, landing on my friends who have followed us into the room. Jade's eyes are sparkling, and Noel looks a little worried. And also fearful. Actually, they all look scared.

"What is that?" Vera asks, pushing farther into the room and past my open-mouthed best friends.

"The shadow creatures," I reply automatically, orienting myself on the couch. Aiden has moved away as if he's been burned by touching me and is now standing by the opposite wall. "They're trying to get past the spell."

"How do you know?"

"I've seen them in person before. I wasn't sure until just now, when I focused on my magic. They're known to syphon magic, and it's the same kind of resistance I found when I looked."

"This building has the same protection as the main school though, right?" Jade asks, taking a seat beside me.

"It does. But I added something extra."

We're all exhausted. There are students huddled all over, wet and shivering from the cold. This attack took us completely by surprise. And that should be impossible, considering we've been walking on eggshells all semester.

"So, does that mean they can't get in at all?" Christy asks from her position by the door. She looks so small, half covered in dirt, with her arms wrapped around her middle. I want to reach out and comfort her, but all I can offer her are my words.

"Someone would have to physically open the door from in here to penetrate my spell. So even if they bust through the school's magic, we have an extra layer of protection." She nods, and I can see her shoulders drop a little. Vera and Noel both look just as reassured as Christy. The shifters, on the other hand, are still on full alert.

"What happened out there?" I ask, directing my question at Ben. But the moment he opens his mouth, Aiden steps in.

"They've been on the outskirts of the magical shield for days," he says, crossing his arms in front of him as he leans against the door. "Headmaster called us in a few hours ago to double the patrols. They were planning some kind of spell when the creatures broke through. They started attacking people directly, and you're right, taking their magic. It happened so fast, it's as if they knew exactly where to find them, and the sudden storm provided the cover."

I close my eyes briefly as he speaks, picturing the scene. I was only privy to our part in it, and it happened so quickly, no one had any time to react. If this is the same around the whole campus, the shadow creatures would have a feast.

The spell Aiden is talking about must be the story casting one the headmaster was supposed to present to the council. Everything is happening at once, no wonder we're struggling to stay ahead of the game. We don't even have time to do proper research.

Just then, another impact shakes the walls around us, and Jade grabs my hand. She's not even hiding the fact that she's terrified. My body feels the drain on my magic, and I feel weaker than I should be. I glance at Aiden who's been watching me this whole time, and I want to ask why he was in the meadow when he could've been stationed anywhere else. But then I notice Christy sliding carefully toward the doors to the hallway.

"Christy?" I call out, and the girl turns right as she steps through the doorway. "Everything okay?"

She gives me the sweetest of smiles before replying, "It will be."

Something doesn't feel right. I untangle my arm from Jade and push to my feet. Somehow Aiden is right beside me in an instant as I wobble, but he doesn't reach for me. However, his presence soothes my nerves, but I'm not about to tell him that. Instead, I push past him and into the hallway.

"Christy," I call out, pausing on the other side of the doorway as the petite girl makes her way slowly down the hallway. "What are you doing?"

She stops right in front of the door to the outside, placing her palm against the wood as if she's feeling the building tremble through her fingertips. Cocking her head so she can look at me over her shoulder, she smiles big and my blood runs cold.

"Letting them in, of course."

Before anyone of us can move, she grabs the handle, pulling it open. My spell dissipates, and with it, our protection.

The traitor has been under our noses this whole time, and she just broke the last layer of our defenses.

Aiden and Ben growl on either side of me before launching themselves forward. Christy raises her hands, and both shifters hit an invisible wall at once, sliding back toward me. I drop to my knees, my hands on each of them as they shake off the impact.

"Funny Maddie," Christy says, and her voice doesn't sound like her own. "Always trying to save people and... creatures." My hand is still on Aiden's upper arm, and I drag him to a standing position beside me. Owen helps Ben up, and both of them take their position at my back, with Aiden at my side.

"It was you the whole time," I say now, and the other girl laughs like she's a villain on a bad TV show.

"Of course it was me. And you had absolutely no idea. You were too busy with your stupid schoolwork and your unrequited love crushes and sucking up the headmaster, you golden child."

It's hard not to look at Aiden at Christy's words, but I can feel his eyes shift to me. I'm sure he's putting two and two together. She's not exactly being subtle.

"Why?" I have to keep her talking while we figure out what to do next. But it's not like I can communicate telepathically with the shifters. My plan will have to be my own. Everyone else has moved away from the main hall as the wind blows all around Christy. If I look closely enough, I can make out the shapes of the shadow creatures at her back, but it's like she's keeping them in check for the moment.

"Why not?" She laughs again, and I'm really starting to hate that sound. "You thought you were the big man on campus after that little spell you and your sisters pulled but look at you now. You couldn't' even see what was staring you right in the face."

I shake my head, amazed at how focused she is on this concept of my popularity. "You really think I wanted all this responsibility?"

"Ha! You've been eating it up all semester. Woe is me, I'm Maddie Hawthorne, a powerful witch with a super cool spell under my belt. Don't look at me. Well, only when I want you to."

Bitterness drips off her every word, and I don't know what to say to that. How can I explain to her my actual feelings on the matter when she has already made up her mind about me?

"Is that what this is all about?" I wave my hand in the direction of the open doors, and the smile she gives me chills me to the bone.

"Of course it's not all about you, Madison," she says my name like a curse.

"So, what was it? Why betray this place? Why now?" I can't risk looking at the shifters, but I can feel them move at my back. Aiden's fingers graze mine, sending a million electric shocks up my spine, and the moment makes me braver. I take a step toward Christy, putting my friends at my back.

"You had to go and open your big mouth." Christy spits in my direction, all trace of that cute, bubbly girl gone from her eyes. "The council has been deliberating, and I can't let them spell extra protection over Thunderbird Academy."

So, Headmaster Marković stayed true to his word and went to the Elders. But how could Christy know any of this? And why is she involved?

"What's in it for you?" I ask, even though I have a pretty good idea.

"Power, of course. Ultimate power. They sure know how to reward their followers. And I? I will have no problem knocking down whatever spell you throw my way. Because I will be more powerful than you."

It's that simple. Power really does corrupt.

I move closer still, and this time, she notices.

"I wouldn't if I were you." She raises her right arm into the air, and I watch as three shadow creatures appear from the darkness at her back. "You know my dear friends, right?" Christy asks, that sinister smile back on her face. "They've been dying to say hello."

Before I can figure out what she means, she flicks her hand, and the creatures attack. Along with the first three, a dozen more pour into the building with Christy standing by the doors, laughing like a maniac. I can't tell if she's controlling them completely or only providing a pathway, but I know I have to get to her.

The chaos around me is a battlefield. The shifters have all turned and are holding their own against the Ancient's minions. I can feel the vibrations of battle magic echoing around me as my friends and fellow students fight the dark creatures. The storm is now inside the building as well as outside the walls. The blackness of the night is seeping into every nook and cranny, as if the mere presence of the Ancient magic is poisoning the land.

"Aiden, watch out!" My heart jumps inside my chest as I thrust my hands out in front of me, throwing up a protective shield right before the creature attacks Aiden from behind. The wolf spits out the creature he has in his mouth, dissipating the magic before he turns to look at me. Even in his wolf form, I see the gratitude and determination in his eyes. Suddenly they narrow, just as I feel something coming at me from the left.

I twist around, throwing up a protective shield, but I'm a second too late. I go flying across the hall, my back slamming into a wall. Dazed, I do my best to get up on all fours, but with my magic drained and my head spinning, I'm not fast enough. The tendrils of a shadow creature wrap around my wrists yanking me back. I cry out, searching for my battle magic, but I can feel it leaving me by the second.

The pain is excruciating, as if one of my limbs is being pulled clean off. Writhing on the floor, I try to clear my mind enough to think, but no dice. It's too much, all at once, and it feels like I'm being torn apart.

Then, just as suddenly, the pain is gone, and I open my eyes to find Aiden ripping the shadow creature apart. Since they're made of magic, all they do is reform somewhere else, but at least I'm no longer attached to one. That's when I realize what I need to do.

"Aiden," I say, getting to my knees. The wolf stops in front of me, and this time I don't hesitate. I plunge my hand into his fur, memorizing the silky texture with this one touch. Electricity sparks between us, but before I can understand it, I breathe easier as I meet his eye.

"Shadows cannot live in the light," I say, staring right at him. He nods, understanding exactly what needs to be done. "Give me five minutes."

AIDEN DOESN'T HESITATE TO STEP IN FRONT OF ME AS I GET TO MY feet. One howl and Ben and Owen are suddenly there as well, protecting me from every side. I glance around, trying to find my friends, and see Jade and Noel battling a few of the creatures farther down the hall. Some students are screaming as the monsters eat their magic right up. The sight breaks my heart, but the only thing I can do for them now is draw out the shadow creatures. For that to happen, I need more power.

"Get me to Jade," I say, and the wolves move as one as I race behind them. Throwing up a protective shield, I wish for more water, but I make do with what I have. The rain outside is enchanted, so it's no use to me. When we're almost to my friend, something knocks me off my feet. I drop fast and hard while my face stings from the impact. With my head ringing, my instincts take over, and I pull on all those hours of working with Aiden.

I'm being straddled, and my neck is wrapped in a tight grip, so I do the only thing I can. I drive my palm straight up with full force and am satisfied when I hear a crunch and then a scream. Christy is immobilized for only a second, but it gives me enough time to find my momentum and push her off me. I'm on my feet as she recovers, blood dripping down her pink shirt.

"You broke my nose, witch," she spits, looking less like a human by the second. She's more of a feral creature than any animal I've ever seen, and that makes her dangerous.

"It looks better that way," I reply, unable to help myself. She doesn't like that, so she launches herself at me with a scream, but this time I'm prepared. Ducking underneath, I twist around, bringing my leg up to slam it into her back. She staggers forward but doesn't drop, and before I can deliver another kick, she's coming at me once more. I block her advances as she continues to swing her arms. For someone so small, she's incredibly strong and quick. I wouldn't be surprised if she's had a few magical enhancements.

When my fist connects with her face, I don't hesitate to grab her hair and pull her down as I bring up my knee. The impact affects both of us, but I manage to stay on my feet. She reaches for my skin, ripping half my shirt off and scratching up my arm, but I'm so focused, I don't even feel the pain. I punch her again before I knee her in the stomach, and I finish it with a jump kick. She lands hard on her back, completely knocked out, and I gulp air like a drowning man.

"Jade!" I call out when I find my voice again, and I turn in time to see Aiden and Ben take care of another three shadow creatures. With two leaps, Aiden is beside me once more, and I swear he looks proud of me when his gaze moves from my face to that of Christy's body.

"I told you I was paying attention," I mumble and then take off toward my friends.

"Jade, Noel, I need you," I shout, stopping near the doorway to the other room. They hear me and instantly move toward me as I turn to study who else is there. Vera has shifted into a hawk, and is a beautiful bird, much larger than any I've seen before. She's holding her own, but I need her witchy powers right now.

"Witches, I need you!" I shout into the room and a few students glance up at me before moving forward. Some are still fighting, but others race to meet me at the doorway.

My thought is simple. If I can call on my ancestors for help, then I can call on my fellow students as well. We need a blinding enough light to drive out the creatures, and I've only heard of the magic my sister's friend created month ago. Now, I get to improvise.

"Join hands," I direct as the shifters do their best to keep the creatures away from us. "I will call on the guiding light, and I need you to let me connect to your magic as an amplifier."

"How do we do that?" Noel asks as he takes Jade's hand. Vera lands elegantly beside him and shifts before she replies.

"Give Maddie permission to enter." She nods at me as she steps over and takes my hand. She's more powerful than I imagined considering she holds her clothes within her shift. That's usually the sort of magic that is earned, and if we survive this, I have a lot of questions for her. Now, I give her a soft smile, and then turn to face the main hallway. Jade grips my hand tightly, and I watch the rest of the witches follow suit.

Now that Christy is out of commission, it's as if the shadow creatures are given to their own devices. Those who are still fighting glance over at us and push the creatures out further, giving us a wider berth. The shifters are right in front of me, holding their own. When I take a deep breath, Aiden turns suddenly, his attention entirely on me.

I meet his eye, as if we're the only two people in the whole world, and this war is not happening around us. I find calm within the storm just by looking at him, and instead of hiding from the feeling or running from it, I embrace it.

It blossoms inside of me like a flower opening its petals, and my magic follows suit. My arms vibrate from the power of it all as I feel the students at my back giving me permission to enter. When I open my mouth, I'm still looking at Aiden.

> *"The night is dark, the evil is Ancient,*
> *"But bonds are stronger than those of the agents.*
> *"The story of old has all but been told,*
> *"And the magic of sunrise has never been wronged."*

The words of the story pour out of me as the ground under our feet begins to shake. The shadow creatures all pause, as if they feel something coming. I'm not about to disappoint them. The simplest of spells are sometimes the most powerful. I grin, my body beginning to glow from within, and then I utter the words.

> *"Let there be light."*

$$\maltese \quad 30 \quad \maltese$$

When the blinding light finally dissipates, I drop down to my knees, completely spent. My friends are there to hold me up and then, so are the shifters.

"Maddie, you did it. They're gone," Jade whispers, hugging me tightly. I can barely hold my head up, but when I do look outside, I find the storm has ended, and it once again looks like a gloomy afternoon outside. I feel a slight bump on my arm, and I look over to find Aiden pressed against me. This time, I'm sure his wolf looks proud of me, and I manage a smile.

"Not bad, huh?" I ask, right before I pass out.

When I wake up, I'm in my room with no recollection of getting there. My body feels heavy, as if something is pressing on me at every side, but I don't actually feel any physical pain.

"You're awake!" Jade exclaims, jumping off her bed and coming to stand beside mine. "Oh Maddie, you really saved us. You're amazing!" She falls right into me, hugging me tightly, and I return the gesture.

"What happened?" I ask when she finally pulls back.

"I can't believe it was Christy all along," Jade comments, tears running down her face. "We trusted her, Maddie. How could we not see?"

"She didn't want us to see," I reply, sitting up fully and reaching for Jade's hand. "What happened to her?"

"Headmaster Marković and the council took her to prison. You really did a number on her. I think she'll be in recovery for a very long time. Part of her punishment is being stripped of her powers, and they're not performing any healing spells on her either."

"What about everyone else?"

"We've all been checked over by the healers. They're more concerned with our safety than anything else. Since the protective wards were breached, it's hard to rebuild them now. Especially since so much of the magic was drained during the battle. Headmaster, along with most of the staff and shifters, has been on patrol nonstop."

"Wait, how long was I out?"

"Almost a full day." Jade squeezes my hand. A day? I can't believe it. I need to get to the headmaster. I need to see what the council said about story spell casting. I need to see Aiden. That last thought comes unbidden, but I can't deny it. Something happened between us in that building, and I can't exactly run from it now. It felt more powerful than magic.

"Aiden has come by to check on you every chance he gets," Jade comments, as if reading my mind. She gives me a small smile, and I return it.

"I need to see him."

Without hesitation, Jade moves out of the way, so I can stand. Pulling on my jeans and a hoodie, I find that even though my body feels heavy, a part of me is energized. Something is happening to me, and I don't know if it's my own magic, or the story spell cast I used, but I feel... right somehow.

"He's scheduled to patrol by the pond," Jade says, as I lace up my boots. "He told me the last time he came in to check."

I give my friend a quick hug before I'm racing out of the room. The hallways are deserted, and I wonder if the students are barricading themselves inside their rooms, or holed up somewhere together. Clearly, we can leave our rooms, but I can understand why they wouldn't want to.

The few who are out and about patrolling don't try to stop me, but

I can feel their eyes on my back. I have no idea if the rest of the school knows what I pulled in that building, but at this point, I'm used to the looks. After everything I've dealt with, I think I can handle a few stares.

I half walk, half sprint to the pond, passing a few of Aiden's pack mates in the process. They all seem to know exactly where I'm going. When I reach the pond, I find Aiden directly by the water.

"You're up," he says before turning to face me. I knew it wasn't just me who was so attuned to him that I could feel his presence. He doesn't move toward me, and now that I'm here, I freeze only five feet away. We study each other as if we've never seen the other person before. It's as if our eyes have been opened to something entirely new, and we're unsure of how to proceed from here.

"Thank you." I break the silence. "For what you did back there."

"I didn't seem to need to do much," he replies, flashing me a smile. I think my heart stops for a second at the sight, my eyes drinking in every detail. It's the first true smile I have seen from him and it shatters me into a thousand emotions. Suddenly, I can't seem to think, and I wonder if I look as flushed as I feel.

"You were incredible, Maddie," he continues, taking a tiny step forward. "I've never seen someone so in tune with their magic and so bold in their execution."

With each word, I think my world is tilting on its axis once more. If we don't get back to even ground, I don't think I'll ever be able to recover. So, I say the first thing that comes to mind.

"But the most important thing is how was my fighting form?"

There's a slight pause, and I think I'm just being stupid, but then Aiden laughs and the sound becomes my favorite sound in the world in a span of a second.

"Your fighting form was amazing. But it could probably still use some work."

It's my turn to laugh, and suddenly, I don't feel so awkward anymore. We were partners on that battlefield, and that means we will never be enemies again. This time, it's me who takes a step forward, and then we're only three feet apart. I don't want to push my luck, but

I have to ask him. I have to know if I'm the only one thinking these crazy thoughts.

"That moment when I touched you, it—"

"I felt it everywhere," he interrupts, speaking softly, and now I know I didn't imagine the electricity rushing through me. He takes another step toward me, and now, the only thing between us is the air we share.

"What does it mean?" I whisper, afraid of the answer and afraid of not getting one.

"It can't mean anything," he replies, cracking my already fragile heart. But somehow, I don't move away, and Aiden is not done. "When I first saw you, it changed everything for me. I can't explain it, but it did. But you and I, we can only ever be this." He waves a hand between us, and somehow I understand. Seeing him has changed me too.

"I am bound by my duties as the next alpha, but I am also bound to the promise I made to make sure you are safe. Know that I will always keep that promise."

I frown at him, unsure of what he means by that last part. I know Natalie is part of his duty as the next alpha, and I know there's nothing I can do about that. I want to ask him about his promise, but just then a wolf runs over, and Aiden is back to his closed off soldier self.

"We need to go. Headmaster is looking for you," he says after he looks over at the wolf. I nod my head and swallow the tears that are threatening to overwhelm me. But before I can take two steps, Aiden does something that breaks me completely. He closes the distance between us and pulls me into his arms, much like he did after the dance. This time, he clings to me as tightly as I cling to him, and in this one embrace, I realize I've fallen in love with the alpha.

"We can't stay here!"

The shouting greets us as Aiden and I reach the headmaster's office. Voices both male and female are talking over each other, and we push into the partially open door without an invitation. The moment we're inside, the arguing stops and the people in the room turn to face us as one.

Some of the teachers are here, but there are a few people I've never seen before. These must be the council members Headmaster was talking about.

"Miss Hawthorne, it is good to see you up and about." Headmaster Marković greets me warmly. I give him a small smile, still very unsure of myself in front of this group. He motions me closer, and when I walk farther into the room, I see that a few upperclassmen are here as well. Including Natalie. The other girl doesn't seem very impressed with me, but then again, I'm not impressed with her either.

"What possessed you to try story spell casting, girl?" One of the older women I've never seen before speaks, her voice full of disapproval. She appears to be in her seventies, her hair pulled so tightly into a bun, it makes my own scalp hurt. Her eyes are dark as she stares at me, waiting for an answer.

"Matilda, please," Headmaster Marković says, waving the woman off. "Miss Hawthorne saved her fellow students at the risk of her own health. That should be admired."

"It should be reprimanded. You have no idea what kind of power you are playing with here." There is so much venom in her words that it takes all the air from my lungs. But then, it makes me angry. This semester has taught me a lot about myself and one of those things is that I am braver than I give myself credit for. I'm not about to cower at the words of some old lady.

"Not to mean any disrespect," I begin, shocking everyone into silence. "But I didn't see you out there in the front lines, fighting to protect the students of this *fine* institution. I hope all the screaming and bloodshed didn't inconvenience you too much."

"How dare you?"

"No, I will not be spoken to like I'm some kid," I say, standing up a little taller. There's a light touch of a hand on my arm, and I realize Aiden is encouraging me with that small move. "I did what I had to do, and I would do it all again."

"Miss Hawthorne," Headmaster Marković interjects, shifting my attention to him. I'm pretty sure there's a gleam of approval in his eye, but I know he's not about to voice it. "What Elder Matilda is trying to say is, there are always consequences to this type of magic. Consequences that may not reveal themselves right away."

"I understand that, sir. And I will answer for those consequences when the time comes. But I will not apologize for saving my friends' lives."

"I told you, Henry. I told you!" Elder Matilda points her finger at the headmaster before she turns back to me. "She is unlearned and cannot be given the responsibility."

"That is your opinion, Matilda," Headmaster Marković replies. "And you are only but one vote."

"Headmaster, could you tell us what's happening?" Aiden says, voicing my own question.

"The council has voted to have Miss Hawthorne perform a story spell casting on the school." My heart leaps in my chest, elevated all at once. They're giving me permission to help. I was planning on doing so myself anyway, but this means I have their support.

"When can I begin?" I try not to sound too eager, but I can't hide my excitement.

"Immediately. We're on borrowed time here, and the wards could break down again at any moment."

"Wait a second." Aiden turns to me. "What exactly is story spell casting?"

"It's vile, and it has no place in this school," Elder Matilda spits, shooting daggers at me. I glance at the others in the room and find that the opinion seems to be divided. Most of my teachers look on with encouragement, as does one of the other Elders in the room. But the rest are very apprehensive, although not as hostile as Elder Matilda.

"It's an ancient way of spell casting that hasn't been performed in generations. But it's powerful, and it's what Miss Hawthorne did at the training building."

"But it nearly killed you!" Aiden's attention is entirely on me now, and he's not even trying to hide the worry.

"I'll be fine. I need to be more selective with my words. I think it only drained me so much because I was the conduit. If I use something else as an anchor, it won't be as bad." I try to reassure him, and I hope I'm making sense, because at this point, I'm making this up as I go.

"You need to be very specific with your words, Miss Hawthorne," Headmaster Marković agrees. "Next time, the aftermath of the spell could be much worse."

I understand what he means. I can die. I read about it in the books, not that I'm about to mention it now. But I don't think I need to. Aiden is a smart shifter. He knows what we're talking about. He opens his mouth to protest again, when the phone on the desk rings. Headmaster answers immediately, and only a few words are spoken before he turns to us.

"You need to start the spell immediately. More are coming."

❧ 31 ❧

They don't let me say two words before Mrs. Hously is guiding me into Headmaster Marković's chair. She hands me a piece of paper and a pen before she squeezes my shoulder.

"To tell a story you need a setting. Use the school as the basis, paint a picture. It doesn't have to rhyme, although poetry has always had the strongest affect in spell casting." She rattles off instructions hurriedly, her eyes shining with unshed tears. "Think of what matters the most. The greatest stories are filled with love and adventure. They're filled with heart. Find that and you will be fine."

My eyes drift to Aiden involuntarily, and I find him staring at me just as intensely. The teachers and staff hurry out of the room as Headmaster begins issuing orders.

"We need to keep the school as safe as possible until Miss Hawthorne is finished. Rally everyone. Every student, every magical being, tell them we are officially at war. I know they are scared, but if they have even a glimmer of magic, they are not helpless."

Miss Cindy rushes over to her desk and then the alarm begins to blare. Those in the room scatter quickly, each heading for their assigned areas.

"Mr. Lawson," Headmaster calls out, and I realize he's the only one, besides the Elders, left in the room.

"I'm staying with her."

He doesn't take his eyes off me as he says the words, and the intensity there takes my breath away. Then, Natalie moves from behind him, placing her hand on his arm.

"Your pack needs you, Alpha," she says, sparing me half a glance that's filled with so much hostility, I think my skin got burned.

"Miss Hart is right." Headmaster steps up, glancing between the two of us. "Miss Hawthorne is in capable hands."

I know he doesn't want to, but Aiden can't ignore the call of the alpha. He gives me one last heated look that's filled with all kinds of promises, before he's out the door.

"Now, Miss Hawthorne—"

"I'm on it."

Ignoring the angry glares from Elder Matilda, I concentrate on the paper in front of me. I am not a writer. Books are magic all on their own, and it's because of hard work and talent that authors create such stories. I think back to what Mrs. Hously said, that the best stories are filled with heart. And I know my heart belongs to this school.

It may not be anything I expected, and I never would've imagined this is where my life would lead me, but I love Thunderbird Academy. This place has been a home away from home, and I will not rest until it is a sanctuary once more.

I begin to write, letting those emotions guide my pen. When the screaming starts, I don't let up. Headmaster and the rest of the Elders, join hands, mumbling their own spell as I work on mine. I feel the magic fill this space, I hear the battle rage all around me, and yet I still write.

"Work faster, girl," Elder Matilda snaps, but even that sounds far away. I completely give myself over to the story. As the building begins to shake around me, I feel my heart bleed out into the words in front of me. When the last dot is on the page, I am spent. I glance up to find the Elders still in the midst of their spell, sweat running down their brows.

"Sir," I call out, afraid of breaking their concentration, but they don't answer me. "Headmaster Marković."

"Now, Maddie. Now," he calls, and I have no choice. Glancing down at the paper, I begin to read.

"There once lived a girl,
With magic in her veins,
Inside a castle made of stone,
On the grounds of Ancient remains.
The place has always been,
And the place will always be,
An institution of knowledge, of honor, of friendship,
Of tranquility.
Until the evil came and fought to destroy,
So, the girl took a stand and wrote a song.
It spoke of her happiness, of the friends she had made,
And it spoke of a boy, who had changed her fate.
She gave of herself, of her magic, her heart,
She did not hesitate to protect, to impart,
This story will not end with failure or pain,
The institution will withstand,
Just like witches, and shifters, and pixies, and fae.
There is nothing more precious than the love of a girl,
And there is nothing stronger than the bonds of a spell.
Protect, protect, protect."

As I read the words, the world around me shifts. I hear someone screaming my name, but I'm too lost in the story to care. It's as if I am singing to a melody only I can hear, and when I'm done, everything feels right again. The paper falls from my hands, and I drop back down to the seat, my heart beating wildly, my body buzzing from the magic.

"Stupid girl, what did you do?" Elder Matilda is screaming as I focus back on the room. The others look horrified, and I don't understand what's happening.

"Headmaster Marković?"

He doesn't meet my eye but continues to stare out the window. I follow his gaze and find a forest I've never seen before on the other side of the glass. I no longer see the campus I have come to love, nor do I hear the sounds of struggle. Confusion clouds my mind as I glance down at the words I've written.

"What did I do?"

No one moves as a knock sounds at the headmaster's door. He walks over to it, pulling it open, and a person steps in. My mouth falls open at the sight, and at first, I think I'm hallucinating.

"Okay, which one of you have decided it would be a good idea to drop Thunderbird Academy in the middle of Spring Court's forest?"

I don't think I hear him right, and then it all falls into place. They warned me to be careful with my words and intentions. I wrote with my friends in my heart.

"Umm, Liam?" I stand, and the fae's eyes dart to me immediately. "I think that was me."

His eyes light up at the sight of me as his mouth breaks into a breathtaking smile.

"Maddie Hawthorne, why am I not surprised? I knew you wouldn't survive the year without me."

MADDIE'S LIST OF OLD SLANG
WORDS/PHRASES

Claws sharp - A lot of knowledge about various things.

Chicks on a raft! And Eggs on a toast! - diner speak, sometimes used as a utterance of surprise.

Made in the shade - Everything is going well and there is not a care in the world.

Don't have a cow - Don't get upset or go ballistic.

Peachy keen - very good.

Tickety-boo - everything is correct or everything is okay (depending on the situation)

Gigglemug - a perpetually smiling person.

Minding you Ps and Qs - "be on your best behavior", "mind your manners".

Dilly Dally - wasting time through aimless wanderings.

Pang-Wangle - live or go along cheerfully in spite of misfortunes.

Source: bustle.com, mentalfloss.com, first hand experiences.

OF DESTINY AND ILLUSIONS

Thunderbird Academy - Book Two

Valia Lind

It is not in the stars to hold our destiny but in ourselves.

— WILLIAM SHAKESPEARE

❧ I ☙

This is the screw up of all screw ups. I have ruined everything. If they were giving out awards for the biggest mess-up of the century, I would be the recipient. Hands down.

I've been sitting in this room for what seems like hours. I haven't seen my friends or spoken to anyone since the Elders and Headmaster Marković were ushered into the Spring Court's private chambers. The large intricate design on the doors does nothing to minimize the fear I feel knowing they're in there, deliberating my future.

My mind drifts to my friends, and I really hope they're okay. If I'm being honest, I have no idea what my spell actually did. Sure, I went ahead and moved the whole school, including the outside campus, right into the middle of the Faery's forest. But that's all I know. My friends were out there, fighting the creatures sent by the Ancients. They could've gotten hurt. Or worse.

I really shouldn't think like that, but my mind is my worst enemy.

When the door finally opens, I think the Elders have come to banish me to some unknown plane of existence, but then Liam slips in.

"Maddie." He says my name softly and then he's across the room in a flash, pulling me out of the chair and into his arms. I grip him tightly, basking in the feel of the comfort he provides.

"I'm sorry," I whisper against his chest, and I feel him stiffen. He pulls away just a tad, glancing down into my face.

"You have nothing to be sorry about."

"Right, can you make sure you mention that to, oh I don't know, everyone?" I step out of his arms, frustration and fear once again ruling my body.

"Maddie, you did the best you could with the information you were given." I glance at him sharply and find that quiet wisdom on his face that I've missed so much. "If Headmaster Marković asked you to story cast, then he should've given you proper instruction."

"It's not like there was time."

"Then they should've found another way."

As he speaks, I realize something. He's angry. In the year I've known him, I don't think I've ever seen him angry. Fae are known for mastering their emotions. It takes a bit to get them rattled.

"Liam, what is it?"

"How are you feeling?" he asks instead, and I narrow my eyes.

"Liam." At first, I think he'll continue beating around the bush, but he surprises me.

"Maddie, story spell casting is dangerous. Especially for the witch who wields the power. How are you feeling?"

"I'm fine, honestly. I felt drained the first time I did it. But not so much now."

My words don't seem to reassure him in the least. He studies me like I'm a bug under a microscope, and I shift foot to foot under the scrutiny. Now that he mentions it, I do feel more tired than I initially thought. But I'm not about to tell him that. It's just the adrenaline wearing off.

"Can you tell me what's happening in there?" I ask instead, motioning toward the closed doors. Liam glances behind him, and I swear his look just got a tad darker. But when he turns back to me, I find no trace of that fleeting emotion.

"You rattled quite a few cages, Maddie." He sighs, taking my hand and leading me toward the love seat positioned under the large window. It's opposite from the doors. I've been trying to stay away from it, if only to keep myself from staring outside and freaking myself out more than I already am.

"I didn't mean to."

"No, but what's done is done." Liam doesn't let go of my hand as we sit, and I'm grateful for the small comfort his skin offers mine. We've never been touchy feely before, but I think he realizes I need this right now. I'm teetering at the edge, overwhelmed by the knowledge of what I've done, of what I'm capable of. It's not an easy burden to carry.

"What do you think will happen next?" I'm not sure I'm ready for the answer, but I need it all the same.

"I think they will ask you to write a spell to take the school back to the human realm. But I'm not sure how effective that will be."

"What do you mean?" It takes him a long time to reply, but I don't push. Something is going on here, and it's up to him to share whatever he deems best. When he finally speaks, it's not what I expect.

"The Ancients are right on the border of Faery, Maddie." His words are heavy with everything he's not saying. "I know everyone thinks this place is impenetrable, but the Ancients' magic is stronger than anything we've ever encountered. And they're getting through. Somehow they're getting through."

This time, I'm the one who offers an encouraging squeeze to his hand, and he grips it tightly. I thought him staying home would keep him safe. Instead, it put him in even more danger.

"Do you think they'll get through?"

"We are not about to let that happen."

The voice comes from our right, and both Liam and I jump to our feet as I turn to watch a group of people walk through the doors. The woman at the front can only be described as strikingly gorgeous. Her porcelain skin and platinum blonde hair glow brightly enough to light up the space around her. Her crystal blue eyes are on me, her lips rosy, as if she's wearing makeup. Except I know better. I'm mesmerized by her, and I can't help it.

"Your Highness," Liam bows beside me, and I hurry to follow suit. So, this is the High Queen of Spring Court. Stories about her do not do her justice. Even her gown is more intricate than I would've imagined. The color is of blooming buds on a spring day, and it seems to flow around her as if it's dancing in the wind.

"Madison Hawthorne." The queen speaks, her eyes piercing me right through. "You have created quite a predicament. What do you have to say for yourself?"

"I'm not a very good storyteller?" I shrug, and for a second, I think she might actually smile. "I'm sorry, Your Highness."

"Do not ever apologize for your power, child." She waves a hand, as if waving away my words. "Come, we have much to discuss."

The headmaster meets my eye over the queen's shoulder with an encouraging smile on his face. I have no idea how I got myself into this mess, but as I trail after the queen, I realize, I will do whatever it takes to turn this into my greatest victory.

After all, I am a Hawthorne. I have a legacy to live up to and an opportunity to create my own.

❧

WE DON'T GO BACK INTO THE CHAMBERS, OR WHATEVER THAT ROOM actually is, behind the closed doors. Instead, the queen leads us outside. I'm too nervous to appreciate the gorgeous castle walls and the beautiful art displayed all around me. My heart feels like it's going to beat right out of my chest. The headmaster, Liam and two of the Elders, Matilda included, are walking a few steps behind me.

Once outside, I take a deep breath, inhaling the freshness of the perpetual springtime. I've never visited Faery before, but it's always been a dream of mine. Especially after I met Liam. I glance back at him, and he gives me a tiny smile of encouragement. He's unlike any fae I've ever read about, his kindness toward me has always come first. But I have no misconceptions about the beautiful creature walking in front of me. The queen would have me killed in a second if it fancied her.

"Madison Hawthorne," When the queen speaks, I understand why songs are sung about fae's ability to draw in humans with just one word. My name sounds like a lyrical poem on her lips. "Look around. What do you see?"

"The school?" Because there it is, situated amongst the tallest trees I have ever seen, Thunderbird Academy stands completely untouched by the effects of my spell. Except for *where* it's standing.

"What do you know about the story casting you performed?" She turns to glance at me, and I feel that look root me to the ground. The rest of our entourage feels miles away as I stare at the gorgeous creature in front of me.

"I'm afraid I don't know much. I never thought I would use it."

"But then you used it twice."

Confusion must be plain on my face because I have no idea how she could know such a thing. Unless the headmaster told her. Actually, I take it back. It was probably Elder Matilda. She's out to get me; I know that for a fact. But then, the queen surprises me with a laugh. It sounds like the first rainfall of spring beating on tender leaves. The sound pulls me in until I don't want to listen to anything else.

"I can see the magic on you, Madison Hawthorne. You almost reek of it."

That snaps me back to reality. I glance down, as if I would be able to see the physical effect of my magic, but of course there's nothing. It takes me a full minute before I can bring myself to look at the queen again. I need to be more careful and not be so mesmerized by her presence. Even though it's difficult, it's possible. My sister's best friend is dating one of the fae from the Spring Court, and I, of course, asked Nolan enough questions to become annoying. Now I'm glad that I have.

When I finally meet the queen's eye, she gives me a cold smile.

"There is knowledge in your eyes, Madison Hawthorne." I have no idea how to take that, so I don't respond. "But there is also immaturity to your magic. You have broken through the Vale in the most unconventional way, which puts the whole realm in danger."

There is not a hint of kindness in her voice, and it chills me to the bone. I don't want to show fear, so I solidify my resolve as much as possible. I'm not sure it helps any, but I don't back down.

"Tomorrow, you are to come see me for a ...conversation." I try not to show the shock I'm feeling, but I doubt I succeed. "That is all."

She doesn't wait for a response but leaves me standing as she turns and walks back into the castle. I'm so flabbergasted, I don't even have it in me to bow. Once she's gone, Liam is by my side, along with the headmaster and Elder Matilda.

"Now you have gone and done it," she hisses at me. "The Queen of the Spring Court is not a fae you want on your bad side, so you better not mess it up."

"I don't understand." I finally find my voice, completely ignoring the woman and looking at my headmaster instead. "What does she want with me?"

"Miss Hawthorne, you..." He stops for a second, as if looking for the right words. "You are a fascinating subject for her, one she plans to study. I am afraid your attendance is required as it is one of the stipulations for us to stay here as free folk."

"You mean, she would put us in prison if I don't go to the meeting?"

"You are correct. The queen is not to be trifled with in any way. This may be the Spring Court, but do not have any misconceptions about the fact that you are in Faery."

He's right. The Spring Court may be one of the nicer ones in Faery, but that doesn't change anything. I let that sink in, my blood cold in my veins. I made everything so much worse. I wish I never would've opened my big mouth. Liam steps closer to me but doesn't offer empty words of encouragement. I'm in big trouble.

"What do we do now?" I ask, looking over my shoulder at Thunderbird Academy, my home away from home.

"Now, we learn all we can about your magic, resume school as usual, and train you to write a spell that will take us home."

"School?" I twist around, not sure I heard him correctly.

"Ah, yes. Unfortunately for us, your spell was a one-way ticket. With the Ancients right on the border, we cannot allow any students back into the human realm. Not yet. So, we are to go about our days, business as usual."

At first, I can't wrap my mind around his words. I thought I'd be the one to stay here and everyone else would be able to leave. To go home or go into hiding. This was going to be my punishment and no one else's.

"Are you saying we're stuck here?"

"That is precisely what I'm saying."

With those words, my already upside-down world completely shatters. Not only have I made myself the queen's personal guinea pig, but I sentenced my friends—and the entire school—to a stint in the Faery Realm. Against their will.

I hope they're okay. I doubt any of them will want to talk to me once they find out.

$\mathscr{K}$ 2 $\mathscr{K}$

Thunderbird Academy cannot be more than half a mile away, but for some reason, it seems unreachable. Headmaster and Elder Matilda have moved farther away, but I can still hear them arguing behind my back. Well, it's mostly Elder Matilda yelling at Headmaster Marković. Not that any of this is his fault. It's mine. I know it. The queen knows it. Everyone knows it.

"How are you holding up, cupcake?" I groan at the hated nickname, turning just a bit to see Liam's grin.

"You're the cupcake, cupcake," I reply, our standard exchange. Honestly, I can't even remember how this started, but it became our thing. He's trying to make me feel better, but I don't.

"I really need you to get that chip off your shoulder, Maddie," the fae sighs. "We already discussed how this is not your fault."

"You say that because you're my friend."

"I say that because fae can't lie."

I glance at him then, noticing the seriousness that has entered his voice. So often, I forget he is not of my world. He's got that breathtaking glow about him that makes it difficult to stare for too long. It's like looking at the sun. But there is also kindness about him that's not typical to the fae. I know he's spent much of his years in the human world, despite his standing within the court. Even in his dark jeans, faded t-shirt, and leather jacket, he looks like royalty. That's when I realize he's dressed in human clothes.

"Why are you wearing that?" I ask, completely distracted now. He glances down at himself, as if realizing it for the first time.

"I had an errand to run."

"In the human realm?" My mind automatically goes to my family. Liam's half-brother is dating my sister's best friend. Wow, that's a mouthful. But it's also a link. "Have you seen my family?"

He shifts his eyes to the side, as if to see who is listening. When he turns back, I know he's not saying anything. Not here or right now.

"It was official business for the queen," he replies, and I nod my head in understanding, even as I try not to feel disappointed. Everything Liam does is calculated. It has always been so, and I know he won't put me in any kind of danger. Even when it comes to information. Yet, I still wish he would give me some kind of an indication.

As if reading all this in my face, Liam takes a step toward me, reaching for my arm. His hand wraps around my wrist, giving it the tiniest of squeezes, and I feel better instantly. Just then, Headmaster Marković comes up, and Liam drops my arm quickly. I don't have to be reminded that my friendship with Liam has always been a bit of a sore spot for his family. But now that his family reconciled with his brother, I wonder if that has changed. Just another question among the millions of questions I want to ask him when we're alone.

"We should get back to the school," Headmaster says, and I look over his shoulder to see Elder Matilda disappearing back into the castle.

"Is Elder Matilda not coming?" I ask.

"No, the Elders have much to discuss," Headmaster replies, his eyes on the school. I can't quite read his features, but he almost looks sad to me. "I am sorry for putting you in this position, Miss Hawthorne," he says, and now his expression makes sense. He feels guilty. Well, get in line.

"It's not your fault."

"Oh, but it is. If I had thought this through, instead of jumping to the first plausible solution, we might not be in this mess."

"Or it would've been a worse kind of a mess," I reply, looking him straight in the eye. "You didn't make me perform a spell. I did that all on my own."

"Yet, I am your headmaster. It is my job to guide you in the ways of magic."

"Not that I'm not enjoying this blame ping pong," Liam interrupts, taking a step forward. "The only party responsible are the Ancients. They were the ones who invaded Thunderbird Academy. They are the ones who should carry the blame. What you need to do is use the knowledge you have gained and make sure next time will be better."

Headmaster and I stare at Liam in silence as I let those words sink in. He's right, of course. But it's the way he says it that really gets to me. There's complete faith in his eyes and behind his words. He believes we can do this, that *I* can do this. I can't let him down. I can't let any of them down.

"I really missed you, Liam," I say, and the fae flashes me one of his heart-stopping grins.

"I know."

⁂

WHEN WE GET BACK TO THE ACADEMY, THE PLACE IS EERILY QUIET. A part of me expected chaos. I should really stop expecting anything at this point. My life isn't exactly anything I would've planned for myself.

Headmaster leads the way toward the large auditorium with Liam and me trailing behind. The fae's eyes keep darting around the area, as if he's waiting for something to jump out at us. It's never been my nature to be paranoid, but I'm rethinking that stand with the current events. Taking a step closer to Liam, I lower my voice and ask, "Should I be looking for something?"

He looks over at me, flashing me one of his quick smiles before replying.

"Nothing in particular. But you're in my world now, so I would advise you to always be looking for something."

Cryptic, but that's fae for you. As we continue walking, a low buzzing sound seems to come from the walls, but I can't pinpoint it. So instead I focus on my friend.

After meeting Liam last year, I did a lot of sneaky research to learn more about his kind. Before him, I never even imaged I would meet one. My hometown hasn't had a fae resident in generations. Not until Liam's half-brother, Nolan, came to stay there. If there is a lesson I remember from my childhood, it's the hierarchy of danger my mother taught me about. Shifters are at the top of that list. But what tops even them are the fae folk. One misplaced word and you can be indebted to them for a lifetime.

Not that I ever had to worry about that with Liam. Although, I'm still cautious. He even tells me to be. And like he said, fae can't lie. It doesn't matter what I think of his people, I'm just glad he's here. The feeling of dread hasn't gone away, and I fear that whatever the headmaster is about to tell the students will be just as earth shattering to me.

"Miss Hawthorne." The headmaster turns as we reach the double doors leading to the auditorium. "Please stay at the back of the stage for the time being."

"I'll stay with her." Liam immediately speaks up while I'm still trying to figure out why he's keeping me in the background. The headmaster gives my friend an affirmative nod before he pulls the doors open and steps inside. We follow close behind, but while he continues to the stage, Liam pulls me to a stop. "Give him a minute."

"Why?"

"Because, by the sound of it, people are not happy."

That's when I realize, the low buzz I've been hearing are people's voices talking over each other in the next room. I creep toward the stage, keeping to the shadows, and I feel Liam's presence at my back. There is unmistakable panic in people's voices, even some animal growls and chirps. That tells me some of the shifters are in so much emotional distress, they can't control their shift.

"Please settle down," Headmaster's voice booms, amplified by magic to be heard in the farthest corners of the room. Everyone quiets instantly, and I wish I could see inside. But we're behind a large curtain, keeping as still as we can. There are plenty of shifters in the room that can sniff me out if I make even a little bit of a noise.

"I understand you are all scared," Headmaster Marković continues, his voice soothing and authoritative at the same time. "Queen Amaryllis has kindly opened up her land as a safe haven for our school. Since the Ancients have overrun our own grounds, I am sad to say, we will not be returning any time soon."

A murmur goes through the room at his words, and my own heart pangs painfully at the thought. I don't care what Liam says, I feel responsible for this outcome. Maybe if I was a better spell caster, I would've done a better job protecting us. Maybe if I was as strong or as smart as my sisters, I would've known my own limitations. No matter what anyone says, this is something I will have to live with. I just hope my actions haven't hurt anyone more than I already know they have.

"The grounds of Thunderbird Academy are protected, and while we are here, it will be business as usual. We will hold classes, we will train, and we will do what it takes to find a way back to our own way of life."

The murmur is much louder now, but I can't shake the feeling that Headmaster Marković is not telling us something vital.

"Since we are on Queen Amaryllis' land, she has asked for some of her court to be allowed to attend classes here. We will adjust accordingly. Now, please report to your rooms and further instructions will be given. Dismissed."

The headmaster doesn't allow for questions. He walks off the stage as soon as he says the words. I can hear the student body shouting at him for more information, but I know he won't provide it. Something else is happening here, and when the headmaster walks by where Liam and I are hiding, I take a step in front of him to block his path.

"What are you not telling them?" I ask, keeping my voice extra low in case any of the shifters can hear me. The headmaster looks me in the eye, and at first, I think he won't answer. But then, it's as if he's resigned to the fact that I need this information. When he opens his mouth, he looks older than I've ever seen him.

"Do not think for even a moment that we are guests here, Miss Hawthorne," Headmaster says, deliberately not looking in Liam's direction. "We have no way out and no choice but to obey. We are bound to this place for the time being, Miss Hawthorne. Please keep that knowledge to yourself."

"So, what you said before about me going to the meetings, it's much more than that. We're already prisoners."

He doesn't wait for a response, leaving me standing in the shadowed room, gaping at his retreating back.

"Stuck?" I turn to Liam, as the fae takes a step toward me. "We're stuck here?"

🙛 3 🙙

"I need to go see my friends," I announce. My mind is on Jade, who's probably full-on panicked by now at my absence. I think of Vera, Noel, Ben...and yes, even Aiden. They're my tribe, my people, and they probably think I've abandoned them. At least Kate is not here to be part of the mess. I just hope she's safe with her family. One day, when all of this is over, I'll find her and we'll catch up on all the things we missed about each others lives. But for now, I have to focus on what's right in front of me.

"I should get back to the castle. Will you be okay?"

Nodding my head is all I can do because, even though I know Liam has my back, a seed of doubt has been sown.

"Maddie." He takes a step closer, peering down into my face, and I have no choice but to look up. I'm blinded by his beauty once more, and I hate that I can't read anything in his eyes. "Everything will work out as it should."

"I like how you made sure to not say everything will be okay." I sigh, but this is just the way of their world. Words have power and when you can't lie, every single one is that much more powerful. Liam smiles at my observation but doesn't correct me.

"Your queen will really keep us here?"

"I told you, Maddie. We're at war. If she believes this is the best way, then that is what needs to be done."

"Even if we become prisoners?"

"We're all imprisoned one way or the other."

I glance at him sharply, surprised by the emotions brewing under that statement.

"We can sit around and be miserable. Or we can make the best out of a crappy situation."

It's difficult not to get inspired by his words. He's always had a way of getting right to the core of things and bringing them to a different light.

"You haven't lost your pep talk skills," I say now, flashing him a quick smile, "This is number five or six since I got here."

"It's what I do," he replies, bowing a little. Suddenly, I want to reach over and pull him into a hug because his arms will make me feel safe. If only for a moment. When we first found the library last year, we spent so much time together, I often forgot there are boundaries between our kind.

I squash the desire before I can take it any further. Maybe in the quiet of the secret library we could be something to each other, but here, in the light of day, we're a witch and a fae and there are eyes on us. No matter how much I have missed my friend, I have to remember where I am. I have to remind myself that I can stand on my own two feet.

"I'll come check on you later." Liam inclines his head before turning on his heels and walking away. After taking a few deep breaths, I make my way to the hallway.

There are a few students here and there, but not enough to make me nervous. No one pays me any more attention than usual, and I wonder if anyone knows what actually happened when the Ancients attacked. If they know I was directly involved.

But when no one starts throwing magic at me, I breathe a little easier and hurry to the staircase that leads me to my floor. There are even fewer people up here, most already safe in the confines of their rooms. No one seems to dare disobey Headmaster's instructions.

Jade is the first to see me. She freezes for half a second before she launches herself at me. I meet her halfway as she throws her arms around me, holding me tightly.

"Oh my gosh, I thought you were dead! I was so worried. We've been so worried. Those creatures seemed to descend out of nowhere, and we did our best, and then suddenly, we weren't there anymore, and the sky looked different, and where have you been?" She pulls back, breathing heavily as she takes me in, head to toe.

"I'm sorry to worry you," I reply, squeezing her hand briefly. "I was with the headmaster."

Thankfully, I don't get to say anything more as the rest of my friends reach us. I get pulled into a hug by Noel, nearly taking me off my feet, before I'm transferred to Vera. Even the hawk shifter seems to be showing an unusual amount of emotion as she gives me a quick hug. Then, I realize Ben is there, and even though he doesn't move to hug me, he gives me the kind of look that goes right through me. There's so much happiness and relief on his face, it almost brings tears to my eyes.

"Please head to your rooms immediately." The robotic voice sounds suddenly, making us all jump. "The lockdown is in full effect. Please head to your rooms immediately."

The rest of the hallway clears within seconds. My friends are reluctant to leave, and now that they see I'm safe, it's probably out of curiosity. Vera waves in our direction, heading off toward her room alone, and I realize she's the most affected by Christie's betrayal. She no longer has a roommate.

The boys are next to leave, after a long searching look at us. Just before Ben heads off, he moves toward me, touching my arm gently.

"I'm glad you're okay, Maddie," he whispers, his eyes intense on mine. "Aiden will be too." Then he's gone before I can interpret what he means by that. Jade takes my hand and pulls me toward our room as the last of the announcement sounds through the now empty hallway. The door shuts behind us and then we're alone.

I lean against the wood, my focus on breathing in deeply and exhaling fully. It feels like my heart rate has been at an all-time high since the moment I realized what I'd done.

"Are you okay?" Jade asks, and I open my eyes to find her sitting on her bed, her attention on me. She looks just as scared as I feel on the inside, so I push away from the door and walk toward her. Once seated, I turn to face her, trying to figure out what to say.

"Are *you* okay?" I ask, instead of answering.

"Honestly, I'm terrified. I know we've been training for battle since school began, but I never imagined it would come to this. And now, we're in Faery. Faery! You need a special invitation and a visa to visit, yet now we're living here. I don't know how to wrap my mind around that."

I can feel the panic creeping into her voice the longer she talks, and I truly wish Bri was here to offer some wisdom. My oldest sister is the best in these types of situations. But I can't seem to come up with anything because all I can think of is how it's my fault we ended up in this situation, and I can't even tell her that.

"We'll be okay, Jade," I say instead, giving her shoulder a little reassuring rub. I'm trying to convince myself as well as her.

"That's what people say when they don't think things will be okay."

"Let's not panic," I try again. I don't want to offer her empty promises, but I have to believe we will come out of this. "I say that because I believe it's possible and because that's the goal. We can and we will be okay, Jade."

She watches me for a long moment, as if searching the weight of my words. Finally, she leans her head on my shoulder and sighs.

"I hope my family is safe. I hope Headmaster finds a way to contact them. I can't imagine what they must be thinking."

It's a good point, but a moot one at the moment. My mind drifts to my own family but only for a second. I can't focus on what I can't control. I already have plenty on that list.

"I'm sure they're safe. And since we've been on minimal communication, maybe they're not worried." Yet. I don't say it, but I don't have to. Jade understands.

"Yeah," Jade sighs again, sitting up. "I can't believe Christie would do this. She was our friend. How could she?"

I've been thinking about this at the back of my mind since she let the creatures into that building. Typically, there isn't a way to truly rationalize someone's actions because they have their own motivations. Always. But in this case, she told us what she wanted.

"Power can corrupt, and I think Christie just wanted it so badly, she didn't think about anything else."

"Like us."

"Yes, like us." I push down the sadness and the disappointment as I stand. "But you know what? That's on her. We did everything right. And we will continue to do so."

Jade gives me a brilliant smile, and I think I helped. In silence, we begin making preparations for bed and tomorrow. With the fae now walking the halls and controlling our every move, this will be the strangest school year. I just hope I don't accidentally send us somewhere worse.

Tomorrow, I will start looking for answers about my powers. Tomorrow, I will figure out how to play this game with the queen. For now, I rest and hopefully, my dreams won't be filled with a certain shifter, who apparently sent his beta to check on me.

❧

THERE IS NO REPRIEVE IN SLEEP FOR ME. I TOSS AND TURN SO MUCH, I end up wrapped in the blanket so tight, I smack myself in the face trying to get out. Some all-powerful witch I am. I tried slipping out to see if I could get to the greenhouse, but the doors are completely on lockdown. It seems this school has become our prison. At least for the time being.

The next morning, Jade and I wake up to a piece of paper being slipped under our door. She picks it up, glancing at it briefly before she walks over to me.

"What is it?"

"A list of things we can and cannot do." She sits beside me as we read, and the feeling of dread intensifies with each word.

"No leaving the premises without specific permission and an escort. Curfew is at exactly nine o'clock. Weekly dinners at the palace are not a negotiation. What's happening, Maddie?" Jade's voice rises in panic, and I reach over, placing my hand over hers.

"They're just rules, Jade. They're not a bad thing. Fae are..." I pause, trying to figure out the best way to tell Jade just how careful she needs to be without freaking her out more. She grew up in a town without fae residents, and until coming to Thunderbird Academy, never even met one. But it wouldn't be smart to lie to her, so I settle on the truth. "Fae are dangerous. They're cunning, and they are not your friends. If the queen put these rules in place, she is doing us a kindness very uncharacteristic of her kind. They also cannot lie, and that means, as long as we follow the rules, we'll be safe."

"You make them sound like villains."

"Because they are."

Jade stares at me in shock, as if not quite believing my words. I stand, moving from one side of the room to the other, feeling restless.

"Don't you for a second think these creatures are on your side. They only look out for themselves."

"But I don't understand. You have a fae friend. There are others here..."

"They're different. We're at the queen's mercy now. She is not our friend."

"Follow the rules, Jade." I point to the piece of paper she's holding in her hands. "Stay away from strangers. Don't make any bargains or promises or wishes."

My words settle over us, and we pause at the reality of what our lives have become. We're in a completely different situation here. And as much as I know about the fae, or even the Ancients, so many students here don't have that same knowledge. Much of this comes from how segregated the magical community has become. My mama told me other covens have a tendency to keep to themselves. Much like Jade's family, students are raised in an environment that is very one sided. It makes me so thankful to know my family made sure I knew the ways of the world.

"I'm scared, Maddie," Jade whispers, and I move instantly to her side.

"We'll get through this," I vow, even more intent on setting this right. For a moment, I consider if I should tell Jade what I did. I'm not sure if the headmaster is planning to keep it silent, or for how long it can really stay under wraps. Both Aiden and Natalie were present when I was told to create the spell. I can't see Aiden telling anyone, but Natalie seems like the kind of person who would. Especially if it benefits her.

As Jade and I get ready to head down to breakfast, my mind drifts to the shifter. Not that he's ever far from my thoughts. I didn't exactly dream about him last night, but he was there any time I closed my eyes.

The look he gave me right before Natalie pulled him out of the room haunts me. There was emotion there I didn't expect but hoped for. Yet, now that the dust has settled, I have no idea if it's all in my head. After all, he hasn't come to see me. I'm not sure why I'm even thinking he would. Just because I've developed some unwanted feelings, doesn't mean he's going to reciprocate them. Even though I think we have a connection.

Why am I even thinking about this?

I yank my sweatshirt over my head, sending my hair into frizzy disarray. I'm such a dumb Dora, I need to get my act together before it's too late. But maybe it's already too late. I'm all kinds of twisted up over a boy. That's as unintelligent as it comes.

"You ready?" Jade's question pulls me out of my thoughts, and I turn to see her standing by the door. She gives me a questioning look, clearly reading something on my face, but I push it all down. Now is definitely not the time to have a heart-to-heart about my unnecessary emotions. We're in a place that is hazardous to our health. We are in a midst of a war. I brought us here, and I should focus on sending us back.

Everything else can wait.

"Let's do this."

❧ 4 ☙

"**M**addie!" I hear my name called the moment we step into the dining room. I turn to see Ben wave as he heads toward us. My eyes instantly search for Aiden, but he's still nowhere to be found. Ben reaches me in the next second, wrapping his arms around me and sweeping me right off my feet.

"Someone is happy to see me," I mumble into his shoulder when he puts me down.

"Sorry," he replies, rubbing the back of his head as he takes a step back. "I'm just happy you're okay. I know I just saw you yesterday, and I knew you were okay, but now you're here and you're..."

"Okay?" I interrupt his babbling, and he gives me a sheepish look. I can't resist that small smile, so I step right back into his arms, hugging him around the middle. "I'm glad you're okay too."

Ben and I have become the fastest of friends, and I'm honestly not sure if I should be weirded out by that or not. He's not like the rest of his pack, and I feel a certain kinship toward him. Which is a bit strange. It's not like I have a tendency to open up to people right away, but it's as if we're on the same wavelength.

"We're going to get some food," I say, motioning toward Jade. Ben nods, stepping aside as my friend and I head for the line.

"Why were you so worried?" I decide to ask as Jade and I pile some breakfast food onto our plates. The academy has gone a little over-board today, probably trying to soothe anyone's worries, but I'm not complaining. Breakfast food is at the top of my favorites. Ben doesn't reply right away, and I look over to see him scanning the crowds.

"Ben."

"Sorry, there have been rumors."

"What kind of rumors?"

"That you had audience with the queen yesterday. And then, no one saw you after. So, I didn't really know what to think."

Great, the ever-present gossip mill is alive and well. That's an annoying turn of events considering I would've liked for people to not know I'm seeing the queen. But there's not much I can do about that now, except try and turn the gossip a certain way. My way.

"Yes, I was with queen yesterday, but it was actually before I saw you in the hallway. One of her nephews used to go to school here and is my friend. I was with him when he was summoned."

"Oh." With that one word, Ben visibly relaxes.

"What?"

"Nothing."

"Ben." I think saying his name in my stern voice is going to be the way to go. He glances at me sheepishly before looking over my head.

"We were just worried, that's all."

"We? What are you not telling me?" I grab one of his sleeves, tugging on it until he meets my eye once more. There's a look there I can't quite place, and then, he's moving away.

"I'll see you later, okay?"

"Ben!" But he's already gone.

"What was that all about?" I ask, turning to Jade, who stayed silent during the whole exchange. We grab our plates and begin making our way to a table. Noel is already seated, so we weave in and out of the aisles before finally reaching him.

"I think it may have something to do with his alpha," Jade whis-pers, leaning closer once we're seated. I glance at her sharply, and then twist to see if Aiden has finally decided to make an appearance. But no. He's still nowhere to be found.

"What do you mean?" I turn back to my friend.

"Just that Ben has always been here to watch over you for him. And he said, '*we* were worried.' That implies more than one person." She shrugs, giving me a quick smile before she dives into her food. I think she's right, of course. Ben has been assigned to watch me. It's how we became friends in the first place. But I still don't understand the secrecy. I knew that, so why not just say Aiden was worried?

Forcing myself to take a bite of the hash browns in front of me, I do another scan of the dining hall. This time, my eyes land on Owen, Aiden's other right hand. He's leaning against the wall on the opposite side of the room, his face turned in our general direction. While I can't exactly see his eyes from this distance, I feel like he's watching me.

It should make me feel safer, but it just makes me feel more nervous than I already am. If Aiden is so set on having me followed, then maybe he knows something I don't. There has to be a way to talk to him, wherever he is. He can't avoid me forever. We still have training, after all.

That's it. That's where I'll talk to him.

He's always taking combat training seriously, and except for a few times, has always been present. Even when we were fighting. No matter what's going on now, he has to be there. He wouldn't leave me unprepared.

Satisfied with that, I dig into my food a little more forcefully. So much is happening in such a short time, it's difficult not to get overwhelmed. But right now, for this one little thing, at least I have a plan. And that makes me feel much better.

❧

AFTER BREAKFAST, EVERYONE CONVERGES IN THE GRAND HALL ONCE again. It has always fascinated me how this room never seems that big, until it fits everyone in it. Now I realize, it's just another magic trick, but what in my life isn't?

"What do you think they want now?" Noel asks, coming to stand on my left side. Jade is basically plastered to my right, with Vera a few steps away with other hawk shifters. She's been keeping her distance a bit, and I'm sure it has everything to do with the fact that her roommate turned out to be evil. I don't think she's trusting anyone right now. I catch her eye, and she gives me a small nod before turning her attention to the front of the room once more. I make a mental point to try and talk to her later. Maybe she'll feel less pressured if it's just me.

"I think they're just making sure we know the plan," I reply, studying the students around me. They all look uneasy, and I don't blame them. This is not exactly what they signed up for when they came to the academy. We were supposed to be safe here; it was supposed to be the safest place for us. But things change. I've learned that better than anyone recently.

The headmaster takes the stage, and a hush falls over the student body immediately. I feel a presence at my back, my heart skipping a beat. But when I turn, my face falls in disappointment. I try to mask it, but Owen doesn't miss a thing. He gives me a small smirk as he takes his place at my back, his eyes on the headmaster. Not that I don't appreciate the silence, but it always amazes me how different Ben and Owen are. Both at Aiden's side as his seconds, but where Ben is a bit like a hyperactive puppy, Owen is a wise old dog.

I shake my head a little, dispelling the analogies. I have an inkling that shifters don't like being compared to pets. Therefore, I should keep those thoughts to myself.

The other thoughts I should keep to myself are the ones currently swimming in my mind, telling me that even though Aiden can't be here, he's still sending his guards to watch me. Does that mean he cares, or is he being cautious because I'm the one with the story spell casting ability? I really need to talk to that shifter and soon.

"Everyone has received your list of school guidelines." The headmaster is speaking, and I force myself to focus on the words. "We understand it may seem like a vast amount of rules, but they are here to help guide you in this new situation."

I wonder if he rehearsed this or if this kind of speech comes easily to him. That's when I notice Elder Matilda lurking in the shadows behind the faculty up on stage. My eyes narrow as I try to bring her fully into focus, but she's too far and too hidden. That makes me highly suspicious. It's not like the school doesn't get an occasional visit from the elders. Why would she be staying in the shadows now?

"Your morning classes have been cancelled, but the afternoon classes are to proceed as scheduled. Those of you with training, you are still to report to your instructors. Please follow the rules, and we will keep you updated as we learn more."

Well, that told us nothing new. He dismisses us then, and the students begin filing out of the room. But my eyes are still glued to the headmaster's retreating back. He stops near Elder Matilda, and the two exchange a few words. With the noise of conversation around me, I can't even focus enough to read lips. Not that I could from this distance. But I want to know what they're saying. This is when being a shifter would be helpful.

"Ready to go?" Jade asks, and her words bring me back to reality. And then I realize something. Spinning, I push through the exiting crowd and stop right in front of Owen who hasn't moved.

"Hi, bodyguard," I greet him, smiling sweetly. "Can you use that super hearing of yours, and tell me what Elder Matilda is harping on about over there?" I nod my head in the direction of the stage, but my eyes remain on Owen. He watches me for a long moment, his intensity making me squirm, but I refuse to budge. I think we're going to stand there forever, but then I see a slight tug on his lips, which tells me I won some kind of a favor. His eyes move to focus on the stage, and I glance over my shoulder to see my friends waiting for me, confused looks on their faces.

"Elder wants an audience with the queen." Owen's low voice rumbles, and I turn my attention to him. "She's not happy being stuck here. She blames you." He glances at me briefly. "She wants favor and a safe passage out. Headmaster won't have it."

I try looking over my shoulder, but just as I do, they move farther off the stage and into the shadows. Neither looks in my direction, but I have a feeling they knew what I was doing. If we're on lockdown, it would be impossible for Elder Matilda to leave. So why is she making such a fuss? Does she know something we don't? I mean, I'm sure she knows something we don't. But this does raise a few more concerns in my mind.

"Always causing trouble, are we?" Owen's question turns my attention back to him.

"Is that a joke? Are you teasing?" I place my hand dramatically over my heart. "I didn't think this day would come!"

He shakes his head, but I have a feeling he's trying not to smile. At this moment, I realize I want him on my side like Ben is on my side. Maybe I can crack this stoic shifter and then I'll have two friends for life.

"Nothing?" I say, keeping a smile on my face. "I'll crack you eventually."

"I doubt it."

"I like a challenge," I say over my shoulder as I turn to rejoin my friends. Even that exchange was more than I've gotten from him since school began.

"What was that about?" Noel asks as I reach them.

"Just a friendly hello," I reply.

$$\text{❦} \quad 5 \quad \text{❦}$$

Classes go by in a blur. I'm hardly paying attention, but I think that goes for everyone at the moment. It would be easy to forget we're not in our realm anymore, if not for all the extra fae walking around. I'm not saying they're making me nervous, but they are making me uneasy. It doesn't matter that those two things are nearly the same, one makes me sound a little braver than I feel.

"Do you have training today?" Jade asks as we head for our room after our last class. Neither one of us felt like eating lunch today, so we grabbed some fruit on our way to our side of the castle.

"I'm supposed to," I reply. "I haven't heard otherwise, so I'm assuming yes."

I try not to let the excitement I'm feeling show on my face. Well, maybe not excitement. Anticipation? I just need to see Aiden with my two eyes to make sure he's okay and then I'll go back to ignoring everything I feel for him. How's that for a plan?

"Yeah, I think your shadow would've mentioned it."

I turn to where Jade is looking and see Owen leaning on the wall by the opposite staircase, his eyes on me. He's been there all day. I haven't seen Ben at all, but Owen has followed me like the shadow Jade says he is. Not that I'm complaining. I do feel safer with him around. I have conflicting emotions on the matter. Aiden should know I can handle myself. Even though I feel like I can't at the moment. But also, having Owen at my back calms me somehow.

The doubts and fears creep in suddenly, as if they were waiting their turn to populate my brain all day. I don't like this feeling. I don't like keeping things from my friends. I don't like having this power inside of me that can ruin everything with just a few words. At least while I was in class, I could pretend I was focusing on the course work. But now, I have no excuses for the thoughts rushing through my mind.

When Jade and I reach the room, we both head for our beds. It's like the day has drained us in more ways than one. Lying down, I look up at the ceiling, my thoughts drifting over to the secret library. If there is a place that has an answer for my predicament, it has to be there. But I have no way of reaching the greenhouse unnoticed. And I can't even be sure the library is there. Maybe the place is more attached to our realm than the school. Or maybe its magic is blocked here in Faery. I'm going to have to talk to Liam about it. If I see him anytime soon. I really thought he'd be joining the academy once again now that we're here, but I haven't seen him since yesterday. I can go over all the ifs and whens until I'm blue in the face, but it doesn't change the facts. I have no idea what I'm doing. Yet somehow, with the thoughts of the fae, I drift into sleep.

There's a thick fog all around me, so much so I can barely see two feet in front of me. With the fog comes the chill of an early morning, but it goes even deeper than that. I glance down at myself and find I'm not wearing my usual clothing. A deep green gown shifts around my legs, and when I move my hands over the material, I find the corset full of jewels. My shoulders are exposed, and so is a good portion of my back. The chill becomes cold as goosebumps race up and down my arms.

Doing a quick three-sixty, I realize I have no idea where I am. There are no markers for me to go off of, just fog and darkness beyond it. Reaching out with my left hand, I lift the dress up with my right. Taking tentative steps, I move forward with my hand outstretched. I haven't taken but few steps when my hand hits something. It's a tree, and that's when I realize I'm in a forest.

Once again, I study my surroundings, but there are no clues for me to find. Even after all the survival lessons, I have no defense over a forest where moss doesn't grow. I have no idea how I got here or why I'm here. Having no other choice, I start moving forward, keeping my steps as light as possible. Automatically, I reach for my battle magic, but I don't feel it. That makes me pause, a burst of panic in my chest, but I quickly push it down. It would do me no good to lose control right here and now. My mind races with the possibilities of what this means. I don't remember this dress. I don't remember getting here. I just opened my eyes, and the fog was in front of me.

That makes me pause.

I stop moving, doing another quick scan before I call on my magic. Nothing happens. That's when it comes to me.

I'm dreaming.

"I wondered how long it would take you to figure it out." The voice comes from beyond the fog, neither male nor female but some kind of distortion in between sounds. It makes me disoriented, so I put a hand out, searching for a tree I can lean against. The moment my skin touches the bark I feel more grounded.

"Who are you, and what am I doing here?"

"Learning. Growing." I don't miss the way the voice ignores my first question. My eyes narrow, as I try to see through the fog, but it's useless.

"What am I learning?"

"The way of the story."

That makes me pause, a million question come to mind. But which one to ask to actually receive an answer I can use? Before I can utter another word, the voice speaks again.

"Do not be afraid of the story. Let it flow through you, and it will be complete."

There is a rush of wind, sending my dress flying as it envelops me.

"Wait!" I call out, but somehow, I know the voice is gone. I battle the dress into submission, but it's no use. The wind is everywhere and then I'm spinning.

I sit up with a gasp, sweat dripping down my neck.

"Are you okay?" Jade asks, looking up from her history book. Glancing down, I see that I'm once again in my dark jeans and blue t-shirt. Reaching for my magic, I feel it dance inside me and instantly feel better.

"Yeah, just a bad dream."

"Sorry," Jade replies, genuine concern in that one word, and I try for an encouraging smile. "You better hurry though. You have training in thirty minutes. I was about to wake you up."

I glance at the clock, realizing the time. With a quick thanks, I jump off my bed and reach for my workout attire. Finally, I'm about to check one thing off my to-do list. It's time to have a conversation with Aiden.

❧

THERE ARE FIVE MINUTES TO SPARE WHEN I ARRIVE AT THE training building. One my way over, I noticed there are hardly any students outside on the lawn. Even though the whole campus was transported to Faery, no one is spending their time by the fountain or the avenue of limes. I think we all feel a little unsure of the air around us, even though the surroundings look familiar.

For just a second, I think he won't be there. But when I open the door, I feel him even before I see him. He's standing on the opposite side by the windows, and when I step inside and shut the door, he turns slowly toward me. I don't have shifter eyesight, but even at this distance, I can feel the intensity in his gaze. There so much emotion there, so much that he usually keeps inside.

I don't know what to do with myself as I try to figure out what he's thinking. My skin goes hot under his gaze, and I keep myself from moving forward before I'm ready. Before he's ready. I'm waiting for him to speak, to do anything, in that way I've only dreamed about. But he doesn't move forward, he doesn't come to me. So, I have to be the brave one.

Tentatively, I take a step toward him as I wipe my clammy hands on my leggings. A drop of sweat runs down my spine, and I'm sure with his shifter senses he can feel the intensity coming off me like steam.

"Where would you like to start today?" I say because the only thing I can do is pretend everything is as it was. I can't think about the fact that I'm feeling all these emotions, or the fact that I am ecstatic about seeing him alive and well. Then, I'm only five feet in front of him, and I don't know if I can get through training without giving something away. We've never been friends, and after Natalie arrived, we can never be anything more. But he stood by me in battle, he had my back in the headmaster's office. That has to count for something.

I open my mouth to say something else, to ask another question, but then his arms are around me, and he's lifting me straight off the floor, and all I can do is cling to him like I never want to let go. He lifts me even higher, burying his face in my collarbone, and I twine my legs around his middle to pull him even closer. I'm not sure who's comforting whom here, but we both need this. So, I don't speak, I don't move, I just hold him as tightly as I can, with his arms wrapped around me.

After what seems like hours, we pull back at the same time. With the way he's holding me, I'm finally looking down at him, instead of the other way around. The colors in his eyes dance, changing from light to dark, similar to the storm that's brewing inside of me. Emotions rise up within me, and I try to fight the urge, but I can't seem to control myself or my emotions. Being a shifter I'm sure he can tell what I'm feeling even more so than I can. One of his arms trails down my back while the other pins me to his front. I shudder, fully aware that I'm putty in his hands, and I don't care. The electricity dances around us, and my magic is doing a rumba within me. When I lean down, he moves to match me and then we're only a breath away.

But before our lips can touch, he jerks away, placing me gently on the ground and moving to the opposite side of the room with his supernatural speed. I'm breathing heavily as I force my legs to keep me upright. The sting of rejection almost takes the breath out of my lungs, but I can't let him see just how much he's affecting me. I think I finally have a hold on myself when the door opens at my back. Twisting around, I watch Natalie step into the room.

Her eyes zero in on me, and it's like she's studying me from the inside out. She carries with her a different kind of an intensity, but after the rollercoaster of emotions I just went through, I'm not backing down. I'm tired of cowering from situations or events. Maybe if I was braver in the first place, my spell would've done its job properly.

"There you are," Natalie coos, walking farther into the room and heading straight for Aiden. He turns just in time to catch her kiss on his cheek and the burst of jealousy that springs up inside of me doesn't go unnoticed. Natalie gives me a smug smile before focusing on Aiden. "I thought we had plans."

"For later," he replies, not meeting my eye. "I have training for the next hour. I'll meet you after."

"I'll just stay and watch..."

"No."

The word is sharp, and even though I'm not a shifter, I can hear the alpha in that one word. Aiden still hasn't met my eye, and I proceed to do stretches as Natalie pouts.

"Awe, but I would love to see these hard muscles at work now. Instead of waiting until later."

I almost face plant as I drop my foot from where I was stretching it behind my back. My eyes stay glued to the floor as I move my arms over my head, but I'm sure at least Natalie is looking at me in that smug way of hers.

"I'll see you after," Aiden says, and this time, he leaves no room for arguments. Natalie does her little disappointed sigh and turns to go.

"See ya later, Maddie," she calls, finally acknowledging my existence.

"Bye," I reply, and thankfully it doesn't come out as bitter as I expect it to. She can tell I'm not exactly her fan. Being a shifter does give her a certain upper hand in these situations.

Aiden and I don't speak immediately after she leaves. I continue my warmup as he walks around the room. I have so many things I want to ask him, but once again, I have no idea who we are to each other. There are words I want to say but won't. No matter how brave I'm trying to be. But this thing with Natalie? I can't let myself forget it. He's promised to her. It's their way. Even if Aiden was into me as much as I am into him, there could never be a future for us.

"I wanted to come see you after." He speaks up, and I stand up straight, all thoughts of exercise forgotten. If this is the only conversation we get, I'll take it.

"Why didn't you?" I'm almost afraid to ask, but I need to know.

"I had to take care of my pack first." He means her, of course. She's part of his pack now. They're merging hers and his together, so Natalie is at the top of his list.

"I understand." Turning away, I reach for my water bottle because suddenly my throat is closing up, and I can't seem to stop the flood of emotions I'm feeling.

"I don't think you do."

His words are so quiet, I know I'm not meant to hear them. But I do. Spinning around, I gasp when I realize he's moved closer. There's something in his eyes I can't decipher, but the desire to reach out almost overwhelms me.

"Then explain it to me," I whisper. He stares at me, rooting me to the spot, and for just a moment, I think he'll give in. That he'll cross the line and tell me everything. But he doesn't.

"I can't."

I nod at that, taking a swig of my water to push the tears down. Maybe it's the aftereffects of the magic, maybe this is what Liam feared. I'm too unbalanced. The magic inside of me is bursting to be set free in a completely new way. I can't tell if it's reacting to Aiden or my emotions or something else. But I'm fighting for control on too many fronts. I don't know if I can win.

"Thank you for sending Ben and Owen to watch out for me."

"Always."

His eyes flash with that one word and my heart thuds in my chest. Words are on the tip of my tongue, but before I can decide if I'll utter them, Aiden attacks.

✺   *6*   ✺

There is no mercy in the way he moves. But after all this time training with him, I anticipate his moves a lot more than I thought I would. He's pushing me to react, and so that's what I do. When he comes at me from the side, I drop to a squat before I roll out of the way. My body has become acquainted with the physical aspect of combat and is reacting almost automatically. I'm on my feet in a flash, and when Aiden's punch comes, I block it with my arm. We dance around each other, him punching and me blocking. His knee comes up, but I bat it down. Sweat begins to drip down my skin, but he needs this as much as I do. I can see it in his eyes. They're almost all wolf, and when I meet his gaze, my own magic flares up.

When the next attack comes, it's much stronger. But so am I. I don't hesitate to infuse my thrusts with magic, giving myself the same power up Aiden receives from his wolf. We're evenly matched in so many ways. I didn't even realize how much I've learned, until this moment.

But my thoughts are a distraction because the next thing I know I'm being tackled. I land hard on my back, with Aiden right on top of me.

The feel of him on top of me is the purest sort of torture. I freeze, afraid to breathe too loudly and distort the serenity I feel with him next to me. He pushes himself onto his elbows, glancing down at me as if he too wants this moment to last a little longer.

Neither one of us understands it, but here we are.

The intensity in his gaze is more than I can take, but still, I don't move. Maybe I'm being a coward, but I don't want to be the one to put a name to whatever is happening here. I don't want to be disappointed when it's not the word I would use.

Aiden's eyes land on my lips before he brings them back up to meet my eyes. My heart stops beating and then restarts with a ferociousness I don't expect. The shifter doesn't miss a thing, and his eyes are all wolf as he looks down at me. One of us is going to break, and I'm afraid it might be me. It's the fear that drives me and then I'm pushing him off me as we roll. He catches on quickly, but not quickly enough, which gives me time to escape.

"I count that as a win," he comments, getting to his feet. My face feels flushed, and I hope it's only red from exertion.

"I don't," I reply before I attack.

There's something freeing in the way we spar. I've never would've imagined myself as someone who loves combat training, yet here we are. Of course, I wish to never have to use it, but I know better than to expect that from my life. It hasn't exactly been all cupcakes and unicorns. Although that last part is probably a good thing since unicorns are vicious.

"You're not focused," Aiden calls out, and I glare at him.

"I'm focused."

"Not enough."

"Oh yeah? And how do you know?"

"Because I know you."

Those words burrow into me and take residence deep inside. Maybe I'm foolish to take these small glimpses of his character, but I can't help myself. When he says things like that, it's like he's talking to my very soul. There's no arrogance, no distance between us. It's a genuine truth, and I hold onto it. Doesn't everyone want to be known, truly known? But I can't let him see how those words affect me.

"Maybe you don't know as much as you think," I reply with a grin and then I throw myself at him. He turns, but as my body connects, I use the momentum to send us tumbling as I wrap my arms and legs around him. We roll a few times, but I don't let go. My arm is wrapped tight around his neck, and my legs are crisscrossed over his stomach. I hold on as he struggles, but he taught me well. Unless he goes full wolf, he's not getting out of this one. When he taps me on the hand, I release, and he tumbles out of my arms and next to me.

We lay side by side, both of us breathing heavily.

"You're getting better."

"I know."

For some reason, both of us find that funny. I laugh, and he chuckles, and this moment is going into my memory box. Because no matter how much we are not meant to be together, he's always going to have a place in my heart.

⁂

As I make my way toward the castle, my body breaks out in nervous sweat. It's not that I've never dealt with the fae before. But this is different. This is the High Queen of Spring Court. She is ruthless and cunning, and she thrives on power. I can't pretend to be brave around her. I have to actually have the courage.

When I'm only halfway across the school grounds, Liam steps out of the trees. I pause, surprised to see him, but I really shouldn't be. He said he'd come see me when he had the chance. And no matter how I feel about the rest of his people, I know he has my back. My two seconds of doubt are not earned. He's never done anything but stay by my side.

"Are you here to escort me to the queen?" I ask as he comes up to stand in front of me.

"I'm here to make sure you're safe," he replies. His quiet words soothe my worries because I know he'll stand by them.

"Did you think I wouldn't be?" I ask, genuinely curious.

"You know better than to assume anything otherwise."

And that's the truth of Faery. No one is safe while we're here. I told this to Jade, and I wasn't exaggerating. He gives me a quick once over, as if making sure everything is as it should be and then turns to fall into step beside me. There's a moment of silence, but then I ask what's bugging me.

"What are you so worried about?"

At first, it seems like he's not going to reply. The fae have to be careful with how much they say, and what kind of questions they answer, because words have power here. I'm not so naive to think Liam has given me his true name. I don't know if anyone knows that. But he has shared more with me than he's shared with probably most people.

When we first met, it was instant kinship. At the time, I was too nervous to question it. I needed a friend, and he was there. But it was easy to be around him, and after I learned more about his kind, I wondered if he did something to make me like him. After the Ancients started their attacks and I became surer of myself and my magic, I asked him about it. He told me he never had to use his glamour to make me like him. He felt connected to me in a way he didn't expect. So, he stuck around to see where it would lead. It led to us finding that secret library and forming a friendship that is odd to a lot of supernatural beings.

That's not to say that fae are unfriendly bunch. Actually, no, they are unfriendly. They keep to their own people. Sure, quite a few cross the boundaries when it comes to shifters, since shifters have some of the same glamour magic running in their veins. And they're just as promiscuous as the fae. But it's never been like that between us and right now, I'm beyond thankful. Especially since everything else is weird in my life, including Aiden, and I need the stability I find in our friendship.

"I don't like her fascination with you," Liam finally replies, and I don't have to ask who *her* is. I'm not exactly thrilled by her attention either, but it's not like I can do much about that. I did kind of drop a whole school into her forest.

"It'll be fine. I know what to expect."

"I don't think you do."

That makes me pause. I stop moving and wait for Liam to explain. He stops but doesn't turn around, as if his mind is lost somewhere else.

"Liam, talk to me."

I need to know what I'm walking into. He seems to have some kind of knowledge he thinks I don't. Having no other choice, I wait him out. This is definitely a skill I developed a little more fully after dealing with Aiden. Silence doesn't have to be filled for it to be powerful. People have a tendency to get unconformable when there's too much of it. Not that I think Liam will fall for that. But he knows what I'm doing, and that's what finally gets to him.

"I told you this when you arrived, you need to be careful with your magic. I don't want you to get hurt. And she," he pauses for a moment before carrying on, "she won't hesitate to have you hurt if it works in her favor. Just remember that when she begins promising you great things."

"She's just as nervous as we are," I say, and Liam's eyes fly up to meet mine. "The Ancients are after all of us. I've never thought anyone on this planet would be as old as the fae, but the Ancients are here now. And they're at the border of Faery. You think she'll promise me great things because she needs me. But that means she can't do this on her own."

"Don't do that, Maddie." Liam moves forward, placing gentle hands on my shoulders. "Don't try to rationalize her behavior or motives. Be smart and always on your guard. That's how you survive."

We stand like that for a long moment, me looking up at him, his hands on my shoulders. There's an understanding that flows between us, and I realize I've missed that. A pure kind of emotion not clouded by anything else.

"Look who it is." A voice sounds from our left, and Liam and I turn as one to watch Natalie step out of the shadows. My heart leaps into my throat when I see Aiden right behind her. His eyes are on me, fire sending the color into disarray.

"I'm Natalie," the shifter announces, looking Liam up and down. The fae has dropped his hands from my shoulders, but he's moved to stand close enough that his arm grazes my own. "I don't think we've had the pleasure."

My magic flares up at her sweet tone, and Liam's hand moves to capture mine. The contact calms me, but then a growl swings my eyes to Aiden once more. His are entirely focused on where Liam's hand holds my own, and I can see the wolf emerging. Instinctively, I release

Liam's hand, but he won't let go. I glance at him and find his hard gaze on Aiden. The two are now in a full stare down, and I'm afraid to see this go any further.

"This is Liam," I say, trying to diffuse the situation with my voice. Aiden's eyes shift to mine, and I almost stumble under the heaviness I find displayed there. "This is Natalie and Aiden."

"Shifter," Liam nods a greeting.

"Fae," Aiden replies, his words full of ferocity. His wolf is close to the surface and a part of me wants to step forward and reach for it. My fingertips long to be buried in Aiden's silky fur, and I curl my free hand into a fist by my side to control the desire.

"It's a pleasure," Natalie says, and it sounds anything but. She doesn't miss the way Aiden is reacting, if the hatred she's throwing at me is any indication. "We should be going."

She wraps her arm around Aiden's turning him in the direction of the school. At first, I don't think he's going to move, but then, as if resigned, he does. Natalie throws another hard glare my way and then they're walking away. I watch their retreat, perplexed by what just happened. One minute, Aiden doesn't want anything to do with me, the next he's ready to get into a battle with a fae. How am I supposed to figure him out?

"So, that's interesting."

Glancing at Liam, I squint at him in question. He gives me a small smirk before pulling me toward the castle, since he's still holding my hand.

"What was that?" I reply, tugging my hand back. This time, he lets go.

"Nothing."

"That wasn't nothing." It's my turn to glare, which earns me one of Liam's rare chuckles.

"No." I grab his sleeve, pulling him to a stop. This is a move I wouldn't try with anyone else but him. "Tell me."

"You've become very demanding, you know that?"

"Yes. Because I deserve to be treated fairly." I place my hands on my hips, trying to make myself appear taller. Liam grins, not missing what I'm trying to do.

"I like this side of you."

"Goodie. Now can you tell me why you were acting like a Neanderthal?"

"Because shifters are fun to mess with."

He takes off toward the castle then, not bothering to explain. I hurry to catch up, burning questions on the tip of my tongue. But then, I see the guards at the front gates, and the questions die on my lips. I have more pressing issues to focus on right now than boys being boys. I'm about to see the queen.

$$\textbf{\textit{\&}} \quad 7 \quad \textbf{\textit{\&}}$$

Liam leads me through the hallways in silence. I'm thankful for his presence, but I'm still nervous. There's no going around that. When we reach the massive carved doors, two guards standing on each side, Liam pauses.

"Aren't you going in?" I ask, glancing behind me.

"This is where I leave you," he replies.

"Oh," is all I can manage, but that's all Liam needs to hear. Stepping forward, he reaches for my hand, giving it a quick squeeze.

"You'll be alright. Just be smart and careful," he whispers just as the guards move to open the door. That's my cue. Quickly, before I lose my nerve, I head for the entrance. The moment I step inside, the doors are shut at my back, and I'm alone.

The room is large, shaped similarly to the secret library, with a big open space and a large dome ceiling in the middle. The one big different I notice immediately is all the drawings. Every part of the dome is covered in paintings depicting the fae world. There are beautiful women in gorgeous dresses, handsome men in their fine coats. There are battles and bloodshed, as well as romance and dancing.

"Beautiful, is it not?" The queen speaks, stepping out of the shadows at the opposite side of the room. I had no idea she was already in here, and it freezes me for a second. Then, I remember myself and curtsy, hoping my little lapse of decorum isn't too noticeable.

"It is. Does it tell a story?"

"It does." The queen continues to make her way toward me slowly, as if she's circling her prey. Which truth be told, that's exactly what I feel like I am. "It is the history of the court and the battles we fought against one of our greatest enemies."

I'm too afraid to ask what enemy that could be. Outside of the Ancients, the fae are the most powerful beings within the realms. I can't image what could be more powerful.

"Come, child." The queen motions me forward as she lowers herself onto a window seat. Tentatively, I walk toward her, taking the seat opposite. With Liam's warnings and my own misgivings, I have no idea how to act or what to say. The queen continues to study me, and I almost ask her what she sees.

In the past few months, I have changed in more ways than one. I discovered more about my magic, and I've had to be stronger about standing on my own. But I've also been in combat training while spending restless nights researching. All those things take a toll on the body, one way or another.

"You are afraid." The queen finally speaks up, breaking the silence. I'm so surprised by the sound, I don't contradict her. Maybe I should. Maybe I should play at being braver than I feel. But I have a feeling she would be able to tell.

"This whole situation is scary." I settle on the truth, without being direct about it. She surprises me by laughing, the sound melodic and hypnotizing as it rings out around us.

"You are a smart girl, Madison Hawthorne. You know the ways of the words."

For some reason, her statement brings a pang to my chest. Maybe it's the memory of my father saying something similar when we were creating one of our slang lists. He always made sure I understood the words I was researching, and so we would construct difficult sentences to help me. Now, it seems that's paying off in more ways than one. His memory emboldens me to utter my next question.

"If I may, Your Highness, why am I here?"

The queen doesn't answer immediately, sending those calculating eyes to study my face thoroughly. It's not my place to question someone of her stature, but I can't keep making up scenarios in my mind. None of them end well.

"I am fascinated by you, little witch," she finally replies, and I can't quite get a read on her tone. Everything she says sends chills up my back. "Your magic has broken through our boundaries and yet, you have no idea how it was done. You do not know your own power, and that is the most fascinating aspect of all."

"You want to...study me?"

That laugh rings out again, sending unpleasant goosebumps to my arms. It's difficult, but I keep myself from fidgeting. At least I can keep the outward appearance of maturity.

"I want to discover more of your power." So, she can use it. She doesn't have to say it; I'm smart enough to figure that part out. But maybe this can go both ways. The fae have been around long enough that they would have information others may not. After all, there was a reason why Liam's brother came to my hometown. He brought some very important pieces of history with him that helped us find a way to battle the Ancients and their minions.

Now I'm in a perfect position to gain more knowledge. I just have no idea how to go about it, besides agreeing to whatever the queen proposes.

"What are you proposing?" I ask before I lose all the nerve.

"You are required to practice your magic, are you not?"

"Yes."

"My proposition is that you do it here, within these walls, with me as your teacher."

"You want to teach me to use my magic?" I'm not exactly sure how that's supposed to work. Fae magic and witch magic are not the same. We follow different rules, we practice it in our own ways. The only similarities we have is our connection to nature.

"I can teach you how to use a type of magic. There are ancient practices that can benefit both sides of the power. While I teach you, you learn more about yourself. We can help each other."

She makes it sound so reasonable, as if this is the easiest decision to make. Why wouldn't I want to learn more about my magic? But I also know this is a bargain in the making, and that is not something I'm prepared to get into. Any bargain with the fae, however small, can result in imprisonment or death. And I'm already imprisoned in this realm. Yet, I also understand I can't refuse her. Doing so can end with me in the exact same position, except minus the knowledge I can glean from her. I really wish I could talk to my sisters and my parents. I could use their guidance right about now.

But then suddenly, I think about Aiden. How he's bound by duty to marry an alpha from another pack. How he's sacrificed part of his happiness to do what is right for his people. Isn't that what I would be doing? Is my staying in Faery so bad if I save my family and my friends?

"I can see you have much knowledge of our ways, Madison Hawthorne." The queen's voice penetrates my thoughts. "I will give you until tomorrow to decide. Then, a decision will be made for you."

She's playing at being nice, we both know that. But I take what I can get. I stand, knowing my next stop is to see the headmaster. Maybe he'll be able to help me make the right decision. Or come up with an alternate plane. I curtsy again before speaking.

"Until tomorrow."

WHEN I STEP OUT OF THE ROOM, MY MIND IS WORKING A MILE A minute. There are so many possibilities here, so many ways being Faery can be the worst thing that has happened to us. Up until this moment, I didn't want to admit to myself just how bad it all can be. Yes, I told Jade to be careful. I listened to Liam's warnings. But sitting in that room with the queen of the Spring Court, it has made me feel powerless. Even with all my magic, I'm nothing compared to her or what she can do to me if she puts her mind to it. And none of my friends is safe. I really screwed up.

So lost in my thoughts am I that when I finally do look up, I'm in a part of the castle I haven't seen. Everything is just as beautifully blinding as the room I left but somehow even more intimidating. The plant carvings that adorned the door spread across the walls here.

When I look closely, they look like vines with leaves and flowers growing out of them, but they're gold. When I touch them, the metal is cool under my fingertips. Even so, the plant seems to be moving and breathing somehow, as if it's alive. I jerk my hand away and proceed to walk farther.

Most of the doors are shut, but there are a few open ones. Even though I'm so curious to go inside, I'm not about to diverge from the main hall. I don't want to get so lost that I can't get out. When voices reach my ears, I breathe a little easier. Maybe I can be pointed the right direction.

But when I reach the open doorway, I stop in my tracks. A group of noble fae sit around the room. Their clothes sparkle with each move they make, some in more elaborate outfits than others, but they all look like magic. They're laughing at something in the middle of the room while drinks are being passed around. The glee is so tangible, I can almost taste it from where I'm standing. Moving a little closer, I try to see the cause of their enjoyment. One of the noble fae moves and then my eyes land in the middle of the room.

A boy, not much older than myself, is at the feet of one of the fae women. He's barely dressed, just a pair of shorts, but his chest is tanned and magnificent. He clearly takes care of himself. But right now, he doesn't look like he's doing so. He's massaging one of the women's feet as she pokes him across his body with her other. However, he's not fazed. One of the others speaks up, and the moves swiftly to begin massaging them across their whole body. At first, I'm confused at why he's being pulled in all directions like a puppet. But then he turns, and I see there's nothing in his eyes but a vacant faraway look.

Instantly, my blood grows cold. They've glamoured him into servitude. I can see it now, as plain as day. Even if I tried going to him, he would reject my offer of help. He's a puppet, and they're enjoying themselves tremendously. Disgust and fear battle for the top place in my emotions, and I think I'm going to be sick to my stomach.

Turning, I race blindly for an exit. I'm not even looking where I'm going. All I can see is the empty face of the human boy as he parades around the fae, servicing them in every way possible. I'm not so naive to think they stop at him fetching drinks or doing measly massages. The fae's cruelty has never been more evident than in this moment, and I brought us here.

Gasping for breath, I stop running and look around my surroundings. I have no idea where I am. The disgust diminishes as the fear takes over. I'm full on panicking now, because if I'm lost in these halls, I may never find my way out again. My father always said if I'm lost in the forest, the best thing I can do is sit in one spot and wait to be found. It does no one any good if I'm wandering aimlessly while waiting to be found. But who's going to find me here? Maybe Liam will eventually come looking for me, but I'm not even sure about that. He has no reason to think I'm lost in the castle when all I was supposed to do is walk in and out of the meeting with the queen.

But it's still my best option. So, I find a spot against the wall where the gold vines don't go as far down and sit. If I had my phone, I could call Liam to come get me. There are so many aspects of this situation that are my fault, I don't care what anyone else says. I can't stop feeling guilty or scared. I guess I'm not that brave after all. The pretense was bound to fail me eventually.

I'm not sure how long I sit in the hallway before I hear someone coming toward me. Refusing to be found wallowing on the floor, I stand, ready for whoever it is. Then, a figure steps forward, and I forget all pretense. I throw myself at him, and he catches me easily. His arms wrap around me as if they're made to do so. He holds me closer than close, my body molding into his, and I feel one hundred percent safe.

"What are you doing here?" I mumble against his chest. I don't care how pathetic I look right now, I need this.

"I felt your fear."

That breaks through my little cocoon of happiness, and I take a step back.

"You might want to explain that to me, Aiden."

$$\text{❅}\quad 8 \quad\text{❧}$$

"There's nothing to explain," the shifter replies, putting a good three feet of distance between us. It's as if we've forgotten to be enemies. This is the second time in two days he's offered me comfort. And I returned the favor.

"Aiden."

"Come on, Duchess. We need to get out of here."

He doesn't wait for a response but turns and walks back the way he came. Seeing no other choice, I hurry to catch up. I open my mouth to ask more questions but one look at his face, and I close it back up. He's concentrating, his senses attuned to our surroundings. With his shifter hearing, he probably hears way more than I would want to, so I stay quiet.

After what seems like hours, we find ourselves outside. I haven't seen this part of the castle, and after a quick study, I realize we're in a garden. The trees are planted in little circles, and there are a few sitting areas and two fountains from what I can see. It's not a large place because from where we're standing, I can see the wall surrounding the area on all sides.

"Aiden?" His name is all I can manage because I have no idea how we're getting out. At least we're not inside anymore. The castle was truly becoming suffocating. The shifter doesn't reply but leads the way to the opposite side of the garden, stopping at the wall.

"Do you trust me?"

The question comes out of nowhere, and while I understand the context, it feels more heavily weighted than in just this moment. But for some reason, I don't hesitate.

"Yes."

There's a sharp intake of breath on Aiden's part, as if he didn't quite expect that answer. I swear his eyes grow more intense, and now I feel unsure of my footing. My body is responding on its own, and I don't think I'll ever understand it. All I want to do is pull him close and never let go. When he does take a step forward, it's my turn to catch my breath.

"I'm going to have to touch you. May I?" He hasn't asked before, but I guess in training, it's just part of what we do. This feels much more intimate. I nod, seeing no other choice, and he steps up close enough that our bodies are flush together. His arms circle my back before he sweeps me right off my feet. I yelp, just a little, wrapping my arms around his neck.

"What are you doing?" My voice comes out breathless, as he holds me like I weigh nothing.

"Getting you out of here."

Then, before either one of us can say anything else, he squats and jumps. I feel the wind on my cheeks and clothes for just a moment before we land on the other side of the wall. Amazed at his power, I can't seem to look away. I knew shifters had some of their animal abilities while in their human form, but I've never seen them demonstrated so blatantly. Now that I think about it, shifters have a tendency to keep those powers a little bit of a secret.

But he let me see it. It feels even more intimate than the fact that he's still holding me in his arms. Something passes between us, something different and new, and I know he feels it as his eyes grow darker. My pulse jumps, and I can't hide it. Not when I'm this close to him. One of us has to break this moment, or we'll stay lost in it forever.

"Thank you," I push past my dry lips, and the sound is enough to bring us back to the present. He sets me down gently, taking particular care to make sure I'm firmly on the ground before he takes a step back.

"You're welcome."

That's all I get before he steps around me and begins making his way deeper into the forest. The forest we're not supposed to go in. Not done with this conversation, and refusing to be left alone, I follow.

"What did you mean you felt my fear?" I ask, not about to let go of that particular piece of information. There are too many unanswered questions in my mind right now. I don't need to add any more to that list.

"Drop it, Duchess."

"You know I won't."

He growls then, which brings a grin to my lips. It's like he brings out the fighter in me. For some reason, when I'm around him, all I want to do is get a reaction from him. He's too unreadable for me to do anything else.

"I could just start making scenarios up on my mind," I continue, smiling sweetly even though he's walking in front of me. "Or I could just bug you until you tell me. Tell me. Aiden. Tell me."

"Are you planning on stopping anytime soon?" Aiden asks, twisting around and making me halt in my steps before I run into him. He narrows his eyes, but I like seeing him riled up. It means he's not as immune to me as he pretends to be.

"I'm not planning on stopping at all. You should just tell me." He grunts again, rolling his eyes before he turns and continues walking. I glance around then, realizing we're much farther from the academy than I thought. I don't see it through the trees anymore. Not that I'm nervous. Shifters have an impeccable sense of direction. Even in places they've never been before.

"Aiden."

"You're annoying."

"Right back at ya, Mrs. Grundy."

That makes him stop. He turns, this time a little slow, and gives me a confused look.

"What does that even mean?"

I have to think for a second which part he'd be confused about. I'm so used to using these terms, I don't even think about them.

"Mrs. Grundy is an oldies slang for an uptight individual," I explain, raising my eyebrows a little. He shakes his head at me before a quick smile blossoms onto his face. It's there, then it's gone so quick, I almost miss it.

"You and your slang."

"You and your avoidance tactics." I'm grinning up at him, and I think he's actually fighting the urge to answer in kind. We've been so off about each other, I'm not sure how to act around him anymore. This exchange is not helping.

"Ever since the dance," he begins, surprising me into silence. "I can tell when you're in danger."

⁂

I HAVE NO IDEA WHAT TO SAY TO THAT. FOR WEEKS NOW, I thought what I've been feeling, this awareness toward Aiden, was completely one-sided. But it's not. He just reacts to it in a different manner.

"Is it just when I'm scared?" I'm almost afraid to ask, but I need to know. If he can decipher my emotions without me knowing it, that would get real awkward, real fast.

"I think it's mostly when you're in so much a distress, it's a physical danger to you."

His words make me want to deny my fear, but if he can feel it, what's the use? But that actually makes me pause for a moment.

"Is this why you've been more standoffish around me?" How I'm asking all these direct questions is beyond me. But I'm not backing down. That much I know. Waiting for him to respond is a new kind of torture, that's for sure. It seems I'm still only reacting to him.

"I'm not being standoffish," he finally says before turning on his heels and beginning to walk.

"Yes, this is definitely the behavior of someone who's not avoiding anything," I mumble to his back, but of course he hears me. Stupid supernatural hearing. He spins and is in my face in a second. The intensity is physically manifested in the way his body is giving off heat. Because we're only inches apart, I feel myself grow hot from it. Or maybe it's something else. I'm too confused to try and figure out where my emotions end and his begin.

"What is it you want from me?" Aiden asks, his breath dancing over my flushed cheeks. Involuntarily, my eyes drop to his lips for a mere half second, but it's enough. His sharp intake of breath tells me he doesn't miss a thing. When my eyes meet his, the fire there nearly brings me to my knees.

"I want us to stop fighting," I answer truthfully, falling deeper and deeper into his eyes. "I want us to work together. You can help me figure this whole mess out."

With every word I say, he seems to move closer and closer. There wasn't much distance to begin with, and now our bodies are separated by a breath.

"I can't do this alone," I whisper, not caring that my heart is in my throat. "I want us to be friends."

The moment I say those words, a shudder comes over Aiden's eyes, and he takes a step back.

"I told you before, we could never be friends." He starts to move away, but I'm not done. I'm tired of this back and forth, and I need him to talk to me. So, I do the one thing you don't do to a shifter. I grab his arm, pulling him to face me. He growls, his wolf clearly unhappy with being manhandled, but he's doing the same thing to me. Expect without actually touching me.

"I thought you were smarter than this." Aiden's voice is dripping with warning, but I don't remove my hand. He feels hotter than I imagined, but it doesn't matter.

"I'm smart enough to know you answer in half-truths and even smaller sentences. Why is it so hard for you to be my friend?" A note of desperation enters my voice then, and it's too late to push back. His eyes soften, and I see the boy who held me in that shed and the one who was glad I was safe.

"I have a duty to my people, Maddie," he says, keeping his voice low. "There are things required of me that others may not understand, sacrifices I must make." For some reason, I know he's talking about

Natalie and their betrothal. It's a sacrifice a seventeen-year-old should not be thinking about, yet, he doesn't have a choice.

"Because," he starts again, and a hint of emotion enters his voice making me hold my breath in anticipation. "Because being friends with you will break me, and I cannot lead my people or win this war if I am not whole."

This time, when he turns to go, I let him. Tears spring up to my eyes, and I desperately try to push them back. Every time I think Aiden and I are together, a new wall is broken down and three more are built up. We will never be anything but what we are now, but it doesn't stop every part of my being from yearning for it to be otherwise. How I have fallen so hard for someone I can never have? It's so tragic of me.

I wish I could talk to my dad. Maybe this is not something most teenagers go to their parents with, but I know my dad would say exactly what I need to hear. Being in Faery, so far away from my family, I just hope they will find some kind of lead, and the next time I'm home, my dad will be too. I spent months trying to find him, and now I'm further away from my goal than I've ever been.

Aiden slows down a little, and I realize I have fallen too far behind. Hurrying, I catch up to the shifter, but I don't speak, and he doesn't turn to look at me. We're back to our corners for now. I need to squish every emotion I have toward him and focus on the problem at hand. He can't deny me that. Not when he's trying to keep his pack safe.

"I need your help," I say, and he turns to glance at me. "I need to get to the library and see if there are any answers about our predicament. Can you get me there?"

Just like that, we're back to business. He watches me for a tense moment before he nods.

"Good. Then let's go."

❊ 9 ❊

"Is this where you've been?" I dare to ask after a few minutes of silence. The forest around us grows darker and heavier by the minute, and while I'm not scared, I would be if I was alone.

"Sometimes," Aiden replies without turning around. "I'm not exactly a big fan of the way of the fae, so I need an exit strategy, if the time comes for that."

That seems like a lot more information than he usually shares, but I'm not going to point that out. If he feels like he can talk to me, I'm going to take it and run with it. There are parts of him that are a complete mystery, even after all the time we've spent together. Maybe that's why I bring up Liam.

"Not all fae are bad."

"You mean like your little friend?" This time Aiden does look at me, but I still can't read what's going on with him. There's definitely history there, but I can't even begin to guess at it.

"Pretty sure Liam is taller than you," I point out automatically before I realize maybe this isn't the time for jokes. He'll shut down again, and I don't want him to. But Aiden surprises me once again. A small laugh escapes him before he replies.

"Yes, fae have a tendency to be giants. Got to have something going for them, I guess."

My nose wrinkles at his statement, but I don't actually hear any hostility in it. I think he might be teasing. When he steals a glance my way, I smile.

"You're hilarious."

"Oh, I know."

While the lightheartedness of the situation doesn't go unnoticed, I still want answers. So, I decide to push.

"Are you going to tell me about your feud with the fae or am I making stuff up again?"

My question makes him pause, and he turns toward me before replying.

"They're not nice creatures."

"This is coming from Mr. Friendly?" While I said the same thing to Jade, my defensive side still comes out apparently. But Aiden doesn't take the bait.

"You know I'm right, even though you're friends with one of them. You're more cautious than not."

"So, what you're saying is that you had personal experience with their...meanness, and thus refuse to give any of them a chance." It's not a question because I know I hit the nail on the head on this one. Aiden gives me one of his intense looks, narrowing his eyes slightly, before he takes a step toward me.

"You are a smart witch, Maddie. Don't let their glamour fool you."

When he says my name like that, it becomes very difficult to keep my hands to myself. It's like it requires a physical response. Instead of doing something stupid, I clench my fists at my sides.

"You're not stupid either, Aiden," I reply, needing him to understand that not everyone is cut from the same cloth. "I wouldn't think past history would keep you from future possibilities."

We're in the midst of a stare down, once again lost in a battle of wills. While I've never been confrontational before, Aiden has a way of getting under my skin. I have a slight inkling that I do the same for him. Although, shifters are already pretty confrontational. We can stand here forever because neither one of us is backing down.

Then, he does something that completely throws me off balance. He breaks eye contact for a moment before coming back and nodding.

"You're right."

"I'm sorry, what was that?" I cock my head in his direction and am rewarded by a smile for my efforts.

"I said you're right," he repeats, this time with a curl to his lips. "I wouldn't be a very smart alpha if I wasn't open to possibilities. But that doesn't mean I have to like it."

"It's a start. Once you realize I'm often right, you'll be even better."

This time, I'm the one who pushes past him and continues walking. It may not seem like a big thing, but it feels like a breakthrough. Every conversation I have with Aiden feels like that. He's a tough nut to crack, but I'm getting to him, and I'm not sure if I should be happy or nervous about that. It's not like we have a future together. Sure, one day our history may bring us an alliance. But that's all we'll ever be to each other. That thought brings genuine sadness to my heart, and I can't shake it off.

"Hey," Aiden's hand reaches for my own, a barely-there graze of his fingers on my skin sets my body on fire. He retracts his touch but not before it becomes an imprint. "Are you okay?"

Of course he can tell my emotions are changing. Not that I think shifters can read the way some witches can, but they rely on their intuition for a reason. So, instead of saying I'm fine, I give him a piece of the truth.

"I'm just worried. About everything. About how I'm supposed to fix this when I have nothing on my side to help me."

"You have me."

The statement is spoken so softly, I don't think he meant to say it out loud. But he does, and it sends my emotions on another crazy rollercoaster ride. There will never be a time when I'm around Aiden and I feel nothing. I know that now, just like I know the sun comes up in the morning and goes down in the evening. But I force myself not to react. Maybe it'll be better for both of us if I pretend I didn't hear it. Even though everything in me yearns for me to go to him and hold him until everything in my world is right again.

Something that can never be a possibility.

"Maybe the library can help. Maybe I will suddenly understand this story spell casting. I just don't want to fail everyone."

Aiden catches up to me then, stopping right in front of me so I'm forced to look up into his handsome face.

"This whole thing, it's not your fault. A responsibility was put on your shoulders in a way that no one should have to carry. No matter how bleak things may seem, you did save us. We weren't going to win, and many lives were going to be lost. But you pulled us out, and while it wasn't what we expected, we're here now. We'll make the best of it."

This, this right here is why I can never imagine him not being part of my heart. We might fight, and we might be frenemies most of the time, but he always says the right thing when I need to hear it. Afraid that I'll say something stupid, I nod instead.

"Let's get to the library," I reply, giving him a small smile.

"Actually, we're here."

❧

AIDEN LEADS ME THROUGH THE BUSHES TO OUR RIGHT, WEAVING IN and out of the greenery. I was so focused on our talk, I didn't even notice the wall-like growth right beside us. The leaves are thicker and larger than I'm used to, but Aiden doesn't offer any caution on them being harmful to us.

"Where are we?" I ask when we finally break though. The forest looks exactly the same on this side, but when I turn, I find the wall of green at my back.

"At the back end of the Thunderbird Academy campus line," Aiden replies before moving forward. "If you walk far enough, you'll discover there is a wall at every side of campus."

"Did the queen put that there or was it me?"

"The Queen. I think it's to prevent anyone from exploring beyond the delegated areas."

"Not that it would stop you."

"Not that it would."

We grin at each other, and as usual, his smile makes me feel calm and excited all at the same time. He motions me to follow, and I have no reservations in doing so. I've trusted him this far, but that doesn't mean I don't have questions.

"What have you found out there?"

"Nothing that can help us, that's for sure." I can feel the frustration in his voice, even though I can't see his face. As an alpha, I'm sure it's difficult for him to not have all the answers. A huge part of me wants to ask how Natalie is fits into all this, considering I saw them step out of the forest together. But I don't think I'm ready to have that conversation.

"The forest is always shifting." Aiden continues, pulling me out of my thoughts. "Every time we explore, it seems different, and it feels different. I think the queen has spelled it to keep us in one spot."

"Imprisoned, you mean?" He flashes me a quick smirk as I don't hide my dislike for her in my tone.

"Not a fan?"

"Not even a little."

She terrifies me. I'd be stupid not to fear her. But I'm also annoyed by her demands. It's not like I planned on bringing us here. And the last part, the very small part that's trying to be braver, is also fascinated. She can teach me so much about magic. Areas that the teachers at Thunderbird Academy would never even mention. After all my studies and conversations with Liam, I know fae have a particular way with the elements. After all, they created the elemental spell my sisters and I used to put a barrier around our hometown of Hawthorne. It's the only part of this whole mess that makes me feel like I wasn't a complete failure. Even though I don't trust her, maybe I can learn something from her. Isn't that the most adult outlook ever? My parents would be proud.

Just like that, my mind is on my family as I trail after Aiden. I can see sunlight on the other side of the trees and know we're getting close to the actual academy. But now I'm sad because even though I'm on campus, I'm a whole world away from my parents and sisters. Well, technically, I have no idea where my father is, so there's that. Inhaling deeply, I force my thoughts to focus on the issue at hand. Exhaling fully, my heart rate slows down just a tad, clearing my mind. It would do no one any good if I started having panic attacks now.

I notice Aiden glance at me from the corner of his eye, but he doesn't comment. He probably felt the change in me, heard the speed up of my heartbeat, but he doesn't comment. Good, I guess we're both pretending at areas in our...relationship? I don't even know what to call us. I just know what I want to call us.

"Let's run quickly," the shifter says as we come to the edge of the forest. "I don't want any wandering eyes seeing us from the building."

"If only I had supernatural speed." I chuckle, shaking out my hands as I get ready for him to say go. But instead, he turns to me with an unreadable look in his eyes. "What?"

"I can... I can carry you."

"What?"

"I run much faster than you, and if I carry you, there's a lesser chance of us being seen."

I stare at him in silence, wondering if he's being serious. When his calm and collected expression doesn't change, I realize he is.

"You didn't before, after the dance." Maybe I shouldn't be bringing that up now, but it's true. If he could've gotten us out of there sooner, why didn't he?

"I could've, but I needed to be able to fight. I wouldn't have been able to do so with you in my arms."

Every time he mentions holding me, I get a little rush of goose-bumps along my spine. Besides my curiosity on the logistics of this kind of magic, I don't want him to get in trouble. If the fae find out he's been sneaking away, it won't be taken well. And there are enough fae roaming the halls right now that any one of them could look out the window. Maybe there's always someone watching. Which is why I say,

"Okay."

I think I take both of us by surprise. But he just nods and steps toward me. His arm circles my back as I reach over to wind my arms around his neck. The proximity is doing crazy things to my heart, and that's when I realize his own is beating just as fast. He crouches for a second, sweeping my legs up with his other arm, and then I'm completely in his arms.

"Hold on tight," he whispers, his breath washing over my skin. I nod, nestling my face into the crook of his neck and then, the wind

＊ 10 ＊

We stop as suddenly as we began. He ran much faster than I anticipated, and I wonder if I'll ever get to experience that rush again. I'd be lying to myself if I said I didn't enjoy it. Aiden doesn't let go right away, and I have no desire to either. After a moment, I lean back, looking into his face, my arms still wrapped around his neck.

"You okay?" he asks, his voice dangerously low. Not trusting myself to speak, I nod, taking a calming breath. His scent surrounds me, and I think of rain and the forest, with a particular musk that's his alone. If it was up to me, I'd stay in his arms forever. But I know better than to wish for things, so I'm the one who moves to get down. He places me gently on the floor but doesn't move away.

"Thank you," I finally manage and then turn to look at the greenhouse. He brought us straight in, and at first, I think we're still outside. Every single plant I land my eyes on has grown tremendously. The trees are to the ceiling, all the flowers are blooming. "What's happening here?" I glance at Aiden and see that he's studying our surroundings with a type of awe as well.

"I have no idea. I haven't been in here in a while."

There's nothing I can do to stop myself from reaching for the plants. The closest to me, a type of ivy, has spread across the table and onto the floor. The leaves are plum and a gorgeous green shade, deeper than I've seen it before. I run my fingers over it gently, and my elemental magic reaches out for the plants in front of me. I feel it in the air as well as the moisture.

"It must be Faery. This realm is the strongest in their natural magics. The plants must be reacting to it." The ivy wraps itself around my hand, as if saying hello, and I smile. Nature has always been part of magical structure, but I've only seen plants react visibly a few times. Mostly in rituals class. This? This is a whole new lesson I want to learn.

Glancing up, I find Aiden has moved closer to the library's opening, and I follow him over to the crates. Without a word, we begin moving the wood away from the rug. Once that's done, I pull up the rug and yank at the door. It swings open, the stale air of the underground hitting me in the face. Without hesitation, I descend with Aiden close behind me. Liam will probably want to come visit as well, although I'm not sure how I'm going to get him in here without being seen.

When we come to the door to the library a few minutes later, something feels off. Reaching out, I place my palm against the door, and let my magic reach for the place that became like my second home. But then, a sharp pain stabs me in the palm of my hand, at the same time sending me flying from the door and straight into Aiden. He catches me easily, placing me on my feet before we both turn toward the door.

"What was that?" he asks, his hand still on my upper arm to keep me steady.

"I have no idea," I reply, the pain of rejection rushing through me. It's like the library is protecting itself against me, and I don't understand. I move forward again, and Aiden squeezes my shoulder to keep me beside him.

"What are you doing?"

"I need to know what's wrong. It's like, it's angry at me."

"It's a door, Duchess."

"Yeah, and a wand is a stick. But we both know of powerful sorcerers who can communicate with it like a friend."

Aiden has nothing to say to that because he knows I'm right.

"Just be careful," he whispers as I approach the door once more. Maybe this is what I felt when we got here, a sort of hostility coming from the library. Headmaster Marković once told me there are areas on this campus that only reveal themselves to special individuals. The library has always been my place, and only when I chose to bring others here did they find out about its existence. The library can't be mad at Aiden, he's been here before, and she's opened herself up to him with open arms. No, I think she's mad at me, and I need to know why.

"Won't you let me in?" I ask, keeping my voice gentle as I stop right in front of the door. The wood glows for half a second, before turning back into its regular brown, and I wonder what the library is trying to tell me. "Please don't be mad at me." I try again, and this time, I run one finger down the middle. I receive no response, but somehow, I know if I tried that again, I'd get hurt. Whatever is happening here, it's not something I'll be able to fix this minute.

"You've always been a friend," I whisper, pulling on my magic to make my words mean a little more. "You have helped, and you have taught. Please help me understand what's happening." I take a tiny step forward, but it's too close. The library's magic flairs up once more, sending me stumbling into Aiden.

"I don't understand." The sadness I feel is like a weight. It's like I've lost another friend, and I have no idea what to do about it.

"We'll figure it out, Maddie," Aiden says, running a comforting hand up and down my back. "All is not lost."

But now I feel more helpless than ever. This was my one chance to get an upper hand in the situation, and now it's gone. Being in Faery is messing everything up.

WE LEAVE THE LIBRARY BEHIND AND HEAD FOR THE STAIRCASE IN silence. There was so much hope riding on me being able to research and learn in that place. In the past two years, the library has become my sanctuary. Now, I can't enter it, and that's hitting me harder than I thought it would. I feel too helpless to be angry. Now, I don't know what to do.

"Do you want to talk?" Aiden finally breaks the silence when we've finished covering up the entrance and are back in the greenhouse. I must look way more lost than I feel for him to be so nice to me. But then again, he's been surprising me a lot lately. This side of him isn't as new anymore.

"Actually, I'd like to punch something," I reply before I recognize the truth to my words. Aiden grins, before motioning for me to follow. Now that we are coming out of the greenhouse, we're not as worried about people seeing us. Although, if a certain someone saw us, I'm sure there would be a lot of questions. Aiden leads the way to the corner of the building, between the academy and the greenhouse, before turning to me.

"Attack me."

"What?"

"Attack me."

"Aiden."

"You want to punch something, so do it."

"I don't want to punch you," I reply, rolling my eyes.

"Well, that seems new." He grins, breaking all my defenses. He has no idea. I sigh heavily, receiving another quick smile before he motions me forward. "Come on, Duchess. Don't tell me you're afraid of me now."

I know what he's trying to do. He's goading me into it, and I already know I'll break. The need for physical release is too loud to ignore. The past few hours have been a tsunami of emotions, and if I don't do something soon, I'll explode.

"Today would be nice."

"You really want to get your butt kicked, don't you?" Not sure where that confidence comes from, but it surprises us both. Aiden laughs, a sound I will never get tired of hearing, and I react. Pushing off my feet, I launch myself at him.

Even paying half attention, Aiden is much faster than I am. He sidesteps my attack, and I roll, getting to my feet in the same motion. Yanking the jacket off my shoulders, I toss it to the side and attack again. This time, my hands are up in front of my body, and my leg is the one that swings at Aiden. He blocks it easily, and we begin the dance.

I kick and twist, blocking and dodging most of the strikes. He's letting me lead the exercise, matching my intensity with his own. When I go to uppercut, he shoots his elbow in front of my move. My knee comes up, and he slams his palms down to block it. The move brings us closer together, so I thrust my hand up, aiming for his face. He dodges before catching my arm in his hand over our heads. Our bodies are flush together, and I try to twist out of his hold, but he yanks my arm down behind my back, bringing his other to catch me, and now I'm against his chest, with both of my arms pinned behind my own back.

"How do you get out of this?" he asks, and I'm breathing so heavily I barely hear him. I almost tell him I don't want to get out of it, but instead, I throw my knee up. He anticipates my move but doesn't move as quickly as usual, and I catch him right in the stomach. He loosens his hold on my arms just enough for me to break free, and that's when I punch him in the face. He stumbles to the side, probably more from surprise than actual pain, but now I'm fired up. I jump up to kick him in the chest, but he's already recovered. I missed my opportunity and he catches my leg, pulling it toward him. I yelp as I fly off my feet and down to my back. I land hard, the air leaving my lungs, but I'm not about to take this laying down. I kick out blindly, and then feel my foot connecting with flesh. Aiden tumbles forward, and then he's on top of me.

He catches himself on his arms, stopping just a breath above me, and we're both breathing heavily now. His eyes are doing that color changing that only comes when his wolf is close to the top. We're both sweaty, and even though it's chilly outside, all I feel is hot all over.

"You're getting better," he whispers, his breath washing over my flushed skin.

"I've had a good teacher," I reply, without thinking. His eyes flash, dropping to my lips for a second before coming to meet my eyes once more. We're back to our standstill, knowing it can never go past this. No matter what this madness is that we're feeling. Because I'm way past pretending Aiden doesn't feel anything. It's no longer wishful thinking. It's a truth I live with now. As well as a burden I carry.

"If you use your magic when you attack, you'll be able to deliver quite a punch." He's trying to make this normal, but the fact that he's still hovering over me doesn't exactly help.

"I'll keep that in mind." I grin and then, I'm rolling out of the way. He moves his arm just in time, landing on his back before he's on his feet again. I adjust my clothing and reach for my jacket before I finally meet his eye.

"Thank you," I say, before turning to flee into the greenhouse. I may be a lot of things, but what I mostly am is a teenage girl in love with a boy I can never have. That will always be a part of me, and it's just another issue I have to deal with in my life. Because there isn't a shadow of a doubt in my mind, Aiden will stay with me for a lifetime.

It's been two weeks since we arrived in Faery and everything seems to have fallen into a routine. We get up every morning, we go to class, we have combat training, and we go to bed. I'm not sure what I expected when we arrived here, but it wasn't this. Everyone is acting like we aren't stuck in another realm. I'm honestly not sure how to deal with that.

On the other hand, I haven't been to see the queen since our meeting that ended with me in the woods with Aiden. She's been called away on some urgent matter, so a big part of me is just waiting for the other shoe to drop. Liam hasn't been around either, and that's making me a little concerned. Not that he owes me anything, but his disappearance isn't sitting all that well with me.

"Did you see Miss Lee's outfit today?" Jade's voice brings me back to reality and I glance up as Vera replies.

"She's wearing a very twenties dress today. Do you think she magically made it appear in her closet or she had it already?"

Thankfully, Vera has returned to our group, and things have been mostly normal between all of us. I can understand how frustrating it might be to constantly be reminded of a time you failed to see something that was right in front of your face. Okay, now I'm being extra melodramatic. It's just so ridiculous that there is nothing I can do about our predicament. I got us into this mess, and I've yet to figure out how to get us out of it. Also, the whole situation with the library is driving me insane. I've been down there two other times since that day, and both times, I ended up across the room with bruises all over my body from the impact.

"I think she had it," Noel replies before taking a huge bite of his sandwich. Since we've come to Faery, he's been training extra hard, and therefore eating a lot more. Even after a few weeks, we can all see the results. Jade, especially, is liking it. Not that they've had any sort of talk about their...relationship. I can't exactly give them any advice, since I know nothing.

Just then, I hear a few chair scrapes and look up in time to see Natalie march over to me. She pushes everyone else aside, stopping to tower over me, her hands on her hips.

"Where is he?" she nearly growls, her voice sending unwanted goosebumps over my skin.

"I have no idea who you're talking about." It's hard to appear unaffected when an alpha shifter is trying to intimidate me, but I'm holding my own. Natalie has had a bad attitude toward me since the moment she arrived. It doesn't help that she knows I was the one in the headmaster's office on the day we ended up in Faery. She hasn't spread that information around yet, but I have a feeling she would one day. Maybe today is the day.

"You know who I'm talking about. He's disappeared. Don't tell me you don't have secret meetings behind my back." Confused, I narrow my eyes at her and then I notice Ben and Owen coming up to the table. Realization hits me hard as I meet Ben's eyes.

"Aiden's missing?"

"Don't play with me, witch," Natalie nearly spits, "you know where he is."

I'm honestly baffled by the fact that she believes her own words. Standing, I'm probably not helping my situation by being confrontational, but I really don't like her towering over me.

"Why would I know where he is?" I ask, genuinely wanting to know. The question doesn't sit well with Natalie as she takes a step toward me. Then Owen is there, putting himself in her path. Ben takes his place beside me.

"Maybe we should talk somewhere else?" he says, nodding his head in the general direction of the rest of the dining room. I glance around and realize everyone's eyes are on us. Owen is close to physically removing Natalie from the room because even I can tell she's losing control. Her wolf is too close to the surface, and if she shifts in here, she won't hesitate to attack.

"Yes, let's talk somewhere more private," I say, nodding at Ben.

"Maddie?" Jade asks as she stands and places a hand on Noel's shoulder. I notice my friend has put down his sandwich and moved to spring up if he needs to.

"I'm okay, guys," I say, plastering a smile to my face. "I'm not alone." I motion to Ben and the guy gives my friends a quick smile. I know it's not ideal, but I'm not about to put my friends in the warpath of a shifter. Jade nods, but I don't miss the worry in her eyes. Owen has already led Natalie toward the outside doors, and Ben and I follow quickly.

"What is her problem?" I ask the moment the doors shut behind us and we're outside. Not that I think certain shifters can't hear us anymore, but I know most of them can't. I look over and see that Natalie has shifted and is racing toward the forest. Ben and I exchange a look and take off in the same direction. Even though Ben can shift, he doesn't, staying beside me instead. We reach the woods at the same time Owen does.

"What's happening?"

"She lost control. Give her a moment," Owen replies.

"Okay, cool. But what's happening with Aiden?"

THE BOYS DON'T ANSWER RIGHT AWAY. EVEN WITHOUT SHIFTER hearing, I can hear Natalie moving through the woods, and I have a feeling she'll be back before we know it.

"Now. I need an answer now."

Ben and Owen exchange a quick glance as I place my hands on my hips. Their caginess is making me so much more nervous. If something has actually happened to Aiden, and they're taking this long to tell me about it, there will be no stopping the wrath I unleash on these boys. I'm scaring myself a little with my thoughts, but the amount of emotions racing through me right now will get no other response.

"Ben." I level my gaze on the shifter I know best. "I know about Aiden's...recon missions. Why does Natalie think I know about his whereabouts? Where did he go?" At first, I think he's going to stay silent, but he finally concedes.

"Since you know, he's been trying to figure out why the fae are keeping us contained to the academy's grounds. We've been taking shifts, running the forest around the school, and past the hedge. Most of the time, we find nothing. Because, as strange as it sounds—"

"The forest changes." I finish his sentence, and he looks at me in surprise. Owen takes a step forward, picking up where Ben left off.

"If he told you that much, then you must know he's been looking into spell casting as well."

"What?" That makes me pause. "He hasn't said anything about that."

The shifters exchange another look, and I swear if they do that again, I'm going to scream. Going against my better judgment I step up, snapping my fingers between their faces. They jerk, swiveling their heads in my direction, and I can see they're as surprised as I am. Even though they're not alphas, they're still powerful beings, and I shouldn't be trying to rule over them in any way. Except, I can't seem to stop myself.

"Sorry, look, I..." My words leave me because I have no idea how to explain what I'm feeling or doing. It's like a tidal wave of emotions is crashing on top of me, and no matter how much I struggle to swim to the surface, I can't get my head above water. There is an elephant sitting on my chest, making me sink farther and farther down. "What is happening to me?"

Ben reaches out, placing his hands on my upper arms as he leans over to look into my face. There's genuine concern in his eyes that pushed away any annoyance he may have had at me trying to command them into talking.

"Maddie, I think you and Aiden—"

"Ben." Owen's sharp voice cuts off whatever my friend was going to say, but I can't even lift my head to look at him.

"She must know."

"She can't. And we don't know for sure."

They continue speaking as if I'm not there, and their voices grow further away with every second. There's a dull noise filling my ears, as if I'm truly underwater. I have to get a grip on myself, or I won't be able to find Aiden. Just with that small thought, the wave crashes over me again, and I stumble to my knees. Ben follows me to the ground, still holding my shoulders, and he gives them one painful squeeze.

"Breathe, Maddie. Don't let this overwhelm you. Don't push it away. Accept it and breathe."

I don't understand his instructions. They seem to contradict each other, but I have no other choice. I'll be completely useless to Aiden if I don't pull myself together. Closing my eyes, I follow Ben's instructions, forcing the air into my lungs. At first, it doesn't seem to be working. I concentrate on the bombardment of emotions, but instead of pushing them away, I let them wash over me like rain. Suddenly, the tidal wave becomes a drizzle and my lungs open up. I gasp, taking in hungry balloons of air before I finally open my eyes.

Ben is still in front of me with Owen hovering over his shoulder. Even the stoic shifter looks concerned. But there's something else in their eyes, a secret they almost discussed in front of me. I feel exhausted, as if I actually fought through that storm.

"What was that?" I finally ask when I think my voice won't come out breathless.

"I think you had a panic attack," Ben replies before standing and helping me to my feet as well. He squeezes my hands in encouragement before letting go, and I adjust my skirt and t-shirt just for something to do. What a day to not wear jeans. It didn't feel like only a panic attack, but I don't think these boys will tell me anything. Even if I ask.

"Are you better?" This comes from Owen, and I look up to meet his eyes. Over the course of this year, I have earned at least a little bit of respect in his eyes, and for a second, I'm afraid it's gone. But it's not. Something else has joined it, and I can't decipher what.

"I am. I don't think I've ever had a panic attack before. I don't know what caused it."

"You're overwhelmed," Ben hurries to say, as if he's afraid I'll think it's something else. "So many people are putting pressure on you, and Natalie isn't helping with accusing you of Aiden's disappearance."

"Why would she think I have anything to do with it?" I still don't understand. Ben opens his mouth to speak, but then I hear a noise behind me. I turn in time to watch Natalie step out of the woods, once again in her human form.

"Because he left to help you."

12

"What do you mean he left to help me?"

I can feel panic rising from the base of my neck, but I refuse to lose control in front of Natalie. She can already smell my fear. I don't need to add any more to her fuel against me.

"Just what I said," she snaps before she gives Ben and Owen a scorching look. "You two are just as whipped as he is." She motions toward me. They don't like that; they don't like that at all. Immediately, both of them take a step in front of me, and growls like none I've heard from either of them, sounds around us. They bare their teeth, and I think they'll shift at any moment. They're ready to attack, and I have no idea why.

"Ben? Owen?" I call out, hoping my soft voice will sooth them, but they won't take their eyes off Natalie. She's glaring right back at them, as if daring them to make a move. Even though she's not their alpha, she is an alpha. She carries herself as such, and I know for a fact she carries the alpha magic in her blood. Enough of it that she can take on these two large shifters without batting an eye.

"Do not disrespect Maddie in that way again," Owen snaps, his words barely audible between his teeth. His wolf is so close to the surface, I can see it over his human form. I take a step back, afraid I'll do something to set them off, but somehow, I know they're not a danger to me. They're protecting me.

"I may not be your alpha," Natalie says, standing a little taller, her own wolf showing through, "But I will be one day, and there is nothing you can do about that. Not even if what you think is true is true."

"You know it is," Ben replies, his own growl bunching up the words. "And there's nothing you can do about that either."

Now I feel like they're talking in riddles. There has to be a way I can take control, or we'll be in this spitting match for ages, and Aiden will be out there, going through who knows what. Maybe this is foolish of me, but I do the one thing I can think of. I step up to Ben and place a hand on his shoulder. He turns in my direction instantly, his features falling back to normal in the same moment.

"Look, I don't understand what's happening," I say, looking at him before I turn my attention to Natalie. "But you came to me for a reason. If you think I can help, then use me. Aiden is my...trainer." I want to call him so many other things, but this is the safest one. "He's protected me before, and if I can return the favor, then let me."

This sounds a lot more diplomatic than I thought I was capable of. Something flashes in Natalie's eyes, and I wonder if it's a bit of respect. No one ever takes a stand against the shifters. Especially not an alpha. But I'm more scared of Aiden getting hurt than I am of Natalie and what she can do to me. I think she understands that now.

"Fine. Tell me what you know," she says, pulling away her wolf and folding her arms in front of her. I glance at Ben and Owen who are back to normal as well, but they're not moving from their position beside me. I have a feeling they're going to stick even closer to me now.

"I don't know anything; that's the problem. You think I do. So, tell me what you think I know, and we'll go from there. What did you mean he left to help me?"

Natalie rolls her eyes, and at first, I think she'll get into another argument. But after she stretches her arms over her head, she levels me with a glare.

"Your stupid spell, the one that brought us here, he's been researching it as much as he can." That's news to me because he never mentioned that. But instead of admitting that, I have a more important question.

"How would he research such a thing in the forest?"

"You really know nothing of this world, do you?" That makes me angry. Even if I studied for a hundred years, there would still be areas of Faery, and its people that I would not understand.

"How about instead of insulting me every ten seconds, you tell me what you're talking about? It'll save both of us a lot of time," I snap. This conversation could've taken half the time if she'd just get over herself. I get it that she doesn't like me, but for an alpha, she's acting a little too emotional. Not that I can talk. I just had a panic attack.

She rolls her eyes again, and I wonder if she can blink like a normal person, or if that's just what she does. But I don't comment.

"The forest here holds many secrets and many doors. You can wander for a mile and find entrances to many dimensions. But you can also find doors full of knowledge."

"You're telling me Aiden found a door like that?"

"That's what I think. There are creatures living in those woods that have more information than we could ever learn in our lifetime. If he stumbled onto one of those, he could be in trouble."

"Because no information is given freely."

"You're not as dumb as you look."

It's my turn to glare at her, but my mind is already lost in thought. If he went into those woods to look for answers, and found someone willing to talk, there's no telling what they would make him do in return. How many times have I told Jade to be careful with her words around the fae? Why would Aiden do something so stupid?

"Why didn't he take one of you with him?" I ask, turning to the other two shifters.

"We always patrolled alone, so we don't raise suspicion," Ben replies, shrugging a little. A part of me wants to yell at them and tell them they should've gone anyway. But I know they won't disobey their alpha.

"Believe it or not, I had no idea Aiden was doing that. The only thing I knew was that he was trying to figure out why we were kept within these boundaries so tightly. But we haven't even discussed that in weeks."

This is probably not what Natalie wanted to hear, but that's the truth. She studies me for a tense moment before shaking her head.

"Well, then you are no help. Not that I'm surprised." I ignore that last remark, and her for that matter, and turn to the boys.

"Could you find his trail? Have you tried?"

"I've tried." Natalie's voice brings me back to her. "It's no use. It ends a little after the hedge. And it gets harder and harder to get past the boundary."

So, there must be magic at work here. Which I guess I already knew. But my mind is full of possibilities. I can work with my magic, that's something I don't fail at on the regular. A tracking spell will be easy to create, especially if I use one of the shifters in front of me as the main ingredient.

"What are you thinking Maddie?" Ben asks, watching my face curiously.

"That I have a way to find him. But I need to ask someone a question first."

"Oh, do you mean your fae friend?" Natalie asks as I turn to head back to the academy. I glance at her sharply as she gives me a pointed look. "Who do you think Aiden used to get through the hedge in the first place?"

"Liam helped him?" I'm not sure I could be any more surprised if I tried. Aiden has a clear dislike of the fae, and yet, here he is working with one. So many questions spring to my mind, and Liam better be ready to answer them. Just as the thought comes to mind, I freeze.

"Wait, when was the last time anyone has seen Aiden?"

"Two days ago," Owen replies, and I try not to visibly react to that. He's been gone for two days, and I had no idea. But then, it comes to me.

"Liam has been gone for that long," I state, and I don't have to explain any further. All three turn their eyes on me, and I meet each gaze one at a time. "We're going after them."

WE GET BACK TO THE SCHOOL, SEPARATING AT THE FRONT DOORS. Each has been given a task, and I have a few hours before nightfall to get my portion of it done. First of all, I need to talk Jade into a) staying and b) covering for me. It won't be easy, considering she told me she's not letting me try any more magic alone.

"Where have you been?" she asks the moment I step into our room. Thankfully, she's alone. I thought maybe Noel and Vera would be in here, but maybe Jade knew I wouldn't talk in front of them. I'm keeping my circle tight, even within my friend group.

"Aiden's missing," I reply, seeing no need to sugar coat it. She opens her mouth, but whatever she was going to say, dies on her lips.

"Are you sure?"

"Positive. And I have a plan for finding him, but I need your help."

"What do you need me to do?" She doesn't even hesitate. For some reason, that brings tears to my eyes, and I step up to her, wrapping her in a tight hug. She holds me back just as tightly as I focus on breathing and not crying. Even though she's not blood, she's become like a sister to me, and her support means the world.

"You're not going to like it," I reply, stepping back.

"I'm one hundred percent sure of that," she says, giving me a quick smile.

"I need you to cover for me. I'm going with the shifters into the forest. That's where Aiden disappeared. I'm going to use one of them as the fuel to my tracking spell."

"You're hoping the pack's bond will help the spell?"

"Exactly." I move toward my closet, pulling out a backpack. I haven't used it since the last time Dad and I went on one of our camping trips. It really seems like another life, one I'm no longer part of. Running my hands over the material, I push the worry away. I can only handle one missing man in my life, at a time. Because this one, I can actually do something about. Quickly, I place essentials in the bag.

"I don't like you not taking me with you," Jade comments from her position on the bed. I knew this was coming.

"You're the only person who can keep my secret, Jade," I say, turning to face her. "I will only be missing Friday classes and then it's the weekend."

"We have an assembly tomorrow. How am I supposed to cover for that?"

That's right. I completely forgot. Headmaster Marković has been holding weekly assemblies to let us know what's going on. Not that he ever tells us anything useful. It's mostly to make people think they're involved and in the know. But most of us are not fooled.

"I don't know. I just know I can't let him stay out there, without even trying to help. He could've gotten himself into a real mess."

I give her a quick run down of everything I learned, and she listens without interruption. For a moment, I think of skipping over my panic attack, but in the end, I don't.

"I have no idea what came over me, or why it was so intense." If anyone can guess, it would be Jade. She's not a Reader, but her intuition hasn't failed us yet. Besides Christie, of course. That girl played her part so well, I think even she believed she was one of us.

"I think it's because you care about him. You can't tell me you two are not connected in some way. I've seen you together."

"No, I can't. But it feels like more."

"And I think you're right. But I can't answer that. The shifters will have to take that one."

"Not that they will tell me. They're being very stubborn."

"Wow, imagine that. Someone being stubborn."

I laugh at that and feel slightly better. Jade does have that effect on me. We kind of balance each other out. And she's definitely knowledgeable enough in magic that she's the perfect person to have on my side.

"What are you thinking?" she asks after I finish packing.

"I need to create a tracking spell, but I won't do it until we're outside the hedge. No need to alert anyone to my intentions." Jade nods at that. I'm especially concerned with Headmaster Marković knowing what I'm up to. He told me once that my magic reads a specific way, and he's been tracking it. It's how he knew I was keeping a secret, even though I can't tell him about the library.

Speaking of that place, it would be very helpful if I could get into it. But I would be foolish to try right now when I'm on such a tight schedule. Also, I don't need it zapping me into unconsciousness.

"What ingredients are you missing?"

I do a quick inventory of everything I have stored up, realizing I'm missing two elements.

"I need barberry root and calamus."

"Miss Lee will for sure have those in her classroom."

Jade's right. We worked with the elements a few months ago. Miss Lee always keeps extra in the closet in her classroom. While we're allowed to be in those rooms after class, everything we do is watched pretty closely. I don't know if we can just walk in and grab them.

"Okay, then I guess we need to sneak in."

❦ 13 ❦

We wait about an hour as I prepare the rest of the ingredients and place them inside my backpack. They need to be separated until the moment I'm putting them together, so I stuff them in different pockets and wrap them in separate sections of my sweater. I don't want any of them to lose their potency.

Once the dinner bell rings, we leave the room with the rest of the students. Owen is in charge of grabbing a few snacks for the trip, since we have no idea how long we'll be gone. There's no doubt in my mind that when we come back, they'll be hell to pay. Especially if the queen finds out about our little adventure. But I'm willing to take that risk for Aiden, and so is his pack.

When Jade and I reach the bottom floor, we follow the rest of the students into the dining room. Ben comes up, and I place a piece of paper in his hand as he says hi and buy. It's a completely normal exchange, so I don't think anyone notices. Once inside, Jade and I wait about a minute standing in line before she clutches her stomach.

"Are you okay?" I ask, adding a note of concern to my tone.

"Help me to the bathroom, please," she replies in mock whisper. Even some of the students who are not shifters have heard our exchange. I place a comforting hand on her arm, and we walk out at a moderate pace, so as to not attract any more attention. We actually walk all the way to the bathroom, and step inside, before Jade stands up normally.

"Now what?"

"Now," I reply, walking farther into the bathroom, "we climb out that window."

Jade looks up at the rectangular window over our heads before she looks at me. While most of the castle has kept its original structure, there were two communal bathrooms built downstairs to help students stay on track between classes. It's a very modern design, complete with the overhead window.

"You're serious?"

"Of course I'm serious. Ben unlocked the window in Miss Lee's class on his way out. We just have to get in there unnoticed."

"Couldn't have Ben also grabbed the ingredients?" Jade asks, coming up to stand beneath the window with me.

"Really? You wanted a shifter to find the right ingredients?"

Jade nods at that because there's no arguing with my logic. I'm not being mean. As witches, we take pride in our work. I'm also nervous about anyone else mixing the ingredients before they get to me. This way, I know they'll be useful.

"Alright. How are we getting up there?" Jade points to the window, and I grin. The window is slightly cracked to let air through, but it's enough.

"Like this."

I take a few steps back, then do a running start, jumping just before I reach the wall. My hands land on the windowsill, and I pull myself up. Satisfied I can do that, I drop back down.

"Wow, someone got strong," Jade comments, and I grin. It's true. Working out with Aiden has made my body more flexible and much stronger than before. I still have curves, but now they're more defined than ever. I'm definitely not complaining.

"Thank you, thank you. Now, I'll boost you up and then follow. Okay?"

"Okay."

Twining my fingers together, I place them down, so Jade can step in with her foot. She does, and I boost her up as she grabs the top. Pulling herself through the opening, I hear a thud and then, "I'm okay."

My turn. I walk a few feet back, redoing the exact same move I did earlier, except now when I grab the windowsill, I pull myself through. When I'm on the other side, I drop and roll, landing in a crouch. After a quick look around, I see that no one is on this side of campus, and I have to be thankful for small favors.

"Come on."

Jade and I stay close to the wall as we race toward the classroom window. Thankfully, the windows are large, as Miss Lee requires extra light for the spells we practice. I cross my fingers, hoping Ben did his part, and when I reach for the bottom of the window, it slides right up.

No one is inside and Jade and I have no problem getting in. I shut the window behind us, just in case anyone looks over and sees it open. We head directly for the large closet at the front of the room when we hear a noise outside.

"Hide," I mouth as we rush toward the closet. There is nowhere else to hide. If it's Miss Lee, she's probably here to do inventory or something like that, so being in the closet is the worst place we can be.

We hear the door open, and we exchange a look. I'm trying to come up with a plausible explanation of why we would be here, but I have nothing. We look guilty.

"Oh hey, Miss Lee." I hear Ben's voice and breathe easier instantly. Motioning for Jade, we start searching through the ingredients. "Can I ask you a random question? It has to do with one of my classes."

"Of course Mr. Light, how can I help?"

The door shuts, and their voices become muffled. It's now or never. My eyes land on calamus, and I grab the bottle just as Jade comes up to me holding a pouch of barberry root. We don't hesitate. Stepping out of the closet, we hurry over to the window, pulling it open quietly. Jade goes first, and I follow quickly, pulling the window closed in the same movement. The door opens in the same motion, and I drop to the ground and out of sight. Jade and I sit on the dirt for a moment longer before we squat and hurry away.

"That was close," she comments, linking her hand through mine.

"But we got it."

Now, I just need to make sure we can get off campus.

WAITING FOR NIGHTFALL IS ABSOLUTE TORTURE. I'M BEYOND restless, and I've been pacing for the last hour. Jade has stopped trying to get me to sit. I know my nervousness is not helping her own. When the bell for lights out finally sounds, it's like the greatest sound in the world.

I have to get out before the lockdown is in place. Jade and I have already said our goodbyes, so I grab my bag and give her a quick wave before I slip out the door. The moment it shuts behind me, it clicks, and I know the spell is in place. Ben mentioned that the spell for the outside doors is a little different, since the patrols have to go in and out. He can get me through, but I have to get there first.

With the added security, it's slow going. The only helpful aspect is a lot of the patrol are fae, and therefore, they don't have shifter's hearing or senses. I can hide behind various structures and statues without being sensed. I just have to be smart about it. A part of me could be worried they'll leave without me, but they have no way of tracking Aiden past the hedge, so I know they'll wait. But with the way I'm moving, they'll have to wait longer than they want.

When I'm finally downstairs, it feels like hours have gone by. I can't take more than a dozen steps before I duck behind a shelf. Glancing around the corner, I see the door to the dining room slightly open. That's where I'm supposed to be meeting Ben. The glass doors that lead out to the yard are the closest to me, besides the front door. There's no way we'd be able to walk out there and make it to the back unseen. I get ready to move again when I hear voices.

Slamming myself back against the wall, I breathe through my nose, hoping it's fae and not shifters on the other side of the hallway. Shifters can probably hear my accelerated heartbeat as I force it to calm down. After what seems like an eternity, the voices move on, and I breathe a little easier. Peeking my head around the corner, I can't see anyone, so

I rush toward the open dining hall door. Slipping inside, I shut it carefully and turn to the darkness.

Without supernatural sight, I can't see anything but the few outlines of the tables and chairs in front of me. Maybe I should call out, but I know that would be stupid of me, so instead, I just wait. When Ben materializes beside me, I'm proud of myself for not jumping. He points down at my hand and I nod, letting him take it. He leads me over to the doors, weaving in and out of the tables without any issues. It takes work to stay close enough to him to follow suit. Once by the doors, he stops, turning to me.

"I'll have to carry you."

The words immediately take me back to when Aiden did so, and I get a chill from the memory. I know it's the only way to merge our supernatural signatures to get through the barrier, but a part of me wants to say no. I don't understand it, but I squish the urge down. This is no time for weirdness. Instead, I step up, nodding my head.

Ben doesn't hesitate to reach over, sweeping me off my feet and into his arms. I wrap my own around his neck, expecting to feel the rush I felt with Aiden. But there's nothing. Ben feels the regular hot of any shifter and smells just as fascinating. But I don't feel anything toward him, not in the way I felt being held in Aiden's arms. I burrow my head into Ben's shoulder and trust him to get us to the outskirts. The wind comes and is gone before I know it, and the shifter is placing me on the ground, right inside the tree line.

"You okay?" he whispers, and I nod, knowing he can see me. Just then, Natalie and Owen step out of the shadow, their own clothes dark, matching my jacket and jeans.

"Let's get past the hedge," I say, keeping my voice low. I don't have to have supernatural eyesight to see Natalie is annoyed with me as we begin moving. The shifters could get there much faster if they weren't staying beside me, but we have no choice. They need me, and I need them.

My mind goes over every possibility of what could happen and the vast majority of that is not good. We could be caught, we could be killed, we could be put into eternal servitude. This is not an easy path, but I know Aiden would do it for us. He's already doing it for me. It's getting more difficult to keep my emotions at bay, but I refuse to have another panic attack. I'm especially not going to lose it in front of Natalie.

The shifter leads the way, staying a good ten feet in front of us, which means I can't really see her. Ben is beside me, leading me through the darkness, with Owen bringing up the rear. I hate the fact that I'm at a disadvantage, but I can't use magic to help me. Not while I'm on campus. I just hope my magic is enough when we're off it.

It takes us a little over half an hour to get to the hedge. When we finally stop, it seems bigger than I remember. I glance to my right, then to my left, and it seems to go on forever.

"Did it get bigger?" I ask, stopping right in front of it and looking up.

"It did. Bigger and stronger," Owen replies. Makes sense. If they figured out someone has been getting through, it's only normal they would make it a bit harder. It's an interesting type of magic. Harper would love to explore it more, since she's the one in my family with the natural elements affinity. Not that Bri wouldn't love to research it.

"Are you ready?" Ben asks, breaking through my thoughts, for which I am thankful. I can't be getting emotional about my family right now. I need to concentrate.

"Yes."

He takes my hand, and together, we step into the bush.

$$\maltese \quad 14 \quad \maltese$$

The branches seem to fight us for a moment, and I think we'll be stuck in the in-between forever, and then we're through. I stumble, and the only reason I don't face-plant is because Ben's hand is holding mine.

"You good?"

"Yes, thank you," I reply, and that's when I notice I can see him better. Glancing around, I realize the moon shines brighter here than on the other side of the hedge. "We should move a little before I try the spell," I continue. "Can you lead us in the direction Aiden went?" The last is directed at Natalie, and she doesn't reply. Just turns and starts walking away. The air is chilly here, and I'm glad I'm wearing my jacket. The shifters run hotter than the rest of us, in more ways than one, but even they have long sleeves on.

In about five minutes, Natalie stops. Without a word, I drop down to the ground and take out the ingredients one by one. The last item is four tarot cards, each with a corresponding ace to mark the elements. I place those at four corners, indicating North, West, South, and East. Then, I motion for Ben to step in.

"Sit right here while I do this," I say, pointing to the center. Once he's seated, I take out a basil leaf, lighting it as I walk around the circle. Owen and Natalie stand to the side, both on alert and fascinated. It's rare for shifters to watch witches cast big spells. It's kind of like me watching them shift. It's a glimpse into the other world for us. When the circle is cast, I take a seat in front of Ben.

"You ready for this?"

"Absolutely." He gives me a huge grin, and I smile back. Even though I didn't feel any similar feelings toward him when he held me, I realize he's important to me. This spell has a better chance of working because of our connection. The air around me is energized from my circle cast, so it's time.

Placing a small bowl in between us, I call on my water magic, holding my hands over the ground. The magic inside of me stretches, as if it's been laying in one spot for too long before it unfurls around us. Turning my hands palm up, I reach for the moisture in the ground and the plants around us. Drop by drop, the water comes, floating up and toward me as I collect it into small spheres over my hands.

When there is enough, I turn my palms inward, letting the water fall into the bowl. Next, I pick up a basil leaf and a lighter. Burning the leaf, I drop it into the water before reaching for the barberry root. I do the same thing to it before I reach for calamus. After all three have burned, I take out hibiscus. This one, I crush between my hands, and motion for Ben to give me his. I turn his hands palms up before I sprinkle hibiscus bits all over them. Then, I take another petal and burn this one, dropping it into the bowl. Last but not least, I take out sugilite and kyanite, placing each in Ben's hands. Both are strong crystals meant for guidance.

Taking my own hands, I put them over Ben's and close my eyes as I pull on my power. Something strong rises in me, and I want to speak words that are unusual. I realize it's the spell casting trying to break through, and I push it back. I'm not about to make matters worse by performing magic I don't understand. Instead, I look for the knowledge shared with me by my sisters and mother.

This type of spell doesn't require spoken word, just intention. I told Ben to think of finding Aiden, and so I follow suit. For just a moment, the magic within me fights itself before settling on what I want. It brings a smile to my face as I feel it tug at my heartstrings. My magic is like an old friend, and while it was drained for a while, it's always been there. Now, I need it to help me find Aiden.

The bowl between us ignites, evaporating the water and sending a sweet fragrance into the air around us. I open my eyes just as Ben does, our hands hot where they touch.

"How do you feel?" I ask, watching him for any reaction.

"Elated." That brings another smile to my face. His wolf likes my magic, that much I can tell. "And determined." I nod at that before I remove my hands from his.

"Place the crystals into your pockets. They'll help keep the spell at bay. Don't move just yet," I hurry to add when he goes to stand. I jump to my feet, grabbing the cards as I walk in a counterclockwise circle. Once the last card is picked up, I turn to Ben.

"The circle I broken. You can stand now."

He does, and I can tell my magic is all around him. He's watching me with a new kind of intensity, and when I glance at Owen and Natalie, I find their eyes on me as well.

"That was pretty incredible," Owen comments, which means a great deal, coming from a stoic shifter such as him. "Does your skin always glow when you do magic?"

"Not always," I reply and turn back to Ben. "Well, what do you think?"

"I can feel a pull in a certain direction. It definitely reads like Aiden."

"Good. That means my magic is not only pretty, it works." Both of the shifters smile at that while Natalie rolls her eyes. It really is her go to response to everything. I'm finding it comforting at this point. "Can you tell how far he is?"

"He's not close." My heart drops at his words, but I'm not surprised. He would've been found by now if he was close. "We should make camp and then start in the morning."

It's not what any of us want to hear, but Ben is right. Although, with the magic awakened in my veins, I'm not sure how I'll be able to sleep. Especially now that I know Aiden can be found.

SURPRISINGLY, I FALL ASLEEP RIGHT AWAY. AND WHEN I SLEEP, I dream.

This time, I know I'm dreaming. The fog rolls in just like the last time, but even so, I get a glimpse of my surroundings and realize I'm in the forest. The same forest I just performed the spell in.

Even though the scenery looks familiar, the feeling it evokes is entirely different. My heart beats loudly in my chest, as if making sure I'm aware of the danger. Because nothing feels safe as I stand surrounded by the thick fog.

A noise comes from my left—or maybe it's behind me—and I turn quickly, trying to see if anyone is there. That feeling of being watched comes over me, and I reach for my battle magic. When nothing happens, I almost growl out loud. I forgot my magic doesn't work here, and that makes me so much more afraid.

"What do you want?" I throw my question out into the space around me, hoping for something concrete. Instead of the half answers I got last time. But no answer comes, and I grow more irritated by the minute. If I'm being pulled into this place, there has to be a reason. But so far, all I'm getting out of it is fear. I don't need to be more afraid than I already am. Plenty of things are going wrong in the real world.

"Stop playing games and show yourself!" I yell, no longer caring about decorum. My fear is making me reckless, but at this point, what else am I to do? I know enough about dream walking to know I can be hurt here, if the dream weaver deems it necessary. But I also know I can find a way to control it, if I'm strong enough. I don't pretend to be, but it doesn't mean I'm not going to try.

"Whatever games you're playing, they stop now. What do you want?"

For just a second, I think I made things worse. The air grows heavier around me, the fog thicker. But then, something happens. To my right, the fog parts, and a shadow moves toward me. Everything in me tells me to run, but I stand my ground. Where would I run anyway? It's not my dream, whoever this is, they would be able to find me. When the shadow steps into the light, I gasp.

"Not whom you expected?"

"Not at all," I swallow around my words, "Your Highness."

The queen of Spring Court smiles, but there's no kindness in that. Her sharp teeth seem sharper, her features more striking. Which makes her appear that much more terrifying.

"Do you really think I do not know of the magic you practice over my lands?" She walks around me slowly, like a hunter circling her prey. And that is

exactly how I'm feeling standing under her scrutiny. My mind races with the possibilities of a response, but I can't lie to her or make up stories.

"I'm sorry, Your Highness," I say, bowing my head a little before I look up and look her straight in the eye. "I made a mistake, and I brought us here. If I don't do everything in my power to right the wrong, I won't be able to live with myself."

She doesn't respond right away, making another circle around me before finally stopping to face me. The gown she's wearing, a light green, that of fresh leaves springing out from a dormant branch, seems to melt into the fog around her. Everything in this forest is an extension of her, and it was my oversight not to remember that.

"Do you truly believe your magic is a mistake?"

The question surprises me. I expected more reprimands, or even threats, but not an inquiry that makes me pause. Do I believe my magic is a mistake? Even when I'm afraid of it, it's still a part of me. An intricate part that I would not untangle, even if I could.

"No," I reply, facing the queen straight on. She smiles again, and it feels even more dangerous than before.

"Good. While most fear what they do not understand, you must embrace it. The magic brought you here for a reason. Learn that reason and use it."

While her words ring true in my mind, I hear an underlying something between them. She wouldn't be as powerful of a queen if she didn't have her own agenda in every aspect of her life. But how do I ask the necessary questions? It really is not my place. But I know I have to because I need to know at least some of her intentions.

"Is that why you have...asked for my presence for lessons?" My question comes out much stronger than I thought it would. A gleam of approval shines in her eyes before she takes a tiny step forward.

"You are clever enough, Madison Hawthorne, to know I have my own reasons for your magic. I am curious about you and what you are capable of. If your magic can help me defeat the Ancients, then we would be in a very agreeable partnership. Why would I not have your best interest at heart, based on that one truth?"

I get what she's saying, just like she expects me to. She won't reveal her plans, but she does have them. No matter how I spin it, I'm under her thumb.

No amount of courage will help me get out of that arrangement. But maybe, just maybe, I can learn how to use her for my own advantage as well.

"Will I be punished?" I dare to ask, knowing full well she's not happy I've broken her rules.

"Maybe. Maybe not," she replies, always the fae. "Since I have been called away, we have not had our meetings. Finish your quest and return to take a room at the castle. All will be determined then."

As I try to wrap my mind around her words, she takes a step into the fog, and as it swallows her up, it dissipates. Just as quickly, my head begins spinning, and I'm thrown out of the dream.

Sitting up, I gasp coming awake, and Ben is instantly by my side.

"Maddie, are you okay?" he asks, placing a gentle hand at my back, as if he's afraid I'll topple over. I look up into his worried eyes, noticing it's a little lighter outside.

"The queen knows what we've done," I say, wiping the sweat from my forehead. "She's not happy, but she's not stopping us."

Natalie and Owen come to stand beside us as I speak, and the shifters exchange a look. Now that I think about it, she didn't mention them, so maybe I can protect them from her. If she's tracking my magic, she won't be tracking theirs.

"Well, let's get moving then," Natalie snaps, turning on her heel and heading to the fire we built last night. Ben rubs small circles at my back, and when I glance at him, his eyes are focused on something far away.

"Don't worry," I say, placing a hand on his arm and bringing his attention back to me. "We'll be okay."

"But will you? If anything happens—"

"Nothing will happen. I've got pretty great bodyguards on my side." I give him a smile, and I hear Owen grunt half a laugh. But Ben isn't deterred.

"We can't protect you in your dreams."

That makes me pause, but no matter how true that is, I won't let them take this as their burden.

"Maybe not, but I can protect myself if I know you're watching my back."

My words come out strong, a note of power I don't expect, and it

❧ 15 ❧

As we begin our trek, the forest seems restless around us. Or maybe it's just me. I can't shake off the dream, or the feeling of being watched. That last part might have something to do with Natalie throwing glares my way every few minutes. It's as if everything I do makes her hate me more and more. I don't understand her dislike of me in the first place, so it's just getting ridiculous at this point.

Ben stays a few feet in front of me at all times. His shifter senses are mixed with my spell, and so his steps are sure in the direction he's leading. The closer we get, the harder my heart pounds in my chest. I can't pretend I'm not scared for Aiden or worried about what he must be in the midst of. And when I think of Aiden, I think of Liam and get angry all over again. Maybe Aiden wouldn't tell me what he's doing, but Liam and I are friends. While I know he's still a fae, he's always been different with me. So why change now? What has happened to make two complete opposites team up and break the queen's rules? It seems my list of questions will continue to grow, with no answers in sight.

At that moment, Natalie turns and gives me her half glare, half roll of the eyes, and I've had enough. Picking up my speed a tad, I snap.

"What is your problem with me?"

The shifter spins on her heels immediately, and while that's very intimidating, I don't flinch. I have plenty of worries to carry on my shoulders and even more areas to fear. I'm done being scared of her.

"Where do I even start?" she growls, when she sees me not backing down. Ben and Owen move to either side of me, strong pillars of support, but I want to do this myself. Natalie, of course, doesn't miss the gesture. She throws her hands up, pointing at the boys. "This is definitely a good place to start."

I glance at Ben and Owen, my brow furrowed at her meaning. They've always been protective of me, but I don't understand how this concerns her. Then I notice the boys specifically not looking at me directly, and I narrow my eyes.

"What are you not telling me?" I ask Ben, but he stays stubbornly mute.

"Of course they won't tell you. They're not about to disobey their alpha. But I have no qualms about that," Natalie says, smiling a very dangerous smile.

"You will not." Owen surprises me by stepping between the girl and me. His body is tense, and I can see the wolf pushing to the surface. My eye snap to Ben, and he looks just as ready for a fight. This is definitely déjà vu.

"Stop it. All of you." I push between Owen and Ben, so I can see Natalie again. "You, stop sending me dirty looks all the time. You hate me? Cool. Then don't look at me. You two." I point at the boys. "What is with this extra macho intimidation technique? I can protect myself, you know."

"It's not that..."

"We know..."

Ben and Owen speak over each other but stop when Natalie's laugh rings out. All three of us turn in her direction, as she levels us with a glare.

"They can't help themselves," she says, pointing at the boys. Confusion clouds my mind, but no one is offering up any explanations. "But you're not as much of a weakling as I thought you were, so I'll give you that."

She turns then, continuing to walk through the forest as if nothing has happened. I glance at the boys, but they won't be sharing any time soon. Ben hurries to take the lead, with Owen falling into step behind me.

My sisters have told me the range of a shifter's emotion. They can go from hot to cold in the span of a second. Their tempers are not something to be trifled with, and I'm sure if my family could see me now, they'd be telling me to back off. But I can't shake the feeling that all three of them are keeping something incredibly vital from me. I felt it when Natalie first attacked me, and I feel it now. But since it clearly has something to do with Aiden, I guess I'll have to wait and ask him myself.

At least Natalie seems to have stopped throwing dirty looks my way. We've been walking for an hour, and she's only looked at me once. Suddenly, Ben stops, his eyes focused on something I can't see. I come up to stand beside him as Natalie and Owen follow suit.

"What is it?"

"There's a small village in front of us," Ben says as Owen nods. Their eyesight is truly awesome. "Aiden's signature is all over it. It's the strongest I've felt."

My heart leaps in my chest at those words, and I try to contain my excitement. We're getting closer. I have no idea how far from the academy we've gone, but the spell has clearly broken through the confusion barrier placed around the school's campus. Even after half a day, I wasn't so sure. But now I am and so are the shifters.

"Not bad, witch," Natalie says as she takes off toward the village. Halfway through the run, she shifts, her clothes disappearing into the shift. Even Aiden doesn't have that capability yet, and I wonder who spelled her to carry the clothes with her.

"She'll recon," Ben comments, turning to me. "Then we'll follow suit."

I nod, trying to keep my excitement at bay. We're getting closer.

WHILE WE WAIT FOR NATALIE TO RETURN, I CAN'T KEEP STILL. THE pacing I've become so fond of has returned, and I think it's making the guys a little annoyed. I keep making noise every time I step on a crunchy leaf, but I can't help myself.

"You know, if you sat in one spot, we would be less likely to get noticed," Owen points out after another five minutes of my frantic movement. Did I call it, or did I call it?

"Yes, but—"

"Maddie, we're all feeling it. But we have to stay calm."

"I am calm. Don't I seem calm?" I ask as I make another pass in front of the shifters. My question makes Ben chuckle, so I stop moving and turn to him. "Sorry, I'm just..."

"We get it. We're close. Either Aiden is there or he's nearby."

For some reason, when Owen says that, it makes me think he means something more than the words he speaks. I'm back to that secret they're keeping from me, but even though Natalie isn't here, I doubt they'll tell me. After all, she's the one who would've, and they keep stopping her. Even so, I open my mouth to speak, but then freeze. Something changes in the air, an intensity that wasn't there before.

"Guys," I whisper and then they're on their feet. They sense it too if their wolf is any indication. Both have opened up a pathway into the shift but haven't taken the leap yet. I've seen them do this a few times already, but it still fascinates me. Their eyes turn gold or silver, depending on their wolf, and their features get a soft gaze of an outline around them. It's as if they're on the edge, and all they have to do is plunge forward to fully become wolves.

"Stay between us, Maddie," Ben commands, not taking his eyes off our surroundings. I bristle at that a little, my battle magic sizzling at my fingertips immediately.

"I'm not so helpless," I say just as a movement to the left catches my eye. Something darts in the trees beyond our minicamp, and I try to follow it as I turn, but it's moving too fast. "What is it?" I ask, hoping the shifter's senses have picked it up. I'm not disappointed.

"It's a troll." Owen says just as it attacks. It's not like any troll I've ever studied. This is more rabid, a short and quick creature, and it's on a mission to destroy without a conversation first.

There is more than one, and they descend from the trees. The creatures drop on the ground in front of us, teeth bared. I've never seen them in real life before, and for a second, all I can do is stare. Then, the closest to me launches himself in my direction, but even as I bring my battle magic up, Owen snatches him from the air. With his teeth. He's fully a wolf now, a gorgeous silver beast, coming up to my waist. Twisting around, I see that Ben stayed in his human form, but he's fast enough that he's dodging the creatures.

Another group of five trolls jump from the trees, but this time I'm ready. I raise my hands from the ground up, and a blast of thunder sweeps the creatures right off their feet and into the air. This time, I sweep my hands from over my head to the ground, and the creatures fly back into the trees, knocking a few over. Calling on my element, a stream of water bursts from the ground before expanding into a line and sweeping the creatures on my left off their feet. Ben and Owen are each holding their own, but I'm not beyond helping.

Pulling the water at the top of my hands into orbs, I thrust them one at a time at the trolls. The impact sends them flying, dropping to the ground or ending up back in the trees. My body feels exhilarated, nearly bursting at the seams with power, and I don't want to stop. It's like a door has opened up inside of me and everything is pouring out. It's been so long since I've felt this in-tune with my magic. It's like I found whatever was preventing the flow and ripped it away.

Another blast and the creature hurry away, dragging their wounded ones behind them. My first instinct is to go after them, but I make myself pause and think. This is not why we've come here. The moment of clarity pulls my magic in, snapping it like a rubber band. My chest feels like it's not big enough to hold it all in. Bending over, I try to breathe, exhausted and exhilarated at the same time.

"Wow, Maddie," Ben says, coming up to stand beside me. "That was impressive."

"Indeed, it was." Natalie's voice sounds as she steps through the trees, two fae coming up behind her. "Impressive enough that you've convinced the villagers to let us in." She motions to the two following behind her and they step forward.

"Thank you for protecting our borders." They bow, and I glance at the shifter smirking beside them. This is not what I expected.

16

This trip is not at all what I thought it would be.

"What are they?" I ask as we take a seat at the table in the tavern. The village is more like a small town. Smaller than Hawthorne but still big enough to house all the amenities. The tavern is one of the biggest buildings, with accommodations for travelers in the upstairs rooms. It's very old-timey but still modern enough that I know we haven't stepped into a fairy tale book. The fae may not have all the conveniences, but they stay up on the times. Considering most of the time, a day in the human realm is like ten years here, and vice versa, depending on the magic. I'm intrigued by the way they adapt.

"Trolls." One of the fae who came to meet us on the outskirts speaks up. His name is Hector, and the woman with him is Alvina. Natalie's recon didn't provide any answers, so she made the executive decision to just waltz into their place of business and ask questions. The art of subtlety is clearly lost on her. But at least it seems to have delivered some results.

"They've been terrorizing our borders for months. The queen was to send soldiers to clean up the woods, but with the war on the Ancients, all resources are being sent there instead."

"A war?" That takes me by surprise. I knew the Ancients were right on the borders, but if they've broken in somewhere, the danger is much closer than I thought.

"It's not just in Spring Court," Alvina says. "All over Faery, creatures we've never seen before are rising up. And those we have seen are meaner and bolder in their attacks. We've always had a troll problem, but it's become a real issue recently."

"We're glad we could be of help," Ben says, his tone diplomatic. It's not like we don't care about the plight of these individuals, but there's nothing more we can do.

"We appreciate it. So, we will return the favor," Hector says, turning to face me once again. I realize then that Liam must've sworn them to secrecy. But since we have done them a service, the magic can be overridden. I'm guessing, of course, but it's the best I have from all the research I've done. When I find Liam, I definitely have some extra questions to ask him.

"A Fae of the royal blood came by with a companion. They have gone to see the oracle in the mountains. That is all we can tell you."

My heart leaps at the words. Liam and Aiden were here. There's no one else who could fit that description. But the mountains? I didn't even know there were mountains anywhere close by.

"I understand," I reply, trying to keep my voice calm and collected. "Would you be able to point us in the right direction?"

The fae exchange a look, and I know their answer before they even speak it.

"We cannot. But the oracle is well known around these parts."

"Can't you just—" Natalie snaps, and she seems ready to launch herself at the two across the table. Not that I fault her. I'm not fond of fae games, but they told us what we needed to know.

"It's okay, Natalie." I interrupt her, receiving a scalding look for my efforts. "We'll find the oracle just fine. We would like a room for the night."

Alvina nods before she stands and motions for us to follow. The boys don't question me, but I can see Natalie wants to. Once Alvina shows us to a room, I take out three silver coins and hand them to her. She nods, accepting the payment without audibly saying thanks, and leaves.

"How come the fae never say thank you?" Natalie grumbles as she drops herself onto one of the beds. There are only two in the room, but the place is modern and clean, so I'm not complaining.

"Because everything is a contract here. Even simple gratitude," I reply as I walk over to the window.

"You sure know a lot about fae, witch."

I turn at that, leveling her with a stare. "And you don't know enough, shifter." She rises at that, as if she's going to attack, but I'm not done. "They're bound to keep Liam and Aiden's secret. But they told us the oracle is well known. It means we can ask someone else."

Natalie huffs at that before laying back down. I turn to look out the window. We're on the fourth floor, so I can see over some of the rooftops. The trees here are so old, they reach nearly to the sky. I can't see a mountain anywhere near us, but that doesn't mean one is not there.

"Tomorrow we ask around, carefully, and we'll take it from there." I say, moving away from the window and toward the other bed. There's no way Natalie and I are sharing. She'll probably smother me in my sleep. But it's been a long few days, and I'm sure they didn't get much sleep last night in the woods.

Ben comes to stand near the bed, and I nod. Owen surprises me by walking over to the other side of the room and settling in a chair.

"Aren't you tired?" I ask, and he gives me a rare smile.

"I'll sleep better over here."

Natalie rolls her eyes but doesn't comment as she rolls away from us and presumably goes to sleep. Ben settles onto the bed beside me, and I can't say that it feels strange. I smile down at him as I sit up cross-legged on my side of the bed.

"What are you doing?"

"Making sure we sleep."

Then, I close my eyes and call on my magic. Now that the adrenaline is gone, the magic feels a little drowsy, like it did after I spell casted. Liam has been worried about the effects, but I haven't given them much thought until now. Maybe something *is* off about my magic. But I can't concentrate on that now. Instead, I call on a protection spell, sending it into the walls, the floor, and ceiling of our room. When that's done, I open my eyes and lay down.

"Thank you, Maddie," Ben whispers before he too gives into slumber. My own sleep doesn't follow as easily.

❧

AFTER I TOSS AND TURN FOR HOURS, LIGHT FINALLY MANAGES TO creep into the room. Thankfully, no one else has suffered from insomnia. I have no explanation as to why I slept in the woods, and I couldn't sleep here.

Actually, as we wash up and head downstairs, I realize it may have something to do with the queen. There were no dreams this time. She's leaving me on my own. I'm not sure if I should be pleased about that or not.

Once downstairs, we don't sit to eat but grab items to go. Contrary to popular belief, most things are okay to eat in Faery. There are only certain foods that should not be consumed by outsiders, and that was the first lesson I learned when I became friends with Liam. He wanted to make sure I was prepared, just in case.

"Where to?" Ben asks as we eat our biscuits. I'm sure the shifters would like something more substantial, but no one complains. Not even Natalie.

"The market?" I reply, looking down the street at what I think is an outdoor bazaar. "There are usually people there who will talk. For the right price."

"Aren't you so smart?" Natalie mumbles before pushing past us and leading the way.

"She's so pleasant in the morning," I comment and watch her shoulders tighten. But she doesn't turn around. Ben, however, chuckles. We hurry to catch up, and even though the boys seem more relaxed than Natalie, I don't miss the way their eyes keep moving, studying everything in our surroundings. They may handle themselves a bit better, but they're still on high alert, and for that I am thankful. Even though my senses seem to be more attuned to danger, the shifters have a much better idea when something is close by.

The market is in full swing. Everywhere I look, there is someone bartering for goods or services. We push through a throng of people, and I try and find someone who would be willing to talk. Without me having to give up my right kidney. Then, I see her.

The moment my eyes land on the older woman, I don't hesitate to walk over to her. Ben stays close behind with Owen bringing up the rear. When we reach the small booth, I glance down at the array of crystals in front of me.

"Are you looking for something in particular?" the old woman asks, bringing my eyes back to her. Somehow, she looks different from the others here. There's a softness about her that isn't usually found in fae. Or other creatures residing in Faery.

"We are looking for the oracle who lives in the mountains. Would someone be able to show us the way?" I ask, carefully choosing my words. The old woman studies me for a moment before she replies.

"You aren't of this world."

"Neither are you." I guess, but I know I'm right immediately. Ben and Owen both swivel to look at the woman as she gives me a small smile.

"You're an intuitive child. What do you have to do with the oracle?"

"We're looking for our...companions." Even though she's not from here, I still need to be careful. She has clearly lived here long enough to know the dangers of this world. To survive, I'm sure she's adapted.

"We will not make a bargain," I continue, "but will pay a sum upfront."

She studies me again, this time, with a new kind of respect in her eyes. Maybe she expected me to not know what to say or do, but I'm glad Liam made sure to teach me the basics. Even though I'm a bit mad at him still, he might eventually get a thank you from me.

"You are a smart one as well," the old woman comments, standing up from her stool. She's not as tall as I thought she'd be, which solidifies my earlier assessment of her not being fae. "Very well. The mountain you seek is beyond that tree line, about a half-day's walk. Trolls and goblins reside there. Along with other creatures."

"How do we find the oracle once we reach the mountain?"

"If you reach the mountain, the oracle will come to you."

The if does not go unnoticed. I take out five silver coins, handing them over. It might be a little steep to pay for the information we received, but I feel for her. She's in a world that is not her own. Although, maybe I shouldn't be feeling sorry for her at all. She seems to be doing just fine.

"You are generous and kind. Both of those are characteristics the fae will use against you. There are no guarantees with them. Not even the ones who show you kindness."

She doesn't wait for a response but takes the coins and walks back to her stool. It's a warning, but also, I think it's a bit of her own history in those words. I don't say thank you as I turn to leave. We take three steps, and Natalie materializes beside us.

"How many of those coins you got?" she asks, nodding her head toward the stand we just left.

"Not too many," I reply, without giving her specifics. They were a gift from Liam after we became friends. He told me I could use them when I came to visit, and we'd go to the market. It never happened, but I'm glad I kept them safe. From what I know, I could've paid with magic. But that's not something I have stored up at the moment.

We head out of the town without a backwards glance. There's no time to waste now that we know where we're heading. Ben fills Natalie in on what we learned, and all I get is another roll of the eyes. The shifter is beautiful, and I'd like to say her negative attitude makes her less so. But it doesn't. She's exotic in every way, while I feel gross after all the walking we've been doing.

I have no idea why my mind has gone to such trivial things. Maybe it's because I'll be seeing Aiden soon.

❧ 17 ❧

This part of the forest is much darker than the one we left behind. The village woman's words echo in my head as I study our surroundings. My battle magic is brewing under my skin, ready to be released at any moment. The shifters are all on high alert, their bodies tense. We walk steadily, but not too fast. We wouldn't want to attract any unnecessary attention.

After a while, it seems that maybe the woman was exaggerating. But then, I realize just how quiet it's gotten. Ben and Owen both move in closer, and even Natalie slows down to create a tight circle between the four of us. When the first shadow darts between the trees, my heart skips a beat. And not in an exciting way. There's another movement to our right, and this time, my magic comes a little closer to the surface. I'm expecting an attack at any moment, but it doesn't come.

"What's happening?" Natalie asks, keeping her eyes trained on the small bodies jumping around the outside of our perimeter.

"I think they're following us," I reply, confused by the whole situation. They stay close enough that we have to stay in a tight group as we move forward, but they don't come any closer. If the creatures are really so bad, they wouldn't be passing up an opportunity to attack. But while the trolls had no problem with it, these little guys are just observing.

"Why would the woman tell us of the danger if there was none?" It's Ben's turn to ask questions, and this time I do look over at him.

"I don't think she was lying," I reply honestly. "Maybe they're reacting differently to us for some reason."

"Or maybe the woman spun tails so she could get more money off you." Natalie smirks, flipping her hair over her shoulder. Even after days, it's still raven black and silky smooth. My hand automatically reaches for my own hair, but I drop it down. It's fine in the braid it's in. What is wrong with me? I need to focus on the issue at hand, and while I think over Natalie's words, I don't agree with them.

"No," I state, receiving a mild grunt in response. "My instincts are telling me she told the truth. Something else is in play here."

"Oh good. We're relying on her instincts now."

I don't get a chance to response as Ben growls, speeding his walk up a bit to catch up to Natalie. Without thinking, I react, running to grab his arm and pull him back.

"My instincts have gotten us this far," I say, squeezing Ben's arm in warning. "You have a problem, you know the way back." Natalie throws some daggers with her eyes at me, but she doesn't comment further.

Truth be told, she's not the only one frustrated. We're constantly playing catchup in this world, and I'm not seeing us getting ahead any time soon. We need to be ahead if we're going to find Aiden and Liam. Or get out of Faery. But that last one, it's truly on me.

"Wait, do you hear that." I pull on the arm I'm still holding, and Ben immediately stops, looking down at me.

"I hear..."

"Water."

The moment I acknowledge it, I feel it. My heartbeat speeds up in anticipation, and I forget all about the creatures in the forest or the danger they bring. My steps speed up, and in a manner of minutes, we're bursting through the trees, a glorious sight in front of me.

A river of clearest blue flows from east to west, separating this side of the forest from the mountain.

"Look!" I point at the giant rock in front of us as if the shifters can't see it. My heart longs for what's out there, but it also longs for the water. I glance down to the river again, the magic dancing at my fingertips. A noise comes from behind us, and we turn to see goblins on the trees, slapping the bark in excitement as their pointy teeth stick out in huge smiles.

"They weren't trying to hurt us," Owen comments.

"No, they were leading us here."

Without another thought, I walk toward the river. When we're on the bank, Ben tries to reach for me, but Owen stops him, as if he too wants to see what I'm about to do. I don't even know what I'm about to do.

It's been so long since I completely immersed myself in my water magic. Sure, I used some on our little adventure. But before then, the last time I can remember is when I lifted the pond straight in the air and then brought the storm. I've been so busy trying to learn this new power inside of me, I've completely neglected the one I already have.

Stopping right on the bank, I lift my arms, stretching them in front of me, palms up. The river rushes by beneath me and I can feel its rhythm like the beating of a heart. Closing my eyes, I call on my magic, and it answers immediately. Everything I've felt in the past few weeks pours out of me, carried by the power inside me.

A gust of wind kisses my cheeks, and when I open my eyes, the river is dancing in the space in front of me. Snakes slithering over the top of the blue liquid, flowers blooming the size of a small horse, bunnies jumping up and down, trying to reach the butterflies fluttering in the air. Each and every one of them made out of the water living in the river. I've never shaped so fully and effortlessly before, and it takes my breath away. I weave my hands up and down in the air, and the water follows, as if it's desperate for direction. A laugh bubbles inside of me, and I let it out, sending the river into the sky like a million stars. Then, just as it suspends above us, I pull it all in, dropping it back into the riverbank.

My heart beats fast and feels lighter. I turn to look at the shifters who have all been standing completely still as they watched my display. Complete and total awe is written all over their faces. Even Natalie looks impressed. But then, just as I register that, her eyes move over my shoulder, and her expression changes to one of surprise. I twist, and there they stand. Aiden, Liam, and a woman who looks to be in her twenties.

"Now that's what I call a welcoming sight," she says, smiling.

❧

I CAN'T STOP STARING AT AIDEN. IT'S AS IF NOW THAT I'VE LAID eyes on him, all the weirdness I've been feeling has lifted, and I'm finally balanced again. The moment that thought solidifies in my mind, I snap out of it. This is definitely not allowed, and here I am, gaping at him like a lovesick kid with a first time-crush.

Forcing my eyes to shift, I glance at Liam. That's when I notice both of the boys look happy to see me for about a spilt second before that look turns to fear. The woman between them keeps smiling.

"What are you doing here?" Liam's voice snaps me back to myself, and I glance at him to find his expression full of panic before the mask falls back into place. I'm instantly on alert, even though I keep my face as neutral as possible. I'm not as good as it as these boys, but I try.

"You've been missing for days. We've come to bring you home," I reply, grateful that my voice comes out strong and sure. The woman standing between the guys hasn't stopped watching me the whole time, a pleased smile on her face. I find it unnerving.

"Unfortunately for you, little witch," she says, her voice melodic and soothing. "These two are unable to accompany you back."

"What does that mean?" Natalie growls over the woman's voice, not even bothering to keep the hostility out of her question. She's taken on the persona of a protector, and I wonder if that's how mates work in the shifter world. She's ready to go to battle for Aiden.

Even though my eyes want to drift his way, I keep them trained on the woman. I'm not naïve enough to not realize the danger around her, cloaked in fine beauty. As I study her, I stand by my first impression, she is striking. But she also looks like a sorority sister dressed for a themed party. While a lot of the fae prefer their hair long, hers is cropped right above her shoulders and arranged in a messy bob. Her dress, while full and shiny, is made of something tougher than silk. The green of the dress dances and sparkles every time she breathes.

"It means that nothing is free here and these two," she waves her hand absentmindedly, "have made their choice."

My heart drops in my chest, blood running cold. There's no way they made some kind of bargain. They wouldn't be so foolish. But as I glance over at them, I realize that's what they feared. Me finding out and doing something about it. Well, good on them. They seem to know me well.

"What. Does. That. Mean?" I snap, taking a dangerous step toward the river. The woman's eyes flash in my direction, and I feel movement at my back. Out of the corner of my eye, I see Ben has moved closer to my side, his body rigid.

The woman doesn't miss a thing. She studies those around me before her cold eyes come to rest on me once more. It takes everything in me, but I don't flinch away, holding her gaze as steadily as possible. Suddenly, her melodic laugh rings out around us, making me jump a little.

"You are not what you seem," she states as she waves her hand in front of her. Roots spring from the ground, weaving together as they reach our side of the river. In less than a minute, an intricate pattern emerges, making a solid bridge between us. Instinctually, I take a step back as she moves across the walkway. With my hand at my side, battle magic sparks at my fingertips, and even though it's not visible, her eyes immediately go there.

"Not at all," she murmurs as she steps off the bridge and onto our side of the river. Both Owen and Ben are at my side, just as focused on the woman as I am. Natalie is on the other side of Ben, having a difficult time holding her shift. I glance at her, knowing I have to do something before she loses it and ruins everything.

"Nat, stand down." My voice is low, but her shifter hearing picks it up no problem, as her angry eyes swing toward me. She doesn't like me, and she has no problem showing me that. But for some reason, she listens. As if my words carry more weight than expected, her wolf settles, but she's doesn't break out of her ready stance.

When I turn back to the woman, Liam and Aiden have joined her on our side of the river. It takes much of my self-control not to rush over to them and either hug them or strangle them. I'm not sure when

I've become this person, but here we are. I'm not the only one surprised by my leadership. The boys both wear surprised expressions on their faces, and I'm sure it has all to do with the fact that Natalie just listened to me.

"You are a curious creature, little witch." The woman speaks again, her eyes on me like I'm some science experiment waiting to be dissected. She still hasn't answered my question, but it's not like I actually expect her to listen to anything I have to say. I'm trying anyway.

"What's so curious about me?"

"There is powerful magic in your blood. Yet, so unlearned."

"So I keep hearing," I grumble, receiving a slight growl from Aiden. He seems to be even more worked up than Natalie, but he's controlling it much better. I can tell because I've seen him in battle. This is another step above that.

"This is a good place to learn." The woman smiles, but there's no kindness in her eyes. For some reason, I think she means to learn with her. So, I play the only card I have.

"Her Highness Queen Amaryllis has taken it upon herself to teach me," I say, holding the woman's eyes steadily. Gasps sounds from all around me, but I'm not sure if they're shocked or if it's all in my head. The woman's eyes flash, and a part of me thinks the hatred I see there is directed at the Spring Court's queen.

"Of course she has," the woman says, her words dripping with coldness. "But there is something I have that you want." She inclines her head toward the boys. "You and I still have a bargain to make."

"No!" That comes from Aiden, and he moves forward until Liam grabs him and pulls him back. Pushing them from my mind, I focus entirely on the woman. She wants something from me, that's clear as day. And if Aiden and Liam are stuck here, then I have to be willing to do whatever it takes to get them out. No matter how much I hate breaking the number one rule of dealing with the fae.

"What kind of a bargain?"

$\mathcal{\$}$ 18 $\mathcal{\$}$

"Maddie, no." Both Liam and Aiden speak, but the woman waves her hand and both their mouths are shut. They struggle against the magic, but it's too powerful to overcome. It's hard not to look in their direction, but I manage. Because this is between me and the woman. I'll deal with them later.

"They came here for information and therefore, I require some as a trade," the woman says, coming to stand just a few feet in front of me. Ben and Owen automatically go to move toward me but can't. I glance at them and see their feet have been swallowed by the grass we're standing in, roots growing over them. Natalie is in the same predicament. How do I stand up to this kind of a power? Fear threatens to overwhelm me, but I search for every lesson, every single word I've ever heard on how not to let it control you, looking for that center. I focus on my breathing, keeping a mental count in my mind, until my mind is settled. The woman doesn't continue, and maybe it's because she's waiting for me to say something.

"What information?" I ask.

"On you, of course. You are an interesting creature, born of past and present. Do you know why your magic brought you to the Spring Court?"

The random question throws me off. Maybe this is just a tactic to keep me on edge, but it's working. The magic inside me is in uproar, scared and ready for battle at the same time. I blink my eyes a few times before I shake my head.

"Spring Court has an affinity to water, the element that fuels everything. You were drawn to it because of your friend." She flicks her hand in Liam's direction. "And your magic was drawn to it because of the power it holds."

If this is the information I'm supposed to be bargaining for, why is she giving it to me freely? Something is missing here, something she's not telling me, and I don't understand how I play into any of this.

"What does it mean?"

"It means you are in the perfect place to learn."

How many times am I going to hear this? Learn, learn, learn. Yet, no one is teaching me anything! Okay, the academy is still teaching me something, but it's not the same. Why are the two most powerful fae I've met so stuck on this one word?

"I can see your frustration, little witch," the woman continues, and honestly, at this point, I think she just likes the sound of her own voice. If I let her fill the silence, maybe she'll give me more than she wants. Not that I actually think that'd work on a master of trickery. It would in the human world for sure.

"Then help me understand," I dare to say. It's not a question but more of a challenge. She studies me again, this time with an intensity that makes me feel like she's looking straight into my soul. My skin prickles under her gaze, and it takes everything in me not to fidget. I can't let myself display any uncertainty. Not when a hunter is looking at me like I'm prey.

"You are to owe me a spell," she finally says, once again choosing what she shares with me. "When I call upon you, you will deliver. A spell of your own particular magic, no questions asked."

I know what she's asking. Somehow, she knows of my story spell casting, and she wants that power for herself. Making this kind of deal, it goes against everything I know. Even though I'm not looking at them, I can feel Aiden and Liam's eyes on me. They're pleading with me not to make the bargain, but I have no choice. I'm not leaving them here. My mind races over all the knowledge I have on contracts with the fae, and then my father's voice comes into my mind. He's been the Watcher of our coven for years, with his family in the position for generations. Watchers are the history keepers and the mediators between supernatural creatures. I realize he has taught me a lot more about the way of the words than I've thought until now.

"You are to give me the information promised to both Liam and Aiden." I speak up, keeping my voice clear and direct. My eyes are on the woman only, a burst of courage burning in my veins. "Along with whatever you were going to keep to yourself as leverage. Once I am satisfied with the knowledge, and you have released Liam and Aiden from their bargain, you will receive the promise of a spell, executed by me of my own magic. There will be no strings attached now or ever."

I link my fingers in front of me, my shoulders back as I look her in the eyes. This time, there's no doubt of the fleeting approval in her. The boys struggle against their magical bonds behind her, mumbling something around their closed mouths, but it doesn't matter. I have spoken.

"I accept," the woman replies, waving her hand in the air between us. I hear a pop and then, before I can ask anything else, she steps forward, placing her hand against my temple.

A rush of magic bursts into me, making my head spin. It feels like I'm being ripped apart from the inside out, and I grit my teeth against the agonizing pain. Tumbling and spinning, the magic takes me on a ride. Even though a part of me knows I'm still in one place, it doesn't feel like it. When images begin to assault my mind, I can't hold back the screaming any longer.

The only reason I stay standing is by the power of her magic. The only sound I hear is my own voice, going hoarse with exertion. And then, just as fast as it began, it ends. The woman takes one long look into my eyes and steps back.

Having nothing to hold me up, I drop to the ground, completely exhausted and then everything goes black.

WHEN I COME TO, THREE PAIRS OF EYES ARE HOVERING OVER ME.

Ben and Liam look concerned. Aiden looks angry. Raising myself to my elbow, Liam hurries to guide me up, keeping his hand on my back for support. I glance around, but the woman is gone. Owen is on my right and Natalie on my left, their eyes on the surroundings.

"Welcome back, Sleeping Beauty," Natalie mumbles without turning around. I roll my eyes but don't engage.

"How long was I out?" I ask instead.

"About fifteen minutes," Liam replies, rubbing my back in a comforting circular motion. His magic seeps into my skin, helping rejuvenate me. All fae carry a bit of healer magic in them, since they're so closely attuned to the nature around them. Right now, I'm thankful.

"Where is she?"

"She disappeared the moment you passed out. Which is when she freed us as well."

I look over at Aiden, who still hasn't said anything, but I can tell he's mad at me. The feeling is mutual right now, so I make sure to send a glare his way. That seems to rile him up even further.

"Let me up," I mumble when Liam continues to hover. Before I can even begin moving, Aiden is there, reaching to lift me up, but I bat his hands away. He growls a little but doesn't press.

"I can stand on my own," I snap in response as I run my hands over my shirt to smooth it.

"Oh, can you? Can you actually do anything on your own? Like make good decisions?" His eyes are dangerously dark, and I can tell he's barely restringing his wolf right now. But for some reason, I'm not afraid of him. Instead, I move toward him, and when Ben reaches over to stop me, I push his hand away.

"A thank you would be appreciated."

"I didn't ask you to come. You should've stayed at the academy."

"And leave you rotting away in the service of the fae?" My hands move to my hips as I stare the shifter down. I have grown a lot in the past few months, and I have never felt it more than I do at this exact moment. The me from before this ordeal would never have stood up to a shifter this way, much less an alpha. But I'm not afraid of Aiden hurting me. Not physically at least. What I am afraid of is him getting himself killed.

"We would've gotten out on our own," Aiden replies, clearly just as angry as I am.

"When? In a hundred years? What were you thinking?" He opens his mouth to reply, but I'm already turning, this time entirely focused on Liam. "And you! You know better. You know better than all of us. Why would you do this?"

My voice has risen enough to be heard in the forest at my back. Even the pack has moved back, trying to stay out of my way. My body is vibrating with pent up energy, mixed with magic, and I'm breathing heavily. I'm provoking two creatures who are much stronger than I, but it doesn't stop me. Real terror grips my heart at the thought of either of them getting hurt.

"Maddie, you don't understand."

"Then, you better explain it to me!"

"We did it for you!" Aiden snaps, and I twist, staring at him as if I've never seen him before. There's so much in his look I can't even begin to understand, but as he says the words, images of what the woman showed me start falling into place.

"No," I whisper, all energy leaving me as I process the information. It's as if she put it all in my head, but until I made a conscious thought to think about it, it didn't come. Now, it's filling me up with knowledge, and that knowledge feels like a ton of bricks sitting on my chest. Liam and Aiden move toward me as one, grabbing my arms as I sway on my feet. "It's not possible."

"I'm afraid it is."

Raising my head, I stare at Liam, at the uncharacteristic sorrow in his eyes. Fae are not emotionless. I've known that my whole life. But they do control their emotions better than anyone else in this realm or the next. For someone in his position to express so much of it on his face makes all of this worse somehow.

"Did you know before this?" I ask, regaining a little of my strength.

"No."

"What are they talking about?" Ben's voice reaches me, and I look over to see him and Owen hovering nearby. I feel a feather of a touch on my cheek and turn in time to see Aiden wiping a tear from my skin. I'm crying, and I didn't even realize it.

"Maddie?"

"My dad." I hiccup over the words. "My dad is in Faery. It wasn't the Ancients who took him. It was the Winter court."

Whatever I thought, whatever I was going to do, all of it fades away as I come to terms with that information. It's what she told the boys; I know that from the images. But she also kept something from them, a prediction she foresaw. My chest fills with so much pain, I can hardly breathe. Before I know it, Liam is pulling me into his arms, and I cling to him like a lifeline.

"Maddie?" his voice whispers over my head, and I hear it rumble in my ear. I don't want to appear weak in front of any of them, but for just this moment, I let myself feel it all. Before I have to face them. Because I do have to face them, and I have to tell them what's coming.

Pushing away from Liam, I wipe at my eyes and straighten my shirt. Taking a deep breath, I roll my shoulders, compartmentalizing everything I've learned. My dad always said nothing is given to a person that cannot be handled. I've always been stronger than I've given myself credit for, and now, I guess I get to see if my dad was right.

"Dad." My voice catches, and I clear my throat before looking up again. "My dad is being held prisoner in the Winter court, and there is nothing I can do about it right now." Liam reaches for me again, but I wave him away. "What the woman did not tell you..." I glance at him, then at Aiden, who has moved to stand with his pack.

"She did not tell you the Ancients aren't the only evil at the borders. A plague has spread throughout Faery, and it is now on the threshold of Spring." The group exchanges glances as I take another pause. "We're in real trouble here."

And once again, it is all my fault.

❧ 19 ❧

Everyone has questions. Even Natalie steps forward after staying quiet for so long.

"We don't have time for this," I interrupt, putting my hand up. I gave them a little longer than I had, so it seems fair. "We have to get back, and we have to warn Headmaster Marković."

"What exactly is happening?" Aiden may still be angry at me—right back at ya buddy—but he's all business now. There's the alpha I know and...*nevermind*.

"When I figure out how to sort through all the information she stuck in my head, I'll let you know. But for now, we need to go."

No one can argue with that logic. I glance behind us at the spot where the bridge of thorns was and wonder what kind of a spell she will require of me. For someone as powerful as she is, why bother with my minuscule spell work? Not that I can do anything about it now. One way or another, I did what I came here to do. I got Liam and Aiden back. I don't care if they're not happy with me.

It doesn't take us long to get back to the village. I scan the area for the older woman we met, but the bazaar is gone. Since we've spent most of the day getting there and back, the sky has grown dark, so we head toward the hotel we stayed at last time. Alvina meets us at the bar, a small smile on her face.

"I knew you'd be back," she calls in greeting before her eyes move over the rest of the group. "And you found your companions."

"Something like that," I reply as Hector comes out from the back. "We would like a room for the night."

"Not a problem." The two exchange a look before Alvina motions us to follow her, like before.

Alvina leads us to the same room we were in before, and this time it's Liam who pays her. Everyone goes to their corners while Natalie follows Aiden to the bed. She's been trying to get him to talk to her, but he's not in the mood. From my position on the other side of the room, I watch as she reaches over, running her hand gently over his hair, neck, shoulder, and down his arm. He inclines his head toward her, and then she's saying something into his ear that I can't hear.

Tearing my gaze away, I push down any sort of emotion that rises up in me. I can't be doing that in a room full of supernatural creatures who can read me like a book. But I know if they start making out, I'll be yelling 'bank is closed' and leaving as fast as my feet can carry me. Actually, that's not a bad idea.

"I'll be back," I announce, and then before anyone can stop me, I'm out the door and down the stairs. Now that I've officially made a fool out of myself...I need a distraction. I need a break from my thoughts and my worries.

If I let myself stop moving for even a second, the plethora of emotions will overwhelm me. I'm barely staying afloat as it is. I can't think about my dad, and I can't think about the plague. All it does is make me want to curl up on the floor and cry. I definitely cannot afford that at the moment. Even though I'm running on empty, I'm still running. I'll take what I can get at this point.

"Is the room not up to your standards?" Hector's voice pulls me out of my thoughts, and I look up to find him before me.

"It's great, th—" I stop myself before I can thank him. "I wanted a glass of water."

Hector nods before walking over to the bar with me on his heels. We've been eating nothing but granola bars and beef jerky since we left the school, and as the smell from the kitchen hits me, my stomach growls.

"Would you like dinner as well?" he asks, clearly not missing the sound. I shake my head, and he takes that at face value. After handing me a mug filled with water, I raise it slightly in the air and walk away. I'm not in the mood to talk to anyone, least of all a fae I'd have to be careful around.

As I walk through the hall, I pass a sitting room. There are plenty of creatures sitting in the main room, but this area is empty. Finding a spot by the window, I settle down and give myself a moment to feel.

I know I promised myself I wouldn't lose it in front of anyone, especially those upstairs, but here and now, alone in this room, I let a tear slip down my cheek. Only a moment, that's all I get, before I have to push my emotions down.

Somehow, I have to figure out how to help my dad. It feels like I've been searching for him forever, and now, there is finally a lead. My family and I were so sure the Ancients took him. He was doing research on them, trying to find something that would help us defeat them. He was on one of his recon missions to one of the covens when he disappeared, leaving all his stuff behind in his hotel room. Mother didn't feel his demise, so we presumed he was taken for something specific. Now I find out the fae had him, and I can't even pretend to guess as to why.

But somehow, someway, I will find a way to get him back. I'll have to get word to my family, but I'm not sure how that's happening anytime soon. Maybe once I'm in the castle, I'll have a chance.

So many things are happening at once, my head spins from thinking about it. I wipe at my tears, taking a deep breath. There's nothing for me to do but focus on one problem at a time. Getting back to the academy and warning them about the plague is the next order of business.

"Do you want to talk about it?"

I'm not even surprised.

I turn as Liam pushes away from the door frame and walks farther into the room.

"How long have you been there?"

"Not long. But I don't have to see you cry to know you're hurting."

He takes a seat in front of me, and I reach over to take a swig of my water before I meet his eye.

"That was a stupid move on your part, Liam," I say because I want him to understand just how foolish it was. Not that it really matters. He'll always do what he deems best.

"I would do it again."

There it is. The expected response. I cock my head to the side, studying him carefully. It's always been true that he's different from the rest of the fae. Both he and his half-brother grew up away from this place, away from the rules of this world. He's always been kinder, softer, which makes it easy to forget he's one of them. But I'm seeing glimpses of it now. Ever since I got here, I've been seeing it more and more. Yet, it doesn't stop me from pushing him.

"Why?" I ask, because I need a good reason. What if Natalie never said anything to me? Aiden would be gone and so would Liam. I wouldn't even know where to look.

"Because you needed answers, and this was the only way to get them." The guilt I carry close to my heart rises up, but now is not the time. Instead, I push further.

"So what? Aiden and you are friends now?" The question isn't hostile exactly, but Liam doesn't miss the undercurrent in my words.

"I wouldn't go that far, Mads. But I also wouldn't let him go into that forest on his own."

"Because?"

"Because he would've gotten himself killed, and you would've been heartbroken."

I bristle at that immediately because Liam is not supposed to know about my confused feelings toward the shifter. No one is supposed to know. Well, besides Jade. But I know she wouldn't tell anyone.

"Come on, Mads. You should know better than to try and keep that from me. I know you."

And he does. Better than anyone in a long time, which is very surprising considering we've only been friends for a little over a year. But maybe it's true what my sisters always say. It doesn't matter how long you know someone, when you click, you click.

"It's not like that," I say anyway because how am I supposed to admit it to him when I refuse to admit it to myself?

"Mhhmm."

"Don't do that, Liam." I point a finger at him before I stand and being pacing around the room. "Don't make this into something it isn't."

"Just because it isn't doesn't mean it never will be."

At that, I spin toward him, amazed he would even say that. He would have to be blind not to see what's happening between Natalie and Aiden.

"They're promised to each other, Liam. I don't play into that equation."

"And yet, he broke the queen's rule and went into the forest for you. Actions speak louder than words, and all that." He shrugs, but I can't allow hope to blossom. Instead of encouraging this conversation any further, I walk over to Liam and sit down next to him. My head falls onto his shoulder as he reaches over and takes my hand.

"Please don't ever do that again," I whisper. I may be mad at him for keeping me out, but the fact that he could've been gone from my life forever overpowers that. I don't expect him to reply because anything he says will sound more like a contract. But then he squeezes my hand and warmth spreads up my fingertips.

"I won't."

❧

THE NEXT MORNING, WE GET UP, EAT BREAKFAST, AND LEAVE without any extra flair. Some have given us weird looks, but we've mostly been left alone. I have to be thankful for small favors. Also, there haven't been any weird dreams. I'm not sure what to think of that. A part of me is glad and another part is worried. I'm not naive enough to think the queen doesn't have something up her sleeve when it comes to me.

The shifters went out and grabbed some supplies, replenishing what we brought, which means I haven't talked to anyone but Liam.

Not that I'm complaining. The distance is good for me. Or it will be. I should get used to not being around a certain someone.

Aiden and Natalie stay to the front of our little group with enough distance between us that I couldn't hear what they're saying even if I wanted to. Which, of course, I don't. Liam walks to my right, Ben to my left, with Owen bringing up the rear. Somehow, I've ended up in the middle, as if they're protecting me from everyone around me. I don't know if I should be flattered or offended. I decide to take it at face value since I have other things to worry about.

We walk through the day with absolutely no issues. I thought the trolls would come back, but I haven't heard anything in the forest around us. The quiet makes it so much harder for me to stay out of my own head. I try to sift through the information in my mind, looking for answers. It's wishful thinking, but I would love for the library to suddenly be available to me now. There has to be something there I can use.

"Should we stop for the night?" Ben asks when the forest grows even darker. Since I'm the only one without extra special sight, the decision comes down to me.

"Let's stop," I say, keeping my eyes directed at Ben. No one questions me, and once the perimeter is set, everyone settles into their corners. Owen is taking first watch, and as I study my companions, I realize they're all feeling it. That foreboding hangs over us the closer we get to campus. It's not fair for me to think I'm the only one feeling all these emotions. They have friends there too, all of this affects them just like it affects me.

"Am I allowed to ask about it?" Ben takes a seat beside me, keeping his eyes trained on the trees. Since we left the village, he's been staying close, but we haven't really talked.

"There's nothing to talk about."

"You know that's not true." He turns, looking me straight in the eye. We have become friends through all this and for that I am thankful. But I can't spill my deepest and darkest to a beta. Especially to Aiden's beta. When I don't speak, he sighs. "I want you to know, Maddie," he begins, keeping his voice as low as possible, "What you did for him, for all of us, it was beyond impressive."

I smile at that and reach over to squeeze his forearm. He pats my hand and stands, understanding that's as much as I can give him at the moment. So much of me is exhausted. I feel as if the last week has lasted a year. Between the attacks, my own magic, and coming here, nothing is what I ever would've expected my life to be.

On their own, my eyes drift over to where Aiden and Natalie are sitting. She's been staying extra close to him, and I can understand that, even though I don't like it. She's his mate, and there's nothing to be done about that. When they move to lay down, I tear my gaze away and look up at the sky. Not much of it can be seen through the giant trees, but I pretend it's there.

I miss my family something fierce. Even though we're not looking at the same sky, I pull on the knowledge that they may be looking up as well. Harper and Bri are probably with their significant others, pouring over books and potions. Mama is probably with the council, researching more ways to keep the town safe. Right now, I wish I was with them. I wish I could talk to them and ask for their advice. My family means the world to me and being this far away from them, it's another weight I have to carry.

But then I think of my father, and the fact that he is under the same sky as I am. Somehow, I have to figure out a way to get to the Winter Court. I'm more than aware of the tension between Spring and Winter, so I know better than to ask the queen for help. But maybe she can tell me something I can use. And maybe a certain other fae can be of help.

I glance over at Liam, and he looks up as if he feels my eyes on him. His eyes narrow, and I give him a small smile. He doesn't look reassured, but he doesn't press it. After the events of the past few days, I know better than ever that he has my back. That's what I'm going to focus on. I may not have my family here, but I have my friends. And they're as good a family as anyone can ask for.

❧ 20 ❧

The moment we step through the hedge, I know something is wrong.

The blanket of danger that's been hanging over our heads this whole time, suddenly covers us without preamble. We're surrounded on all sides. The shifters move to attack as I raise my hand.

"Stop!" I shout, freezing them in their tracks just as a guard steps forward. His uniform is custom tailored, the dark green adorned with gold thread. Before he speaks, I know what this is about.

"By the order of the Queen, Madison Hawthorne, you are to come with us immediately."

Nodding, I move toward him when Aiden's hand is suddenly on my arm. Turning, I find his eyes full of concern and caution.

"What are you doing?"

"I'm going with them."

"No, you're not."

That protective streak of his is much adored but also very frustrating. I shrug off his hold, receiving a slight growl.

"It's part of the deal, Aiden," I say, keeping my voice low but urgent.

"What deal?" he and Liam ask in unison as the fae takes a step toward me.

"The deal I made with the queen. Go back to the academy," I plead, hoping this once they listen to me. "Let Headmaster know what's happening, and see if you can find out more information."

"Miss Hawthorne." There's a hint of threat in the guard's voice as he says my name again.

"How many bargains did you make?" Aiden asks as I take a step away from them. Raising my eyes, I look him dead on, so he knows just how much I mean what I say next.

"As many as were necessary."

I turn then and rush to the guards before I say anything else. Especially something I'll regret later. A shout comes from over my shoulder, and I twist to see guards stepping from the side, grabbing my friends by their arms.

"What are you doing?" I yell, rushing toward them. But the leader of the guards has already grabbed me around the middle, and he's dragging me back. My magic flairs up as I watch Aiden and Liam being restrained, but right before I can let loose, heavy metal falls on my wrist, cutting off whatever I may have done. I glance down to find a shackle around my skin, and my magic freezes.

"Stay in line, Miss Hawthorne. Or someone will get hurt."

The last thing I see is Aiden's panicked look as the guards swallow me up and carry me to the castle. I wonder if I'll have to struggle for miles, but then a portal opens up and I'm pushed through.

When I land on the other side, the image of the group I left behind is still vivid in my mind. Even Liam looked scared, and that's not something I expect from him. Honestly, I probably should rethink my stance on everyone at this point. Liam looking worried is almost as weird as Aiden looking panicked.

"You better not hurt them," I snap, writhing my arms away from the guards holding them. The head guard steps forward again, a face full of disdain. He clearly thinks I'm below him, and I wonder if he'll strike me to keep me silent, but then he straightens and moves away. For the first time, I look around the room. I'm in a large office with bookshelves on each side. It's bigger than the last room I was in but similar. Then, my eyes land on the other person in the room.

Queen Amaryllis, ruler of the Spring Court, rises slowly to her feet and makes her way toward me. Everything about her is smooth and tailored to make her look regal. She looks like she's gliding across the floor, and for a moment, I wonder if she is. The fae often use their magic absentmindedly, and in a way that makes them one up each other. The queen is a master of that, as she would be.

"Your friends are fine," she says before taking a seat on a purple velvet armchair. It looks like it costs more than half the buildings in my hometown. The queen inclines her head toward a bench with a cushion, and the guard at my back pushes me forward. I glare over my shoulder as I take a seat. They really need to knock it off with manhandling me.

"Please tell your guards to stop pushing me around. I am perfectly capable of following directions on my own." The anger gives me a voice, and the queen's eyebrows raise a little at the tone. But I'm not backing down. I'm done being afraid. This won't end well for me if I don't stand up for myself. The queen waves her hand, and the guards melt away into the background. I guess that's as good as I'll get, but I'll take it.

"I am glad to see your journey was a success," she continues, and I wonder if that's really true. There's an underlying current to everything she says, and I wait for the other shoe to drop. "We can begin our partnership now."

And there it is. She may say partnership, but I'm not stupid enough to believe that.

"What is it you ask of me?" I already know I won't like the answer.

"You are to remain at the castle for as long as I require. We will begin magic exercises immediately. We must learn what we can about your...abilities."

All the words she's saying are pretty, but it still makes me feel like nothing more than a science experiment.

"And if I refuse?" I dare to ask, and the temperature in the room drops immediately.

"I would advise against it."

The threat has been given, and there's nothing I can do to protect myself except learn how to use my magic more effectively. Maybe there's a way I can use this for my own agenda; although, I know the queen won't hesitate to sacrifice me when the time comes. She needs me for a purpose, and the best way I can help myself and my friends is to learn what that is. Steeling myself against whatever may come, I look her right in the eye and say,

"When do we begin?"

BEING AWAY FROM EVERYONE HAS BEEN HARD. IT'S BEEN A WEEK, and all I've done is try to stay afloat without completely losing my mind.

Headmaster Marković came and visited earlier yesterday but could only stay for a few moments. He couldn't even talk to me without the watchful eyes of Queen's Guard lingering near. I've been assigned the captain of the guard, and he's been staying especially close. The queen called him Kurtis, but I doubt that's his true name.

I asked about my friends, and he said they're doing fine. There has been no sign of the plague the Oracle mentioned, but Headmaster isn't dismissing it. He knows better than anyone that what she says will come true. They've made preparations, and what I'm doing here, the training the queen is giving me...I hope it helps.

"Your Highness." I greet the queen as I step into the library. I wonder if I'll ever see past these few rooms. I go from my room to the library and once to the throne room. But that's it. Today Queen Amaryllis is wearing a bright pink dress, the brightest of colors I've seen on her. The sleeves are long and made up of sheer material, with patches of lace here and there. The skirt is full, but as she walks, I see there are slits all throughout. For some reason, the dress makes me think of Jade and with it comes a touch of sadness.

My own outfit consists of a dark blue, off the shoulder, embroidered dress. The neckline is v-shaped with long sheer puffy sleeves, and the skirt is layered with tulle. The queen has provided a wardrobe, even though I told her Jade could put together a bag for me. Queen Amaryllis wouldn't hear of it. She has a specific view of who I am, and nothing is going to change that.

I miss my jeans. In the sixteen years of my life, I've never worn so many dresses. They're beautiful, of course. The fae have a way with style. But they're not me, no matter how much the queen tries to make it so. The only aspect of my new wardrobe I do enjoy is the killer hooded cape. It makes me feel like Robin Hood or something.

"We will begin with a simple exercise," Queen Amaryllis says, and I turn to focus on her. She walks over to a large bowl in the middle of the room, and I come to stand beside it. "You know what to do."

I do because we've been starting every lesson with this exercise. Closing my eyes for a second, I find my center. My magic has seemed to replenish itself in the last few days, and I'm thankful. Ever since we came to Faery, I've been a little worried.

When I open my eyes, I raise my hand, and the water follows suit. It grows into a column in front of me as I watch the droplets sparkle in the afternoon light coming through the window. Twisting my hand at the wrist, I let my fingers flutter up and down, and the water moves with them. I've come to do this exercise whenever I'm around liquid. It soothes me in an unexpected way, like stretching a muscle after sitting in one spot for too long.

"Multiply it."

Bringing my other hand up, I pull the water apart, spreading it into a long line, hand length across. I haven't been able to create animals or objects like I did by the river, but the water listens to me more than ever before. With my left hand, I throw the droplets into the air, and as they fly, they become a sky full of stars. The other half of the water hangs in an orb over my right hand. As I hold the droplets over my head, I turn to the orb. Calling forth a little more of my magic, I watch as the orb grows in size, doubling almost immediately. Then, I swing my left arm, pulling all the droplets from the air and slamming them into the orb. The water explodes as it comes together, and I mold it into a pillar once again, before it can get anything wet.

"Now, use your words."

At first, I want to protest. We've tried it once before, and it made me so tired, I couldn't think straight for the rest of the day. But this is why I'm here. I don't want to find out what she'll do if I resist.

"What are you asking me to do?" I ask instead, hoping for more direction. That's the thing about lessons with Queen Amaryllis. She's not really teaching me anything. She watches as I practice my magic and then demands I do certain types of spells. What I wouldn't give to have someone who understood my story spell casting explain to me exactly what it means and how it works. Instead, I'm making up my own rules.

"Multiply it."

Great. She just expects me to know my onions. It's frustrating, and it's infuriating, and it's— I take a calming breath before I do something I'll regret. Turning my focus back to the pillar of water still holding strong in front of me, I think back to the river. I felt my magic explore itself, like it was growing and blossoming on its own. Maybe I can replicate that here, without too much of the story spell casting magic. It's worth a try.

> *"You move and you grow,*
> *You tumble and you flow,*
> *But with words you'll come before,*
> *And dance like flowers after snow."*

The part of my magic that I keep under lock and key bangs on the walls, desperate to get out. But I do my best to push it back, to keep it contained. My words bring the water higher and higher before it splits into a meadow full of flowers. The moment the blooms open, a pain sharper than any I've felt before doubles me over. The magic boils hotter. It spreads throughout my body like it's demanding to be felt. I yelp, unable to contain myself, and I thrust my arms in front of me, pushing them toward the water. The rush is instantaneous, and my head spins with the feel of the magic pouring out of me.

I scream as I try to reel it in, but it won't listen. The water multiplies by ten and then it bursts in every direction, covering every surface and pushing all the furniture against the wall. The pain resides, and I drop to my knees, breathing heavily.

"Now, pull it all back." The queen speaks up, and I glance over to find her completely dry while I'm drenched. I didn't have enough power to protect myself from the blast, but she clearly did.

"I can't."

"You will."

There's no kindness in her gaze, just cold command. Knowing I can't refuse her, I reach for the water with my right hand, calling it to me. At first, there's a moment of resistance, like a petulant child who doesn't want to come inside after playing with his friends, but then it drags its feet toward me. I hold steady, my whole body filled with exhaustion, but I don't stop until every single drop is in the bowl. The volume of water diminishes, and it's only what we started with. Unable to stand on my feet, I stay on all fours, my head spinning.

"That's a start," the queen says and walks out of the room.

🕊 21 🕊

When a knock sounds on the door, I jump. I'm not exactly expecting any visitors. After my water disaster a few days ago, the queen has continued to push me, but my magic hasn't been responding as well. Yesterday, she announced there would be no lessons today because I am required to attend a celebration. Hours after getting up, I'm still trying to figure out what I'm supposed to wear to this ball. Or why it's so necessary that I go.

"I'm coming!" I call out when the knocking becomes insistent. Pulling the door open, I gasp before I'm swallowed up in a tight hug.

"What are you doing here?" My voice is mumbled as my friend holds me tight.

"I'm here to get ready for the ball!" Jade replies, pulling back and giving me a once over. "You look good, by the way. I had these night-mare-esque thoughts that they were starving you or something."

I laugh, my first real one in a week, and reach for her again. It feels so good to be held by someone kind. Not that I'm being held by anyone, and that's the problem.

"But how?" I lead her farther into my room as she gazes around. She's as impressed as I was, but she doesn't comment. She knows me well enough to know that any kind of praise for this place will not sit well with me right now.

"Headmaster Marković requested it. We're all required to go to this ball anyway, so he just made sure I could come get ready with you."

I don't even want to know how he managed that. But the headmaster has been around for a lot longer than I can imagine, so it's not like he'd be making dumb mistakes when it comes to the fae.

"Did you bring anything to wear? I have nothing here but the clothes they've provided."

"Which looks amazing on you," Jade comments, giving my yellow dress another look. The queen seems to enjoy me in yellow, even though I've never been a fan of the color for myself. It's really more of my sister Harper's color. But it's as if the fae royalty want to make sure I'm as far from myself as I can be while I reside in this castle.

"Thanks, but—"

Another knock sounds on the door, but this time, whoever is on the other side doesn't pause. Three fae walk in carrying various items including two large boxes. They place the items on the bed, turn, and walk out without a word.

"That was strange," Jade comments as the door shuts behind them.

"Actually, that's pretty normal," I reply, walking over to the bed. After popping the lid off the box with my name on it, my breath catches. The material inside is made of the night sky, full of stars and magic. As I pull the dress out, it grows in size until it's a full gown, falling around me with flair.

"Wow, Maddie. That's...gorgeous," Jade whispers, the look on her face full of awe. I walk over to the mirror, holding the dress up to me, and I have to agree. The shoulders are bare, with quarter sleeves running down the arms. The skirt is full, with a layer of mesh and lace over it that seems to move on its own. The desire to wear it right this minute is almost overwhelming, but I push it away. Putting it on will be the last thing I do before we go to the ball.

I turn just in time to watch Jade pull her dress out of the box. It's dark pink, and it complements her complexion perfectly. The sleeves are long, and there are jewels all over the outer layer.

"I'm supposed to wear this?" Jade asks, completely amazed.

"That's the plan."

After we lay our dresses out on the bed, I go through the rest of the items that were brought over. There are shoes, hair oils, and makeup.

"Wait, is that mine?" Jade grabs the bag, and I realize it is. They went into our rooms and brought us our own hygiene items. I'm not complaining about that part, just the part where they were in our space. Not that we truly have our own anything while we're in Faery.

"Please tell me how you've been," I say, sitting down in front of the mirror with my makeup bag in hand. I only use a few items from it usually, but tonight, I want to match the intensity of the dress.

"It's been strange, Maddie," Jade begins as she settles on the bench beside me. The mirror is large enough for the both of us, and I'm grateful for small favors. "Everyone is on high alert even though no one has mentioned any real danger. We still have classes like nothing is happening, and the teachers are trying to keep a smile on their faces, but we can see they're strained. It's like there's something they're not telling us."

I keep my face as neutral as possible because if the headmaster decided not to tell the school about the plague, I won't be doing so either. Aiden and his pack are good at keeping secrets, so I didn't expect there to be any leaks in the information. The thought of him makes me pause as I reach to apply eyeliner. I've been working so hard to not think about him.

"Vera is mostly back to her old self, although still a little more private," Jade continues, and I force myself to focus on her words. "Noel and I have been spending extra time together. I do like him; I just don't know if now is the right time."

That doesn't sit well with me, and I turn to Jade immediately.

"You can't wait for the perfect time," I say, my words coming out a little more forcefully than I intended. I dial down immediately. "I mean, you don't know what tomorrow holds. You guys are great together. I don't want you to miss out on something just because you're afraid of what could be."

She's silent for a moment as she studies me. It's difficult not to fidget under her scrutiny. But it's as if she's working up to say something I won't want to hear.

"Like you and Aiden?" she finally asks, and I shake my head immediately.

"Aiden and I are nothing like that. We have no future beside the trainer/student relationship we've been in. You and Noel are more than that."

"I don't think that's true, Maddie, and neither do you. Not the Noel part," she hurries on to add, reading the situation and where I was going to take it perfectly. "There's more to you and Aiden."

"Maybe on my part. But he—"

"He went to the forbidden forest for you," she interrupts. "I may not know everything that happened, but I know he made a bargain to help you. That's way more than just trainer/student."

I realize if that's all she knows, then she doesn't know about my father. There's a part of me that wants to dwell on her words, but I can't think about Aiden and what he means to me.

"He's been a moody mess since the queen took you. He's raged about it on more than one occasion. The pack have all been walking on eggshells around him."

"Jade, please stop," I whisper, not able to take any more of it. How I feel about the shifter is almost overwhelming. I can't allow myself a glimpse of hope because I know it won't do me any good. It'll just hurt so much more in the end.

"I'm not saying this to be cruel, Maddie." She reaches over, wrapping me in a side hug. "I just don't want you to regret not going after something that was important to you because you were afraid."

Well, she basically just threw my words back at me, but I'm not mad at her. She's right, and I'd be a hypocrite to say otherwise. But no matter how much I don't want it to be true, Aiden is promised to another. That's something I have to come to terms with before I ruin my heart forever.

"Jade, there's something I have to tell you." I say instead, knowing she needs to hear this from me. I won't tell her about the plague, not yet. But I will tell her my other secret.

"What is it, Maddie?"

"I know where my father is."

A FEW HOURS LATER, JADE AND I ARE SITTING IN THE CHAIRS NEAR the fireplace, both of us adorned in our gowns. The feel of the silky material against my skin is the purest form of pleasure. I keep running my hand over my stomach, mesmerized by the way the material twinkles. It's like there are actual stars on my midnight blue dress. We've talked about my dad, but mostly, it was me sharing memories of him.

"I feel like I understand you a little better," Jade comments with a small smile. "You'll get him back."

Before I can say anything, a knock on the door comes right before it opens. Kurtis, the head of my protection detail, steps through as Jade and I stand.

"I have come to escort you to the ballroom," he says, giving me a quick once over. While there is usually cool detachment in his gaze, this time, a spark of something almost close to approval comes over him before he's back to his stoic self.

"Jade, this is Kurtis. My personal warden." I smile sweetly, knowing just how much he hates it when I call him that. Or use his name so flippantly. While I know it's not his true name, the fae guard that more than life, it makes me feel better not calling him guard.

"Wow, he seems cheery," Jade comments as we follow him out of the room and down the stairs.

"He's a ball of laughs," I reply to his back, but he's too used to me now to even bother turning around. Not that I ever get under his skin. He's as cold as they come. When we finally reach the outer doors to the ballroom, I pause.

"Are you okay?" Jade asks, bringing Kurtis' attention to us. He doesn't look happy, but he also doesn't push me immediately into the room.

"I'm nervous. I haven't seen anyone in over a week now." My breath catches as I try to breathe and calm my nerves. A chill comes over my naked shoulders, traveling down my arms and spine. The dress has quarter sleeves, but I'm still cold all of a sudden.

"You look amazing, and everyone is eager to see you," Jade

comments, reaching over and taking one of my hands in hers. "Let's do this."

I smile gratefully and grip her hand tightly. It used to be that I was the brave one, but apparently, I've lost some of my edge. Kurtis pushes the doors open, motioning us inside. For some reason, he showed me this small kindness and I'm thankful. I give him a quick nod and then Jade and I are inside.

The room is huge, much larger than what it looks like from the outside. I'll never get over the underhanded way the magic works here. The ceiling has chandeliers that twinkle, the walls are adorned with murals and live vines blossoming with flowers. The queen stands on the other side of the floor, and as I look over, Kurtis takes his place beside her. Both of their heads are turned in our direction, and even though I can't meet her eye, I know she sees me. I incline my head in greeting, and she answers in kind before she lifts her hand and waves it in my direction. The magic reaches me instantly, and I try to figure out what she did.

"Maddie, your skin," Jade whispers, her voice full of awe. I glance down at my arms and find them covered in tiny glitter. Jade pulls out a small mirror from her pocket, because both of our dresses have them, and I look to find my cheeks and lips are covered in it as well. I look...ethereal. The queen gives me another nod as I glance at her, and this time, I return it with a little smile. I still have no idea why she's treating me this way, but for this one moment, I'll accept it.

Tables are set up on the outer perimeter, and there is dancing happening in front of the throne. Already, the room is filled with laughter and talking. The fae love their parties, and this one is no different. When I hear my name called, I spin around in time to be lifted straight off the floor by two strong arms.

"Ben, put me down!" I laugh, feeling like myself immediately. "You have got to stop doing that."

"Never!" he replies immediately before sobering up. "Unless you mean it. Then I'll stop."

"No." I squeeze his forearm reassuringly. "Never stop." He grins in response, and my heart fills with warmth at the sight of him. I've missed him.

"Move over, shifter," I hear and then Vera steps around Ben and is reaching for me as well. I hug her, then Noel, and everything seems to fall into place.

"Castle life has been good to you," Vera comments, looking at my dress and face.

"Today has been a good day," I reply, as vague as possible. I don't exactly want the queen to overhear me talking bad about this place. Not that she doesn't know I hate being here. "Let's dance!"

I'm soaking up every single second of the time I have with my friends, and I will do it to the fullness of my ability. Vera and Jade both grab my arms, and we stumble onto the dance floor. The music is louder in this part of the room, kept so by magic, no doubt. This isn't a typical ball that I've read about where everyone is dancing the same waltz. This is a place where everyone lets the music guide them, and that's exactly what we do. The boys join us, and as I bump into Ben, he lifts me and spins me around. My eyes catch on Owen who's watching from his position against the wall, and he smiles at me, almost making me stumble. He won't join us, but he's happy to see me.

Music gets louder as the voices rise up, and I don't care what I look like as I get lost in the moment. Because if I don't let myself go, I'll be too focused on the fact that Aiden is nowhere in sight.

❧ 22 ❧

The Spring Court sure knows how to party. My head is spinning from all the dancing and laughing. There's a sheen of sweat over my skin, and it only makes me glow in the low light. I haven't felt this much myself since before the Ancients came into the picture. It's as if all my worries have been stripped away. It's just me, my friends, and a world of possibilities.

Our group stumbles over to the nearest table, sweat dripping down our backs, laughing loudly. Well, Jade, Noel, and I are a little sweaty. The shifters regulate their temperature much better. Even so, when I wipe at my face, none of the glitter comes off, and at the moment, I'm thankful. I've felt the queen's eyes on me for most of the evening, but she hasn't asked me to approach. Thankfully.

"I'll be right back," I almost shout into Jade's ear as I push past the throng of people toward the closest door. My skin buzzes with adrenaline, my heart beating a mile a minute. When I glance back, my friends are all laughing, and it brings a smile to my own face. I push through the doors, almost tripping over my own feet, and the instant quiet hits me immediately. There's a magic in that as well as I look back past the threshold and into the ballroom. The contrast is staggering. Being out here in the quiet, my mind instantly clears.

I take a deep breath, turning to study my surroundings. The

hallway opens up in three directions, with the party at my back. Surprisingly, Kurtis hasn't followed me out, but I doubt I'm truly on my own. The queen has eyes everywhere, and I don't want to make things worse for myself by wandering somewhere I shouldn't be. But then I realize this area looks familiar, and my feet move before I even tell them to.

Walking over to my right, I come to a set of doors I've seen before. Without a second thought, I push them open, and the fresh air hits my flushed cheeks. I realize I'm in the small garden Aiden and I rushed through barely two weeks ago. The thought instantly makes my heart heavy, and I curse him for not being at the ball. I have no idea how he got away with it, maybe he's on patrol, but even though I know it would hurt me, I still want to see him.

Now that my head is cleared and my skin is less flushed, I feel more like myself. Even my magic seems more settled inside me, as if it needed this little reprieve as much as I did. I walk over to the nearest bench, settling myself on it slowly. Arranging the dress around me, I lean back, looking up at the night sky. It seems there are way more stars in this realm than at home, and the thought is bittersweet.

"It's strange, isn't it?"

His voice reaches me right before he steps out of the shadows. I should know better than to be surprised. Somehow, he always finds me. My heart leaps at the sight of him, the messy dark hair, the dark suit he wears. The top button of his dark blue shirt is unbuttoned, and it somehow makes him look even better.

"What is?" I ask as Aiden makes his way toward me. He takes a seat beside me, and I curl my hands, fisting the material of my dress to keep myself from reaching for him. Maybe some of my inhibitions are still lowered because it's a harder battle than it should be.

"How beautiful this place is but also how deadly."

I glance at him out of the corner of my eye and find him already watching me. Now that he's close, I can tell just how tired he looks. Underneath all this glitter, I carry the same bags under my eyes. My heart squeezes for him, and the desire to fall into his arms intensifies.

"Would you like to dance?" he asks suddenly, completely disarming my defenses. Aiden stands, placing his hand in front of me like a proper gentleman, and against all my internal alarms, I reach for it. His skin feels like heaven as his fingers wrap around mine, and he pulls me to my feet. Aiden's other hand slides across my back, pulling me against him as much as the dress allows. Even though I'm wearing wedges, he seems taller somehow. He begins to guide us in a simple waltz, something we all learn very early on in our covens. It's tradition, and he seems to be just as skilled in it. We don't need music, as we move to the rhythm of our hearts. The hearts that are beating in sync.

I thought I knew magic. I thought I understood the physics behind it. But now, I realize I've never known true magic until my heart is one with Aiden's, and we're gliding across the paved ground under the moonlight.

As if we're both overwhelmed by what we're feeling, we stop, and I raise my head to look into his eyes. There's a storm brewing there, and I feel my own eyes answer in kind. It's so hard to keep myself from moving closer, from closing the small space between us and finally knowing what he tastes like on my lips. His eyes flash, as if he can read my mind, and my skin flushes hotter. There's only one way I can stop this, and even though I hate myself for it, I ask the question anyway.

"Where's Natalie?"

Aiden narrows his eyes, not missing my tactic. Maybe it'd be better if I put some distance between us, but it's like I can't move away.

"Is that really what you want to know?" he replies, his gaze unyielding.

"It doesn't matter what I want," I say before I can stop myself. He spreads his hand out on my back, and I move just a fraction closer to him.

"Why doesn't it?" he asks, and we both know this is a dangerous game to play. Every time we've ended up here, it hasn't ended well for either of us.

"Have you found a way to stop the plague?" I ask my next question in the arsenal of dodging-the-issue-at-hand questions. A small chuckle escapes him at that, and I fight the urge to smile.

"It's always business with you, Duchess," he comments, finally releasing me from his hold. Yet, I still don't move.

"Someone has to keep an eye on the ball," I fire back, which earns me another chuckle.

"If you weren't wearing that dress, we'd see just how committed you are to keeping your eye on the ball."

That makes me stop. "What is that supposed to mean?"

"It means we haven't had a training session in days. Who's to say you can even handle yourself anymore." There's a gleam in his eye that I'm not used to. That's when something dawns on me. His inhibitions are lowered too. He's acting like Ben and Vera, freer than I've seen them in, well, ever.

"Aiden, I think the party may be affecting you."

"Maybe. Or maybe I'm just saying all the things I've been holding back."

I freeze as he comes close again, his breath washing over my cheeks. He raises his hand, running his fingertips over my cheek, a complete look of awe on his face.

"You look like magic," he whispers, filling my chest with so much emotion, I think it's going to choke me. "You always look like magic."

"Aiden." But he doesn't seem to hear me as he continues.

"The kind of magic that takes your breath away, but it's also unattainable. Like something from another world." His hand moves over to my hair, holding a strand between two fingers as he plays with it almost absentmindedly. "The first time I saw you, you took my breath away."

My emotions are beyond torn. I want to stop him, to keep him from saying something he'll regret later. But the selfish part of me, it wants to know what he truly thinks of me.

"You hated me on sight."

"I hated that you mesmerized me, and I could never have you."

Tears well up in my eyes at the raw emotion in his voice. I can't stop myself from reaching for him. I take his face into my hands, a palm at each cheek, as I pull his attention to me.

"You have no idea what that means to me," I say, trying to keep my tears at bay. Maybe if he doesn't remember this, I can show him a glimpse of my own feelings as well. "You will always have a place in my heart. But you need to let me go now. You're not yourself. You don't know what you're saying."

"My mind has never been clearer," he replies, shaking off my hands from his face and taking them into their own. He holds them over his heart, the heat from his skin sending pleasant sparks up my arms. "I am bound by duty, but my heart belongs—"

He doesn't get to finish his sentence as the screaming begins.

❦

I RACE INTO THE BALLROOM WITH AIDEN ON MY HEELS. THE SENSE of urgency has seemed to clear his mind enough to go fully on alert. We stop right inside the doors, a scene like something out of a horror movie opening up in front of us.

Every creature, fae, shifters, and witches alike, are screaming and writhing on the floor. About half of them are throwing up blood while the others are trying to help. My eyes search for my friends, but I can't see them.

"Aiden, where's your pack?" I ask, turning to the shifter beside me. He narrows his eyes, using his supernatural sight to see something I might not, and then he's reaching for my hand.

"Come on."

He leads me through the throng of people, his grip firm on my hand. A sea of bodies opens up in front of us and there they are. My eyes immediately land on the body on the floor and then I'm the one pulling Aiden behind me. Dropping to my knees, I slide right up to my friend, reaching for her. But before I can touch her, Aiden is there, wrapping his arms around my waist and pulling me away.

"Don't touch her!"

"Let me help her!" I scream, trying to get out of his tight grip. Jade doubles over with pain before she turns to her side and vomits blood. Vera, who's the closest to her, jumps back, completely horrified.

"We don't know how this spreads. You can't help her if you get sick too," Aiden hisses into my ear, and I go slack in his arms immediately. Getting in her blood would be the surest way to get sick, if we aren't already.

"Where's Noel?" I ask Vera as I look around me once more.

"He went to get a drink with Owen. Then this started, and—" She trails off, looking lost. Not that I blame her. I think at this point, Aiden's arms are the only thing holding me together. I give myself another second before I turn and look him in the eye.

"You can let go now. I'm okay."

He doesn't do so immediately, as if afraid if he does, I'll fall apart. Or disappear. Then, after a firm nod, he releases me, and I find my footing. Every part of me wants to reach for Jade, but I don't. I have to be smart about this.

Glancing up, I look for the queen. I know she was here when we first came in, but now she's gone. Probably ushered to her chambers for safety. I see some of the teachers on the floor as well, but no head-master. Or any of the Elders. Granted, I haven't seen them since the first day we got here. Some of the guards who are not sick have begun giving orders, trying to keep everyone under control, but it's not doing much.

"We need to get her out of here. And find the rest of our friends." Aiden nods before he walks over to the closest table and rips the table-cloth from it, shattering the dishes. Then, he walks back over to Jade, careful not to get into any of the blood. Placing the tablecloths over her, he lifts her into his arms, and I reach over to cover her face as well.

"You'll be okay, Jade. We'll make sure of it."

We turn to go with Vera behind us, and I still don't see Noel or Ben or Owen anywhere. But there are so many creatures around, I can hardly see the walls. I'll have to use my magic to get us out of here, but when I raise my hand to call on it, a loud boom sounds throughout the room. Jade is lifted right out of Aiden's arms, and before either one of us can do anything about it, we blink and we're no longer in the room.

Twisting around, I find that we've all been transported into the throne room. Well, all the healthy creatures at least. The throne is empty, but then the noise brings my attention to the balcony, and I see the queen stand.

"It seems a plague has come into our court," she says, her voice clearly heard by every single creature in the room. "The sick are to be kept in the ballroom, quarantined for the time being, as we search the cause of this sickness." There are murmurs all around, but all she has to do is clear her throat and everyone falls silent. "Leave and return to your rooms and houses. Interactions between other individuals are to be kept to a minimum."

Just like that, everyone disperses. I turn to Vera, her eyes huge and filled with worry and fear.

"Get back to the academy," I say, giving her a comforting smile. "I'm sure the headmaster will have more information for you there."

"You can't come with me?"

"I can't."

We embrace then, even though we're not supposed to be touching, and she follows the rest of the student body out the door. Aiden doesn't move, staying as close to me as possible as the room empties out. I'm hoping he forgot our exchange, even though I will never be able to. But that's just another burden I will bear for the both of us.

"Go find your pack," I say, hoping they're okay. I couldn't see if they were in the room or not, so I still have hope.

"What about you?"

I look over my shoulder and find the queen's eyes on me.

"I have to get back to my room," I reply, turning back to Aiden. He studies me for a tense moment, and it's like he wants to say something, but at the last moment changes his mind.

"I'll come see you the moment I can," he says before turning on his heels and sprinting for the door.

I watch his retreating back and then, once again, I'm all alone.

❧ 23 ❧

Before I can take two steps in any direction, Kurtis is there. I don't even ask why, just motion for him to lead the way. The castle staff moves around me in a control frenzy as the quarantine is put into place. I wish there was a way I could see if the rest of my friends are in that room, but when the queen summons, I don't say no.

"Madison Hawthorne, your prediction seems to have come true," the queen greets me as I step into her chambers. I've never been in here before. We usually keep our lessons to the library or the gardens. This room is larger than any I've been in, besides the throne and the ballroom. Her bed sits to one side and could probably fit a dozen people easily. Everything is adorned in throws and there are pillows on every surface made for sitting. The fireplace is on the other side of the room, and it's taller than I am. The gold design almost blinds me as I do a quick scan. This is definitely a room fit for a queen.

"Not my prediction, Your Highness." I feel inclined to point out. I never quite know how much I can get away with when talking to her, but I'm not about to take ownership of what happened in that room. My heart squeezes just thinking of my friends and the rest of the students who have gotten sick.

"Maybe not, but you brought the message to me, and now it is here." Her eyes are cold as she watches me, and that's when I realize what she means.

"I didn't make this happen. You said you can feel my magic. Have I used it?"

Her eyes narrow, but she doesn't answer right away. I glance over at Kurtis, but as usual, I can't tell what he's thinking. I can't let myself forget in how much danger I am constantly in. But right now, the worry overpowers everything.

"You have not," the queen finally answers, and I breathe a little easier. I need to be more careful. I know that. "Now, you will."

"What?"

"You will write a story to cleanse my court of this illness. And only my court." At first, the words don't register.

"I can't," I stammer, looking at the queen as if she's lost her mind. Not even two days ago we had an exercise that went poorly, and now she wants me to use my magic on people.

"This was not a request," the queen states, her cold stare going right through me. I understand what she wants, but I'm not ready for that kind of magic. I've been exhausted for days after the last exercise. A part of me is not even sure I'll be able to do it. Even if I wanted to, which I absolutely don't.

"My magic is weak, it wouldn't work."

"Your magic may be weak but only because you refuse to use the proper channels. Do not think I do not know you have been trying to substitute your Hawthorne water magic for the story spell casting. I can read you like a book."

"Then why let me?" I raise my voice, throwing my hands in the air. "Why am I even here? My spell brought us to Faery, and I am sorry I have messed up your way of life, but all I want is to get back to my school and to my world. Why keep me here?"

"Because you are valuable!" Queen Amaryllis' voice booms around me, shaking the walls. Her eyes flash, and I can taste the raw power of her magic. "You are a tool, and I will use whatever means necessary to ensure my court is the last one standing. If you want to keep your precious school safe, then you will do as I command."

My body shakes as she speaks, from anger or fear, I can no longer tell. A million things rush through my mind, but I can't seem to articulate any of them. It doesn't matter anyway because she's not done.

"You have till tomorrow morning to speak your decision. Go!"

With that, she turns and leaves the room while Kurtis steps forward. I put up my hand, stopping him from reaching for me. But I realize I have no idea how to get to my room from this part of the castle, since I've never been here before. So instead of storming out of the room, I wait for Kurtis to lead the way. I'm surprised to find my room is actually quite close to the queen's chambers, only two hallways away. But maybe, I shouldn't be surprised at all. She has me here for a reason.

When I step through the doorway, the door shuts at my back with a slam. Alone for the first time, I drop to my knees, hiding my face in my hands. The plethora of emotions overcome me all at once, and I find it difficult to take in a full breath. Tears smear my mascara as I cry for everything that has happened and everyone who got hurt.

My heart bursts with pain as I think of Jade. I have no idea who else is sick, and I'm afraid that when I do find out, it will already be too late. If I could write a story spell to wipe it all away, I would. But I'm not strong enough to do something so...risky. Because the last time I tried, I brought us to Faery. What if I try to erase the sickness and instead erase my friends?

The sadness is quickly replaced by anger, and I get to my feet only to grab the closest thing to me and fling it across the room. There's a thud as the decorative pillow hits the wall but I'm not done. I kick at the chairs, turning them over as I fling a tapestry off the wall. I wish I could punch something. I wish I could stop being so useless. The rage builds and builds until I can't take it anymore. I drop down to all fours, not sure what I'm going to do. But then, something stops me.

When the knock sounds, it's so faint I barely hear it. Then, it comes a little more insistently, making me sit up. I glance at the door and listen, but when the third knock sounds, it's not coming from the door.

Quickly, I jump off the floor and hurry to the window. Pulling the curtains back, I gasp as Aiden smirks at me through the glass. I unlatch the lock, swinging the window open, and Aiden lands softly on his feet right inside my room.

Since I'm on an upper floor, the queen didn't deem it necessary to lock the windows like she locks the doors. Which I am truly grateful for at the moment.

"How did you..." I begin to ask when Aiden places a finger to his lips and motions toward the door. Before I know what to do, the shifter dives under my bed just as the door swings open, and Kurtis walks in.

"Can I help you with something?" I ask, not disguising the annoyance in my voice. Kurtis' eyes swing to the open window, and he marches over to it to look out. "Hello?"

"Why is this open?"

"Because I needed some fresh air," I snap, placing my hands on my hips. It takes serious self-control not to glance at my bed and make sure Aiden is hidden. But I trust him to take care of himself, at least in this situation. Kurtis gives me a suspicious look before pulling the window closed and latching it again.

"Leave it until the morning. You need to go to bed," he commands. He motions toward my dress, and I realize I haven't changed after the ball. Quickly, I reach for my nightgown, holding it in front of me, but Kurtis doesn't move. Annoyed and a little terrified he'll search my room further, I step behind the changing curtain and quickly strip and put on the nightgown.

When I step out, Kurtis hasn't moved. He gives me a quick once over and then marches out the door. I stay in my spot, not daring to even breathe for fear of giving something away, even after the door is closed. It's another few seconds before Aiden stands in front of me.

"That answers that then," he comments, giving my room a once over.

"What?"

"I wondered if the windows had a magical alarm system like the doors. It seems so."

Truth be told, I'm not surprised. The queen watches me like a hawk. I guess it's too much to ask for her to trust me with an open window.

"Is he always like that?" Aiden nods toward the closed door. I cross my arms in front of me, realizing I'm wearing little besides this cloth.

"Basically." That doesn't sit well with the shifter, so I hurry to change the subject. "What are you doing here?"

"I told you I'd come see you as soon as I could." He shrugs as he proceeds to walk around the room. I follow his line of sight, trying to see this place from his point of view. It might seem glamorous, and yes, it is, but it's still a prison. A prison made up of pretty walls. And a little messy from my earlier outburst.

"What have you found out?" I ask, not sure what to do with myself now that we're alone in my room. I realize it's been weeks since we've spent any time together like this. Not that I'd tell him, but I miss our training sessions.

"Noel and Ben are both sick."

His words squeeze at my heart, and I shake my head, as if I can make the truth disappear. Walking over to the chair in front of the fireplace, I sit, my emotions high.

"Owen?"

"He's fine."

"Natalie?" I almost don't ask, but I have to know.

"She's sick."

"I'm sorry." And I am. No one deserves what they're going through. It seems I'm continuously helpless to do something about it. Unless I do what the queen commands. "She wants me to write a spell."

"No!" The outburst surprises me. I look over at Aiden, and the fear in his eyes, before he manages to mask it.

"What do you know?" I lean forward, my full attention on him. He looks away, as if he said something he shouldn't have. "Aiden."

"Liam and I talked about..."

"About me."

"Yes." He turns to face me again, leaning forward as well. "He said story casting is dangerous. It...it takes something from the storyteller."

"What?"

"Part of you. Part of your story."

The words slam into me, making the room spin even though I'm sitting down. Aiden is kneeling in front of me in a flash, his eyes full of concern. For someone who guards his emotions so carefully, he's letting me see too much.

"What does that mean exactly?" I whisper, staring at the flames over Aiden's head.

"He doesn't know. He just knows it will steal parts of you and your magic. Every time you cast."

I guess it makes sense if I think about it. Liam was so worried about me after I brought the academy here. And after, he kept asking about my magic. It's true that it took longer for it to replenish itself, and that's not something I've experienced before. But everything seems to have gone back to normal.

"The queen has commanded me to story cast the sickness out of her court. And only out of her court. She wants to use it as a battle tactic."

Aiden and I stare at each other, realizing at the same time the amount of magic that would take. The toll it would have on me.

"I don't know how to get out of it," I say, honestly. She let me go tonight, but tomorrow, she'll be back to demand her spell, and there's nothing I'll be able to do about it.

"We'll figure it out," Aiden says, bringing my attention back to him. He takes my hands in his, holding them on my lap. This is the side of him I've only seen once. He's gentler with me than he's ever been, and it brings tears to my eyes. "We'll figure it out," he says again, and I nod, swallowing the sadness. This is no place or time for such frivolous emotion. But his kindness disarms me, and I don't know what to do about that.

I lean back, closing my eyes because it's harder for the tears to leak through. Aiden gives my hands a gentle squeeze before I feel him moving away. I've taken the coward's way out. The moment could've turned into something, but it's not something we could come back from. Well, not something my heart would be able to recover from.

It's been days since I've slept well, but with Aiden here, I feel safe for the first time in forever.

"Will you stay?" I ask without opening my eyes. It's safer this way, at least for me.

"I don't think I have much of a choice." I roll my head to the side, meeting his eyes briefly before I close mine once more. He's right of course. If I open the window again, Kurtis will come back, and I doubt Aiden would be able to get away. "When was the last time you slept?" the shifter asks, and I smile.

"I don't know. I haven't felt safe enough to really try."

Maybe it's my tired brain talking because I don't mean to reveal that much. At least I'm not looking at him, so I can't see what he thinks of my small confession.

"You can rest easy, Duchess." His voice is soft, and it's like the first drops of rain on my heated skin. I've come to love that nickname, even though I don't agree with it. "I'll keep watch."

Settling a little more comfortably in my chair, I smile without opening my eyes.

"Tell me a story."

I'm not sure what possesses me to ask, but the words are out, and Aiden surprises me once more when he complies.

"Did you know that when I was a young wolf, I was terrified of witches."

"You? I can't imagine you scared of anything." I chuckle, already being lulled into slumber with the sound of his voice. There's a small pause before he speaks again.

"You'd be surprised." I want to comment on that, but I'm already fading. "There wasn't a coven anywhere nearby, so I grew up with a very skewed view of witches. The first time I met one, she was angry at my father for something and came barreling down toward us with wind flying all around her. She looked enraged, and I shifted immediately and hid behind my dad. My dad made up with her, and she ended up being a babysitter of sorts anytime he needed to go into the city."

There's sweetness in his memory, and I can hear the smile in his voice. The next thing I know, strong arms are lifting me up, and I barely open my eyes to find my body cradled against a strong chest.

"You're buff," I say to his chest and feel him chuckle. "And brave," I mumble as I feel myself being placed carefully on soft sheets. The presence of him beside me makes me feel invincible, so when he moves to go, I grab his arm and pull him onto the bed beside me.

"No, stay. Safe."

He chuckles again but doesn't move away, just stretches out beside me. My eyes open just a crack, and I find myself looking up at him. Satisfied, I let my eyes drift shut and snuggle deeper into the covers.

"Strong and brave," I mumble. "Protector." Silence greets me, and soon, I'm back in dreamland. But through the fog, I hear a gentle whisper.

"If you only knew how terrified I am when I'm around you."

24

When I wake up, something is missing. My hand runs over the space beside me, and maybe I dreamed being curled up against Aiden in the night. But then I hear a noise. I glance over to see him tending to the fire, and I know I didn't. He stayed with me, and he held me while I slept. It was the first fully restful night in ages.

"How did you sleep?" he asks when he sees that I'm awake, and I stretch my hands over my head before I reply.

"I actually slept, which says a lot."

"I'm glad."

We stare at each other, a new kind of intensity between us, and I don't know what to say or do. Do I say thank you? Or do I ignore the fact that I overheard him confessing how scared he is around me? Instead, the decision is made for me when I hear the clock chime.

"Oh no," I say, jumping off the bed. "You have to get out of here before they find you."

I hurry over to my closet and pull out one of the dresses the queen has given me. When I turn, Aiden is standing in the middle of the room, staring at me. Electricity sparks between us, and if I could bottle it up, it would make my magic seem like child's play.

"Go, Aiden. Before you get in trouble."

He nods, moving to the window. After another searing look at me, he reaches for the latch.

"Promise you won't spell cast," he says when I join him at the window.

"I'll do my best," I reply before yanking the window open. He jumps from the ledge without a word and hurries off. When he's out of sight, I pull the nightgown over my head just as the door opens at my back, and Kurtis walks in.

"Maybe knock!" I exclaim appalled as I pull the dress in front of me. Not that he cares, since he's fae, and they run around naked sometimes. Just for fun. For some reason though, he gives me the decency of turning around, and I hurry to pull the dress over my shoulders. Once I'm done, I close the window and walk over to the mirror to pull my hair back into a ponytail. I'm not about those fancy hairdos, that's for sure. I'd rather leave it down, but if I'm to fight battles today, I need to look ready for one.

"Are you ready to begin?" the queen asks when I step into her chambers. I frown, confused at her tone.

"I thought I had time to decide."

"We both know what you're going to decide," the queen replies, walking over to the large window and looking out. There's something so unnerving about seeing her this nonchalant. Her court is in grave danger, and she seems to not have a care in the world. Treading carefully is a must when it comes to her, but I already decided to be firm.

"Then maybe we don't have the same idea of what that is."

Her laugh surprises me, sending a chill down my spine. There is always a sense of otherworldliness about her in the way she moves and the way she speaks. But at this moment, there's a touch more of it, and it turns my blood cold.

"You are an interesting creature, Madison Hawthorne. So much raw power, so untapped." She turns to me then before she waves her hand, and the doors on the opposite side of the room open up. She walks through, and when Kurtis almost pushes me in, I follow. It seems to be a portal directly to her throne room. It's why I've never seen her walk the hallways. She doesn't have to.

Once there, I'm surprised to find the room empty. I'm not sure what I was expecting, but maybe something to convince me to do the spell. The queen walks over to her throne, taking a seat as if nothing is the matter. She doesn't speak, and I don't volunteer either. We stay like that for a few very tense minutes, but I have no idea what she's doing.

"You really do not want to help your friends?" she finally asks, turning her full attention to me. Today, she's wearing a deep green dress, and the gold crown on her head seems more intimidating than ever before.

"Of course I want to help my friends."

"Hmm, yet, here we are. If you do not cleanse my court, and only my court, you cannot save your friends."

The threat is evident, and I'd be stupid not to heed to it. But I don't know how to do what she asks and not lose myself in the process. My magic is already unstable, and after what Aiden told me, there isn't a way for me to do what she wants and not hurt myself in the process.

"Your Highness." I have to make her understand. "My magic is unconventional and confusing. I need more information. Maybe if you let me go back to the academy, the teachers there would be able to help me find out more about it. Maybe then I can—"

"You think they know more than me?" she snaps, cutting off my plea. "You do not learn from those who do not understand."

Confusion clouds my mind as I try to figure out what she means. How could they not understand? And why would she? Forgetting all protocol, I have no choice but to call her out on it. If I'm punished for disrespecting her, then so be it. I need answers.

"You have never explained to me why you decided to teach me." I stand up a little straighter, hoping my voice sounds as confident as I wish it to. "You basically imprisoned me within these walls and made me play with my magic in front of you and never gave me an ounce of direction. How can I learn if you don't actually teach me? How can you understand if this magic is so rare?"

Her eyes flash, and for a moment, I think she'll strike me dead right here and right now. But then she leans forward, her complete attention on me, and I feel her magic rising up inside of her.

"Silly child, no one has ever been truthful with you, have they?" What an odd question, but I don't get a chance to comment as she continues. "Story spell casting is as ancient as the creatures waking up all over the world. The evil that brought you to my doorstep is the same evil that created what is inside of you."

"I don't...I don't understand."

"Story spell casting has been around since the world began, and it was first spoken by the Ancients. I know it because I too possess a pinch of it. Not as powerful as you, of course. It is not my main magic. That is reserved for the Ancients."

At first, I don't think I hear her right. What she is saying can't be true. But fae can't lie.

"No, that's not possible. I can't be...evil."

Her laugh rings out all around me, sending a chill down my spine.

"You are not evil, child," she says. "But you can be. With the right direction."

That's what she's been trying to do? She's been molding me in her own way, and I haven't even realized it. I wonder if anything we've done helped her cause, but how would I even be able to tell?

"I see the horror on your face. It is a sight to behold." The queen smiles, and there is no kindness there. "Now, I believe you need an extra motivator."

She flicks her hand and the doors to the left open. My heart drops in my chest as two guards walk in, dragging a body between them.

"Aiden!"

I move toward him, but my feet won't cooperate. Glancing at the queen I find her hand raised, holding me in place. Aiden is dumped at the foot of the throne, and I can't do anything but watch. He raises his head slightly, and I can barely see him through the tears pooling in my eyes.

"What game are you playing?!" I scream at the queen as I fight against my magical restraints. She leans back on her throne, flipping hair over her shoulder as she grins at me once more.

"Does it really matter? I intend to win."

"WHY CAN'T YOU UNDERSTAND THAT I DON'T KNOW WHAT YOU

want me to do?" I yell, straining against my invisible restraints. The queen flicks her hand again, and Aiden screams, his body twisting with agony. "Stop, just stop!"

I'm showing all my cards, but I can't bear to see him like this. There are cuts all over his body, as if he's been whipped repeatedly. He has shackles over one of his wrists, and I recognize them as the ones they used on me to keep my magic dormant. Aiden can't shift, and if he can't shift, he heals much slower.

"You do know what to do," the queen says, leaning to one side as she watches me. "It is buried deep in your blood. All you have to do is reach for it."

"I don't know how!"

"You do."

Another wave of the hand and Aiden is lifted straight up before being slammed to the ground. My throat is hoarse from all the screaming, and I can't see well through the tears. It feels like my heart is split in two, and it's bleeding all over the place. Aiden grunts, rolling over to the side. At first, I think one of his arms is broken, but then, he moves it, opening his eyes and looking up at me.

"I'm okay," he mumbles over the blood pooling in his mouth, and I can't take it anymore. His words burn through me, and I scream, thrusting my hands in his direction. My magic leaves me with the speed of a bullet. Before it can reach Aiden, it dissipates. I look up at the queen as she narrows her eyes at me.

"That is not the magic I am looking for." She curls her hand into a fist, and Aiden jerks in pain again.

There's annoyance in her voice now, and I can see her growing impatient with every moment I don't deliver what she wants. A part of me can't even understand why she doesn't do something herself. She has plenty of magic, and yet, she wants mine. Just then, a guard rushes into the room, and the queen snaps her attention away from Aiden.

"Your Highness." The guard bows as the queen raises her hand, this time in the direction of the guard. "The general has requested your presence immediately."

The general? The queen stands, retracting her arm and magic from the guard. Her cold exterior doesn't change, but something tells me she's not happy with the turn of events.

"Take them to the dungeon while I deal with this mess," Queen Amaryllis says, descending the stairs and walking out the room without another glance at me. Kurtis waves his hand, and the guards surround us, grabbing me by the arm with a familiar shackle clicking into place over my wrist.

"What's happening?" I ask my guard, but he ignores me. They drag us out the throne room and toward a door at the back of the hallway. Without much fanfare, I'm half carried down the stairs before they deposit me on the cold floor. They're a lot less gentle with Aiden, and as he lands beside me, I crawl over to him. "Jerk," I mumble, glaring daggers at Kurtis. He gives me one of his steady looks before he shuts the bars and leaves us behind.

"Aiden, can you hear me?" I ask as I turn him over and cradle his head on my knees. When he looks up at me, it takes me a moment to collect myself. He looks even worse up close. "I'm sorry. I'm so sorry you're in this mess because of me." I place my forehead against his, the tears running down my cheeks and into his hair. A feather of a touch on my elbow brings my attention up, and I look over to see him reaching for me. He pulls me down as I hold him close, wishing there was a way I could take it all away.

"Don't cry, Duchess," he says, his words a little muffled by his bruised face. "I'll be good as new as soon as I shift."

"You shouldn't even be here," I reply, raising my head to look at him. "What happened?"

"They grabbed me as soon as I stepped into the forest," Aiden replies before he moves to sit up. I guide him up, and we scoot enough that his back is against the cell's wall. "It's like they knew I would there."

"She's always one step ahead." I shake my head, frustration burning in my veins. "No matter how hard I try, I can't win against her."

"You didn't do the spell."

"No. I would've. When I saw you..." I stop, swallowing hard. "I don't know what she wants from me, and she keeps saying that I do, which makes me even more confused." I need my family. I need them to be here so we can figure this out together. But I feel a million worlds apart from them. No one is coming to save me. I have to do that myself. But I have no idea how. We stay like that for a while, and then, when I can't hold them in anymore, the tears come again.

"Hey." Aiden reaches over, wiping another escaped tear off my cheek. "We'll get through this."

"Don't be nice to me," I reply, hiccuping over my tears. "It confuses me."

He smiles then, or tries to, and it breaks my heart all over again. I will never understand the magic I feel when I'm around him, will never be able to explain how we got here, but it's like he's my person and that's where it starts and ends. He must see a change in my eyes because he cups my face, bringing it closer.

"Let me try something," I say, getting to my knees and reaching for his shackle. He nods, giving me permission to do whatever I'm about to do. Closing my eyes, I search for that energy within me. With my own shackle over my wrist, I'm not sure if this will work, but I have to try. I can't stand the sight of him so broken.

Opening my eyes, I wrap my hands around the metal, and it heats up under my touch immediately. Aiden looks up surprised, but I shake my head. I need to concentrate.

> *"Things that are closed must be opened,*
> *And that which was padlocked must be unlatched.*
> *These are the rules that I have spoken,*
> *And they are to be obeyed and done."*

The metal shakes under my hands and then, it snaps open. Aiden glances at me as I grin tiredly, even that much magic took something from me.

"You shouldn't have——"

"Shift, Aiden. Just shift," I interrupt, and as I watch, he does.

His wolf is more beautiful than I remember. As I slouch against the wall, he moves toward me, nuzzling against my hand. Smiling, I run my hand over the soft fur on his face, then down his back. As I lean forward, he changes back to human and our faces are only inches apart. His face is clean of all cuts and the color is back in his eyes.

We watch each other with a new kind of an awe, saying a hundred things without any of them being spoken. His hand reaches for my cheek once more, and I lean into it, needing the feel of him against my skin.

"Can I kiss you?" His whisper washes over my flushed face, and time itself seems to stop.

"I insist that you do," I reply, right before his lips crush over mine. There is no awkwardness of a first kiss, no fumble of hands. We fit together as if we've been made for each other, and it's a special kind of magic all on its own. I pull him close, wrapping my arms round his neck, as he picks me up and places me on his lap. We're hungry for each other, and I'm not sure which one of us is the predator and which one is the prey. All I know is that I never want to stop kissing him.

"You seem to have found your motivation." A voice sounds at my back, and I pull away to watch Kurtis step into the light. "Now, we should probably be going."

❄ 25 ❄

"What are you talking about?" I ask, standing up and facing Kurtis straight on. Aiden rises beside me, a steady presence at my back. My skin feels hot, and I'm probably blushing, but I need to push all that away and focus on the situation at hand.

Kurtis doesn't answer right away but walks over and unlocks the cell's door. Stepping inside, he motions me forward, pointing to the shackle around my wrist.

"May I?"

I'm so surprised, I don't question him. He takes the shackle, unlocking it with a key, before he walks back over to the doors.

"We need to go. Now."

"I don't understand."

"Quick recap. I'm getting you out of here. Since you used your magic, the queen will think you did it on your own. She feels you using the magic, she doesn't know how much. So, let's get you back to the academy before she realizes something is amiss."

"Why?" I have to know. I don't trust anyone but the boy beside me right now.

"Because you can help us defeat the Ancients. But you can't do it if the queen is using you as her own puppet. There are much greater stakes involved here." He glances up, as if he hears something we don't. "We need to go."

I glance at Aiden, gauging his reaction. He looks at Kurtis before looking back at me. Then he nods, and I take that at face value.

"Lead the way," I say, motioning Kurtis forward. We follow him out the door and up the stairs. At the top, he motions for us to wait as he steps into the hallway. Aiden presses close beside me, and it's difficult not to look at him and think of what we just did. That kiss was made for storybooks, and I feel it in every part of me. I think I always will.

Aiden's gaze is as heated as my skin. He looks down, and I see him reaching for my hand. He holds his own out, as if asking for permission. Without hesitation, I place my own in it. The moment our skin touches, sparks shoot up my arm and over my body.

"Let's go," Kurtis says, popping back in, and we don't hesitate to follow him out.

"Where's the queen?" I ask, keeping my voice low.

"The Ancients have reached Faery," Kurtis replies, keeping his movements swift as we rush down the hallway. "There have been battles all across our lands for weeks, but now, the plague has weakened our defenses, and the Ancients are ready to take their place as rulers."

"I thought they wanted to destroy," I say as Kurtis pulls a door open, and suddenly, we're outside.

"They want to cleanse. Your world will fall first, then Faery. Then all the other worlds in between. They're powerful and hungry. Faery is the one place where magic is not diluted. They're taking its power from it."

"They did that in Hawthorne," I realize, thinking back to what my family has told me. Being here, I was so focused on my own problems, I forgot there's a magical war going on.

"How does Maddie play into that?" Aiden asks as Kurtis stops at the outer wall of the castle grounds.

"Your story spell casting is part of the puzzle. It's powerful magic, and it's as old as time. The queen wants to strike a bargain with the Ancients. If you write a story for her, one they cannot get out of, she will gain their favor and protection. She's been looking for it for a long time, and you've been on her radar. It's always about power, and you have a good chunk of it."

I let that sink in, realizing that maybe us ending up here wasn't so much only my doing. If she's been looking for my exact type of magic, it could've affected my spell without me even realizing it.

"Why are you really helping us?"

Kurtis moves his hands over the wall and then a door appears. He pulls it open, and the forest greets us on the other side.

"Liam wasn't the only one to grow up outside of this place," the fae guard finally says, a bit of sadness entering his voice. "I've done some terrible things to prove my worth to the queen, but I don't regret the choices I've made if it means saving the world I left behind. "

For some reason, I don't think he means just the world. He left someone behind, and the fae, they live for hundreds of years, and their memory lives on even longer.

"I appreciate what you have done," I say as Aiden ducks through the door. Kurtis nods but doesn't say anything else. I wish I had time to ask him all the questions I want to ask. But I don't. As Aiden and I run into the woods, the door shuts behind us.

My head spins with all the information we've learned, but my heart is heavy for the people we left behind. Our sick friends are still in there, and I just hope Kurtis stays out of the queen's way. I can't have anyone else on my conscience.

"We need to hurry. If he's right, the queen is already looking for us," Aiden says when I pause. But something is amiss, I can feel it in my bones.

"Aiden, wait," I say, pulling him to a complete stop. The forest is dark around us, even though I think it's still early in the day. I don't know how long we've been in the dungeon, but it couldn't have been that long. The feel of danger hangs low in the air, but as I look around, I don't see anything.

"What is it?" the shifter whispers, his eyes on my face.

"I'm not sure. Something is coming."

We exchange a look and then I let Aiden lead me toward the academy. Everything is happening at once. I have no idea if I'll be able to handle it, or if Kurtis got us out for nothing.

WE RACE THROUGH THE FOREST WITH AIDEN LEADING THE WAY. MY head feels a little light, but it's better than what I expected after the use of my magic. In fact, the lightness is more of a buzz. As if I'm getting a power up instead of a drainage. Nothing is what it seems and everything about my life stopped making sense a long time ago.

The queen knew about me. Somehow, someway, she knew about me. I can't stop thinking that maybe I didn't ruin everything with my spell. Maybe it was always supposed to go this way.

"We're almost there," Aiden says after about ten minutes of weaving around the trees. He said we had to take the long way, just in case, and I trust his judgement. He hasn't let go of my hand since he took it. Not that thinking about that kiss is appropriate right now, but I can't shake it. I don't want to shake it.

"What are we going to do when we get there?" I ask a few minutes later when Aiden pauses.

"Go to Headmaster?" he replies, giving me a quick smile. "Whatever it is, we'll figure it out. Let's go."

I nod, and then we burst through the trees. The school looms in front of us, and the sight makes my heart leap with joy. I never thought I'd be this happy to see the academy. There's help to be found there and hope. We can save our friends; I just know it.

However, before we're even halfway across the lawn, that feeling of danger overpowers me and then I'm lifted into the air. Aiden is ripped away from me right before we're slammed into the ground. Disoriented, I push to my feet, my head spinning from the impact. Aiden gets to his feet as well, and then he growls, his attention on something over my shoulder.

I turn slowly to find Queen Amaryllis and her guards walking slowly out of the forest. My eyes narrow, but I don't see Kurtis with them, and I wonder what that means for the guard. The man that walks beside the queen now looks about fifty years old, with silver hair and an outfit full of armor. This must be the general.

"Aiden, get inside."

"What? I'm not leaving you."

"Please, this is between me and her."

"No." He grabs my hands, spinning me around to face him. "I stand by your side. Always."

Looking at him now, I wonder how I was ever going to survive not being with him. I know that's still on the table. After all, he's promised to another. But the fact that he cares, the fact that he's there for me, it makes all the difference. But I won't let him get hurt. Not again. I reach for the magic inside of me, and it answers happily.

"I'm sorry," I say, receiving a confused look, right before I push the magic at Aiden. Water rushes out of the ground, picking him off his feet and carrying him right into the school's front doors. He lands on all fours and jumps up quickly. The panicked look in his eye is evident, even from this far away, but I'm done putting those I care about in danger. He moves forward, but I slam the water and the doors, shutting them in his face.

"This door locks and keeps him safe," I mumble, hoping that's enough to keep the academy on lockdown.

"Someone is feeling a little more powerful," the queen says, broadcasting her voice toward me. I turn slowly, the energy of the water magic running all through me. I've been so afraid of what this can do to me and to my loved ones, I forgot the part where it can save them. Breaking that shackle didn't feel like a chore. It felt natural and easy. Not something the queen or the headmaster was making me do, but something I wanted to do.

"I'm not helping you," I say, knowing she can hear me. "I'm done being a puppet. For you, for the academy. I'm in control of my own magic."

"What changed?" the queen asks, and I think she's genuinely curious. She couldn't break me with her exercises and her threats. I found my center all on my own.

"I did," I say, a smile splitting my lips.

That doesn't sit well with her. She raises her arms, and with them, roots spring up from the ground, racing toward me. I focus on the moisture all around me, and just like that, I feel it everywhere. Thrusting my arms in front of me, the moisture flies toward me and turns at my shoulders, racing toward the queen. The thorns and water clash, sending a small earthquake through the meadow. The guards stumble while the queen and I stay upright.

"Why are you doing this?" I shout as I pull up a wall of water between me and the queen. There's so much hatred on her face, it shocks me into stillness. That's all it takes. One of her roots get through, sweeping me off my feet. I drop to the ground, but I don't let go of my magic. The magic and me are one.

"I will not be played for a fool," the queen roars, sending another wave of her magic toward me. I block it, my battle and water magic merging together for a stronger shield. I think I hear shouts coming from behind me, but I'm not turning away from the issue at a hand.

"You want me to help you defend the Ancients, I can. But you can't hold me and my friends prisoner."

"I want your magic, you fool. I do not need you to save me."

But she does. No matter how much she talks, that's all it is. I realize she's worried. Worried that her court will not withstand, that she will be the one to fall. She was working to make my magic take pieces of me until there was nothing left. Until she could take my magic. It's like a rubber band snapping into place. Everything seems to make sense, and I don't know where the clarity is coming from, but I'm grateful for it.

Embrace your heritage. Embrace those who have come before you.

It's like there is a voice speaking directly in my mind. I realize that's what I've been missing. Connection. My magic connected to the story spell casting which connected to the history it carries with it. Maybe that's where this sudden knowledge is coming from, from those who've come before me. But I know what to do.

I still my heart and think of my friends and my family. The queen is shouting orders, and I feel her magic pulling at my water shield. The guards are running toward me, ready to take me down, but I don't move. I find my center and I speak.

> *"When Winter leaves, Spring takes its place,*
> *When snow melts, flowers grow in its footprints.*
> *There is no power stronger than that of love,*
> *There is no story more interesting than of us."*

I glance back at the academy, at the faces pressed against the glass as they watch helplessly. I find Aiden, the look of fear and rage on his face, and I smile.

"A girl learned a secret; she carried it in her heart,
She worried, and fretted, and hid,
So, no one would be the wiser and they would never be torn apart.
But a queen found a loophole,
And tore at the seams.
The girl learned another secret, but still, nothing was as it seems.
But that time has come for the words to be spoken.
And the girl, she's no longer afraid or broken.
She found herself and the secrets within,
She's more than she seems and so are they.
Her home is a place, but it's also a people.
And the queen is not welcome, nor is she able
To break through the bonds of love and friendship.
To destroy the sanctuary the girl is creating.
The girl says, Leave! And the queen obeys.
This is now her place and she is the one who holds the keys."

My head is thrown back as I utter the last word, and then my body feels like it's being torn apart. I scream as light and water twirls around me like a tornado and then, just when I think I can't take it anymore, it bursts from me, sweeping across the meadow and the school. There are screams, but I can't see past my own magic. And then, just as suddenly as it began, it stops. I'm lowered gently to the ground. Then, it's just me and the queen in the meadow.

I can see she's struggling with some unseen force as it pushes her away from me and from the school.

"This is not over," she shouts, anger dripping from every word. "Your friends are still within the castle walls. You have nowhere to go and nowhere to hide."

"I'm not hiding," I reply, projecting my voice loud and clear. "I will get my friends back, and I will heal them. But you are no longer welcome here, and you will never control me again."

With that, the queen's strength seems to give out, and she flies back into the woods before I can even blink. My bravado leaves me the moment she's gone, and I drop to my knees, trying to catch my breath. There's still a buzz over my skin, and I am attuned to every water molecule in the area. Breathing deeply, I try to calm my racing heart.

Aiden is suddenly there, followed by Liam, as they reach for me. Aiden sweeps me into his arms, while Liam takes one and holds it tightly.

"That was some magic, Mads," Liam says, a bit of awe in his voice.

"I think, we haven't seen anything yet," I try to smile, but then sleep takes me away.

❧

FIVE DAYS LATER I'M IN THE HEADMASTER'S OFFICE, LOOKING OUT the window. I still haven't been able to find a way to get my friends out of the castle. The queen has sent word to the headmaster saying the plague has taken lives, but that's all we know. I don't even know if my friends are alive.

I'm trying not to think about them, or my father. If I let myself dwell on all the things I can't control and all the people I can't save, I become useless.

"Have you had any luck with your research?" The headmaster asks from his position behind the table. In the last few days, I've learned that the Elders were able to escape before the queen put a lock on the portal, and the headmaster hasn't been able to speak with anyone from our world. He and the teachers have been doing their best to keep the students in line, but it's getting harder by the minute.

"No. I still can't get in."

I've tried the library a dozen times, but even with my more focused magic, something is preventing me from entering. So, the boys and I have started pouring over every book we can find within these walls. We've read through a lot of what the headmaster carries in his office, and we're no closer to any answers.

"You will figure it out, Miss Hawthorne. I have no doubt."

"That makes one of us," I mumble as I head for the door. We've been having these early morning check-ins, and I'm not sure they're doing me any good. It's just a reminder of everything I haven't accomplished. Even though there's probably more he'd like to say to me, he doesn't stop me when I leave.

As I walk the halls, everyone is so much more subdued. The fae who weren't originally enrolled in the school have all gone after the spell I cast. As far as I know, only the original students remain. Plus, Liam. I trust him, so I guess my magic caught on to that.

The kids know about half of what's going on, but no one tries to stop me as I head toward the back doors. The teachers are doing their best to try to keep moral high, but even though there are still classes, they've been reformatted for our current situation. More battle training, more potion creation. We're getting a crash course in our heritage because all of us will need to know how to fight if we're to get back to our own world.

My feet carry me across the grass and to the outer building I know so well. Since the academy became a sanctuary, and I took a five-hour nap after casting the spell, my combat training has been in full swing and slightly modified.

"You sure about this?" Liam says in greeting as I walk into the room. Aiden turns at his words, his eyes finding me immediately. We haven't talked about our kiss, or all the little ways we told each other about our feelings. But there's a new kind of an intensity whenever I'm around him, and I feel him so much more, even when I'm not with him.

"I need all the skills I can get on my side," I reply with a shrug.

"Very well."

Liam hands me a sword, and I take it with both hands. Even after we started combat training, I never thought we'd resort to swords. But this is the weapon of choice in the magical community, and it's the one that can inflict the most damage. That's what I'm looking for. Aiden and Liam are both skilled, so they're the perfect people to teach me.

As Liam talks me through the basics, my gaze keeps jumping to Aiden. A part of me is glad we're not alone. We haven't been since we were locked in the cell together. But the other part wants him all to myself, and I know he feels the same. That awareness that has always been present is more intense than ever. Sometimes I find myself catching my breath because being near him is so overwhelming.

"Aiden will attack, and you will block." Liam's voice instructs, and I force myself to focus. The shifter comes to stand in front of me as I grip my sword a little tighter.

"Don't tense so much," he says, and his voice does funny things to my stomach. "Move into the motions, don't force them."

I nod, and he attacks. He swings his sword overhead, and I raise both of my arms to block. He does it again, and I block again. He's not putting all his strength into the swing and still, each one vibrates my body. Liam moves to the side, giving us the floor as Aiden and I dance around each other.

To some degree, he's still angry at me for locking him inside the academy. But I think to the other, he understands. It's the alpha in him that wants to do the protecting, but that's my job now. No matter what happens, he will always have me watching his back. Maybe one day, I'll be able to tell him. Maybe one day, I'll be able to tell him just how much he means to me.

"Good. Now—" He trails off, catching himself and I narrow my eyes. "We're going—"

"Aiden?"

He leans on the sword, his other hand at his chest. That's when I notice he's a lot more sweaty than usual, droplets of it running down his temples and down his neck.

"We need—"

Suddenly, he drops to his knees, and I'm at his side in the next moment.

"Aiden?" I reach for him, cradling his head on my knees as he convulses under my touch. I blink the tears away as I try to hold him together. "No, Aiden. No."

"Mads, let go of him." Liam is there, trying to pull me away, but I won't go.

"No!" I scream, tearing myself out of his grip. "We have to help him. He's just—"

"He's got the plague." I know Liam says the words, but they don't register.

"He's fine. He's just tired. He's okay." My words tumble over each other as I wipe at his face. The shakes stop, and then start up again, and he rolls to the side, vomiting up blood.

"Maddie."

"No, he's okay!"

I don't even care if I'm getting blood all over me, I hold him close as his body shudders once again, and then he goes still.

MADDIE'S LIST OF OLD SLANG WORDS/PHRASES

"Bank is closed!" - what you say to someone to stop making out

Berries - denotes that something is good, desirable or pleasing.

Dumb Dora - an unintelligent woman

Mrs. Grundy - an uptight or very straight-laced individual

"Know your onions" - to know what's up or what's going on

Source: thoughtcatalog.com

OF STORMS AND TRIUMPHS

Thunderbird Academy - Book Three

Valia Lind

Without love, our earth is a tomb.

— ROBERT BROWNING

❧ I ❧

The cold snakes under my clothes, digging into my skin like little worms burrowing in the ground, chilling me to the bone. I have no idea how long I've been huddled under this tree, or if it's day or night. There is no light in this part of the forest.

I know my friends are going to be angry I left. But they'd have to be alive first. When the Ancients began rising from their slumber, our world delved into careful chaos. We were still living. We were still going to school and running our businesses. But then they started sending their minions our way, and even though we were trying to find a way to coexist with this war, we're still losing.

Rubbing my hands over my upper arms, I wonder if the noises I hear are actually all around me, or if they're part of my sleep deprived imagination. It feels like someone's out there, right beyond my line of vision, waiting for me to finally fall asleep. Being here, alone with my thoughts, I can't help but think of all the ways this is my fault.

Thunderbird Academy is my home away from home. I thought I was doing what's right. I thought I could protect my friends from the darkness. So, I wrote a spell using the oldest magic of story spell casting. Instead of sending the monsters away, I brought the whole school to Faery. For just a moment, I thought Faery would be okay, that we would be safe here. But the Ancients are the first of the magical creatures who've walked the earth, and they have walked in Faery too.

Now, the danger is here, and that's exactly how I've ended up in the middle of the dark forest, slowly dying from the excruciating cold.

"No," I say out loud, breaking the shadows with my word, "I will not die here. I will not give into this self-pity. I am stronger than this. I am."

Speaking helps break some of the tension but not much. I have to keep going. There's a reason I'm here, and I can't really rest until I reach my goal.

The Oracle has been visiting me in my dreams. I promised her a spell in exchange for freeing my friends, and now it's time to pay up. She has guided me across the same river we met at and into the forest on the other side. I have to be getting close to the mountain now. But with no light to guide me, it's been difficult telling the days apart.

Slowly, I get to my feet. That's enough rest for now. I close my eyes briefly, reaching for my magic. There is a stream deep underground that leads from the river to the base of the mountain. I've been using it as a guiding string toward my destination.

When I start walking again, my body is stiff. I'm almost out of the granola I brought, and even that hasn't been sustaining me well. I'm exhausted for more than one reason.

Sadness can take a lot out of a person.

I shake my head, refusing to allow myself go down that road. If I start thinking about it, I won't stop. I'll curl up in a ball right here on the ground and cry until I can't feel anything anymore. It'd be easier if I couldn't feel.

My magic flares up, buzzing over my skin as I walk slowly, with my hand outstretched in front of me, one step at a time. The trees are a little farther apart here, but the grass and bushes are taller. They spring up on me unawares, since I can't see past about a foot in front of me. And even that is just outlines.

After I've taken a few steps, I realize the noise I thought I was imagining is real. Something is stalking me.

I try to remain calm as I scan the area very discreetly. My father would be proud of the survivor I've become. I've picked up a few skills he hasn't gotten around to teaching me yet. My heart thumps in awareness. I'm so worried about him, I can hardly breathe. But I have to focus on one thing at a time. After I save my friends, I'll find a way to get my father out of the winter court.

The noise comes again, and I realize it's a slight scratching on the bark. Whatever is out there, it's climbing the trees to keep pace with me. I wish I could use an illumination spell and create an orb, but light in this dark place would just make me a target. Or a bigger target than I already am. But that's when it dawns on me. I can use that to my advantage.

The creature keeps moving closer and closer as I walk, as if it's getting ready to pounce. I'm afraid to be the first to make a move, but I need to know what I'm up against. The next time I stop to rest, whatever is out there will be on me, and I will have no way to protect myself. When I think I've finally reached a good place, a small clearing where I can stand up a little surer, I reach for my magic once more. This time, instead of looking for the stream, I look for the light.

"Light the way, please," I barely whisper, keeping my movements small.

An orb forms quickly, and as soon as it's between my hands, I throw it in the air. It flies up, illuminating the immediate area. It takes a second for my eyes to adjust, and when I do I see them. The trolls. Up in the trees. Now completely fascinated by the orb hanging over my head. But then, it's as if this was their cue. Their little heads turn toward me as one, and they attack.

The scream that pierces the dark sends shivers up my spine. It's hard keeping the orb overhead as I bring up my other arm that is readying with battle magic, but I've been practicing. One of the trolls hits my magic and goes flying in the opposite direction. Another jumps, landing in front of me. I pull on my magic, pushing him back. Before I can do anything else, the third troll drops down and lands on my back. I scream, falling to my knees from the impact. My concentration breaks. The troll scratches at my back and neck, pulling on my hair and yanking the backpack off as I try to get him off me. But he won't budge.

My mind goes over my options as I keep twisting, but I can't see the others anymore. I stumble over something on the ground and realize this place could be useful. With one arm, I reach out, trying to find a tree. The moment my hand connects, I step up to it and swing my body with full force in its direction. There's a thud and a scream as the troll slams into the wood and flies off my back. Quickly, I reach for my orb, lighting it again to search for my backpack.

I find it a few feet away, snatch it up, and start running. I have no choice but to move fast now. Keeping the orb lit, I search for the stream below the ground, and when I find it, I run faster. The screeching is right at my back, but I don't turn.

My body screams at me to slow down, to take a breather, but I can't. If I die in this forest, my friends are doomed. If I die here, Aiden will never come out of his coma.

❧

WHEN I THINK I CAN RUN NO LONGER, THE FOREST OPENS UP IN front of me. I can hear the rush of water without my magic, and I blink a few times to orient my eyes to my surroundings.

The clearing in front of me is small, but it's right at the base of the mountain. I twist to glance back into the forest, but the trolls don't follow. They stay in the shadows, watching me with those beady eyes of theirs.

I'm on my knees before I know it, breathing heavily. Shedding my backpack, I try to keep my head from spinning, but everything seems too much. If something attacked me right now, I don't think I'd be able to withstand it.

"You are a strong one, little witch."

The voice comes from my left, and I glance up to find the Oracle walking toward me slowly. She moves with such grace, it seems as if she's floating. She's just as beautiful as I remember, her short hair blowing in the wind she carries with her. This time, her dress is maroon and way more revealing, with slits and cutouts all over her body.

"Why put me through that?" I grunt, slowly getting to my feet. Everything the fae do have a purpose. There has to be one here.

"You are unlearned and undisciplined. The forest teaches many things."

The fae are also freaking riddle masters, and I have never been so irritated by words as I've been since coming to Faery. Dad and I love words. We love collecting old phrases no one uses and reviving them. But these, these fae are masters at word play and masters at not answering direct questions... well, directly.

"Great. Did it teach me how to outrun trolls who want to eat my face? Because that's all I got out of that lesson."

"Are you sure about that?"

"I don't understand."

"Of course not, little witch. You have much to learn."

I grunt again, this time even more feral-like. Ever since I came to Faery, everyone keeps mentioning how unlearned I am. Especially the Oracle. I already feel useless with half the things going on. I don't need an extra reminder.

"You don't like that."

"Of course not," I snap, pushing the hair out of my face. The last six months have taught me to be a little bolder as well, and at least for that, I am thankful. "What's the game you're playing? The dreams and now the forest. What do you want from me?"

The Oracle doesn't reply right away, watching me carefully. I'm not sure what she's deciding about me, but I honestly can't see any of this ending well for me. I shouldn't have come. Even though I had no other choice, I still shouldn't have.

"Come with me, little witch. There's much to be discussed."

She turns then, walking back toward the mountain, leaving me no choice but to follow. I grab my backpack from where I discarded it and throw one last look at the forest. The trolls are still there. If I actually survive whatever the Oracle has for me, I'm really not looking forward to going back into that forest.

I just hope my friends are still hanging on. And my dad. Too many people are tied to my decisions at the moment. What I wouldn't give to be able to talk to my sisters right now. I need their comfort almost as much as I need their wisdom.

The Oracle steps in front of a rock wall, and I glance around to see if there's an entrance somewhere. The mountain's base is much larger than I thought, and it spreads out across the plains, as far as my eye can see. We would have to climb to get anywhere, but when I look over at the Oracle, she waves a hand, and the rock in front of us ripples. Without hesitation, she gives me a quick smile and steps right into the rock wall. Rolling my eyes at her tendency to show off, I follow.

When I step through the wall, I expect to end up in a cave of sorts. What I find is a great room with large windows and huge bookcases. There's a love seat and a full couch along with tables and chairs. It looks like an elaborate study, and there are flowers on every surface. I glance to my right and find a doorway and a hall opening up beyond it.

"You didn't actually think I lived in a cave, did you?" The Oracle laughs, the sound melodic to my ears. Of course that's what I thought. It's what I've been told. But once again, it's ridiculous of me to trust anything the fae say or do. It's time I try and take this situation into my own hands.

"Why am I here?"

I seem to repeatedly ask her the why questions, but I need something to go off of. I'm not naive enough to think she's not playing some kind of a game.

"Because I may be of some help."

That makes me pause, my heart thudding loudly in my ears.

"What does that mean?"

Reaching into a pocket in the folds of her dress, she takes out a small glass bottle. The liquid inside sparkles in the midday light coming through the large window.

"This will heal one individual from the illness. But only one."

"What?"

"It is your choice to make, little witch."

"I don't understand." My mind spins with possibilities. We've been searching for an answer to this sickness for days, and here she stands, holding the answer. "If you can help, why won't you?"

"It is not my job to take care of the Spring Court. Or to save humans from their demise. That would be a full-time job."

"But it's not just humans in trouble. Every magical being at my school...and fae, they're all sick."

"They are of no concern to me."

I can't wrap my mind around this, can't understand why she would keep this magical elixir to herself. The fae are cunning, of that there is no doubt. But how would she have this knowledge? And why only share a bit of it with me? This brings up way too many questions.

"Time is ticking, as you humans like to say. Your shifter doesn't have much time."

My head snaps up at her words, my heart dropping. No, she can't know that. There's no way. The last update Liam gave me was that Aiden was stable, just like the rest of my friends. But then again, why would she say it if it wasn't true? Fae can't lie.

"But if I save him, what about the rest of my friends?"

"That's a puzzle for you to solve, little witch."

I can tell she's already done with me. She places the bottle on the table between us before walking slowly away, as if she's giving me privacy to decide what to do. I have no choice but to pick up the bottle, the glass cool under my fingertips. The liquid swishes back and forth, mesmerizing me with its glitter-filled movements.

"Why are you doing this? Did you bring me all the way for this?" I raise the bottle in her direction, but it's like she can no longer be bothered by my presence. She reclines on the sofa, her gorgeous dress spread out around her.

"Why do I do anything these days?" she muses. "For entertainment, of course."

Her answer doesn't surprise me, just that she even bothered to say anything. The fae, precisely this fae, is in it for herself.

"But also," she continues, sitting up just slightly to lean on her knees. That piercing gaze roots me to the spot as I wait for her to say whatever she's going to. "You are such a curious creature, Madison Hawthorne. I wanted to know what you are made of."

"So, it was a test?"

"Life is a test, darling. The sooner you learn that, the better off you'll be."

She sounds like one of my sisters, and the pang of sadness is sharp and instant. She stands then, not giving me a chance to reply.

"It is up to you to decide what to do with what you have been given. I'll be calling on you again when I'm ready."

"Wait, I have more questions!" I exclaim, even though I know how dangerous they can be. But she's not listening. She waves her arm and then her other comes up, sending a wave of magic at me. I stumble under the weight and then I'm falling. I think I'm going to land on the table, but then I'm on the floor, and a portal opening closes above my head.

"Maddie!"

I twist to the left to find myself in Aiden's room with Liam standing up, staring at me as if he's just seen a ghost.

"Hey. I thought I'd drop in," I reply before plopping down more fully. Today has been exhausting.

❧ 2 ❧

Exhaustion is heavy on my bones, and I give myself just a moment of reprieve. Then, I get up without looking around me and hurry to the door.

"Maddie, wait!" Liam's voice follows me as I stumble into the hallway. He's two steps behind me and then he's blocking my path.

"What?"

"You haven't seen him in days."

I close my eyes briefly, trying to keep the panic and anguish at bay. Being strong is a funny thing. Sometimes you forget how to be anything else and you push people away. But I can't do that with Liam. I have to give him at least some of the truth.

"I can't, Liam."

Moving around him, I try to flee, but he's not done.

"Why can't you?" His voice is low and gentle, and it breaks me.

"Because if I see him, any of them, it will shatter me. And I can't help them if I'm in pieces!"

My words echo around us in the near empty hall. Thunderbird Academy used to be so full of life, and now, it's become a tomb.

"Mads,"

"No, Liam. I have to figure this out. I have to..."

"Wait, where were you?" It's like he's finally taken a good look at me. I glance down and find that I'm covered in mud. When I meet Liam's eyes, they're a mixture of outrage and concern. The regular two emotions he's been experiencing toward me recently.

"I went to see the Oracle."

"Alone? You know how dang—"

"Spare me the lecture, Abercrombie. I did what needed to be done."

Liam looks confused for a second, but he won't let my weird word usage deter him. "And what exactly was that?"

Because I know I can't keep this a secret, I reach into my pocket and pull out the glass bottle.

"Get an antidote to the sickness?"

I don't think I've ever seen Liam this shocked before. He takes a literal step back, his eyes going from me to the bottle and back to me.

"She just...gave it to you?"

"I made sure to not say thank you," I reply, before stepping around him and moving down the hall. He falls in step beside me, and I wait for the tirade of questions to descend. But he stays quiet. When we reach my room, the emptiness of it comes like a hit. It's a reminder that Jade is not here, that's she's sick, and I have to choose who to save.

Liam closes the door behind us, but I don't even slow down. Yanking open my dresser, I pull out clean clothes and then head to the bathroom.

"I need a shower," is all I say before I shut the door and lean against it. A pressure starts up in my chest, but I refuse to let it out. However, the moment I step under the water it's like my own floodgates open up. The feel of the drops against my skin is comforting, and the tears that come will not be denied.

I cry for myself, and I cry for my friends. I cry for all the things that have happened and for all the things yet to come. Never would I have ever imagined myself with this power, with this responsibility on my shoulders. I'm terrified I'm going to mess it all up. In front of the headmaster, even in front of Liam, I have no choice but to put on a brave face. But here, standing under the spray of hot water, I can let myself feel.

What I told Liam is true. I'm afraid I'll break apart, and no matter what I do, I won't put myself together in time. Not seeing Aiden has been killing me slowly, but I think seeing him would do it all at once. I failed to protect him. I failed to protect Jade. And Ben. And even Natalie. Yes, a rational side of my brain tells me there's no way I could've known. But the rest of me just thinks if I was smart enough or powerful enough, I would've kept the sickness from reaching the school.

My magic boils inside of me, just as frustrated with me as I am. Besides what happened in the forest, I've been keeping it as shut down as I've been keeping my emotions. It's the only way I can deal with all this. But right here and right now, I need the release, and so I don't hold it back. The magic spins out of me like a twister, sending the water dancing all around me. I grab hold of it before it can get out of control and push all the water to the left before I bring it to the right. Up and down. Left to right. I repeat the process a few times before I send the droplets into suspension around my body. Slowly, with one finger, I draw a heart as the water creates it right in front of my eyes. Then, I shift and repeat the movements, this time creating a flower. My own magic is mesmerizing to me. It twinkles even in the dimness of the bathroom.

The more I play with the magic, the calmer my heartbeat becomes. It's like I've been holding onto everything so tightly, the pressure has become too much. But now, it's like I can roll my shoulders again and stretch. I really should learn by now that denying myself my magic is the worst thing I can do.

I bring it all back, letting the water run its course, and I wipe at the tears. Thankfully, they get mingled with the water, and for a second, I can pretend everything is alright.

❧

"SO, WHAT DO YOU WANT TO DO?" LIAM ASKS THE MOMENT I STEP out of the bathroom. I'm going to be honest, I kind of hoped he'd go do something else while he waited for me. But that was futile. He's been my shadow for weeks now.

"Honestly, I want to not be the person that makes this decision." I drop down on my bed, as dramatic as I can manage. I'm not trying to be difficult. This is just a difficult situation, and I'm overwhelmed. I'm still allowed to be overwhelmed, right? Liam doesn't comment, just sits down beside me, and we stay like that for a few minutes.

"I think you're the perfect person to make this decision." He finally speaks, and I jerk my head to the side to look at him. But he's not looking at me. His gaze is somewhere far away, and I wonder what he's thinking about. I could ask him, but that feels like an intrusion, and we've had too many of those lately as it is.

"I don't agree with your statement," I say, sitting up and turning to face him. He follows suit until we're face to face.

"Maybe not. But it's still the truth."

"Liam, how am I supposed to know what's the right thing to do here? How do I choose who lives and who dies? Because that's the choice!"

"Is it?"

"Of course it is! We have no idea how this sickness works, how long anyone has until it finally takes them. And what if I save someone and someone else is much further along, and it's my fault they die? How can I live with that?"

"You'll live with it like the rest of us live with our choices. You're right, we don't know anything about this sickness. But we know that we have an antidote."

"But do we?" I jump to my feet, starting to pace. There's not much space in my small room, but I need to move. "We don't even know if she's telling the truth. She might be playing with us. I wouldn't put it past her."

It's true, I'm not about to trust her blindly. But I also don't know of a way where we can find out what's in the elixir. We don't exactly have a science lab attached to the academy. There might be a magical way about it, but I'm scared to mess with the ingredients. Magic can be dangerous. We've been learning that firsthand here for a while now.

"If it helps you to know, nothing has changed while you've been gone."

"How long was that?"

"Almost three days."

Wow, I'm a little surprised I can still stand up straight. The exhaustion weighs heavily on my shoulders, and I think if I laid down right now, I'd sleep for days.

"Mads, how about I go get you some food and you rest? You won't be doing anyone any good if you collapse."

I want to argue with him, but I can't. He's right. I nod my head and he gives my upper arm a quick squeeze before he heads out the door. Sliding farther up on the bed, I tuck myself into a ball, my mind racing with ideas. There has to be something I can do to find more information. I could ask Headmaster Marković if he knows anything, but I feel like if he did, he would've done something about it by now. This means none of the staff will be helpful.

It would be ridiculously helpful if I could talk to my family. My dad probably knows the most, but Bri would be a good second. She's a pro at herbs and spells. Even talking it over with her would help. But of course, that's not an option. The communication lockdown is really starting to get to me. Who am I kidding? I've been mad at it from the beginning.

The only place I can think of to go for help is the library. But it hasn't exactly been my friend lately, and I'm not sure I can get in. So basically, I have nothing. When Liam returns with food, he sits beside me as I devour the sandwich, but he doesn't ask me a million questions, clearly reading my mood.

Once my stomach is satisfied, I lay back down. Liam pulls the covers over my body because I can't even find enough strength to do that for myself. I'm still berating myself in my mind when he leaves, and I fall into a dreamless sleep.

❦   3   ❦

Maybe in another fifty years I'll look back at this and appreciate the lessons it taught me. But it's only hindsight that's twenty-twenty. The rest of it? It's torture, and I can't see past it. The vexing spirit inside of me has taken over my complete makeup. I wish I could say I'm handling it well. But I'm not. I won't lie to myself, no matter how much I would like to appear strong.

Standing in front of the library door, I can't help but feel frustrated. I've tried everything. In the last two weeks, I've begged and pleaded. I allowed my magic to do the same. I even did a spell where I showed the library all that has transpired, including the sickness. It's like she's completely unresponsive to me. So, I left her alone.

But now, more than ever, I need to get in there. I need to know that this miracle elixir won't kill whoever drinks it on the spot. Our own library has yielded nothing. This is the only avenue we have left to explore. Well, the only one I have left. Liam is doing what he can from his side, but he's not exactly on the list of Queen Amaryllis's most favorite fae at the moment. His friendship with me and his upbringing in the human realm, makes her doubt everything about him. He took a stand to help me and a huge risk that I hope I'm worth.

Taking a full calming breath, I let it out slowly. I have to try. And my only option is story spell casting. Something I said I wouldn't use again.

Stepping as close as I can to the door, I close my eyes. Focusing on my magic, I let it expand, taking up every part of my being. But I don't force it out like I've done before. I allow it to settle over me, as my mind looks for a way.

There isn't a guide for me to follow, no step by step instructions when it comes to this place. My sisters would probably have a better chance, but they're not here. I have to trust in myself. It terrifies me to open myself up to this magic. Especially after all the warnings Liam has shared with me. But this is something only I can do. So, I open my eyes, and I tell a story.

> *"A grand wooden door,*
> *With secrets held dear.*
> *She stands in between,*
> *The truth and the fear.*
> *With time running out,*
> *She opens the lock.*
> *To give life a chance,*
> *To teach, to help.*
> *No thanks could express,*
> *The gratitude within.*
> *But the witch tries,*
> *Bowing deep to her knees.*
> *The door swings open,*
> *And the secrets are told.*
> *The thanks are given,*
> *And the answer is formed."*

Out of breath, I stand still, letting the magic infuse my words. It never fails to amaze me how the words just come to me the moment I call for them. It's as if I don't have to think about it because they already live deep within me. As I wait, the current of the magic races through me and through the story I told. When it seems like nothing is going to happen, the door shudders and clicks open. I grin and take a step forward.

As it swings inward, the pain comes.

I grab my temples as pain pulses, while I grind my teeth together to keep from screaming. I've been very careful to not use story spell casting unless it's absolutely necessary. But the last time I used it, the pain wasn't this sharp. It was more of a headache, instead of the pulsating pounding I feel now.

Dragging myself forward, I'm through the door and into the library. The door shuts behind me, and I wonder if I passed out here, if anyone would be able to find me. Liam knows of this place, and so does Ben. But neither one remembers it or would be able to enter. I could die here, and no one would know. That can't be my story. Not when I have so many people counting on me. Stumbling over my own feet, I finally make it to a chair before I collapse.

I HAVE NO IDEA HOW LONG I'VE BEEN PASSED OUT. WHEN I FINALLY come to, I'm half off the chair, leaning on the table in front of me. My head is still hurting, but the pain has receded to a dull awareness. Sitting up slowly, I roll my shoulders, trying to orient myself.

This place hasn't changed a bit. All the books I left out on the table are still there. My notebook with randomly scribbled notes is still open to the last entry. I expect it to be covered in dust, but it's not. It's as if I was just here. Instead, it's been weeks. Maybe one day I'll solve the mystery of this library, but for now, I have plenty of other mysteries to solve.

Flipping through my notebook quickly, I think that it's a waste of time until I notice an entry that makes me pause. It's only a few sentences, but I read over them three times. I sit back, mulling over what I read. Somehow, I completely forgot that Hawthorne has battled with sickness twice. I mean, I think I vaguely remembered it, but not to a point where it was useful. Until now.

Krista healed the town, but I have no idea how she did it. And it's not like I can ask her. Slamming my notebook shut, I cross my arms in front of me and lean back. Why does it seem the closer I get to an answer the further away it seems? Like with my father.

I know he's in Faery. I have no idea how he ended up here, but he is. And I would give anything to go visit every court right now and try to find him. The biggest clue we had points to the Winter Court, and I'm ready to go break down that door. But I can't. I'm confined to this campus just like those in quarantine. If it wasn't for the Oracle sending me back through the portal, I doubt I'd be free right now. Queen Amaryllis can sense my magic when I'm in her land, and she does not have any kind feelings toward me. Not since I decided to show her up and ban her from Thunderbird Academy.

Restlessness is heavy in my veins, so I get to my feet and start pacing between the tables. After a full minute, I find some sense of control and head toward the history section. Last time, that's what yielded the most information. Human history.

Back in the olden days, people were more aware of magic and more afraid of it. So, the human historians and coven leaders alike kept a pretty concise record of the time. There is a lot more magic hidden in human history books than anyone would imagine. It's how the whole story spell casting was even found. And how Liam and I found the information needed for the spell performed in my hometown.

Now, as I stand in front of the vast wall, I have no idea what I'm looking for. But then I realize I'm in the wrong place. Pivoting, I head toward the opposite bookcase, which is filled with medical books from all over the world. If this is a sickness, maybe there's some mention of it here.

Pulling out a bunch of books that seem to fit the timeline from when my parents first encountered the disease, I settle myself at the desk and begin to read. It would go so much faster if I could bring my friends down here. But I guess that wouldn't even matter now since only about three of them are awake.

The thought brings instant sadness to my heart that I try to push away. I can't afford to give into emotions, not when so much is resting on my resolve to stay focused. I've become a ping pong ball, volleyed back and forth between being an emotional mess and being a hardened warrior. Because that's exactly what I've had to become. Dad has always said I had an old soul. Well, it's never been truer. I've become older than my years.

Shaking my head, I bring my attention back to the words in front of me. There are so many diseases, I don't think I'll ever be able to find anything useful in these pages. After a minute, I stand, spreading out the books on the table. Then, I climb on top of it as well, standing between the stacks. I tried this once before, with Ben, and it worked. Maybe it'll work this time as well.

Closing my eyes, I call on my magic. The other power answers the call instantly, but I lock it down. It's not happy to be shut off, but I can't afford passing out right now. My water magic bubbles to the surface, eager to be of use. With a few deep breaths, I ask for guidance and let the magic seep out of me. I feel it as it travels over each manuscript, leafing through the pages, and moving on to the next book. It's much easier letting it explore, and I don't have to do much but trust it to guide me.

That's the biggest difference between my water magic and the story spell casting. Anytime I story cast, I feel the intensity of it in my very blood. With water magic, it's such an extension of me, it's like moving my fingers or toes. Maybe I just need more practice, but since I'm a little banned from using story spell casting, I can't exactly get much of that.

When I feel a tug on my magic, my eyes spring open. Expecting one of the books below me to glow like last time, I jump down from the table, searching for the sign. But I don't see anything. The tug is still there, but it's not coming from the books in front of me. Raising my head, I search for the source. When I finally locate it, I see one of the books on the shelf to my right is glowing.

Quickly, I walk over, afraid I'll lose it. But I shouldn't worry. My magic is firmly attached to the book until I have it in my hands. The moment I touch it, it sends a little spark over my fingertips before settling to an open page.

"This is definitely not what I was looking for," I say, my own voice jarring me after the quietness of the room. It's a story.

"Soulmates?"

❧ 4 ❧

Istare at the page like I've never seen words before.

What do soulmates have to do with the sickness? Or the Ancients? The questions I asked, the energy I sent out, had nothing to do with this. It was about helping those I care about. Not looking for some love story.

Of course I know the gist of it. My sisters have found their true soulmates. Even though we didn't really get into it when I was home months ago, I've heard about it. It used to be a fairytale, just like the Ancients. But now, both are a reality. I shut the book, ready to put it back, but it springs back open.

"Okay, fine. I'll read it."

It's not like I really have a choice. I asked the library for help, and she's giving it to me. In her own weird way. Walking back over to the big window, I sit down on the plush window seat. I don't think I've ever actually sat here before. I've never been able to find an exit or figure out if the forest outside the glass is actually real. But this feels like the perfect place to read this. Glancing down, I begin.

Once upon a time, in a land beyond imagination, lived a prince in a big castle. He was a kind prince and took care of his people in the best way possible. He visited the villagers, and he held open balls, inviting everyone in the kingdom. His parents doted on him, and he was never without a friend.

But the prince had a secret, like most people do. The secret, however, wasn't like that of most people. In the depths of his being lived a beast, which could not be tamed. So, every night, after the curtains were drawn and the doors were locked, he let the beast free.

I glance up from the page, my mind mulling over the words. If what I'm reading is what I think I'm reading, the prince would be a shifter. Maybe this could be helpful after all. Getting a little more comfortable, I continue.

No one knew of his predicament, only his parents. They guarded the secret as closely as they could. They wanted their son to have all the advantages in the world. They were afraid of how the kingdom would see him were he not the perfect man that stood before them during the day. It is a fear as old as time; and therefore, it was a secret that had to be kept.

Even though the prince's life was a grand one, he longed for a connection like no other. He had watched the love between his parents, and he wanted the same for himself. He was ready to love someone, but how could someone love him back if they could never know him for who he truly was?

Not long after his twentieth birthday, the prince was out in the village, visiting the market. The bazaars were always his favorite pastime, as it gave him a chance to not only get to know his people but to help them by buying up trinkets for the palace. His people were of a talented sort and made tapestries and paintings that belonged in the grandest halls.

That particular day, the prince was walking through the stalls with his captain of the guard beside him, when a stand caught his eye. The most beautiful cloth he had ever seen danced in the breeze, pulling him toward it. The designs woven in and out created an explosion of color like no other. The prince instantly knew he had to buy a few pieces for the palace. When he walked around the stall, eager to purchase the tapestries, he came face to face with a fair maiden.

The maiden was the most beautiful creature he had ever laid eyes upon. The tapestries around her failed in comparison, but so did the moon and the sun. The maiden smiled, bowing deeply, and it was as if something clicked within the prince's heart. It was like a melody had started playing all around them, but only he and the maiden could hear it well enough to dance. They spoke only briefly as the prince paid for a few tapestries, and money was exchanged. She was friendly, just like they were all friendly to him, but there was a pull about her that the prince did not understand. He had met beautiful maidens before and none of them ever fascinated in the way that she did.

Before walking away, the prince invited the fair maiden to a ball at the palace. When she promised she would try to come, the prince walked away with a happy heart.

But that night, just like all other nights, the prince locked the doors and became a beast.

No one could understand why this happened to him, no one had a way to stop it. He had no control. Just the knowledge that once the moon was out, so was the beast.

The ball was to be held and days later, the prince was still thinking about the fair maiden. Would she come? He did not know. But he knew that he would wait for her.

When it was time for the ball, in the early afternoon as usual, the palace had never looked better. There were candles everywhere, and the palace looked like it was filled with the night stars themselves. The ball was always early, as the prince had to excuse himself once the sun was down.

The people came and the ball began, but there was no sight of the fair maiden anywhere. The prince greeted the guests and talked to the musicians. He made sure there was enough food brought in from the kitchens and enough seats set up for rest. Still, the fair maiden was nowhere in sight.

The sun started to go down, and the king and queen begged the prince to retire to his chambers. But he insisted on waiting, just a few minutes longer. He waited and waited, and when he could wait no longer, he excused himself and rushed to his chambers. But before he could make it to that wing of the palace, the fair maiden was there in his path. She was wearing a sparkling green dress, her long brown hair falling down past her waist. Her cheeks were flushed from running, but she looked like she was glowing.

Apologizing profusely, she told the prince that her mother was sick, and she had to take care of her before she could slip away for the ball. The prince smiled, enchanted by her even more. But there was no time. He had to get to his rooms before the shift came. He excused himself, even though it pained him to do so, and raced toward his rooms. The maiden, worried something was wrong with the prince, followed. After all, she had been taking care of a sick mother. She thought she could be of some help.

The prince rushed through his doors, but before he could close them, he was on his knees. The time had come, and there was nothing he could do about it. His skin began to ripple, his spine began to fold. A soft gasp sounded from behind him, and he turned, only to see the fair maiden looking at him from the doorway. Terrified of what she would think of him, he tried to retreat, but she surprised him.

"I am not scared," she whispered, holding her hands out in front of her. Those four words, the words the prince had wanted to hear all his life, burrowed right into his heart. The fair maiden took a tentative step forward, then another, until she was right in front of the prince. With shaking hands, not because of fear, but of emotion, the fair maiden reached for the prince. His own hand reached out and the moment their skin touched, it was like the brightness of the sun had entered the room.

Everything seemed to stop. Not only time itself, but his shift. Glancing down, he watched as his body became his own again. When he looked up, there was pure happiness shining in the maiden's eyes, which was mirrored in his own. She raised her other hand, and a spark of magic danced at her fingertips.

"You are a witch," the prince said, his voice full of awe.

"You are a shifter," the maiden answered in kind.

The two were complete opposites, yet two pieces of a puzzle, fitting together perfectly. She was his anchor and he was her sever. Her magic unleashed when they came together, and his was tamed. From that day on, he could control his shift and learned to call upon it whenever he wanted. The two became one, and it would not have been possible without his true mate.

For that is what the fair maiden was. A soulmate, his true mate, the one which was made for him and he for her. Their friendship grew, and then their love, and in seasons time, they had their happily ever after.

When I finish reading, I sit frozen for a while. It may have been hours for all I know. I can't get the image of the prince and the maiden out of my mind, or the story itself. I see myself in her, even though there is barely any description or words spoken on the page. It's as if the story has seeped into my skin, and I see images instead of words. The library has tried to show me something, something I don't think I'm ready to know.

Jumping off the seat, I leave the book behind and head toward the door. Liam and I have training, and right now seems like the right time to go. But before I leave, I turn to the library, and I whisper a quick thanks. Somehow, I know I learned important details here today. I just have to come to terms with them now.

❧

WHEN I GET BACK TO MY ROOM, IT'S MUCH LATER THAN I THOUGHT. Changing into my workout gear, I'm braiding my hair on the run. I feel that constant tug toward the side of the school with the quarantined, but I race past it. Now is not the time to suddenly change my stance on seeing my friends.

Once I finally make it to the workout room, I see Liam is already there. He doesn't look upset, just a little worried. Which goes away the moment he sees me. I guess me not showing up could mean a bunch of things right now.

"Sorry, I lost track of time," I say, and Liam just nods, letting me decide if I want to share more than that. As I walk toward him, I know I'll tell him about the library, just not the story I found. That, I still need to digest on my own.

"I was able to get through," I begin before the magic of the place stops me from going any farther. It gets really difficult to keep talking in circles, but I guess that's how the library stays hidden all this time. Even though Liam has been down there with me, he wouldn't be able to find it on his own. Only I can do that. But he knows exactly what I'm talking about, if the excitement on his face is any indication. I had to remind him I had a place I can look for answers, and he seemed to have retained that information.

"And?"

"All wet." He crinkles his forehead at me and I smile, before translating. "No good. No specifics, no instructions. I could read for days, and I doubt I'd be able to find what we need."

"It was worth a shot."

"I'll keep trying. If I can."

I realize I don't know if the library will let me back in. But it's not like I can share that with Liam either. He would not be happy with me if he knew I had to story spell cast. Instead of worrying about everything I can't control, I focus on the here and now. Liam has been teaching me how to wield a sword. He hands me the weapon, and the moment my skin closes around the steel, I think back to our first few lessons. When Aiden was still here.

There I go again, dwelling on aspects of my life that are extra painful. So smart of me. I should pat myself on the back.

"You with me?" Liam's voice breaks through my self-loathing and I nod, shifting my feet into the start position. We've been doing this at least once a day, and even though my body is already exhausted from barely sleeping, I welcome this particular exertion. This is the kind of weariness that leads to something good. And I can use a little more good in my life right now.

"Let's start with drills."

We go through a series of exercises, stretching and prepping our bodies. Not that Liam needs much of that. He's in excellent shape, like every fae I've ever met. But since he did mostly grow up in the human world, he actually does exercise like us mere mortals. I snicker at that, and he gives me a questioning look, but I'm not about to share my thoughts with him. I'm having a very difficult time keeping my brain from overheating as it is. It seems to be jumping from subject to subject without any coherent thought. Maybe I should be taking a nap instead of sparring. Not that I could actually sleep.

"Maddie, if you're not up for it?" Liam once again has to bring my attention back to him, and I shake my head.

"I'm here. No worries. Let's do this."

He gives me one long look and then he attacks.

I expect him to do so, but somehow, he still takes me by surprise. It just shows how exhausted I really am. I've taken a few steps back before I manage to bring my sword up to block his swing. The impact jars me, like it always does, because I told Liam not to hold back. I know he still does, but he doesn't baby me and for that I am thankful. It's my turn to jab, and when I do, he blocks me easily. The familiar exhilaration starts boiling in my veins. It's the kind of fuel I need. Stepping forward, I swing low, slamming my sword against his. We continue our dance, middle to high to low, before I twist around. Close left, close right, then side. We've trained with different swords, but long sword is what he prefers. There are plenty of guards but knowing the basics is what I asked for. I don't need to be the best. I just need to know how to sneak up on someone enough to cause damage.

Aiden is just as good with the sword as he is at personal hand to hand combat. The image of his face flashes before my eyes, the memory of us in this very room, sweat dripping off our bodies after we sparred. With the image comes the pain in my heart, and it's enough of a distraction for Liam to almost get a hit in. I block him just in time, but the impact still sends my body a few feet back.

I plant my feet before I can fall, and then I'm swinging again. My body has learned how to move, but my mind is too full of Aiden to be of much help right now. The next time Liam swings, I don't catch it. He pulls back at the last second, and only grazes my shoulder. Still, it's enough to send me flying, my own sword clanking against the floor. The only thing that saves me from bleeding is the training spell we put in place when we first started practicing. Even so, Liam is beside me in a flash.

"Are you okay?"

"Just embarrassed," I reply, getting to my feet slowly.

"What you are is exhausted. When was the last time you actually slept?"

"When was the ball? A day before that."

I'm not about to lie to Liam. He can sniff that out like a hound dog. But the moment I tell him the truth, I regret it. Because I know what comes next.

"Mads," he begins, before stopping and looking for the right words. "We're done for the day. We're not practicing again until you've slept."

He means well, of that I am sure. But I know myself. Every time I close my eyes, I just see my friends on the floor in front of me, vomiting blood and guts, and I can do nothing but stare. Even when I try, I can't shut those images off long enough to truly fall asleep.

"I know you don't want to hear it," he continues, "but maybe you need to go see..."

"No!" I cut him off before he says the one thing I don't want to hear. "I'll go lay down."

He studies me for a moment, as if deciding how much truth is in that statement, but finally he lets me go. I give him half a smile before

❧   5   ☙

The sleeping doesn't go well, as I expected. After I left Liam in the training room, I head to take a shower, thinking it might help me relax. But it doesn't. However, I don't break down crying this time, so I call that a win.

After a nap doesn't work, I get up and start reading the same books on magic I've been reading over for days. When the dinner bell rings, I almost don't bother going downstairs. So few of the students and faculty remain healthy, it's more depressing than not going downstairs. But then I realized Vera will be waiting for me, and I need to see her. For selfish reasons as much as for her. It's her friends who are sick as well.

"Hey, Maddie," Vera calls out as I step through the doorway to the dining room. As predicted, there are barely any people in here. I think most just grab some food and leave to go back to their rooms. It's safer that way. Groups I never thought I'd see have formed, staying together in each other's rooms and walking in packs. Those who never shared two words with each other are now confidants. It's a truly upside-down world we're living in.

"How are you doing?" I ask, reaching over to give her a quick hug. She looks pale, mirroring the same bags under the eyes that I'm wearing.

"I'm okay. They're not getting any better." She's the one who keeps me up to date with our friends' predicament. I'm not sure if she understands why I can't go see them, I'm not sure I fully understand besides the part where I'm trying to keep myself together. I guess that's a good enough reason, but it's not like I'm proud of the fact that I think I'm too weak to see them. That may brand me a coward, but I don't pretend to be who I'm not.

"What about worse?" I ask, almost afraid of the answer.

"Same." She shakes her head, and I breathe a little easier. That means I have more time. I can figure this out. Or maybe the headmaster will. He's been working with the Elders and the teachers, doing what he can from his side of things. I truly expected him to just take over and fix everything. But he trusts me to learn about my power and to see if I can help. It's scary to think they're not powerful enough to make this go away. I don't want to fail him any more than I want to fail my friends.

"Let's get some food," Vera says, leading me to the buffet. The magical supply of food still seems to be holding, which makes me thankful for small favors. I fully expected Queen Amaryllis to have blocked that magic by now. But I guess the banishing spell I cast really does keep her out of this school and its dealings. We grab a few things, bagels and some fruit. Neither one of us seems to be hungry, but we know we have to eat.

"How are you holding up, really?" I decide to ask, because I want Vera to know I'm here for her. Her roommate ended up being a spy for the Ancients, and then the rest of her friends end up sick. I can't imagine what's going through her mind. She's a powerful shifter, but even powerful beings need friends.

"I don't know, Maddie. It's all so scary. Every time I go to visit, I'm afraid they'll be gone. Most of my kind...they're not handling the sickness well." She sighs, looking down at her food. I'm not sure if it's because they shift into birds and those are smaller creatures, but I've heard most of the avian shifters are pretty bad off.

"I'm sorry, Vera," I say, reaching over and giving her hand a quick squeeze. She's typically not big on physical touch, but I think we both need to know the other is present because she covers my hand with her other and returns the gesture.

"I'm sorry too. I wish there was something I could do to help."

"Mrs. Lee hasn't been able to find anything?"

Just like I am doing research for the headmaster, the remaining students are working with various teachers to help find some answers. Vera shakes her head in response.

"She and Miss Housely have been trying to find something from the witch's point of view, but no amount of potions seem to do anything. The virus is a whole different breed of magic they can't seem to get a grip on."

"We'll figure it out," I say, sounding a lot more confident than I feel. Vera usually has no problem with confidence, but I'm the first to admit this ordeal has changed us all.

"We will," she agrees, but I think, only because she has to.

There isn't much to be said after that. I don't want to give her more empty promises, and she doesn't seem to want to share any false hope. We nibble on our food, just content in the presence of the other. My mind once again drifts to how crazy our lives have become. A year ago, I couldn't even imagine us in the midst of Faery, battling a disease from what seems like another life.

But that's who the Ancients are. They are the first creatures, the beginning to all of this. Their magic is older and stronger than anything we've ever seen, and this is just one example of it. Who knows what else they have up their sleeves? Their greatest strength is that even though they've been asleep for centuries, they are still adaptable. They know magic better than we do and they know how to make it work for them, even in this new world they've woken up to.

There has to be an answer in all of this. I just can't find a way to ask the question that would yield it to me.

THE NEXT MORNING, I'M UP BEFORE THE REST OF THE SCHOOL. OR so it seems. The academy's halls have become so empty, I can't really be sure. Some students are huddled together in each other's rooms.

Others are working with teachers, trying to find answers. The upper-classmen have been assigned to help take care of the sick, but even they can't do much. It's mostly maintenance, making sure they're comfortable. As I walk down the empty hallway, the heaviness settles over me. We're all trying to do our part and none of us is helping.

I didn't sleep the night before. Maybe a few minutes here and there. But I kept thinking about the Ancients and Queen Amaryllis and how similar they truly are. Both hungry for power, both willing to do whatever it takes. Then, naturally, my mind drifted to my family and then to my friends. Before ending with Aiden. I try so hard not to think of him. Especially when it comes to the kiss we shared. But the feel of his lips on mine has been seared into my being and there is nothing I can do to remove it.

Without even trying, my mind shifts to the story I found in the library. It's difficult not to connect the two together. The balance the story spoke of, it's what I feel around Aiden. And yet, I can't be his soulmate. That's Natalie's spot. No matter how much my heart wishes for it not to be so.

The exhaustion I've been carrying with me for days is making my magic a little bonkers. The best way I know how to calm both myself and the magic is to let it run free. So, as light begins peeking through the trees around the academy, I slip out the front doors and head toward the pond. The walk isn't long, and the air is the perfect temperature, like it always is in Spring Court. Yet I'm so worked up, I'm sweating a little.

I haven't been able to find a balance between my magic and the story spell casting magic. Often, I'm not sure which one I'm using, and that's the reason I have to keep it all under wraps. But I need a release, and I know the pond is the place for it. After all, it's not the first time.

When I reach the water bank, I sit down as close as I can to the edge with my legs crisscrossed. Taking a few calculated breaths, I stare at the water and reach for it with my hands. There's a moment of still-ness right before the water shoots toward me, slamming into my open palms and then flying straight toward the sky. I chuckle at the excite-ment I feel coming off each drop. The stream slows down, letting me mold and shape the flow any way I'd like.

The last time I was here, the last time I let myself go, Aiden was here. He thought I was in trouble, and he jumped right into the tossing waves to try and save me. The water begins to dance faster and harder in front of me, answering to my emotions without me having to say anything. I let it play, keeping the storm anchored to the pond, but other than that, I give my magic free reign.

The movement of the water, the electricity in my veins, it's exhilarating. The exhaustion seeps away, renewing my strength for this one moment in time. Suddenly, there aren't ancient evils to battle or a broken heart to mend. It's just me and my magic, and I let it fly.

When the time comes, I think I'll be able to use the magic in the way it is intended to be used. But until then, I will try and practice. After all, it's just like an untrained muscle. I have to work at it to make it strong.

Closing my eyes, I let the magic sweep me away. Images play out in front of me, and I feel the water create the shapes, even though I can't see them with my eyes closed. Before I can make myself control it, the images become the visuals from the story I read. But this time, the prince is clearly Aiden, and I am the fair maiden. Opening my eyes, I watch their meeting, created by the pond like a little miniature theater. The maiden bows, and the prince returns the gesture. Then everything shifts and suddenly they're at the ball. She's wearing the gown, and he's running away. The shift comes, but she stays.

I don't realize there are tears in my eyes until my vision blurs. Blinking them away, I blink the pictures away as well. I have to stop dwelling on the story. It won't do me any good. Nothing good can come from two people whose destinies are not meant for each other.

Once the water is dancing without the images, I close my eyes once more and let the magic heal me. If only it worked for my sadness just like it works for my injuries. But I wouldn't want a world without sadness. Because it's that emotion that makes us appreciate the happy times that much more.

{ 6 }

"I have an idea."

With my eyes closed, I don't hear him coming. Liam seems to materialize next to me. Settling down beside me, he sounds more excited than he should be able to at the moment. He waits for me as I take a deep breath and bring my magic back into myself. The water floats down gently and then I turn to him.

"It must be a good one."

"Well, of course it is. But that's besides the point. I didn't think it would be possible, but I figured we could give it a shot."

"Just spill it already."

He blinds me a little with his grin, leaning toward me.

"You know how you said your sisters are very knowledgeable in all things Ancients?"

"Yes?"

"And how their help would be just perfect right now?"

"Liam!"

"I think there's a way we can contact them."

"What?" I don't think I hear him right at first. My head spins with possibilities. If what he's saying is true, then I could figure out this whole sickness thing. The selfish part of me that has missed them just wants to see them. But before my mind can run away with me, I take a deep breath and focus on Liam. Who's still grinning at me.

"Are you sure this is possible?"

"Not a hundred percent." He sighs. "But do you remember when you showed up here, and you asked why I was wearing human clothes?" I wave a hand in his direction, up and down his body, because he's been wearing human clothes the whole time I've been in Faery. Well, besides the ball.

"It's easier to blend in at the academy."

"I'm not against it," I hurry to reply, "I'm just saying..."

"Okay, well that time you saw me. I went to visit Hawthorne."

"That's right. You did mention something. Vaguely."

"The queen isn't really a fan of me doing my own thing." I nod at that, but don't interrupt again. I'm waiting for him to get to the point. "I went through a portal. Not one of our regular ones, but one of my family's."

I lean a little closer, hand on my knees as I listen. The even slight possibility of seeing my sisters has me hyped. I could tell them about our father. Even though I don't know much myself, talking to them could help me figure more things out.

"Each royal family in Faery has their own ancestral magic. Even though it's ours, we still have to run everything by Her Highness. But, with everything that's been going on, I'm thinking we can sneak under the radar and try it. It might be shut down by her magic, but it might not be."

I'm already nodding, the possibilities swirling inside my head. It's difficult to not get excited. Maybe this will be the break I need. Because after all the research, all I am is more confused. The elixir the Oracle gave me is still in my pocket. It seems that no matter how hard I try, I can't reconcile myself to the decisions I must make.

"So, let's go. What are we waiting for?" I ask, jumping up to my feet. Liam follows more slowly, glancing around quickly.

"It's not exactly safe for you to leave the premises of the school," he comments, lowering his voice. "We'll have to travel by foot because you can't use the portals. The queen would know and would be waiting on the other side."

Queen Amaryllis and her need for control is really getting on my nerves. It's why even traveling through the forest to meet the Oracle was such a risk. I could've been found out at any moment. Not using my magic is the only way I can think of to sneak around her. But that becomes a problem when my magic is what I need.

"Okay, we'll go in a few hours, once it's dark out," I say, turning toward the academy building. The comforting brick castle looms before us, the mismatched architecture a bit of comfort at the moment. I miss my family; I miss my home. I miss my friends being well. But at least I have the comfort of knowing I will be sleeping in my own bed at the academy. That's more than some can say.

"Have you been able to figure anything out about..." Liam doesn't have to finish. I know what he's talking about. Maybe I should mention what the books showed me in the library, but I'm not even sure what it all means. I searched for answers and all I got were stories. And more questions.

"No, and I need to go see the headmaster for our status report."

"Will you tell him about it?"

"I don't know."

That's my standard answer for everything right now. I'm not sure who to trust, and that makes it difficult to make any sort of progress. Even though a part of me keeps forgetting Liam is fae, I'm not afraid of him betraying me. I may not be the best judge of character, but I trust him. Right now, he's the only one I trust. Still, I'm keeping some information from him. At this point, I'm not sure if it's to protect him or myself.

"I'll meet you in the greenhouse?" he asks, breaking through my thoughts. I realize we've arrived at the front doors of Thunderbird Academy. I nod, and he hurries off, leaving me to go inside alone.

Once I'm through the main doors, that tug on my heart begs me to turn right and go up the stairs. But I push it away, just like I've been pushing away all my emotions. I can't see him right now. I need to focus on how to save them all first.

So, against my own heart, I turn left and head down the hallway. Headmaster's office doors loom in front of me, and at the last moment, I almost stop. Seeing him, it just reminds me how many responsibilities rest on my shoulders. How much this whole mess is my fault. But I don't turn away, I don't leave. Instead, I raise my hand and knock.

❧

THE MOMENT I'M INSIDE THE OFFICE, I'M CAUTIOUS. THE DRAPES are closed, shutting off most of the light coming through the windows. There's only the small desk lamp lit on the table, casting everything into shadows.

"Headmaster Marković?"

"Come in and take a seat." The voice comes from behind the desk, and I walk forward to take a chair on the opposite end. The last time I was in the office, the lights were on, and Headmaster Marković was hard at work. Right now, it feels like I walked into a tomb, and all my internal alarms are going off.

"Headmaster Marković, what's going on?" I'm almost afraid to ask, but it's not like I can beat around the bush. There's a long moment of silence, as I try to squint through the darkness. But all I manage is to make out the outline of the headmaster, nothing more.

"I am afraid the Elders are not as immune as they surmised." When he finally speaks, it makes my blood run cold. Even before he leans over, I know what I'm going to see. The headmaster shifts in his seat and then his face comes into the light. The pale skin, the bloodshot eyes, the sweat running down his face. He's sick. The magical sickness that has been spreading through the school has reached him.

I'm at a loss for words. I just sit here, staring at him as he works to meet my gaze. The darkness in the office makes sense now. The sick are much more sensitive to light. It's why his office feels so dreary.

"Headmaster, you should be in bed, resting," I finally find my voice, while I swallow down the panic. So many of us thought the Elders were immune. I remember my sisters mentioning something about a spell our parents cast over thirty-five years ago that protected those who have now become Elders. I should've asked more questions, but of course, I didn't. Headmaster Marković has been around for generations. This sickness shouldn't be able to reach him. And what about the other teachers?

"It does not matter where I am, Miss Hawthorne. The sickness can reach me there. Here, I can at least try and help."

But he's not helping. I can see that as plain as day. He seems to be confined to the chair, barely staying awake. Even though it's not my place to tell the headmaster what to do, I feel like I must.

"You're no good to anyone if you don't take care of yourself. Maybe with a little rest, you can renew your strength and get back to work." Even as I say the words, they don't ring true. But what else could I say? My mind is still trying to wrap around the fact that this school is about to be without a functioning headmaster. A part of his magic keeps this place safe. And if he's not immune, that means the rest of the teachers aren't either. The chaos of the past month is about to go up a notch. Or ten.

"Have you been able to find any more information?" The headmaster completely ignores my comments. Not that I'm surprised. I sit up a little straighter, almost ready to tell him about the library's findings and the elixir, but something stops me.

"Nothing yet. But I'm still working on it."

Headmaster stays quiet, and I can't even tell if he's breathing anymore.

"Do what you can, Miss Hawthorne."

I've been dismissed. Saying my goodbyes, I head to the door. With one last look at the darkened office, I slip outside. Once I shut the door behind me, I lean against it. He was the one keeping this place together. The leader who was front and center, keeping everything running. With this new development, I'm scared to find out what will happen next.

But just like it's become my constant, I can't dwell on this situation. I have to figure out what's next. There's a plan to be made and a battle to be won, but I would give anything to not be responsible for making this decision. Taking that nap is sounding better and better by the minute. I haven't slept well in days, and it's definitely coming across in my actions and decision making. I wish there was some way I could pass out already.

Straightening away from the door, I square my shoulders and take a deep breath. That was my moment of self-pity, and now it must be pushed aside. I think if my family saw me now, they wouldn't recognize me anymore. I'm not just a sixteen-year-old girl going to school. I've become an adult almost overnight, and I have to make decisions that affect everyone. No one has asked me if I can carry the load. It was handed to me, and I either carry it or drop it. And if I drop it, my friends and family will be gone.

I can't let that happen.

❧ 7 ❧

After dinner, I'm once again in my dark sweater and jeans, boots laced up at the ankles. Not that it was truly necessary, considering no one is around to see me sneaking off anyway, but it seems appropriate for the occasion. Of course, I'm still very careful as I make my way across campus. Even the rebel kids won't come out after curfew. This sickness has truly made all of us equals.

When I finally reach the tree line, night has fallen. I've heard Faery operates on a different set of night and day rules, but since we've been here, it's been pretty close to what I'm used to. I'm not sure if it has anything to do with the academy or not, but right now, it's appreciated. I like having the darkness as an extra measure of protection.

"Mads." Liam's voice reaches for me through the shadows and then he seems to materialize out of the trees.

"Nifty trick," I comment, and he shrugs, looking pleased with himself. That's a very fae thing to do, so I just shake my head. He motions for me to follow him, and we slip farther into the forest.

"You sure about this?" Liam asks when we've walked a few yards.

"Yes. It's actually the perfect time. I unleashed a lot of magic earlier today. It should solidify my location to the queen, if she decides to do her spying." I have no proof of this, of course, but I won't put it past her. Knowing what goes on in her land is her job.

"Since we can't take any of the doorway portals, it's about a forty-minute walk."

"I'll survive, Liam. Don't worry about me."

I would walk much farther for a chance at talking to my family. He's still worried, that much I can see, and I try on one of my reassuring smiles. Not sure if he buys it or just decides to take my words at face value. After a moment, he begins leading the way.

It's so much darker between the trees. Last time I was in the woods, just a few days ago, I didn't stop to think about all the creepy crawlers hiding in the shadows. But then the trolls attacked, or whatever those creatures were, and now I'm more aware. Liam's steps aren't full of hesitation, like mine seem to be. It appears that I have to remind myself to be brave continuously.

We stay quiet, to keep alert in case anything does decide to jump out on us. The quiet just makes my thoughts louder. So instead of dwelling, I hurry just a few steps to catch up to Liam.

"What are our chances here?" I ask, keeping my voice low. He glances at me before replying.

"I don't know. This could work, this could be an epic fail. But I owe it to you to try."

"Hey." I grab his arm, pulling him to a stop, confusion furrowing my brow. "You don't owe me anything."

"That's not how I meant it." Liam sighs, which means there's clearly something on his mind. Instead of pushing, I wait him out. He used to always be able to talk to me. He should still talk to me. But maybe we're both being cautious.

"I just feel like I failed you, Mads," he finally says, leaving me completely flabbergasted.

"What does that mean?" I ask, when it's clear he's not going to continue without a little prompting. For someone who carries himself a very particular put together way, he looks pretty unsure of himself at the moment. "Liam."

"I didn't return to school. I left you all alone to deal with the Ancients. And even after I found out about your father, I didn't come. I'm sorry for that."

The apology freezes me in place. Fae don't apologize. They never put themselves in such a vulnerable position. But Liam does. For me.

"Liam," I begin, unsure of how to put into words what I'm thinking and feeling. I take a step forward, reaching for his hand. "You didn't leave me alone. You stayed to take care of your family. You helped my sisters when the time came. I can't hold it against you, not when what you were doing was your duty."

I've never felt abandoned by Liam. Just sad that he wasn't there in school. He's one of my closest friends, the first guy I've been this comfortable with and someone who's kept my secrets better than anyone else. Of course I'd be bummed he wasn't there. But I could never fault him for doing his duty.

"I still wish I could've done more."

"And you're doing it now."

He's stood by me through all of this, I can't believe he would be feeling like this. But I guess that shows no one is immune to self-doubt. Not even beings as powerful as the fae.

"I hope it works," he says, and I give his hand a quick squeeze before letting go.

I do too.

✥

I STAND IN FRONT OF THE OPEN DOORWAY, SWEAT POOLING AT THE back of my neck. I'm so nervous this won't work. I'm so nervous it will, but the queen will know somehow and come take me away. Every single bad scenario is rushing through my mind, and it's like I can't change the channel.

"Are you ready?" Liam asks, coming up to stand beside me. Not trusting myself to speak, I nod. He steps up to the doorway, and I can feel his magic in the air. Fae have a certain frequency about them. Ever since I started using story spell casting, I've been more attuned to the magics around me. He mumbles something in a language I don't understand before waving his hand in front of the doorway.

At first, nothing happens. And then, the longer we wait, the more disheartened I become. Liam says something else, but I can see it's not working. I'm ready to turn away when I hear it. A voice.

"Liam?" Nolan, Liam's brother, steps up on the other side of the doorway just as a ripple of magic washes over the empty space. It's as if a coin has been tossed into the water in the middle of the doorway and the ripple effect opens up the way.

"Nolan!" Liam and I say at the same time, stepping closer to the doorway. The older brother gives us a shocked look, before he races out of the frame. I move to follow, but Liam grabs my hand.

"We can't. It wouldn't open as a doorway. Just a... video chat."

I nod, letting him know I understand. It's probably why it didn't work right away. We're already playing with fire here. This is a dangerous endeavor. But then, I hear another voice, and I don't care about the danger.

"Maddie!" Bri, my oldest sister, runs into the frame with Harper right behind her. I stare at my sisters, tears springing up in my eyes and falling down my cheeks. I don't even care that everyone can see me crying, I'm just so happy to see them.

"Bri, Harper, hi!" I manage, hiccupping over my tears. Liam steps beside me, and I grab his hand, just so I can stay grounded on this side of the door. I'm afraid that if I even get a little too close, it might disappear.

"We've been so worried, Maddie," Harper begins, words tripping over themselves. "Your school disappeared. No one knew what happened. We've been scrying but nothing. We thought you..." She pauses, trying to compose herself, and I realize she's crying too. Harper is the middle sister, and she's always been the outgoing one but also the one that keeps her emotions in check. She's not being so careful now.

"We thought you disappeared like Dad," Bri finishes, and I hear what they're not saying. They thought I was dead.

"Oh my gosh!" I exclaim, everything I need to tell them tumbling out at once. "I know where Dad is! Well, kind of. He's here in Faery. Which is where I am. It's too much to get into, and I'm not sure how long we have, but I accidentally transported the whole school, along with its campus, to Faery. Apparently, I have story spell casting abilities and the Ancient's were close, so I did a spell and here we are. But now everyone is sick, and we're trying to find a cure. I'm not sure what to do. I miss you. Where is Mama? I miss you all so much."

My sisters just stare at me for a moment, trying to digest everything I dumped on them. And then they start talking at the same time.

"Dad is there?" "Do you know where in Faery?" "What kind of sickness?" "Are you using story spell casting? Because that's dangerous."

"I know!" I raise my hands, trying to ward off their worry. "I'm trying to not use the casting, but I might have to. It's another long story, but an Oracle gave me this cure." I pull out the little bottle I've been carrying with me everywhere. "It's only good for one person, and I don't know what to do. How do I choose who to save? And how do I get us out of this mess? I wish you were here. I made a mess of everything. I can't handle it. I can't handle all this responsibility. No one asked me, they just made me the center of it all, and I keep making the wrong decisions."

There's a moment of silence and then Bri takes a step closer to the portal.

"Maddie, you can handle this. You are a Hawthorne. Never forget where you come from. That's Hawthorne blood in your veins, and that's our family's brain in your head. Use that brain and that heart to guide you. We may not be there physically, but we are a part of you. You are not alone."

I take a deep breath, now crying more fully as I let Bri's words of encouragement settle over me. I'm having a pity party for myself now that my sisters are in front of me. I don't even care that Liam can see.

"So, who do I save?"

"Who do you want to save?"

"Everyone."

"Maddie." This comes from Harper. "Be honest with yourself. Who do you want to save?"

I know what she's asking, but I'm not sure I'm ready to give her that answer. I'm not sure I'm ready to admit it to myself. But I know I have to. They can't help me if I'm so stubborn I keep lying to myself.

"Aiden," I finally say, just his name on my lips feeling like too much. "And Jade. And Ben. I don't want to have to choose between them."

"But you already have. Your heart clearly belongs to one." Harper smiles, and it's a sweet smile of someone who knows that kind of a connection to another being.

"How do I sacrifice one over the other? I love them all. They're my friends." And that's not even half of it. They've become more than friends. They're family.

"Every choice you make will sacrifice someone. It's up to you to decide."

"That's not helpful."

"Maybe I can help." Another voice reaches me and then Krista steps into the frame. She's been Harper's best friend since basically birth, which means she's an unofficial third sister to me.

"What do you mean?" I ask, a note of hopefulness entering my voice. I was going to ask them about her and what she did for the town. My mind was so overwhelmed at seeing my sisters, I forgot all about it.

"This Aiden," she begins, and I cock my head to the side in confusion. "He means a lot to you?"

I glance over at Liam, and he squeezes my hand in encouragement. It really is past time I stop running from my feelings.

"He does."

"How much?"

"I don't know."

"I think you do."

I pause for a moment and then decide to just lay it all on the line. I can't keep doing this to myself.

"I asked for certain guidance," I begin, once again unable to mention the library. "But what I received was a story. About a prince and a fair maiden. Soulmates."

"Ah," Krista smiles, just as my sisters exchange a look.

"What?"

"Maddie," Krista begins, looking me straight in the eye. "When I healed the town from the sickness, it was because the soulmate magic unlocked something in me. I had to come to terms with who I was and what I was willing to do. I thought I'd have to sacrifice myself for

Nolan. When I trusted him and accepted that, our bond was solidified. You should trust your heart and the magic to see if maybe this boy is more than you think."

"You think, if he's my soulmate, maybe I can heal them too?"

"I don't know, Maddie." Krista shrugs, a movement so like Harper that it brings fresh tears to my eyes. They're all together, and I'm so far away. "But I know that we have to trust what is in our hearts. Either way, you will know. Your magic will guide you."

Maybe this is what I truly needed. A bit of a pep talk, because they haven't really said anything I didn't already know.

"Mads, we have to hurry," Liam suddenly says, and I look up to see the portal ripple.

"Look," I say, needing to get as much of this out as I can. "I have no idea where Dad is, just that he's here. If there is a way for you to find out more information, please do."

"We're on it," Bri replies.

"Is the spell still holding?" I ask, since I know the spell I helped my sisters put over the town isn't a permanent solution.

"It's holding, and we're still fighting off some attacks. Other places haven't been as lucky. The Ancients are sneaky. They infiltrate where they can."

"Don't we know it." I glance over at Liam, and he gives my hand another squeeze. I told him about Christie, so he knows what she's done.

"Maddie," Bri's voice brings my attention back to her. "I know you're scared. And I know you haven't been to see your friends. You're a lot more like me than you think," Bri adds when I open my mouth to ask how she could possibly know that. "Go see your friends. Make decisions by trusting who you are. You will make mistakes. There's no going around that. But you will learn with each one. We will see what we can do on our end about your predicament. And we'll look for Dad. We love you."

"We love you," Harper and Krista echo.

"How is Mama?" I ask, just as the portal ripples again.

"She's stronger than all of us," Bri replies. "But she misses you and Dad. She loves you."

"Tell her I love her. I love you."
And then, the portal closes.

❧ 8 ❧

I stand frozen, staring at the now empty doorway, tears still flowing freely down my cheeks. After I don't know how long, I feel Liam move toward me and then I'm the one who basically throws myself at him. He catches me easily and holds me close, letting me cry all my frustrations out.

"Thank you for that," I finally say, pulling back and wiping at my face. I probably look ridiculous, puffy, and red, but he doesn't seem to mind.

"We'll try again. I don't know if it'll work, but maybe if we're careful."

"Thank you," I repeat, and I realize I'm thanking a fae but it doesn't matter. I need him to know just how much that meant to me. He wipes at the lone tear trailing down my face and gives me a small smile.

"Anytime. Now, I think we should stay here for the rest of the night and set off first thing in the morning."

"You sure it's safe?"

I'm afraid the queen will know of what we did and will come to take me away. I only banished her from the academy grounds. Here she can reach me.

"I think it's safer than wandering the woods," he replies. "This place is more protected than most. When Nolan was still banished, he could come and visit here. It's been spelled."

That makes sense. Nolan is Liam's half-brother, and I know he wasn't allowed in Faery for a very long time. There's a lot of family drama that Liam had to live through. I don't know the half of it.

"Okay."

Liam leads me to a huge poster bed that can probably fit ten people and pulls back the covers. I take off my shoes and get under before I reach over and pull the covers back on the other side. Liam glances over, waves a hand making the lights go out and then he's getting in beside me. Flipping onto my back, we lay like that for a while until I think he's asleep.

"You know, what they said about Aiden?" Liam's voice reaches me in the dark. "I think it's true."

"Why?" I'm almost afraid of the answer, but I ask the question anyway.

"I've seen a lot of magic in my day, Mads. You and him? You have a special kind of connection when you're around each other."

My heart squeezes, and I think I'm going to burst from all these emotions.

"He's promised to another."

"It's a business contract. Nothing more."

"You don't even know..."

"I do know how he feels," Liam interrupts, clearly reading my mind on that one. "I think everyone else can tell, besides you two."

My mind instantly goes to the kiss we shared and how it made the world right again. Ever since I've met Aiden, there was an undeniable pull between us. But I never would've imagined anything as great as fate.

"Why are you so nice to me, Liam?" I ask, turning toward him, so I'm lying on my side. He doesn't hesitate with his answer while he turns toward me as well. I can barely make out his outline in the darkness.

"Because you're my best friend, and I don't have many friends at all."

He says it so matter of factly, but that just makes it so much sadder.

This boy, this fae, deserves much more than he's been given. I reach across the bed and find his arm, running my fingers down to the wrist before I grip his hand.

"I can't imagine growing up in two worlds the way you did," I whisper, and I hear him exhale. It must've been lonely, not belonging to either place. Fae aren't known to be too affectionate as it is, and both Liam and Nolan had to suffer that.

"It doesn't matter anymore. I'm only looking forward."

He sounds so strong and so brave. I squeeze his hand, letting him know without words that he means so much to me. I've never had a brother, but I imagine this is what it would feel like. Having someone at your back, knowing that they have your best interest in mind. And then, I realize that I want to say the words.

"You're my best friend too, Liam. That's now and forever."

It's a promise to a fae, but it's a promise I intend to keep. When the sleep finally comes, I'm still holding his hand.

❧

We wake up early, and head back to Thunderbird Academy without any major issues. I slept better than I had in days. There were no disturbing dreams for once. I'm not sure if it's because I saw my family or because Liam was right there beside me. Either way, I'm a little sharper, and I'm thankful, considering what I have to do today.

"Are you sure about this?" Liam asks, as we reach my room with absolutely no issues. The academy isn't even awake yet. He takes a seat on my bed, while I look for fresh clothes. Liam got to change at his house, but I feel uncomfortable.

"It's the only choice I have right now." I shrug before I duck into the shower. In almost no time at all, I'm dressed with my wet hair braided, and Liam and I are heading to the headmaster's office.

Sometime during the night, I decided to give the elixir to Headmaster Marković. The school needs him. The disarray has already begun, and it's only been two days. I heard more arguments before dinner yesterday then I have in days. People have noticed his absence, and it's not sitting well with them. He needs to be here to keep everyone calm. It pains me to make this choice, but my sisters told me to trust my magic and my upbringing. That's what I'm doing here.

"Headmaster Marković?" I knock on the door with Liam by my side. I think we've decided to stick together a little more, without really talking about it. Maybe he's nervous to see what I'd do if left alone. I *am* becoming more reckless. When the headmaster doesn't answer, I push the door open, slipping inside.

The office is even darker than last time. Liam closes the door behind us and leans against the wood.

"Whoa."

"I know what you mean," I mumble before raising my voice a little. "Headmaster Marković? I brought you something to make you better."

"Miss Hawthorne." The voice comes somewhere from the direction of the desk, but it sounds nothing like Headmaster Marković. The voice is so raspy and old, it's like he's aged a hundred years in a day. "What is it?"

Taking a quick breath to calm my nerves, I step closer to the desk, my hand closing around the vial in my pocket.

"You need to drink this," I say, thrusting the vial in the general direction of where I think the headmaster is. After what seems like an eternity, an old wrinkled hand reaches out to grab it. The rough skin feels gross against my own, and I surrender the bottle immediately.

"It will work?"

"It will."

Of course, I'm not too sure. But I can't exactly tell him that. A lot of magic relies on confidence. Maybe if he truly believes it it'll work, it will get the job done. At least, that's what I'm hoping. I take a hurried step back until I reach Liam.

"Feel better."

And then we make our escape.

Maybe I should've stayed longer and watched him actually take the medicine. But I couldn't stand being in that office any longer. There was so much heaviness in there, I had to get out. Liam seems to share my sentiment. We exchange a quick look, and I wonder if it would be too much to ask to go back to my room so I can shower again. But I immediately decide against it.

"What now?" Liam asks as we leave the headmaster's office behind.

"Now, we try out that other thing my sisters talked about."

He nods in reply, and we head to the wing of the school with all the sick people. It really is past time I stop running. I'm about to see my friends.

❧   9   ❧

We start slow. We head to Jade's area first. She looks like I remember her but also worse. Her skin is too pale, her lips too purple. It's as if her whole body has been painted in some otherworldly hues. I want to reach out and take her hand, but I'm not allowed. If there's a chance this spreads by contact, I've already had plenty of that. But I stick to the rule, if only to keep myself from being kicked out. I sit with her for a little bit, talking about nothing at all.

We go see Ben next. He looks much worse. He and Noel are near each other, and it hurts my heart to see them so unresponsive. One day, they're so full of life, and the next, they're barely clinging to it. I can't wrap my mind around that, and I don't want to. I want to fix it.

"Do you want some privacy?" Liam asks as we reach Aiden's room. Since he got sick after the majority of others, he's been kept in his own room this whole time. I shake my head no.

"It works or it doesn't. I want you there."

When we step inside, I notice right away how dull the space looks. It's not that it doesn't look lived in, like any boy's room would. It's just it's missing something, and that something is lying unresponsive in his bed.

Walking over to him, I almost stop and flee. If it was heavy in the other room, it's almost unbearable here. Aiden is the alpha. He's the strongest of the pack. But here he looks like he's wasting away.

His skin is so pale, it's nearly translucent. I can see just how difficult it is for him to take each breath, his chest rising and falling in jerks. For some reason, he's so much worse off than Jade.

"He's so sick. And he got it after the others," I comment, coming to stand near the bed. Liam remains at the door and doesn't speak. When I glance over at him, he gives me a small shrug before transferring his gaze back to Aiden. It's his way of encouraging me because we both know why I'm here.

Taking a seat on the bed, I reach for Aiden's hand. But before I can take it, I stop. It seems like such an intimate gesture and a part of me is still questioning just how much I mean to him. Or maybe I'm just scared of how much he means to me. Not sure if it matters either way. This whole soulmate thing, I don't really believe in it. Which is strange considering I've seen it with my own eyes. Maybe it's that I don't think I deserve it, but I have to give it a try anyway.

"Hi, Aiden," I begin, not really sure what I'm doing. It's not like I got a set of steps to follow. Even Krista wasn't that much help. But I think maybe I can make my magic do the work for me.

"This is strange, I know. I don't even know if you can hear me. But I've been looking for answers. And everyone seems to be telling me about this soulmates thing." I swallow hard, looking over at Liam, and he gives me an encouraging nod. It might've been easier to get this all out if he wasn't here, but I find his presence more comforting somehow. As if, maybe his belief in this thing can make it happen even if mine can't. Not sure when I became such a cynic, but if I had to guess, I'd say it was about the time my school ended up in Faery.

"I don't even know what I'm doing anymore, Aiden. I could've saved you, but I gave the one cure we had to the headmaster. It felt like I didn't have a choice. He's an elder. He needs to keep this place together in a way no one else can. And Jade. Ben. Noel. They all need it, and I don't know if I'm making the right decisions, but I'm doing the best I can."

I take another deep breath, trying to keep myself from panicking.

"I talked to my family, thanks to Liam. Krista, my sister's best friend, battled a similar sickness in Hawthorne and won. She said the connection she felt for Nolan opened up a magic inside of her that she didn't know she possessed. So, I should do the same. I should be honest.

"So here it goes. You're the most frustrating boy I know." I hiccup, tears running down my cheeks as I try to form the words. "I have never felt so much until I met you. You push me outside my comfort zone, you help me when I'm too stubborn to ask for help. You have a tendency to get under my skin, but you also help me see myself in the best light possible. If I knew story spell casting would work and not make you worse, I would use it in a heartbeat. Even knowing the risks to myself. I..." I pause, not ready to say the words. "I won't say it until you wake up, okay? There's something you need to know, but you need to wake up so I can tell you to your face. Do you hear me, Aiden? I need you to wake up so I can tell you."

Having spent all the words I had stored up but the three, I take his hand into both of mine and open up my magic. It flows through me and over him, like a blanket tucked over his body. I close my eyes, focusing on the intention, on healing him from inside out. The magic shifts back and forth between us, and I don't know how long we sit like that. Until I'm completely spent.

"Hey," Liam is there to catch me when I slouch down, dropping Aiden's hand in the process.

"I'm okay."

"You're anything but okay. Let's get you some rest."

"I can't, I have to..."

I glance over at Aiden, hoping to see some difference in his coloring at least. My heartbeat speeds up as I watch him take a breath, but then, his body jerks and all hope vanishes.

"It was stupid for us to try," I say, getting to my feet. Liam reaches for me as I stumble, keeping me upright.

"It was good of you to try. You've exhausted yourself. You just need rest."

"No," I say as we make our way out of Aiden's room. I can't even bring myself to look at him again. I feel like such a failure. "I need water."

Liam seems to understand, so instead of heading for my room, we head outside. I cling to my friend, trying to keep the tears at bay. If I felt like a failure before, nothing compares to how I feel now.

❦

LIAM HELPS ME TO THE BANK OF THE POND BEFORE LEAVING. I KNOW he wants to stay, but I need to be alone. The tears won't stop, just like the blame. I blame myself for everything. If only I was smarter, braver, stronger... Maybe I could do something to help my friends. But all I've done is bring false hope to my world.

Reaching for the water, I submerge my hand almost up to my elbow. The cool liquid feels nice against my overheated skin, as much as it soothes my magic. Maybe I can just stay here forever. Half in the water, crying myself to full exhaustion. I'll just lay here until nothing else matters.

Sitting up, I take off my shoes and jacket before I lower myself into the water. There's a small hiss in the air, as if my body is actually giving off a bit of steam. My magic begins doing summersaults all over my essence, ecstatic to be in the water. The connection to nature is the strongest when I'm like this, and my magic can feel it. Leaning back, I begin to float, giving the magic the time it needs to replenish.

Being in the water, I start thinking about all the things that happened to me in the last four months. In the last year, really. I've come so far, have learned so much. I've grown as a witch and as a person. But now, here I am, in the pits of my despair, being all dramatic and sad. If my sisters could see me now, they'd say I need to get out of my funk and act like a Hawthorne.

Funny enough, when this school year started, that's what I was most afraid of. Being compared to my sisters. Now I wish I was half as good as them. Taking a deep breath, I plunge into the water, frustrated at myself for all this self-pity I'm feeling. Completely surrounded by water, I swim farther and farther down, enjoying the quiet. It's as if there's a barrier between me and the rest of the world, and it's the safe haven I've been looking for. I can stay here forever and hide from the world.

The moment the thought enters my mind, I push myself to the surface. Breaking through, I tread water, wiping the droplets from my eyes. I can't believe I would think such a thing. It's the most giving up thought I could've had, and I'm ashamed at myself for thinking so. This is not who my mother and father raised me to be. Through this whole ordeal, with every battle I had to fight in this war, I resolved on being strong and doing what needs to be done. But here I am, being nothing but a whiny kid.

"I'm sorry." I say the words out loud because I need to hear them. "This is not the kind of a witch I want to be. This is very un-Hawthorne of me. I'm stronger than this, and I will prove it."

I have no idea who I'm making the promise to. Myself? My heritage? But it feels like exactly what I need. Because no matter what happens next, I will have to fight. I can't spend my time feeling sorry for myself or my situation. I am stronger than that, and I'm determined not to lose sight of that again. It's the easiest thing, to become bogged down by all the problems. But it's the strong person who pushes past the weight and rises anyway. That's who I want to be. I will study harder, push myself more, and I will figure out this sickness. Then, I'll figure out how to protect myself from the queen so I can go search for my dad.

As if my magic hears my promise, it opens up. It flows freely out of me, filling the pond with its power. I smile before taking another deep breath and diving under the surface. Somehow, that small pep talk lifted a thousand pounds off my shoulders. I just needed a moment with my magic and a stern talking to, apparently. Flipping around, I dance a little, surrounded by the water, as my magic continues to grow around me. It's as if it's feeling better as well. It's so easy to forget just how much you can handle when everything seems to be going wrong. But I'm going to try to keep it together. And I'm not alone. I have to remember that too.

When I break the surface for the second time, I feel lighter somehow. Swimming over to the shore, I pull myself out of the water and then use my magic to dry off. Putting my shoes on, I shrug on my jacket. My plan is to go back to the sick wing of the academy and try again. Or maybe, just sit with my friends for a little while. I'm done hiding from them too.

But as I turn to go back to the school, something stops me. A ripple of unease in the air, a tug on my magic. Slowly I turn, scanning the area around me, trying to pinpoint where it's coming from. That's when I see her. Queen Amaryllis steps out of the shadows at the edge of the woods, watching me steadily. She can't enter the actual campus, but she's come as far as the magic allows.

Without hesitation, I move toward her, needing to know what brought her this far. She wouldn't have ventured out here if it wasn't important. Maybe the Ancients have reached the border. Maybe the queen found a cure. A hundred scenarios rush through my mind as I stop a few feet in front of her.

"You are causing problems again, Madison Hawthorne," the queen says, her gaze as cold as ice. Confused, I furrow my brow, unsure of what she means. She might know about my venture into the woods to see the Oracle, but I don't see how that's a problem.

"I have no idea what you mean." I decide to be honest. My guard is still up, for I don't trust this fae and never will, but I need her to be truthful with me.

"Are you really that dim or do you truly not know what you have been doing?" She cocks her head to the side, studying my face, and it's difficult to not fidget under her scrutiny. I raise my chin a notch, keeping my gaze leveled with hers. It takes so much out of me, but I'm not flinching.

"Maybe explain yourself, *Your Highness*, before you start throwing accusations around," I say, folding my arms in front of me. She watches me for a moment longer before replying.

"You really have no idea about the amount of magic you just sent out? The whole court felt it. Whatever games you are playing, Madison Hawthorne, you better be careful. Your little banishing spell will not last forever." She seems to want to say something else, but then her eyes zero in on a spot over my shoulder. Not completely trusting her, I allow my battle magic to flare up at my fingertips before turning around. What I see almost makes me stumble. Not caring about the queen, I leave her behind and sprint forward. The moment I reach Jade, I throw my arms around her, as she hugs me just as tightly.

"You're okay," I mumble into her shoulder. "You're okay."

"Thanks to you."

"What?" I pull back, giving her a quick once over. She looks a little pale but otherwise well.

"I felt your magic, Maddie. You healed me. Us. You healed us." She points behind her, and that's when I see Noel, Ben, and Vera walking toward us. The moment they see me, they take off running. Then I'm being hugged, and we're tumbling to the ground, and it's the best feeling in the world. I don't even notice the queen retreating into the woods.

❧ 10 ❧

Everyone is talking at once, but I don't care. Just the sound of their voices makes me smile. We're still sitting in the grass near the pond as they bombard me with a million questions. I try not to dwell on the fact that Aiden is not here. But I see other students walking out of the school, so it seems everyone has been healed.

"I don't know how it happened. I thought...I tried something, but it didn't work." I say, swallowing around the lump that's growing in my throat. Glancing over at Ben, he notices my look and gives me a firm nod. He knows what I'm asking without having to say the words. So, Aiden is healed. He just didn't bother to come with the rest of my friends.

"Maybe it was just a delayed reaction," Jade replies, squeezing my hand tightly. I'm still a little amazed that she could feel it was my magic that did it. But she has always been very sensitive to people's magics. I think that's why Christie never used any around her, or we would've been able to tell she was going to betray us. Before anyone else can say another word, three chimes sound from the academy and the robotic voice announces a meeting.

"That was expected," Vera comments as we all get to our feet. I'm a little surprised she came out here with the rest of them, instead of going to her shifter friends. But maybe we have reached a new friend-ship status with her too. We begin to make our way toward the school, and I'm the last to follow. Noel waits for Jade, and then, ever so care-fully, reaches for her hand. The gesture makes me smile because I've been waiting for this. It's a little sad this is what it took for him to finally be brave enough, but I've learned people react differently to trials. I, apparently, went on a rollercoaster ride of emotions. From brave and strong to a mini depression to hopefully brave again. It seems I'm constantly fighting a personal battle in the midst of all my other battles.

"I knew you could do it," Ben comments, falling into step beside me. I bump my shoulder with his, giving him a small smile. He doesn't have to be a mind reader to know what's on my mind. "He gave me permission to come find you. He stayed with the pack."

My heart squeezes to hear the words, now knowing that he is truly awake and well. But it doesn't diminish the hurt I feel. Because if he's with the pack, he's with Natalie. No amount of confession would change what he is required to do. And I have to live with that.

The rest of the school is moving toward the doors as well. It seems that everyone needed a breath of fresh air after they came out of their sickness. I notice most of the shifters are shifting back to human form. I bet their animal counterparts missed them.

"Did you shift?" I turn to Ben and he nods, grinning.

"It was the first thing I did. The first thing all of us did." He motions with his head, and I turn to see a pack of wolves making their way out of the woods. I don't have to see Aiden in his human form first to know which one is he. His wolf form is just as imprinted in my mind as his human one. I swear, even across this distance, his eyes find mine. But I don't have supernatural sight, it might just be my wishful thinking.

Once the student body is inside the grand hall, I notice the teachers up on the platform smiling. The noise level is almost over-whelming after a week of near silence. The teachers keep scanning the crowd, as if they're afraid this is all a dream. And I can understand that. It feels surreal, even to me. Then, a hush falls over the room as Headmaster Marković steps up to the front of the platform.

"It is good to see you," he begins, his voice amplified by magic as usual. There is a note of raspiness there, and I can see he's recovering, just like the rest of them. "We will continue to stay vigilant, and there is a routine checkup being set up as we speak. But we will take the next few days to recover. Please take the time to rest, even though you have been in bed for days. We are still guests of Faery, and we will continue to update you as we learn more. Go have fun." He smiles then, which is a bit uncharacteristic of him, before walking off the platform with the rest of the teachers following behind.

There's a pause in the air, as if we're not sure what to do with what we've been given. I expected a longer talk, but maybe the teachers just needed to see everyone for themselves, and we'll get a longer announcement later.

"Did Headmaster Marković just basically give us permission to party?" Ben asks, giving me a slight wink.

"I feel like he definitely did," Jade replies, clapping her hands together. "I think we should listen to him, don't you?"

The rest of my friends grin and nod as they start making plans. The student body begins moving out of the room, a happy chatter of background noise as we exit. My eyes seem to scan the room automatically, looking for a specific shifter, but I don't see him. As we step through the doorway, Mrs. Lee appears beside us.

"Miss Hawthorne, could you please come with me?"

My friends stop, giving me a look, but I motion them to go ahead. I knew this was coming. The faculty has to have questions about what I did. But as I follow Mrs. Lee, I honestly don't know if I have any answers.

⚜

WHEN I'M USHERED INTO THE HEADMASTER'S OFFICE, I'M NOT SURE what to expect. The last time I was here, I dropped off the elixir, and the room was so dark I could barely see a foot in front of me. Now, everything seems to be back to its regular bright lighting and open curtains. Headmaster Marković stands behind his desk looking over some papers, but he raises his head as soon as the door closes behind me.

"Miss Hawthorne," he greets me, a full smile on his face. Something about it unsettles me, but I can't put my finger as to why. "You did it. You managed to find the magic you needed to find."

"I'm not so sure about that," I reply, walking over as he motions for me to take a seat. By my quick study, Headmaster Marković seems completely healed. Even more so than the students. There's more color to him, more liveliness. "Did you take the...medicine I gave you?"

"I did. But it is clear to me that I did not have to. You came through."

"You really think it was my doing?"

Headmaster walks around the desk, perching at the edge of it as he meets my eye. He doesn't speak up right away, as if he's trying to figure out the right words to say.

"Your magic is powerful. Your ability to call on that which is important to you will never fail you. In this case, it proved to be true."

It takes me a moment to decipher his meaning, but then it hits me. He thinks I used the story spell casting. I open my mouth to protest, but then stop. Maybe it'll be better if he doesn't know. At this point, I'm not trusting anyone or anything, and sadly, Headmaster Marković has joined those ranks. I don't want to be suspicious of him, but there is one thing I've learned through all of this, I have to trust my instincts. Right now, they're telling me to be careful. I'm not sure if it has anything to do with the headmaster himself, or the fact he drank the elixir given to me by the Oracle. Either way, I need to play my role as a dutiful student and then get out.

"I guess I really don't know what my magic is capable of," I say, shrugging a little. That seems to satisfy him somehow as he stands and gives me another smile.

"You will figure it out when the time comes." He walks back over to his side of the desk and takes a seat. "Maybe you are ready to write another spell for the academy?"

The question takes me completely by surprise because after all we've discussed, me writing another spell is not on top of the list of things we were going to do. Finding another way was the plan, considering we have no idea what another story spell casting can do to the school and the students.

"I'm still doing research," I reply carefully. "It's important to get everything right, if it's going to work."

"I suppose you are right." Headmaster Marković leans back in his chair, linking his fingers together over his chest. "Well, I just wanted to check in and to say thank you. You have done a good job."

"Thank you, Headmaster Marković."

Just like that, I'm being dismissed. He motions to the door before glancing down at the papers in front of him again, and I stand immediately, ready to get out of the room. Absently, I wonder where the rest of the Elders are, or the staff that I expected to be present. Maybe I'm overthinking everything. It's not the first time, and it most certainly won't be the last. The room is leaving a bad taste in my mouth. I'm just ready to be back in my dorm.

With a quick look at the headmaster, I slip out the door.

❧ 11 ❧

When I step out of the headmaster's office, the feeling of unease doesn't leave. I should be ecstatic about everyone being healed and my friends being awake again, but something just doesn't feel right. Before I can think too much of it, I hear arguing and my head snaps up at the sound. I'd know that voice anywhere.

"I'm doing what's right," Aiden says, his voice calm but with a touch of power in it. He's every bit the alpha as he towers over Natalie. The girl isn't small either, and she holds her own. After all, she's an alpha too. They're off to the side, but even at this distance, I can feel the frustration between them. A few students have stopped to watch, but they're steering clear at a wide berth.

Neither of them has seen me yet, as I'm mostly hidden by the archway separating the hallway from Headmaster's waiting area. My heart beats faster as I study Aiden. There's still a little paleness to his skin, but the color is returning. He doesn't seem worse for the wear, and I'm thankful. The sickness could've turned out completely different for everyone. But Aiden looks just how I'm used to seeing him. Tight dark shirt over his biceps, hair falling into his eyes in disarray, his body tense with anticipation.

"You're doing what you want." Natalie's words interrupt my gawking. Owen is leaning against the wall behind Aiden, but his eyes are trained on Natalie. He doesn't seem to like whatever she's saying.

"Nat, it's not fair to the pack, and you know it."

I try not to cringe at the nickname, at the familiarity between these two, but I'm only a teenage girl. The pang of jealously comes before I can stop it.

"You think this is better? You're not being rational."

"No, you're not being rational. You're acting on feelings, and that's not how an alpha operates." The words are delivered with a punch, loud enough that even I hear every word.

"Oh, and you're not?" Natalie stares at Aiden for a long moment before she says something else that I can't hear. With the distance between us, I can't quite make out the look in Aiden's eyes, but he doesn't seem happy with her.

"You're going to regret this," she announces before she spins on her high heels and marches in the opposite direction. Immediately, I hug the wall in front of me, afraid Aiden will look over and see me. There may be a small part of me that's ready to face him, but not the main part. I'm still confused by my own responses to him. It's irrational to think he would've come to me the moment he woke up. He has responsibilities I can't even imagine. But the uncertainty I feel toward him hasn't diminished just because I've admitted to myself how I feel about him.

I don't have time to deal with my dumb feelings right now. With the sickness situation taken care of, at least for now, I have to focus on my dad. There has to be a way for me to find him, and I'm going to put all of my energy into that. I know the headmaster said to keep working on story spell casting, but I'm not taking this school anywhere until I get my dad. I can't afford to spend that amount of magic right now. If that makes me selfish, then that's what I am. This is the safest place for everyone right now and until that changes, I have to shift my focus. I can't wait any longer.

Moving away from the wall, I peek around the corner, but the shifters are gone. Breathing out a sigh of relief, I head for the stairs. Jade is probably already in the room, waiting for me. We haven't really had any proper time to catch up. I'm sure she has many questions.

As I make my way back to the room, I'm amazed by how different the academy feels. It seems that most people are still staying in their rooms, but there's a buzz of conversation behind closed doors, and it makes me smile. It was quiet, but I didn't realize how much more life this building has with the students in it. I love this school, and I should appreciate it more often. And now I'm getting sappy because it's the best way to keep myself from falling into other kinds of feelings I shouldn't be thinking about right now.

"Maddie!" Jade exclaims, jumping off the bed and rushing to me. "I know I've already hugged you, and you've probably been hugged a lot, but I just wanted to say thank you. You saved us. I don't know how you did it, but you did. So, thank you."

"That's the thing, Jade," I say, as Jade pulls away. "I don't know if I did."

"What do you mean?"

We walk over to my bed, climbing on top of the covers as Jade grabs one of my pillows to hug to her chest. The motion is so Jade that it brings moisture to my eye. It's like we haven't skipped a beat, even though it was almost two weeks since she got sick.

"First, how are you? How are you feeling?" I ask instead, not because I want to steer the conversation, but because I'm genuinely curious.

She sighs. "I'm so tired! That's where everyone went. Well, besides Ben. I'm not sure where he went. But it's crazy that I'm this tired after sleeping for so long."

That answers that. Ben probably went to find Aiden. Just the thought of the alpha sends my head spinning, I really need to focus.

"I think it's normal. I'm always tired after being sick."

"Makes sense." Jade shrugs. "The whole school is basically taking a nap right now. But I had to wait for you to come back. Now tell me what you mean!"

I smile at her insistence because I missed this. I missed her. She's a little like Harper in that sense. Her energy is exciting and tiring at the same time.

"Honestly, Jade, I'm not sure," I begin, trying to figure out how I'm going to put these fears into words. "Something just feels off. When I was talking to the headmaster, he still didn't seem like himself. I can't put my finger on it, but..." I take a deep breath and then dive in. I tell her as much as I can about what I've found out and about what I've done. She listens, only asking occasional questions, but I can tell she's bursting. When I finish, she sits quietly for a second, before she explodes.

"You and Aiden kissed? You think you have a soulmate connection? That's the craziest thing I've heard—"

"Jade—"

"And the truest. It seriously makes so much sense!" I was going to interrupt again, but her words stop me.

"Wait, what to do you mean?"

"Exactly what I said. You guys make so much sense, I thought you'd both burst if something didn't happen soon. And then Natalie came along. Which now that I mention it, how is that going to work out? It doesn't matter, I mean—" She shakes her head, but her words have extinguished the flame of hope that ignited.

"No, you're right. It won't work out. There's Natalie. He has a duty to her."

"From that argument you heard, maybe he's changing the contract."

Sliding off the bed, I get to my feet. The energy inside of me is a nervous mess. For this to be actually true would be my greatest desire. But if these last few months have taught me anything, it's that we don't always get what we want. Sometimes that's okay, and sometimes it'll break our hearts. Either way, it's not healthy for me to dwell on this. I have another item to check off my list.

"Listen, Jade, you're not going to like what I have to say next, but it's what needs to happen."

My friend perks up immediately, leaning forward. I do a mental checklist to see how many shifters reside on our floor, but I don't think anyone is close enough to overhear. Either way, I perch on the bed, lowering my voice.

"I'm leaving. In the next few days. My dad is out there, and there's no one else that can go and find him. I had no idea how I could, but then the headmaster mentioned something that has given me an idea."

"Maddie." Jade reaches over, placing her hand over mine. "I want to try and talk you out of it, but I know better. How can I help?"

Grinning, I squeeze her hand as my heart feels lighter. A part of me was a bit nervous she *would* try to talk me out of it. I'm still not sure when I decided this is my next course of action, but maybe I did just now. After I saw that my friend is okay. Or maybe I'm just running. It doesn't matter. Now that I have an idea, I have to follow through with it.

"I have to get down to the—" The dumb spell is still preventing me from telling anyone about the library, so I improvise. "Books. And do some research to make sure my idea will hold up. After that, I'll let you know."

She nods, accepting this as is, and this time, I'm the one who reaches out to hug her. She's the closest thing I have to a sister here. Nothing can replace Bri and Harper, but having someone beside you who has your back? That's something as special as magic.

Just then a knock sounds on the door, and I jump up to answer. When I see Liam, my face splits with a grin, and I throw myself at him. He catches me easily, lifting me from my feet. But then I feel it. An awareness that is acutely specific to one shifter. However, when I glance over Liam's shoulder, there's no one there. Even though I could've sworn someone was just a second ago.

Liam places me back on the floor and steps back.

"Not bad for day's work," he comments, looking into my room, and I turn to see Jade give him a little wave. Which he returns.

"I think maybe you should come in," Jade says, getting up and walking to her side of the room. "Maddie here has much to tell you."

Then, she grabs some toiletries and heads for the bathroom.

"What does she mean by that?" Liam asks, and I sigh deeply. He's not going to like this.

❧ I 2 ☙

"Are you out of your freaking mind?" he exclaims for the fifth or sixth time. Jade has returned from taking a shower and is now lying on her bed, enjoying the show. Liam is pacing, while I stay seated, giving him time to digest.

"No amount of shouting or logic will talk me out of it," I reply calmly, and he throws such a glare my way, it sends a shiver up my spine. He looks very fae right now and very dangerous.

"Mads."

"I can't just sit here, Liam. I've sat here for long enough. He might not even...he might not—" I can't make myself finish that sentence, but I don't need to. Liam understands. He takes a step forward, reaching for me, but I don't need his pity.

"I'm doing this. You can help, or you can get out of my way. I had a bit of an epiphany at the pond. I'm done feeling sorry for myself, and I'm definitely done being this weakling. I have to try, Liam."

"Okay, okay," the fae replies, throwing his hands up in the air. "Did you practice that speech?"

"No, but it's a good one, don't you think? I might have to use it again." I grab his arm, pulling him to sit beside me on the bed. "We'll have to find a way to sneak out without the queen finding out."

"Mads, you know everyone will know you're gone the moment you leave."

"Then we'll figure out a way that can buy us some time." I pause for a moment, a little afraid to ask but needing to know. "Will you come with me?"

"Really, Mads. Do you even have to ask?" Liam bumps me with his shoulder and the simple gesture, and the sincerity of his words makes me feel better instantly.

"Okay, then we plan. I'm going to see if I can find any clues and—"

"I'll do the same. And we'll go from there."

We share an understanding between us that's unlike anything I've known before. He's got my back as well, and I really am the luckiest person when it comes to friends. I don't appreciate them nearly enough.

"I have to go. But I'll be back first thing tomorrow morning," Liam says, before saying goodbye to Jade and leaving.

"He's a good one," my friend comments after the doors close and an announcement for the lockdown comes over the loudspeakers. I was hoping to sneak down to the library, but that will have to wait. Laying back on my bed, I stare at the ceiling.

"He's the best," I reply because it's true. Jade makes a little noise and then I hear her pull the covers over her head. My lips curl up in a tiny smile, the dream of having her just a few feet away finally a reality. I allow my eyes to close, and an image of all the students come to mind. I still can't believe that the sickness is gone. Even though I have so many questions, I decide that for right now, I'm just going to trust it.

As my body begins to relax for the first time in days, an image of Aiden takes front and center. He's never too far from my thoughts. I'm not sure I'll ever be able to close my eyes and not think of him. He's a part of me, and somehow, I'll have to deal with that.

Tomorrow, I make plans. Tomorrow, my reality shifts. Tomorrow, I'll think about him.

But for now, I sleep.

THE NEXT MORNING, THE SCHOOL'S ENERGY IS AT ITS HIGHEST. THE dining room is filled with students and staff, there's conversation all around us and people are laughing more than ever before. I sit at the table, surrounded by my friends, and for the first time in weeks, I feel like everything will actually be alright.

The feeling is fleeting, but my mind is still cataloguing everything into its memory banks so that I can look back at this and have hope in the darkness. Because when I leave this academy to search for my father, there will be nothing but darkness. The moment I go there, I know I can't keep sitting here and enjoying myself. With no classes, it'll be more difficult to sneak over to the library, so I need to do so now.

Scanning the students, I contemplate on how many may be missing. I know some are outside, others in their rooms. There must be others in the greenhouse. But I have to try now, before it becomes harder. Just then, my eyes land on the table by the windows and Natalie. She's already looking in my direction, eyes hard, and I do the only thing I can think of. I incline my head in her direction and smile. She doesn't like that, but she's also not about to jump across the tables and attack me. She wants to though; I can see that in the way she grows rigid in her seat. Owen leans over, saying something to her over her shoulders, and she jerks her gaze from me. My eyes shift to the Owen, and he gives me a quick smile as Natalie turns back to the table. So maybe I shouldn't be antagonizing the female alpha, even with all the distance between us. He probably saved my butt just now, and I return the smile in thanks.

I also realize Aiden is not there. Neither is Ben for that matter. Half of the regular pack is missing from the table, and I wonder if the headmaster and the Elders are keeping the grounds extra patrolled right now. It would make sense. But a part of me, that part that I constantly try and ignore, is disappointed he's not here. This is kind of my one opportunity to be in the same room as him before I leave. But I guess that's just my life right now. I should be thankful. In light of the big picture, it's probably better I don't see him at all.

It's time for me to go anyway. I lean over to Jade, giving her a little tap on her thigh as we preplanned. Her official job is to cover for me with our friends and the rest of the school. No one knows of my involvement in the academy's predicament, or the sickness, and it's best we keep it that way.

"Oh Maddie, is your meeting this morning or later?" Jade asks, completely natural in her deliverance. I'm slightly impressed, but I try to appear thoughtful.

"It's actually now. Thanks for the reminder."

Standing quickly, I apologize and say bye to my friends before walking at a moderate pace toward the doors. No one seems to be paying any particular attention to me, and that's what I need. Just before I slip out, I glance back to the shifter's table and find Owen's steady gaze on me. He doesn't do anything but watch me, yet somehow, I think he knows exactly where I'm going.

The hallways are mostly empty as I head toward the greenhouse. I probably should go and see the headmaster, but I kind of don't want to until it's absolutely necessary. I don't think he'll try and stop me, but I'm not taking any unnecessary risks. I have plenty risks to take as it is.

When I reach the hallway leading to the greenhouse, I find it empty. Honestly, I'm a little surprised, but it's my best-case scenario, so I shouldn't look gift horse in the mouth. Stepping into the room filled with plants, I do a quick scan and am amazed by the fact that there's no one inside. I walk through the aisles, to still double check. When I finally make it to the corner of the greenhouse, I almost pat myself on the back for not waiting any longer. Then I freeze.

Aiden is leaning against the wall at the far corner, arms crossed over his strong chest, his eyes on me. Sighing, I berate myself for not knowing better. There is no way I could've avoided him forever, and of course he'd be the one to know where to find me. Although, that makes me pause.

"What are you doing here?" I ask, keeping my voice as neutral as possible. He pushes away from the wall, coming further into the light, and I fight the urge to jump him right here and now.

"I knew you'd have to do research sooner or later."

His voice travels over my skin, igniting every part of me with just a few simple words. Even if I tried, I don't think I could take my eyes off him right now. He looks strong and comforting at the same time, like a safe haven I've been needing. Clenching my hands at my sides, I push past those thoughts and zero in on his words. Which is when it hits me.

"Aiden, how do you remember the library?" Just asking the question is usually forbidden, but the words roll off my tongue with no problems. My question does catch him off guard because he stops to think about it for a moment.

"I'm not supposed to know about it, am I?"

"Not usually."

We stare at each other as I let that thought settle over me. Something changed. Something happened that gives him this knowledge, and I have no idea where to even start to try and figure out what. Maybe the library itself can yield some information. But as soon as I think that, I push it aside. I have a different mystery to solve and it's much more important than this.

"Did you keep everyone away from here on purpose?"

He nods, and now the empty hallway and room make sense. Somehow, he remembers, and that's a conundrum I'll have to figure out at another time.

"Well, it was good to see you." I try for a very nonchalant tone. "I'm glad you're better. But I actually have work to do."

I move past him and toward the trap door, but he's not to be deterred apparently.

"You mean finding a way to find your father?"

Dropping the handle of the door, I spin around, not realizing just how close he is to me. I have to look up to meet his eyes, and my body shudders at the proximity.

"What do you know about my father?"

"Just what you do. And that you're leaving to go find him."

"How could you possibly know that?" I narrow my eyes because unless he was listening outside my door yesterday, he should have no knowledge of this.

"I have my sources." He shrugs, looking boyish and adorable, and I really need to tell my hormones to chill. But then, I'm hit with a realization.

"Who told you?" Aiden loses eye contact the moment I ask, so I know I'm right. And then I know who it is. Because it could only be one person. "Liam is going to get it."

Aiden glances down at me, and I think he's about to deny the accusation before he shrugs. "He's worried about you."

"Oh yay." I roll my eyes, turning back to the door. "You guys are such pals now. Well, go tell your bestie that he's uninvited from my mission. Maybe you guys can hang out while I'm gone. Do each other's hair or throw a ball around."

I'm a little angry, that's evident. Without a backward look, I descend into the tunnel below the school. If I'm hoping Aiden would just leave, I really should know better. He drops in behind me in the next moment, not even bothering with the steps.

"What are you doing?" I ask, exasperated as I turn to face him. We're completely alone down here, cocooned by the walls on every side, and I try to not let that get to me. It's been weeks since I've been alone with him.

"I'm coming with you," Aiden replies, his eyes shining in the dark light.

"You weren't invited."

"I invited myself."

With each sentence, we move closer and closer to each other, until there's only a little space between us. All I have to do is breathe in deeply and our chest will bump. But for some reason, I suddenly lose all ability to do so.

"You should probably un-invite yourself," I manage, looking up into his gorgeous eyes. There's a bit of amusement there, and so much emotion it nearly blinds me. He doesn't allow himself to show anything, but here, he's not even bothering to hide.

"I'm not about to watch you put yourself in danger without backup."

"I can take care of myself."

"I never said you couldn't. But it never hurts to have someone in your corner."

"Are you in my corner, Aiden?" I barely whisper, because my lungs are screaming for me to breathe, and my head is spinning from the way his essence surrounds me.

"Always, Maddie," he replies. And even though his voice is low, there's so much conviction in it, it slams right into me. I'm not sure what to say or do at that, but then Aiden makes the decision for me. His left arm reaches for my hair, gently tucking it behind my shoulder before he runs his finger down the length of my arm. The barely-there touch sends goosebumps over my skin, and then he takes my hand in his, tugging me forward. Our chests bump, as his other arm wraps around my waist, locking me in place. Raising my head, I find him already looking down at me. In this moment, everything else stops, and it's just us in this small world, the beating of our hearts syncing together. He lowers his head, and I think if I don't taste him right now, I'll explode.

But before his mouth can touch mine, his head snaps up, glancing toward the opening. I'm instantly on alert because his shifter senses are much more attuned to everything around us. His body goes rigid under my touch, as if preparing for an attack.

"Come on," he says, before tugging me behind him as he heads for the opening. We climb fast, and when I'm standing next to him, I do a quick sweep of the greenhouse, finding nothing amiss.

"Aiden?"

He looks down at me and then the announcement bells sound, right before the headmaster begins speaking. Aiden must've heard the other bells when we were below ground. He still hasn't let go of my hand, and I don't move to extract it, turning my attention to the headmaster's voice.

"We are happy to announce that the sickness has been eliminated. The queen of the Spring Court has made an announcement as well, stating it to be gone from the lands. While we cannot predict the continuance of this healing, we hope for the best and for traveling back to our realm as soon as possible. Miss Hawthorne is still in the process of reversing her spell and the staff and faculty are all here to make sure you are taken care of to the best of our ability. Please, do not hesitate to reach out to the office. My door is always open."

The announcement ends, but I don't think I can move even if I tried. My whole body has gone cold, fear gripping my heart and head.

"Maddie, did he just—"

I glance up at Aiden, finding confusion and anger on his face matching my own perfectly. I nod.

"He just told the school it's all my fault."

There's a pause and then Aiden springs into action.

"We have to get you out of here."

❧ 13 ☙

"Maybe we're overreacting?" I ask, pacing in front of Aiden. "Maybe it'll be okay. Maybe—" I pause, not sure what else to say.

"If you truly believe that, then let's go to the dining room. Rip the bandage right off."

I throw a quick glare at Aiden, but he's not wrong. If I do think it'll be okay, then shouldn't I just get this over with? When I first came back to school for this year, I hated all the stares from my fellow classmates. They watched me, expecting me to do great things just because I'm a Hawthorne. But now they know I'm the one who put them in this predicament. I have no idea how they're going to react.

"It doesn't matter right now. I need to get to the library and see if I can learn anything that would help me."

No sooner have the words left my mouth, Aiden twists toward the entrance of the greenhouse, his body fully on alert. Without hesitation, I freeze, watching him for my next cue. Then, Ben rounds the corner.

"Ben!"

"You have to get out. People are so angry, and they're looking for you," the shifter announces, glancing between Aiden and myself. Then, he notices the open door on the floor behind us. "What's that?"

So, I guess the library is still forgettable to everyone but me and Aiden.

"Never mind that," Aiden says, moving to close the hatch and cover it from everyone else. I let him do that while I turn to Ben. He's already forgotten about the door and is looking at me imploringly.

"I overheard some of the fox shifters talking to the northern witches. They're blaming you for everything, Maddie. They want to hold a council." My heart drops at his words. A council is a magical trial, and it can last for a day. Depending on the species involved, there is often magical torture. Northern witch covens are especially acquainted with the Dark Ages and their ways. I don't have time to stand trial, and I wouldn't be the same when it was done.

"Then, we have to go," Aiden says, coming up to stand beside me. Being an alpha, he knows of the council and the ways of magical trials. I can see the concern on his face already.

"It's not like you did it on purpose though," Ben comments, and I want to hug him and his little puppy tendencies.

"It doesn't matter. It could've been not even my fault, and they still would crucify me. People don't react well in stressful situations. After being away from their families and quarantined, they now have a name to put to all their troubles."

"Why would the headmaster say anything?" Ben asks.

"That's what I'd like to know," Aiden replies, the hardness in his voice could cut down a tree. He's gone from confused to angry, and I'm following that path.

"You better hurry," Ben says, turning his head toward the door. "People are coming."

"I'm not ready!" I exclaim, feeling overwhelmed. I have research to do. I need the information beneath our feet in order to save my dad. I move toward the door, but Aiden blocks my path.

"We have to go."

"I can't."

"If you go down there, you won't be able to come out again. We both know this. They'll put a magical lockdown on the school, it might happen any moment, and then you won't be able to help your dad. Is that what you want?"

"Of course that's not what I want," I snap, my mind racing. "But how am I going to help him if I don't even know how to find him?"

Aiden moves toward me, placing his hands on my upper arms. "We will figure it out, Maddie," he says, looking deeply into my eyes. "Together."

As I stare at him, I see that he means every word. And then, I hear it. People coming down the hall. If I can hear them, they're already too close.

"Let's go." I nod, moving toward the outer door exit. "Ben—"

"I'll take care of it." He pulls me into a quick hug before letting go. "Good luck."

Aiden is already waiting right outside the doors, and when I reach him, he gives me a quick encouraging smile. I'm too shocked to return it. This is not how I planned for everything to happen. But that's life, I guess.

"Duchess, may I?" His soft question snaps me out of my panic, and I watch as he reaches for me without touching. I realize what he's asking me to do and I step into his arms immediately, winding my hands around his neck. He hoists me up and I wrap my legs around his middle, and then he's running.

The academy grows farther away with each step, and just as we reach the woods, I see a bunch of students spill out of the greenhouse. Yet, Aiden doesn't stop. He runs through the woods, still in his human form, but much faster than I can ever run, holding me close. Burying my head into the crook of his neck, all I can do is hang on and hope this will all turn out fine. Because right now, nothing feels sure but Aiden's strong arms around me.

❦

I'M NOT SURE HOW LONG AIDEN RUNS BEFORE WE FINALLY SLOW down. We're way past the protective spell I cast on the academy, past the hedge and the border of Queen Amaryllis' palace grounds. Aiden takes a few more steps with me in his arms before he stops. I stay plastered to him, taking comfort in his strong arms before I pull back and allow him to lower me to my feet.

"Thank you," I say, keeping my voice low in case there's anything out here with us.

"Anytime, Duchess," Aiden replies, his grin lighting up this dreary forest. Because dreary it is. Taking a step back, I do a quick study of our surroundings and see that there are trees everywhere. Nothing looks familiar, but it's not like I know these woods as well as I know the woods in Hawthorne. My mind is finally catching up with everything that's happened, defeat rising up to choke me. And with it, panic.

"I can't believe this. Why would he tell the school? Why? All my plans are destroyed. We left with nothing. No clothes, no food. No idea where to go."

Aiden doesn't interrupt, just lets me vent as I pace the small space around him.

"We're fugitives! We can't go back. They'll put in me in jail. We ran, so we're guilty. That's how it looks. We—" And then I stop. Because it's not we, it's me. I'm the one everyone hates now. Spinning to face Aiden, I march right up to him.

"You have to go back. You're not part of this. You'll be fine if you go back."

"Maddie—"

"No, I'm serious. No one knows you've helped me. Besides Ben. But Ben is on my side anyway. And he would never go against his alpha. So, if you go back—"

"Are you done?" Aiden steps right into my personal space, halting my panicked ramblings. "I'm not going anywhere, Duchess. You'll have to get used to having me around."

For a second, I don't say anything, just stare at him as if he's lost his mind. He's letting so much ride on this. The school can expel him for helping me. He's a future leader of his pack. He can't afford to have any bad blood between him and the Elders.

"Why, Aiden?" I whisper, because my traitorous heart wants to hear all the words he can never say. I can't let my imagination run away from reality. But the way he's looking at me, as if he's ready to go to war on my behalf, sends my heart beating a thousand times a second.

"Because..." There's a small pause, and I think the forest is holding its breath right along with me. "We're in this together. I told you I'm in your corner. Do you really expect me to walk away right now?"

"No. But Aiden..." It's my turn to pause. I don't know how to tell him what I'm thinking and feeling without actually telling him what I'm thinking and feeling. "You're putting a lot on the line. I can't ask you to do that."

"You don't have to." He reaches for my hand then, wrapping his fingers around mine. "When you care about someone, you make their needs a priority. There's no ifs, ands, or buts. People who are important to you are people you take care of. I can help and because I can help, I'm asking you to please let me stay."

The tear slips past my defenses, racing down my cheek before Aiden catches it with his finger. The gesture is so gentle, I have to swallow the flood that almost overwhelms me. He's placing my needs above his own, and he's still letting me make the decision. The three words I've been carrying around in my heart threaten to come out, but I won't let them. We're not making forever promises to each other. He's being a good friend. I can't let his good intentions be overshadowed by my overactive imagination.

"If I say yes, I'm being selfish," I reply instead, and Aiden surprises me with a quick grin.

"I give you permission to be selfish. For once. I think it'll do both of us some good."

If I was truly selfish, I'd grab his face and kiss the smirk right off it. But instead, I squeeze the hand he's holding and smile.

"Then, stay. Please."

"I'll stay."

❧ 14 ❧

We do a quick sweep of our immediate area, making sure nothing was hiding in the shadows, before we find a spot to settle down and plan. With nothing to aide our journey, I'm not even sure where to begin.

"Do you know where we are?" I ask as I take a seat against a tree. We found a few trees closer together, so it provides more of a wall. One of them can be scaled up if we need to hide, so I'm feeling better. Not only are all of my lessons from dad returning, but I have a shifter by my side. This is more his element.

"We're straight north from the school. About six miles or so."

That's half the distance I had to travel to reach the Oracle. But that was in the other direction. She could possibly be of help, but I don't think I can handle making another bargain with her. I'm still waiting for her to collect on the first one.

"I don't really have a plan here, Aiden. This just seems surreal." I swipe my hands over my face, frustration running through my body. I know nothing about the land around us, how am I supposed to know where to go?

"Hey." Aiden scoots a little closer, peering down into my face. "You were going to the library for a reason. What was it?"

"What?"

"You snuck over to the greenhouse during the day. That's risky. Why?"

I stop fidgeting, my mind racing. It's still strange to me that Aiden remembers the library, but he's right. I was there for a reason. What was it?

"Oh!" I exclaim, remembering the idea I had. "It was actually because of something Headmaster told me when I met with him. It was such a weirdly specific statement that it stuck with me. He said, 'Your ability to call on that which is important to you will never fail you,' which I honestly don't understand completely. But. Every time I've been in the library and searched for answers, I called them to me. I thought maybe I could call on some help in order to find my dad. Now that idea is a dud."

"Well, maybe not entirely."

"What do you mean?"

"I mean, just because you're not in the library doesn't mean you can't call on answers."

"Okay, but in the library I can pick up a glowing book and read the answer. What am I going to pick up here? A rock?"

"Your sarcasm isn't helping the situation," Aiden points out, cocking his head to the side.

"But it is part of my everyday vocabulary, so tough luck."

Aiden shakes his head, but I can see the ghost of a smile on his lips. He's enjoying this as much as I am, and I'm not sure what that says about either of us.

"Sure, no books to pick up here. But who knows what's possible? It's magic, right?"

I can't really fault him for that logic. Except I don't really know where to start. Every time I use my magic, it's something new. Well, I would say besides the water magic, but even that has been surprising me lately. I'm changing, not just physically or mentally, but magically. That much I can see.

"I don't know what to do," I say honestly, hitching a breath when Aiden reaches over and places his hand on my knee.

"What does your magic tell you to do?"

"That's not how it works." I half laugh as I try not to focus on how hot my skin is becoming under his touch.

"Then explain to me how it does."

He sits back, and I seem to find my ability to breathe again. If I don't pull myself together, I'm going make a fool out of myself. The woods never felt so claustrophobic before. Shaking myself mentally, I try to figure out how to explain my magic to him.

"It's more like it listens to my inner thoughts and takes them as their own. I don't have to tell it to create, I have to make a definite intention. We're one and the same, so it's not like I go around telling myself to do something. I'm not explain it correctly," I grunt, hanging my head.

"No, you are. I understand. It's similar to my wolf. We're two, but we're one. And it works. Perfectly."

Raising my head, I give him a small smile. Maybe he does understand. But it still doesn't help me find my dad.

"What are you suggesting?"

"I'm suggesting you try calling on needed information and see what happens. As long as you don't use your story spell casting."

At that, I sit up rigid straight. Of course he would know about that.

"Are you and Liam serious besties now, or is this a fleeting thing?"

"I was thinking we're buds for life." That comes from the woods to our right, and both Aiden and I jump to our feet immediately. When Liam steps through into our little circle, I do nothing but stare.

"What? Do I have something on my face?" he asks, snapping me out of my daze. I throw myself at him, and he catches me easily, dropping whatever he was holding onto the ground. I hear the thump from the impact. He cradles me close before setting me gently to my feet.

"What are you doing here?"

"And why didn't I sense you coming?" I glance over at Aiden and find him staring at Liam.

"One, you didn't sense me because I've been cloaked. And two, I brought you supplies. You can't be fugitives from the law without proper supplies."

He points to the ground, and that's when I notice a backpack and two swords. The items bring a huge grin to my face, and I want to hug him again.

"How did you know where we were?"

"I followed your scent."

"What?"

"It's not that strange. You know Queen Amaryllis can sense your magic."

"Yes, which is why I haven't used it."

"Well, it's kind of stays around you anyway, like a scent. Because we're close, I can pick up on it, even when the queen can't."

"How is that possible, Liam?"

"Because he's royalty. Right?" This comes from Aiden, who is now sitting on the ground, going through the backpack. I glance between the two boys before rolling my eyes.

"I hate that both of you know more about fae than I do."

"Well, I kind of have to," Liam replies, and I bump him with my shoulder.

"Does that mean Queen Amaryllis knows I'm gone?"

"I don't think so. I was coming back to you when I saw you speed out of the greenhouse. Ben was right inside, and he explained to me what happened. It didn't take long to find Jade. She was hiding in Noel's room. People were harassing her to find you."

My poor friend. Once again, she's been put into a difficult situation because of her association with me. I have no idea why anyone wants anything to do with me after these things keep happening.

"She's a strong girl, Mads," Liam continues, clearly seeing the distress on my face. "She'll be fine. She packed the bag, and Ben and Owen snuck over to grab some weapons. It's the best we could do. I had to get out of there before your headmaster shut down the school."

"He did?"

"Yes. He sent everyone to their rooms, putting in place a lockdown until dinner time. Giving people time to cool off. But I honestly think it's making things worse."

"How?"

"People don't do well being locked in cages," Aiden comments, and I realize he's been watching Liam and I as we talked. He must've found the items in the bag to his liking because he gives Liam a quick nod.

"What do we do now?" I ask, feeling completely defeated. I'm the kind of person who needs a plan. And I really don't have one.

"You do what you were planning on doing," Liam says, his voice firm.

Aiden leans toward me, his own eyes shining with determination. "He's right. We go find your dad. That's our priority now."

"Okay," I say, my heart full from the way the two are looking at me. "How do we do that?"

☙❧

WE STAY QUIET FOR A MOMENT, EACH OF US MULLING OVER OUR next move. The only thing I keep coming back to is what Headmaster said to me in his office. But I'm not quite sure how to use that to our advantage.

"Do you think you can call your dad to you?" Aiden asks, breaking the silence. At first, I think he's reading my mind, but then I realize we were just talking about it.

"My sisters have tried that. So has Mama. I don't see how it would work for me and not them. I was hoping the—" With Liam here, the library is once again a protected secret and won't let me speak about it. Aiden and I exchange a look and Liam prompts me.

"What?"

"Sorry, I was hoping for more information on it. From a specific source." Liam narrows his eyes at me but doesn't question further.

"But your sisters didn't know where to look when they did the spell, right?" Aiden continues, bringing my attention back to him. "Now that you know he's in Faery, maybe it'll work."

Glancing between the two boys, I can't believe I didn't think of that. But I guess that's why we have people in our circle. Sometimes they're just there to point out the obvious. But it doesn't mean I can just do a spell.

"The spell is to call on a lost witch. There are variations of it in every culture. But Dad isn't a witch. He's a watcher. They don't necessarily have magical powers."

"But they're blood, Duchess," Aiden says, taking a step toward me.

"There's nothing stronger than blood. You carry that part of him within you. Always. So, is there a way to channel that part of your heritage?"

His faith in me is shining in his eyes, and it's the most beautiful sight I have ever seen. There's no doubt there, just complete trust in my abilities and in me. He's thinking smarter than I, and it's irritating me, but also giving me hope.

"Why haven't I thought of this?"

"Because you're too close to it," Liam comments, pinning me down with his gaze. "We'll help you see the bigger picture."

"Which I am grateful for," I reply honestly, "but there's still the issue of me using my magic. The moment I do, the queen will descend. She'll probably throw me in the closest jail and throw away the key. I can't exactly help anyone if I'm locked up."

And that's really the big issue here. I probably would've tried a hundred spells by now if I wasn't worried about the queen.

"I actually have an idea about that," Liam comments, a glint of mischief in his eye.

"Well, don't keep it to yourself," Aiden says, giving the fae an annoyed look. Liam doesn't seem bothered. I can't figure out the dynamic between them, but as long as they're not full on battling each other, we're good to go.

"Remember how I said my house is protected from the queen?" I nod, and he continues. "We have place close to the border of the Winter Court. Well, it's Nolan's grandparent's place. I don't think going to my house is smart. The queen will look for you there. But if we can get to the border, you can practice your magic there. It's very protected."

I study him for a full thirty seconds before I reply.

"What are you not telling me?"

Liam's eyes stay steadily on mine, which doesn't take my suspicion away. Just raises it. When he can see I'm not about to budge, he sighs.

"Why is it you are never intimidated by me?"

"Because I know you're a softy. What's the catch, Liam?" I ask, placing my hands on my hips. He shakes his head a little before replying.

"It's not that it's a catch, but it's a long journey. And we can't portal there. It would take you at least two days to get there. No one lives there during this season. They're with my parents, visiting the Summer Court."

"Two days isn't that bad," I reply, my mind already working on a plan. "Is there a village between here and there at which we can stop for supplies?"

Liam nods. "There are two or three. Depending on how straight your journey is. It's almost a straight shot from here. East."

I glance over at Aiden, who has stayed quiet during the exchange, but I can feel his eyes on me even before I turn. He's letting me take the lead on this, and I can't even imagine how difficult that is for an alpha. I want to ask him a hundred questions as to why, but instead I just ask one.

"What do you think?"

"I think that I don't mind a two-day hike through the woods."

Truly, that's all I wanted to hear. I'm not ready to do this alone, but I don't have to. Glancing back over at Liam, I give him a small smile.

"Point the way, cupcake."

✢ 15 ✢

We spend the next hour hashing out all the details. The hardest part of it all is that Liam can't come with us. The longer he's with me, the greater the possibility of us getting discovered by the queen. While Liam is cloaked from everyone else, royal blood is more easily tracked by other royals. Especially familial blood. Since the queen knows of our friendship, now that I've gone missing, she'll be looking at him. She's been looking at him this whole time.

"I'm sorry I've put you in this situation," I say when it's time to say our goodbyes. He'll be meeting us at the village close to the estate in two days. First, he has to go back to the school, and when the time is right, Jade will create a diversion for him to portal to us. We have one chance at this, and we're going to do it right. Well, as right as we can manage.

"You didn't put me in any situation I don't want to be in," Liam replies, taking my hands into both of his. I smile, even though all I feel is sadness and worry. I keep putting my friends in dangerous situations and they keep trusting me to get them out of these messes. "You'll find your dad, Mads. And then, you'll get back to the human realm and be with your family. I believe it."

"If you say so."

"I know so."

Stepping forward, I allow his arms to come around me, and I hold on tight. Our friendship will always be risky, a witch and a fae, but it's a friendship that has taught me the most in my life. I will never take for granted all that he's done for me. He taught me that people aren't just a product of their heritage. They get to become whoever they want to be. If only they make the choice.

"I will see you soon, Mads," Liam says, stepping back. He gives Aiden a quick nod and then he's gone. I don't move, watching the place where he walked into the trees until Aiden comes to stand right behind me. I can feel the heat off his body reaching out to me, and all I want to do is lean back and find comfort. But now is not the time. Sucking up all my emotions, I resolve myself to what has to be done next.

"We have a few hours of daylight left. We should get going," I say, turning to face him. He's only a few feet behind me, and I have to look up to meet his eyes. When I do, I almost give in to the urge to close the distance between us. Liam isn't the only one who has put his faith in me. Here stands an alpha, a boy who was my frenemy for weeks, who now is my closest companion. Life really doesn't turn out the way you plan.

Aiden doesn't comment on Liam's departure or the way he keeps looking at me. He reaches for the backpack at the same time I do, swinging it over his shoulder first. After a quick smirk, he hands me a sword, and I strap that to my back without hesitation. Aiden's is already situated under the backpack within easy reach.

"Are you ready for this?" he asks when we turn in the direction Liam pointed us in.

"No. But that's been my answer to every situation I've been in so far."

Aiden smiles at that and then we're off.

It feels weird to be in the woods with him, so close yet so far away. Because even though he's right here, there's a distance between us that I've put in place. If I don't do that, I would want to hold his hand and that seems like a disaster in the making. I know eventually we'll have to talk about what happened between us before the plague came.

Neither one of us breaks the silence as we make our way through the forest. It helps having a shifter by my side, because even though I can survive and find my way on my own, he has an impeccable sense of direction. I don't need to cast any spells to help us out. He and Liam talked it out, with the fae giving Aiden all the information he may need to guide us to the right place.

"Thank you for doing this." I finally speak up after about an hour. The sun is setting lower now, casting more shadows through the trees. Even though I'm feeling awkward around Aiden, I'm also feeling exhilarated by his presence. I'm filled with a weird combination of emotions. It's getting more difficult to keep them to myself.

"I meant what I said, Duchess," he says, eyes forward. "I'm on your side."

"I know." I swallow hard, not sure if this is the right place or time but needing to clear at least some of the air. "But I also know we wouldn't be here if it wasn't for me. I'm responsible for a lot of this mess, and I wouldn't fault you for blaming me."

He stops so abruptly I almost run into him. Turning to face me, there's so much intensity in his gaze, it steals the air from my lungs.

"The only fault here belongs to the Ancients. No one asked them to mess with our lives. They could've woken up and lived peaceably alongside us. But their need for power, the same need that sent them sleeping last time, drove them to destroy our cities and target our forests and attack every single magical create known, in every realm. All you've done is try and help. I can't fault you for that."

The emotion behind his words, the way he's looking at me like he's willing me to accept each statement as my own truth, it sends my head spinning.

"You never blame me. Even when it's my fault."

I think of the spell that brought us here and made us prisoners of Faery. The whole school is now in an uproar because of the magic I used. And yet, Aiden isn't angry with me. He never was. From the very beginning.

"We all make mistakes when it comes to our magic, Maddie. You should've never been put into that situation in the first place. That's on the headmaster and the Elders. Not you."

Liam said something similar to me from the beginning as well. He was angry with the leaders of the school, just like Aiden seems to be now.

"Maybe I should've said no."

"Would you have though?" Aiden cocks his head to the side, studying me carefully. "When those who should know better tell you this is the way to go, the right thing to do, would you really have said no? Whether you like it or not, you protect those who are important to you. You do anything in your power to make sure your people are taken care of. That spell, while it wasn't what it could've been, is exactly that. You protecting those you love."

The moment he says that four letter word my mind is filled with him. For weeks now, I've longed to tell him exactly how I feel. I've been saving it because it's a precious truth that I've never experienced for myself before. It's a gift I wanted to give him when he's conscious enough to receive it. But now, I just stare at him, in awe of his faith in me once again. My chest grows heavy, but I settle on a simpler truth.

"In all of this, I would be nothing without the people by my side. Thank you."

We stand frozen in time for a moment longer, the forest growing more rambunctious around us as the night falls. Then, as if we both come to a conclusion, we turn back to the path in front of us and keep walking. For now, these are the only words that will be said. No matter how much I want to say the others.

❧

WE STOP FOR THE NIGHT AFTER FINDING A CAVE SYSTEM WITH A few openings. Aiden does his shifter thing and checks to make sure nothing is going to jump out at us while I go through our supplies. My friends managed to sneak us some sandwiches, so I pull those out first. Unless I spell them, they'll be bad in the morning. So, when Aiden comes back, I hand one over.

"I figured these would be good for now," I say as Aiden unwraps his sandwich and takes a bite. We eat in silence for a few minutes before I speak up again. "I'm assuming you didn't find anything?"

"Nothing. Not even any residual scent that might point to someone or something coming back."

"That's good. Do you think we should start a fire?" Already the temperature is dropping the closer we get to Winter Court's border. When I traveled to see the Oracle, I was nowhere near the border and the nights were still colder than I expected. I can't really pretend to understand the way this realm works, or why it does the things it does.

"I don't think that's the best idea. Unless we go farther in, we're still pretty exposed."

And I don't want to go farther in. I want to have an easy out in case we need to pick up and run. I was already thinking fire would be a bad idea, but I needed to hear that out loud.

"Do you know how to make fire without magic?" Aiden asks after a few moments of silence. It's not an unkind question but a genuinely curious one.

"I do," I reply after I finish off my sandwich. The memory that springs up brings a smile to my face, and I decide to share. "I was about six when Dad taught me." Pulling the sleeves of my flimsy pullover down to my wrists, I settle in a bit more comfortably. Aiden finishes off his own sandwich, turning his full attention to me. "My sisters were always about the magic. Bri is the next in line to be the coven leader, and she's had to work extra hard her whole life. She didn't awaken her active magic until Mark came along." The idea of soulmates and their power instantly draws my eyes back to Aidan. And now I can't seem to look away. "Harper was always the adventurous one with magic. She loves to explore and more often than not, she would end up in some magic conundrum. Both of them stayed by my mama's side, but I was a daddy's girl.

"He doesn't have the typical kind of magic. He comes from family of Watchers, and that's how my parents met. He's learned everything about survival without magic because he never wanted to be a nuisance to my mama. Not that he could ever be anything but the love of her life."

Suddenly, my cheeks feel wet, and I don't realize I'm crying until I swipe at my chin. Lately, they've been coming more often. As if I've been holding it all in for so long, the cup has finally overrun and is spilling over the sides.

"He taught me how to live among the trees, how to find water, and which way is north. He taught me basic self-defense skills and how to love research. I love my magic, but I love the fact that I don't rely on it. When I was younger, sometimes I forgot it was even there. During actual magic lessons, I would do things differently, but mama never reprimanded me for it. Just reminded me that I am a child of both worlds, and it's important to practice characteristics of both."

I pause again, trying to get a hold of myself. It's more difficult than I thought it would be, as I force myself to swallow the tears. Aiden doesn't comment, giving me the time I need to process my own emotions.

"I miss them so much, Aiden," I finally manage, looking up into his face. "My family. But most of all my dad. Because at least I know my sisters and mama are safe. But Daddy, he's out there, somewhere, being held and maybe tortured, maybe... I don't know. And all this time, I've neglected looking for him. I've neglected doing my part, and I don't know if I can ever forgive myself for that. Not if something has happened to him. Not if I'm too late to help..."

My voice trails off into hiccups and then Aiden is there, pulling me into his arms. I tumble against his chest, grabbing his shirt as I pull myself closer. When my grip tightens even more, he lifts me right off the ground and into his lap. I burrow myself into him, as if he can protect me from every bad decision I have ever made. He doesn't offer words of comfort, just makes trails up and down my spine as I cry myself out. The solidness of him around me is everything I ever wanted, and I feel at home in his arms.

I'm not sure how long we sit like that. Now that he's holding me, the world doesn't seem as bad, and my tears slow. When I finally loosen my grip, I wipe at my face with my free hand.

"I know you want to say something," I say, not meeting his eye, my head still on his chest. The beating of his heart is calming, just like the patterns he makes with his hands. "It's okay. I can take it."

"I have nothing bad to say, Duchess," he replies softly, and this time, I do look at him.

"Then say whatever else is on your mind."

He stares at me for a long moment, and I'm sure I look like a mess. But I don't pull away, letting him glimpse every part of me, raw and open.

"I can't tell you how to feel, Maddie," he begins, sighing a little. "But I wish you wouldn't blame yourself for making decisions that would make your dad proud."

"What do you mean?" I sit up more fully, needing to understand what he's trying to say.

"He raised you to be a strong woman, powerful with and without her magic. The kind of person that befriends strangers and takes care of enemies. You haven't looked for him as much as you think you should've because you've been too busy keeping all of us alive and safe. If your dad could see you now, he'd be proud of the person you've become. He wouldn't blame you for doing the exact thing he taught you to do."

Aiden's words are so matter of fact, it's like he's talking about the weather. He's not trying to convince himself or me that this is truth. He already knows it is. That brings fresh tears to my eyes.

"Thank you," I whisper, leaning my head back against his chest. Exhausted from the day's events, my eyes close on their own, and then I feel Aiden's lips against my head. Or maybe I imagine that. But the next thing I know, he's lowering both of us to the ground, me still cradled against his chest, the warmth of his shifter magic encompassing the two of us.

"You are always welcome, Duchess," I hear Aiden whisper right before I slip off into a dreamless sleep.

❦ 16 ❦

I'm awakened suddenly, pulled from my sleep with a tug on my magic. Aiden sits up right away, glancing at me in question. But then, it's like he feels it too. I grab for my sword just as he shifts into his wolf form. Once again, I'm amazed at just how beautiful he looks, but I push the thought away quickly, focusing on our surroundings.

Not daring myself to speak, I call on the magic inside of me but only slightly. If push comes to shove and I have to battle with it, I will risk it. But for now, I just make sure it's there, ready to go. I stand with Aiden beside me, my sword in one hand, battle magic ready at another, as the space in front of me shimmers.

Confused by the phenomenon, I watch it closely before I take a step back. Whatever this magic is, it's not like anything I've seen before. I have no idea how to protect us from it.

"Get ready to run," I whisper, barely making any noise, but Aiden's supernatural hearing picks up every word. The space in front of us shimmers ones more, and I prepare myself to move when I'm suddenly pulled into the magic. A scream rips from my throat as I hurl through the air. I think I'm about to slam into the other side of the rocks, but then I'm landing on a floor, in a well-lit room. The impact knocks the wind out of me, but I don't rest, getting to all fours just as Aiden lands beside me.

"How nice of you to join me," a voice above me says, and I don't have to look up to know who's speaking. First, I check on Aiden as he shifts into his human form. He gives me a quick nod and only then do I meet the eyes of the Oracle.

"Welcome back, little witch. I believe you owe me a spell."

The anger I feel at being pulled away from my mission once again is almost overwhelming. Getting to my feet, I'm still gripping my sword, and I'm more than tempted to use it on the fae in front of me.

"I wouldn't do that if I were you." She wiggles her finger in front of her, glancing ever so briefly at Aiden. But I catch her meaning immediately. There's more on the line than just me here.

"What do you want?" I ask, knowing full well I can't plead with her to let me go. If I bring up my dad, she'll just remind me that he's the reason I'm here in the first place. She's the one who revealed he was in Faery.

"A spell. I heard you managed to get the plague removed. Soulmate magic is something, isn't it?"

Aiden's head whips toward me immediately, the question on his lips before he can help himself.

"Soulmate?"

I don't turn to him, keeping my eyes on the fae, as she glances between the two of us. The mischievous sparkle in her eyes tells me this is exactly the response she expected.

"Ah, Maddie here hasn't told you everything," the Oracle says, getting up from the couch she's been sprawled over. "How typical of her."

"If you know so much, then you know I was on my way to find my dad. So, can we get this over with?"

"Little witch, you really don't understand what is right in front of you, do you?"

"What does that mean?" Her insistence on using riddles and questions instead of coming straight out and saying what she means is infuriating. She can tell it's frustrating me, and she's enjoying my response immensely.

"I will tell you, after you make good on your promise."

The glare I throw her way is deadly, but she doesn't care. She finds me as amusing as a bug on a windshield. Aiden moves closer to me, standing right behind my left shoulder, and I can feel intensity coming off him in waves.

"Don't keep me in suspense. What is it you need?" I sheath my sword at my back, placing my hands on my hips. It's the best power pose I know, and the Oracle doesn't miss the strategic move. At times, I truly think she seems impressed by me. But then I remember she's fae. They're not impressed by anything except themselves.

"First, I'd like to know who got the dosage of my special medicine." She glances over at Aiden again, and I move ever so slightly to put myself more fully in front of him. I don't like the way she keeps eyeing him.

"Headmaster Marković," I reply, and the Oracle's gaze jerks to mine. If I hadn't been watching her so closely, I would've missed it. The quick twitch around her mouth, as if she's genuinely surprised. There's a moment of silence, just a second of time, but I realize she thought I'd give it to Aiden. She planned on me giving it to Aiden.

"Not who you expected." It's not a question, and she doesn't bother answering. She recovers from her surprise quickly, already back in charge of the situation.

"It doesn't matter, little witch. I'll make do with what has been given to me."

Her words are confusing. I have no idea why it matters who received the elixir. The sickness is gone. I could've waited and not given it to anyone.

"Whatever that means, I don't care. Can you make your wish already so we can be on our way?"

"You have really become something, little witch," the Oracle comments, as she begins walking around me in a wide circle. Her eyes roam over me, as if she's cataloguing every feature. I want to squirm under the gaze, but I keep myself firmly planted on the ground. No need to show her how she unnerves me. Aiden growls beside me, and I reach out, placing a hand on his arm. He calms instantly, and the touch sends sparks up my skin immediately. I try not to shiver under the sensation, but I have a feeling he felt it too.

"So interesting," the Oracle comments, stopping right in front of me. "A part of me wants to commend you on your bravery. You sure have learned how to hold your own."

"You know nothing about me," I snap, fire in my eyes.

"Oh, you'd be surprised."

She turns suddenly, making a beeline for a cart full of glasses on the other side of the room. Pouring herself a drink, she gives me a mischievous smile as she sips. I'm getting really sick and tired of this show.

"Are we getting on with this or what?"

"I wonder if you'd be so eager if you knew what I'm going to ask of you."

"If you tell me, we can both find out."

Honestly, I have no idea where all this bravery is coming from. But I'm not backing down. Maybe I cried all my cowardliness out when I was in Aiden's arms, but this is one fight that I'm not losing. Whatever she does next. Her grin is almost blinding as she takes a few steps toward me. She truly is a beautiful creature, all poise and venom rolled into one.

"I want you to tell me a story with your magic." She pauses for dramatic effect. "Of how the Spring Court fell."

❧

"WHAT DO YOU MEAN?" I ASK, WHEN I'VE PROCESSED HER REQUEST. In my mind, there's only one thing she can be asking for. She wants me to strip the court of all the defenses placed on its borders. That's the only way it can fall. Which means it would leave Thunderbird Academy unprotected.

"Exactly what you're thinking, little witch." She smiles again, pleased with herself. "Strip the court of all its protective barriers. May there be nothing between the court and whoever deems it their desire to cross the borders."

"Why? Why would you want your own court to fail?"

"Who said anything about it being my court," she snaps, her voice as cold as ice. Sometimes when she talks, I can almost forget she's a powerful fae. But just then, I see the darkness in her. The darkness the fae carry right underneath their pretty exteriors.

There's only one thing that can drive someone to such hatred. One mission that overshadows them all.

"It's revenge," I say, looking right at the Oracle. "A vendetta against the court and its queen. Why?"

"It is not up to you to ask the questions, little witch. It's for you to deliver on a bargain. Or I can go ahead and take back the memories and the shifter."

"Maddie, you don't have to do this." Aiden speaks up, a feather of a touch on my hand. I still haven't looked at him, afraid I'll blurt out all the things I've been keeping inside. How do I make him understand I have no choice but to follow through on the bargain? I can't stand to see him hurt.

"I do," I reply, my eyes on the fae. "The words were spoken."

The Oracle nods in approval, her eyes shining with excitement. I dare one glance at Aiden and find worry there. All directed at me.

"I can do this." I feel the urge to insist.

"Of course you can," he replies without hesitation. "You are more than capable. But the consequences of what you're about to do..." He trails off because he doesn't need to continue. We both know what could happen. But just like he has faith in me, I have faith in him. We can fight whatever battle comes our way. But I can't do that if he's in the Oracle's clutches.

"I know," I say, my gaze steady on his. "But we'll get through it. Together."

Just one word, but I think he sees the true meaning behind it. And just like always, he gives me the freedom to do what I deem is right. Even though my decision making has left us on the wrong side more than once. He's still trusting me.

When I turn back to the Oracle, that curiosity is back in her eyes. She's been watching our exchange, and I wonder what she sees. But I won't ask her any more questions. I just have to deliver on this one bargain and then I'm done.

"I'm not sure my magic will answer when I call." I let her know because it's the absolute truth.

"Give it a try, little witch. No hesitation. No caution. Trust that the magic inside of you knows what you are asking of it."

The instructions feel strange coming from her. She says it like my sister would, and I'm not sure how to take it. I guess we're about to find out.

Taking a step into the center of the room, I close my eyes. I can feel Aiden's gaze on me like a hot touch, and when I open my own, I see his eyes are on me. There's no need to coax the magic awake, it's been shimmering under the surface this whole time. I'm never too sure what to do with my story spell casting magic, but it always seems to deliver. So, I do what I always do. I ask it to tell me a story that I can tell the others. It seems to take forever, the buzz growing stronger over my skin by the minute, but finally, the words come.

"Once upon a time,
the court's walls stood high.
With buds of leaves,
And blooming flowers to the sky.

Then the knocking came,
To open the door.
It was up to the queen to let them in,
And having no choice,
She opened from within.

The door stood ajar,
The wall no longer a barrier.
The borders were open,
So, the land was less merrier."

THE MOMENT I UTTER THE LAST SET OF WORDS, MY MAGIC BURSTS out of me, draining me to the bone. I stumble forward, and if Aiden wasn't here to catch me, I would've face-planted.

"Interesting choice of words," the Oracle comments, watching me with that unblinking gaze of hers. "Three sets instead of one continuous rhyme. Curious, little witch. I'm very curious."

"Happy to be of service," I spit out, leaning heavily on Aiden. The weariness I feel after using story spell casting is so intense it's becoming pain. Gripping Aiden's arm, I try to push it away. I can't fall apart in front of the fae.

"You were of service and a great one at that." There is evil lurking in her smile, and it sends a chill down my spine. I fear she'll keep me here, keep us both here, to chain me to do her bidding. But then, she glances at me, speaking again. "I can almost taste the magic at the tip of my tongue," she says, running a finger over her lower lip. "Such a lovely taste. One day, it'll be intoxicating."

"I did what we agreed upon," I say before she plays more word riddles. It's getting harder and harder not to pass out, but I need to get us out of here first. "Let us go."

"Oh, I will. Don't you worry about that, little witch. I just want to enjoy you for a little while longer."

"Let us go." I grit my teeth, the full extent of my hatred for her displayed in my eyes. There's a flash of something in her gaze, and at first, I think she'll keep this up, but she surprises me. The Oracle comes to stand right in front of us, reaching for my face and bringing it level with hers. Aiden goes rigid, and I know it's her magic keeping him from attacking her.

"You amuse me, little witch. And because of this I will give you one tidbit of advice. Your father is much closer than you think. The gorgeous flower can hide a variety of sins."

The shimmering starts up again, this time to the left of us. I want to ask her what she means by that, but I'm barely hanging on to consciousness.

"Until we meet again, little witch." With a wave of her hand, Aiden

❊ 17 ❊

When I come to, it's Aiden's voice I hear first.

"Duchess, come on. Wake up."

Opening my eyes, I squint up at him as he comes into focus. We're still in the forest, the sun now shining through the trees, and I'm laying half on the ground, half in his arms.

"What happened?"

"The fae pushed us through the portal, and you passed out," Aiden replies as I push myself to a sitting position, with his help. He guides me up, hand on my back, peering down into my face. "You were out for at least an hour."

"What?"

The sharp turn of my head sends the pounding to new levels of annoying, and I place a hand against my temples to offset the pain.

"It's the magic. It drained you." He's not asking because he already knows. He looks at me in that way that's somewhere in between wanting to strangle me and wanting to protect me. I feel like this is becoming a standard response I receive from people.

"I'm okay," I manage, finally meeting his eye straight on. "Just tired."

Aiden watches me steadily, and that's when the reality of what I've done finally settles. I brought the barriers down. Spring Court is now

483

open for business and once again, I'm the one responsible for the mess.

"You had no choice."

"When does that excuse lose its value?" I snap, but I'm not mad at Aiden. I'm mad at myself. I'm mad that I couldn't find a way out of the bargain.

"You did it to save Liam and me. Would you have done things differently?"

"No." The answer is instantaneous, and I see Aiden grin out of the corner of my eye.

"See, then there's nothing to regret. We'll get through this. Whatever comes next."

I want to believe him. The way he's looking at me, and the gentle way he's been holding me, it's difficult not to give in to the pull of him. But I have to stop this.

"Where are we?" I ask instead, getting to my feet. Aiden helps me up before he takes a step back from me. "Wait, I know these woods."

I do a slow spin, studying the trees around us.

"Are you kidding me? She dumped us right by Liam's house."

"Why would she do that?"

"Because she's diabolical."

If I keep trying to find a reason for everything the Oracle does, I will drive myself crazy. For a second there, I thought I knew what her intentions meant, but then she threw all of that out the window. At this point, she has set me up to take the rap, and there's really nothing I can do about it.

"Once again, this was a trip for biscuits, and I have no idea where to go from here. At this pace, we'll never reach the Winter Court. And who's to say we could even manage to get halfway there now that the barriers are down?"

I expect Aiden to comment, but when I turn, he's just watching me curiously.

"What?"

"Trip for biscuits?"

"A task that yields nothing," I mumble, forgetting once again that not everyone studies old slang as one of their hobbies. Aiden chuckles, and even though I'm frustrated, I'm glad I can bring a smile to his face.

"Let's make something out of it then," he begins, coming to stand beside me. But then suddenly, his head jerks to the side, as if he's hearing something beyond my capabilities.

"What?"

"Come on, I think we need to see this."

He reaches for my hand and then we're moving through the forest, me following his lead, trying to stay as quiet as possible. What we find not even five minutes later stops my heart in its tracks. There are creatures everywhere.

⚜

WE MANAGE TO CREEP AROUND THEM, MOVING TOWARD THE school. It takes us a good fifteen-minute trip, before I hear noises rise up in the forest around us. Getting as close to the border as we can, Aiden leads me in and then I can do nothing but stare.

As I study the academy, my heart hurts at the damage that has already been inflicted on it. The doors are still on lockdown as far as I can tell, but the walls look weathered from the constant beating. I can see faculty and staff at various windows and can feel the magic that's protecting the building. Some students can also be seen, but I can't decipher much more than that.

"Aiden?"

"From what I can see, they set up protective barriers as far as halfway around the building. I can feel my pack shifted, at least half of them, patrolling the halls. But I can't sense much more than that."

My head spins with the information and the picture in front of me. Once again, I've put my friends in danger with my magic. Will I ever stop making these mistakes, or will I always be cursed with being put into situations I have no way out of?

"It's not your fault."

"You keep saying that," I reply, crawling backward and out of the bushes. "But I don't think it means what you think it means."

He rolls his eyes at my lame attempt at humor, but he's not to be deterred. He wants me to understand that I'm not at fault, even though I am. I know I am.

"We need to find our friends. We should head to Liam's and see if he's there. I don't think he'd be at the academy. Not after Headmaster Marković put it on lockdown after we left."

Aiden watches me for a tense moment before inclining his head. For an alpha, he's too accepting of my leadership, and this isn't the first time. I wanted to ask earlier, but I didn't think it was the right time. Maybe it will never be the right time. Maybe I should just start diving into these situations without overthinking them.

"Why are you so quick to follow my lead, alpha?" I blurt out as Aiden moves to walk past me. He freezes in place, his eyes on me, and for some reason I think that whatever he's about to say will change things for me. He's thinking about it, I can see it. I can also see the moment he decides he's not going to answer, shutting it all down. But I'm not going to let him get away with it.

"Aiden," I whisper, taking a step torward him, my hand on his upper arm. Even through the material of his shirt, I can feel heat coming off him. "What is it?"

"Now is not the time nor place," the shifter replies, giving me such a piercing look that I catch my breath. Everything in me wants to push, but something stops me. Maybe it's just the simple truth in knowing that I can't make him tell me something he's not ready to say. No matter what kind of scenarios I make up in my mind.

"When we get through this." Aiden speaks up again, since he can read my disappointment without me having to speak it. "I will tell you everything. And you can decide what to do with that information."

I nod my head, and he turns to head toward Liam's without another word. I'm not sure what this push and pull is between us, but I'm trying not to focus on it too much. There's a war going on, and I need to figure out how to fix all the mistakes I've made before I can figure out what to do about my ever-growing feelings for Aiden. With one last look behind me at the academy, I hurry into the woods.

❧ 1 8 ☙

I
t doesn't take long to reach Liam's place because we walk at a much faster pace than before. The mansion is situated between the tallest trees, almost blending in from the forest into the building without a pause. From the last time I was here, I know the back of the house opens up into a cleared off area for a garden, fae's version of a backyard. But the front area goes forest to building immediately.

"I know he has protective wards in place." I halt Aiden before he steps out of the shadows. "I'm not sure what kind. Or how they would react to us passing through."

"Okay." Aiden immediately stops, his eyes scanning the area around us. "What do you suggest?"

"I need to find a way to contact him. It's not like I can call him up and see if he's home."

Honestly, I have no idea what to do. If we just step onto his property without knowing the magic used, we could be in big trouble. Fae magic is already unpredictable, especially when mixed with everything that's been going on. Who knows what Liam may have cooked up to keep the queen from reaching his borders?

"Wait," Aiden suddenly says, his nose in the air as if he's sniffing the space around him. I don't interrupt while he does whatever shifters do. When he turns his eyes on me, they're shining. "Ben and Owen are here."

"What?" I stand up straighter, glancing back at the house. "Can you..." I turn to ask, but Aiden has already shifted, and his wolf form takes my breath away, as always. I don't think I can ever get tired of seeing him like this. His wolf is bigger than any I've seen, coming up past my waist, his grey fur the silkiest thing I've ever felt. Even now, all I want to do is reach out. As if he's reading my mind, he takes a step forward, bumping my hand with his head, and I sink my fingers into the fur instantly. Both of us seem to sigh at the same time, as if this is what we both needed, before he steps back and focuses on the house. He raises his head next, letting out a howl that is somehow quieter than I've ever heard, but also resounds in my mind. I visibly jerk at the sound, and he whips his head in my direction, as if he's surprised by my reaction. But before either one of us can do anything else, the front door of the mansion opens, and Ben is there. He scans the area around him, and I know the moment he sees us. He yells something back into the house before he's racing out the front door.

A ripple of magic passes over me as the barrier Liam put up comes down and then Ben is there. He's out of breath with excitement, glancing at me and then Aiden as his alpha sheds his wolf form and is standing beside me once again.

"You're both here," Ben says before bowing his head in submission to Aiden and then to me. Confused, I open my mouth to speak up, but Aiden makes a noise at the back of his throat that I'm sure I wasn't supposed to hear, making Ben stand up straight immediately. The beta looks at me a little sheepishly before grinning.

"We've been worried."

That's when I notice Liam at the front of the entrance, with Jade and Noel coming to stand behind him. The moment Jade sees me, she's running toward me and I to her. Then, we're hugging, and I feel so much better knowing my friends are safe.

"What happened?"

"Oh, Maddie. So much! We have to tell you everything." Jade links her arm through my elbow, turning us toward the doorway. When I reach it, Liam is still standing there, his eyes on me. I don't think he's blinked since he saw me. Now that I'm in front of him, he reaches out and takes my hand, squeezing it tightly. He doesn't have to say the words, but he knows. He knows I did something, and he's worried. As he should be. We all know I shouldn't be allowed access to magic at this point.

"Come on," Jade says after Noel gives me a quick hug. "We have so much to catch up on."

I follow my friends into Liam's house, heading for his sitting area. The last time we were here, I didn't take the time to look around. But now, as I study the elaborate walls and the old-fashioned furniture, I feel like I've stepped into the early 1800s.

"You know this is not my type of decor, right?" Liam comments when he sees me gazing round.

"No? You're not a fair maiden with love for old classical literature?" He rolls his eyes at me, which makes him look so human. I often forget just how much fae he is. But the small joke does put everyone at ease somehow. As if it's a reminder that we can still be us, even in the middle of a crisis.

"Well," I say, taking a spot beside Jade on the love seat as the rest of the gang takes their appropriate places. Aiden stays by the doorway, in direct line of sight from me, and I can feel his eyes taking in everything as well. Mostly, me. He can't seem to look away from me for more than a few seconds, and I feel exactly the same. But I force myself to at least focus on Liam as he begins to speak.

"After I left you, I got back to the academy. It was still on lockdown, but your friends managed to get out before your headmaster completely shut the campus down."

"How?"

"Ben and Owen got us out. There's a door on the opposite side of the building..."

"For when we're on shift, patrolling," Aiden finishes, realization dawning on him. He glances over at Ben, giving him a firm nod, and I can see Ben's entire essence light up at the acknowledgment from his alpha.

"Wait, where is Owen?" I ask, suddenly realizing what's been missing. "And Vera."

I don't have a huge number of friends, just my tight knit community, and I'm okay with that. But that means every single person is that much more important.

"Vera stayed behind," Jade says, brining my attention back to her. "The hawk shifters wanted to fight, and she stayed to help."

"Owen is out patrolling," Ben chimes in. "We've been taking turns."

That gets another glowing review from Aiden, and I smile a little. He's a great alpha, of that I have no doubt. I love seeing his pack appreciate him and seek his approval. He gives it readily, as any supportive leader should.

"What's happening at the school then?" Aiden asks, turning the conversation back to the issue at hand. I still can't take my eyes off him, and it's pretty obvious. I have to focus.

"After everyone started looking for you, and we ran, the headmaster put the school on lockdown. Liam came back to get us." Jade takes over the story, giving my fae friend a quick smile. "And he brought us here. We were attacked in the woods, though. A bunch of magical creatures are roaming around all of a sudden. The academy got surrounded, and we barely got through. We have no idea what caused it, but we've only been safe here because Liam's family magic is powerful."

Aiden and I exchange a look because we both know what needs to be done. After I tell them, they might not want anything to do with me. But I can't keep the information to myself. Needing the distance, I stand, walking over to the other side of the room so I can face my friends. Aiden doesn't hesitate to come stand by my side, and I almost reach out and take his hand. Not knowing where we stand, I don't, but I don't have to. Because he reaches at the same time, entwining our fingers together.

"What is it, Maddie?" Jade asks, concern shining in her gaze. She glances down at our joined hands before looking up again.

"What I'm about to tell you, I'm sorry," I begin, my eyes going to each one in the room before finally settling on Liam. "I'm so sorry. But it's my fault the academy is being attacked and why the creatures are roaming freely in the woods. I... I promised the Oracle a spell, and I delivered on that promise."

"Mads, what did she ask you to do?" Liam hasn't taken his eyes off me either, and I meet his gaze steadily.

"To bring down the Spring Court's barriers."

❧

I EXPECT HIM TO BLOW UP AT ME OR FOR PEOPLE TO START panicking, but neither thing happens. There's complete silence in the room, as if everyone has been frozen into statues. Aiden's thumb continues to make comforting circles on my skin, and I hold on to that feeling with all my might. I want to offer up a million excuses, but I know that's not what my friends need to hear right now. I'm not sure what they need, but it's definitely not my lame apologies.

When the silence is finally broken, it's by Liam. He moves toward me until he's standing right in front of me.

"You didn't know." His words shock me, stopping the apology that was right on the tip of my tongue. Out of everyone here, he can blame me the most. I let the Ancients into his court, into his home. But I've always known Liam isn't like the others. And he continues to prove that to me every day.

"Liam, I..."

"If anyone is to be blamed, it's Aiden and me. We went into that forest looking for answers."

"Answers for me!" I wrench my hand away from Aiden, putting distance between us as I wrap my arms around me. "If I didn't need answers so desperately, you wouldn't have gone. You did it for me!"

"And you made the bargain for us." Aiden speaks up from where he stands next to Liam. Turning, I look at the two complete opposite boys in my life. One dark, with shifter blood in his veins and blue eyes that make my skin hot anytime he looks at me. The other, light and so beautiful it hurts to look upon, with green eyes the color of freshly blooming leaves. Yet, both not what I expected. Both willing to risk it all to protect me and to make sure I'm taken care of.

"I don't know how to fix this," I whisper, glancing between the two. I love them both, in different ways, and I can't imagine my life without them in it. Yet, that's what it might come to if I don't fix this mess.

"We fix it together," Aiden says, taking a step forward. "We do what we do best. We learn, we grow, and then we fight. Together." He glances at the fae behind him, and that right there makes me believe anything is possible. They started out as enemies, and now they've become allies.

Not that I should've expected anything different, but Aiden and Liam seem to always be on my side. I guess it's how you know you've found your people. Even if, in this case, my people are a wolf shifter and a fae. But it's those who stand by you no matter the circumstances that truly make a place in your heart. There's nothing I wouldn't do for them. But they're not the only ones I have to worry about.

Walking back over to the other side of the room, Liam and Aiden flank me as I focus on the rest of my friends. No one has moved from their place, as if they needed to work through everything before they could. I meet Jade's gaze as my friend finally looks up at me. I have no idea what I'd find there, but once again, it's just my own insecurities that are creeping up. Because she doesn't look at me like she hates me.

"I can't even imagine what it took for you to do that spell," Jade says, twisting a bracelet on her wrist. "I'm with the boys on this one. We'll figure it out. Together."

A grin splits my lips and then I'm hugging her, as she hugs me back just as tightly. This is exactly how my sisters would react, and this is what I needed. When I glance over at Noel and Ben, they both shrug.

"You already know I'd follow you anywhere," Ben comments, receiving a slight growl from Aiden that just makes me grin. I walk over and give him a slight shoulder punch that makes Ben smile.

"Noel?"

"Well, I can't be the oddball out here. I get it. We all make mistakes. I can't exactly punish you for being human." He shrugs, and that's as much acceptance as I'll get from him. We're not as close as I am to the others, and he still has my back. If that doesn't show just how amazing these people are, I'm not sure anything will.

"Don't worry, witch," a voice comes from the doorway, and all of us turn as one. "I can do the punishing."

Without a moment to spare, Natalie launches herself at me.

❧ 19 ☙

The shifter is so quick, she's on top of me before I can put up my shield. Her body slams into mine, still in human form, and we roll over the couch and unto the floor. She swipes at me, but there's a reason why I've spent all that time training with Aiden. I block her easily, before slamming my elbow into her neck. She stumbles off me, and I jump to my feet, this time prepared.

Out of the corner of my eye, I see Aiden ready to pounce, but Liam is holding him back. This is my fight. Everyone in the room knows it. And we're doing it the old-fashioned way. Hand to hand combat.

"You think you're so perfect. Everyone will just automatically forgive you for the crap you've done to the school."

"Not to shatter your illusion of me, but I have never pretended to be perfect, and I'm only forgiven because I have amazing friends."

"Right, because you don't just expect people to fall at your feet."

"I think you have us confused on that one." I smirk, which sends her into another rage. She attacks, swinging with her right then left arm, but I block both. I don't actually want to fight her, but I know if I back down now, I will never earn respect in her eyes. My friends have all moved out of the way and are watching. A part of me wants to show Aiden what I can do. I want to make him proud after everything he's taught me.

Natalie twists around, kicking out, but I duck at the last minute. The movement brings me below her, and she takes advantage. She kicks again, this time straight out, and I barely block it with a cross in front of my face. The impact sends me sliding across the floor, and she advances on me without a pause. Jumping to my feet, I get a punch to the gut, the wind knocked out of me. She grabs my hair, yanking it back so I can look up at her.

"How will you ever stand up to the evil out there if you can't even stand up to me?" Natalie all but spits out at me, and the dig has the desired effect. My own anger rises up. I've done nothing but try to protect my friends and family. Sure, I've made choices I'm not proud of, but I will never be ashamed for trying. But I also want to prove myself, so I don't hold back.

Swinging, I punch her right in the stomach, making her drop my hair. Before she can recover, I kick her once, sending her backward. I swing to punch her, but she blocks me, grabbing my right arm with her hand. Instead of trying to get out of the hold, I step closer, grabbing her right shoulder. Then, I bring my knee up, yanking her down at the same time. She yelps in pain as the two connect, and then I round-house kick as she flies backward, slamming into the wall. There's power behind my moves, but not of magic. My own power, one I created by training hard and believing in myself. No one can make me doubt myself like I can. But also, no one can believe in me enough to make me see the bigger picture. I have to see that for myself. I have to be the strong one.

I'm ready to go again, but then Natalie gets to all fours, spitting a little blood out and starts laughing. I freeze in my tracks before I reach her, confusion plain on my face.

"That's a lot better," she says, getting to her feet and facing me. A little blood is still on her lip, and she wipes it away before she situates her clothing.

"What is your problem?" I ask.

"It used to be you," she replies, cocking her head to the side. "But now I think you might just be able to get us out of this mess." She glances over at Aiden, giving him a tiny smile. I look over at the shifter and see Liam and Ben have both been restraining him. Not that they really could've held him back if he wanted to. I think he could take on both of them to get to me. But he trusted me to take care of myself, no matter how difficult it was to watch.

"I'd just like to point out, it wasn't my idea." Owen's voice comes from the doorway, and I turn to see the shifter walk into the room. Spinning around, I glare at Natalie, pieces falling into place.

"This was some kind of a test?"

"Of course it was. Everything is a test," Natalie replies, righting a chair so she can sit. "You were in the midst of your woe-is-me attitude and frankly, it's so annoying it makes me want to puke."

"So, you thought you'd come in here and attack her?" This comes from Aiden, and there is no doubt in my mind that's alpha I hear in his voice. Ben and Owen instantly cower a bit, but Natalie is an alpha. She looks Aiden straight in the eyes and smiles.

"It was a lesson for all of us to learn. If she is to take my place, I think the pack needs to know she will not be a liability."

The words are uttered firmly, and at first, I'm not sure what they mean. I hear Jade gasp beside me, but I can't take my eyes off Natalie and Aiden. There's some kind of an understanding that passes between them, and then, he's looking at me. Only for a moment, but there's so much emotion there, I nearly collapse from the impact.

"You are out of line," Aiden states, giving Natalie a hard look.

"And you, alpha, are too scared to admit what is evident to everyone else in the room. I'm done standing in your way. Now it's your turn to man up."

With that, Natalie stands, walking over to Liam. "Do you think I can clean up somewhere?"

My friend gives me one piercing look, and then leads the female alpha out.

"Want to explain?" I turn to Aiden.

"Not really," he replies before he shifts into his wolf and races from the room.

ABOUT TEN MINUTES LATER, LIAM FINDS ME IN ONE OF THE UPSTAIRS rooms, pacing. I've been switching between staring out the window and making circles in the carpet. Everyone else is resting downstairs. I asked for the time alone. Well, everyone but Aiden, who's gone on patrol. When Liam comes in, I'm not even surprised. I figured he'd be the one to come talk me out of my spiral. Because that's exactly what it feels like I'm doing, just spiraling out of control.

"I see you're handling this well," Liam comments, taking a seat on the bed. I'm not sure who's bedroom this is, but it felt like a safe place, so I commandeered it.

"Don't give me that sarcasm, cupcake," I reply, rolling my eyes at him. "I don't need it."

"Oh, I think you do, cupcake."

My lips twitch involuntarily at the stupid game. Every time this powerful fae uses the term cupcake, I want to laugh. Which was the whole point of the game. But right now, I want to stay frustrated. It's fueling me into...some kind of action.

"I don't understand any of this, Liam," I say, running my hand through my hair. "The reason behind the Oracle's spell, why she would send me back here instead of just dropping us off where she found us."

"Aiden."

"Don't..." I point a finger at him as the smirk on his lips infuriates me further.

"Mads, you're not doing anyone any good by freaking out. You need to rest. The spell you performed, I heard it took a lot out of you."

"Ah, yes. Because you and Aiden are now besties."

"We will always bond over the fact that we care about you."

"Does he?" I stop pacing then, glaring Liam right in the eyes. "Because I can't get a read on him at all anymore. I thought we were...but he hasn't said or done anything since...and I'm only confused and frustrated. I can..." At a loss for words, I just throw my hands up in the air before plopping down beside Liam. "I'm a mess."

"That you are. But all the best people are, so don't sweat it."

He bumps me with his shoulder, and I smile for the first trime since fighting Natalie. That brings another question up.

"Where is she?"

"I left her downstairs with the others. You know they're all worried about you. But at least now they know firsthand that you can take care of yourself."

I sit up a little straighter, turning my head so I can see Liam. There's definitely something in his demeanor that tells me he knows exactly what that whole show downstairs was all about.

"Are you going to tell me?"

He doesn't even ask what I mean. "No."

"Liam."

"Mads, it's not my conversation to have."

Of course he means Aiden. But the alpha is nowhere to be found, and I tell him as much.

"Maybe he's scared."

"Please, Aiden isn't scared of anything."

"You'd be surprised."

I wait for more, but Liam won't meet my eyes, continuing to stare toward the window. I place my head on his shoulder, giving myself this moment of rest. He's right, as usual. The spell did take a lot out of me. But I have no time to rest now. We're so much farther away from the border now, it'll take me at least three days to get there. And with the Ancients and their minions now roaming free across the lands, I'm not sure I would make it.

"Liam, why would the Oracle tell me where my dad is, but then send me in the opposite direction?"

"Are you sure she did?"

"What do you mean?" I ask, sitting up.

"Just that you know fae can't lie. She told the truth from the beginning, it was just how she told it that gives us any clues. That's usually how you find out anything around here."

Once again, Liam coming in with the wisdom. There has to be a rational reason for why the Oracle does the things she does, but then again, maybe not. She likes games, of that I am certain. Would she really help me?

"She's entertained by me," I say out loud, letting my thoughts be spoken into words in case Liam can offer some insight. "She doesn't respect anything about me, except for my story spell casting. But she's helped me more than once. That doesn't really make sense."

"That's because she hasn't," Aiden's voice comes from the doorway, and I twist to watch him walk into the room. There's something in his eyes I can't quite decipher, and I keep in place, so I don't spook him. There are a million questions in my mind, but I wait for him to continue. "There is someone who would like to talk to you, Maddie."

"Who?"

He beckons me to follow him, and after exchanging a quick glance with Liam, I do. We pass the sitting room where everyone else has gathered and head for the back of the house. Once outside, I give Aiden a puzzling look.

"Aiden, what are we doing?"

He looks down at me, scorching me with his gaze before turning toward the forest.

"We're waiting for her," he motions, and I turn just in time to see Queen Amaryllis step out of the shadows.

❧ 2 0 ❧

t first, I think I'm not seeing things correctly. But when I blink and she's still there, I think she's lost her mind.

"What are you doing here?" I ask when we're only a few feet apart. Liam and Aiden have stayed by my side while Ben and Owen are a little ways back. Glancing behind me, I see Jade, Noel, and Natalie are at the doorway, and they seem ready to fight, if it comes to that.

"I am here because we need to talk," the queen replies, and I realize she doesn't have any guards around her. Narrowing my eyes, I study her for a moment before I speak up.

"We said everything we needed to say to each other."

"That is a very false statement, Madison Hawthorne. I think it would be best if you let me in, and we can discuss this like civilized individuals."

"I'm not about to break a barrier to let you come in, Your Highness," I snap, my mind trying to figure out all the possibilities where this won't go well for us. There are a lot of them.

"Not even for your father?"

"What do you know about my father?" I almost step closer to her, my eagerness a little too evident. I have to rein it in.

"Quite a lot, Miss Hawthorne. Now tell me, why did you bring down the barrier?"

Of course she would know it's me. She can taste my magic. A part of me wants to lie to her, but I don't think that would yield us any results.

"Because I made a bargain for a spell and had to deliver."

If I didn't know any better, I would say the queen just paled. "Who did you make the bargain with?"

"The Oracle."

I don't think I've ever seen a fae display this much emotion, but the way Queen Amaryllis is looking at me, it shows a little too much into what her mind is doing. There was a glimpse of panic there before she pushed it down and that regular mask of indifference falls into place.

"What are you not telling us?" I ask, because I can see she isn't going to offer up any information without prompting. "Queen Amaryllis, I understand that we're not friends and never will be. But the Ancients are everyone's problem. Even yours. That's one thing we have in common. If the Oracle made me bring down the barrier for the Ancients, shouldn't you give me all the information I need to try and prevent serious war from happening?"

"We are already in a serious war, Madison Hawthorne," the queen snaps, her eyes full of fire. "You made sure we had no defenses against it."

"If a few measly barriers taken down by one witch is all you had as a defense against the Ancients, you've got way more problems than I thought."

The queen is visibly taken back by the harshness of my tone, and maybe I surprised myself a little as well. But this isn't a game, and even though I take much of the responsibility for what I've done, she can't put the safety of the whole court on me. Her barriers were going to fall, one way or the other, and if she has no contingency plan...then everyone is in serious trouble.

"You have really become something, Madison Hawthorne."

"And what's that?" I ask, placing my hands on my hips.

"Something of a leader."

It's the highest praise I will ever receive from this fae, and I'd be lying if I said it didn't feel good having her acknowledge me in that way.

"Glad you're finally realizing this," I say, keeping up the bravado display, since it's clearly working. "Now, how about some answers?"

As I say this, a loud boom sounds around us, echoing through the forest. We all jerk as one, ducking, as if it's going to attack. There's some shouting and then the screaming begins.

"Maybe we can take this inside?" the queen comments, her eyes on me. But this is not a decision I'm going to make. Turning to Liam, I say,

"It's up to you."

He stares at me for a tense moment, mulling over our options. We both know we can't stay out here in the open. The house is the safest place right now and even that won't last. But we also need answers. If the queen can provide even a few of them, we should take the risk. Maybe. Maybe I shouldn't be making any decisions.

"Only if you let me bind you," Liam says. The way the queen jerks at his words would be comical if we weren't in a middle of a crisis. I've heard about binding. It's not exactly a wildly popular concept because it binds one's fae magic to the other. It would give Liam full control, even though it's for a small period of time.

"You are anything but worthy of that kind of an honor."

"Glad you think so much of me, Auntie. But it's not about honor. I'm going to protect my friends first and foremost."

"Going against your own kind for the likes of them." The queen glares at me and no one else, and the sudden courageous side of me smirks. She doesn't like that. But then again, she doesn't like me.

"I'm protecting what's mine. Take it or leave it."

They glare at each other in a standoff, but then another scream echoes in the forest, and there's no choice left. The queen resigns to her fate.

"I accept the binding," she utters and then Liam is reaching across the barrier to hook his hand over her forearm. He whispers a few words that I can't understand, and then there's a pop in the air, and the queen visibly shudders. Liam glances over at me and nods. The queen steps through the barrier, her magic now subdued by Liam.

"How long?" I ask, because unless it a full-on ritual, the binding time is short.

"I'd say fifteen minutes at the most."

"Plenty of time," I say, glancing at the queen before I turn and lead us all back into the house.

❦

"Owen, Ben," Aiden calls out the moment we're inside, "I need you at the east and west side of the house. Natalie—"

"I'll take the south." She doesn't hesitate, racing for the back of the building. Jade and Noel stand at attention as well, looking between the group.

"Maddie?" Jade asks, and I turn to Aiden.

"Where do you want them?"

"Upstairs."

Noel and Jade don't hesitate either. Once they're gone, I turn to Queen Amaryllis. She's looking around the room as if she's a little fascinated. When she catches my eye, she does a very un-queenly thing and shrugs.

"It's been a very long time since I've been here."

She glances at Liam, but my friend isn't budging into a trip down memory lane. There's determination on his face, a readiness to do whatever it takes to keep us safe. Of that, I am sure.

"You think we're about to be under attack?" I turn to Aiden as he takes his place beside me.

"I think it's highly likely. So, let's hurry."

I can tell he's nervous...well, maybe not nervous. Tense. Ready to pounce. I'm not sure if that's directed at what's going on outside or at the fae queen in front of us. We're all on edge and having her here is not helping.

"Okay, we don't have much time," I begin, facing the queen head-on. "What are you not telling us?"

She watched me for a long moment, and I think she's about to play some of her games. There is something in the way fae handle their affairs. They are all about games. The yelling and fighting is getting closer outside. The whole of Faery seems to be on our doorstep. I can't let myself dwell on the blame; I have to focus on finding solutions.

"First, you need to tell me what the Oracle has told you." The queen surprises me with her words.

"This is not about me."

"Oh, but it has always been about you. Your family to be exact."

"I don't understand."

"No, you would not."

"So, tell me." I take a step closer, a note of pleading entering my voice. I've been searching for answers for so long, I'm not sure if I'll ever stop searching. But if she can give me even a glimpse into the answers, I will take it. Asking such a thing of a fae queen is dangerous though. She may require a bargain, and I'm not about to make that mistake twice. But then, she surprises me again.

"Your family is a name many have feared over generations," she begins, walking slowly over to one of the seats and placing herself there in all her regal glory. Even in the simple-for-her green dress, she looks like a queen. She always carries herself as such. It's almost mesmerizing, and I wonder if I'd ever be able to carry myself with half of that grace.

I can't imagine why anyone would fear my family. True, my sisters and mama are beautiful and powerful. My mama is one of the strongest coven leaders out there. But I don't see how that would play into anything here in Faery.

"Why would we be feared? We're nothing special. At least, I'm not."

A tiny growl comes from my left, and I glance to see Aiden's gaze on me. He doesn't seem pleased with my assessment of myself, but no matter how much that scorching look sends my body a few degrees higher in temperature, I can't dwell on that. I tuck that into my heart to examine later.

"Your blood is one of the most potent conduits of magic. It is why you can story spell cast. Why your sisters could both hold their own against the Ancient's minions. It is supercharged, from generations before. The Ancients thirst for it."

"Wait." I put out a hand, my mind racing. "You're telling me the

Ancients want to suck my blood like some vampire?"

"Vampires had to originate somewhere, do you not agree?" She seems so nonchalant about that, but I can't seem to stop the freak out. Sure, there are vampires in the world. But I haven't exactly met any. They always seemed like monsters we don't talk about.

"But why? And how does that have anything to do with the Oracle? All she's done is help me." Which I still don't understand. But I'm hoping I'm about to.

"The only thing that witch did is help herself." Queen Amaryllis gets to her feet, pacing across the room in agitation.

"But she told me about my father..." I trail off because has she really? Mostly, she just used my need to find him.

"And what exactly has she told you?"

"That's he's in Faery. Possibly the Winter Court, being held captive."

When Queen Amaryllis's laugh rings out around the room, I freeze in my tracks. This is not the reaction I expected.

"What's so funny?" Liam ask, his voice cold and dangerous. I think he really would hurt his queen in order to protect me. He's getting just as fed up with her as I am.

"The witch did nothing but play on your most evident emotions. Even when you were not searching for your father, the thought was still there, was it not?"

"Well, of course."

"She preyed on that, preyed on your vulnerability when it comes to family."

"So, you're saying my father isn't in Faery?" My heart drops even as I ask the question. Because if the Oracle wasn't telling the truth, we're back to square one. I'm not sure I can survive that kind of heartbreak. Not with everything else going on.

"I am not saying that. Fae cannot lie. But she may not have been completely upfront about what she knows."

"Fine, she didn't give me all the info." I throw my hands in the air, frustration coursing through me. "How does that answer any of the questions I asked? What does she want from me?"

Queen Amaryllis meets my eye head on, a small smile forming on her lips. She looks powerful and dangerous, the kind of confidence I wish I could portray right now. But the best I can do, is not look away from her stare. She seems satisfied with that, before she finally answers.

"To suck your blood, of course."

＄ 21 ＄

I 'm not sure I heard her correctly.

"You're saying the Oracle is a—"

"An Ancient." The queen inclines her head, still not breaking eye contact.

"But how is that possible?"

"Anything is possible in Faery, Madison Hawthorne."

"But the villagers talked about her as if she's always been there."

"Stories hold power," Queen Amaryllis says, walking over to stand right in front of me. "The story of her being there has been passed down through the generations. And when the Ancients began awakening, she simply took the spot in the story."

"How can you know all this?"

"I've been around a long time, Madison Hawthorne. I have seen my share of Ancients."

"You mean this really isn't the first time they've awakened?" This comes from Liam, but it's the same question I would've asked.

"Of course not. They are too powerful to stay asleep indefinitely. Every now and then, an Ancient or two rises. But not as many as this time, all at the same time."

There's a loud boom, and the walls of Liam's house shake from the impact. The battle is right on the outskirts of the forest, it seems. My spell did that. Or so I thought.

"When I brought down the barriers—"

"The Oracles used that magic to cast a spell of her own. Her minions infiltrated the whole court in minutes, and the fighting began. She is not here to lead her army, but someone is doing it for her. I thought it was you. But now I see it is not."

"Wow, thank you so much for realizing I'm not an evil Ancient's helper," I say, just as another boom shakes the house. It's feels like magic, but I'm not sure where it's coming from. Sharing a glance with Aiden, I take another step toward the queen.

"So, if it's not me, then who?"

"I have no idea." I can see the frustration in her eyes. The queen has lost control of her court, and I can't even imagine that feeling. I find myself deep in self-pity and regret when I lose control of just one aspect of my life. But then again, this is why I'm not the queen. But I am a witch from the Hawthorne bloodline, and apparently, that means even more than I previously thought.

"How do we figure it out?" I ask, because I'm not about to fall into a pit of despair. My friends and I are here to do whatever it takes to fix this. Of that I am sure.

"It would have to be someone who she had access to. Which besides you, I cannot imagine anyone else. Unless you have passed something along."

I open my mouth to ask another question, but then the queen's words become clearer in my mind. Someone the Oracle has access to. Sure, there are magical ways to connect people, but it would require a conduit. A connection between point A and point B. And right then, I realize what that is.

"I know who it is," I whisper as three sets of eyes swing to focus on me. Glancing at Liam first, I turn to Aiden. "It would've been you, but I didn't give you the elixir."

"Mads." Liam's voice sounds over my shoulder, and I glance at him as he comes to the same realization as me. "You mean—"

"Yes," I look back over at Aiden. "It's why she was so confused when she saw you," I say to him.

"I don't understand."

"The Oracle gave me an elixir, a medicine of sorts to help one individual. To save one life during the sickness. She thought I would give it
to you. But I didn't."

Aiden's eyes stay on mine, and I think I'll see pain or disappointment there. But I see neither. He's still supporting me, trusting me
that I made a decision that would've been the best one possible.

"Who did you give it to?" Queen Amaryllis asks, pulling my attention to her.

"Headmaster Marković."

There's a short pause as I say his name, but then the queen nods.

"It makes sense. She needed someone on the inside, and now she
has one of the best choices she could have picked," the queen mulls
out loud, walking over to the other side of the room. I let her be as I
turn back to Aiden.

"I'm sorry. I mean, now I'm glad I didn't give you the elixir, but I
doesn't mean that I didn't want to. I—"

"You made a choice for the good of the school." Aiden interrupts
me, reaching for my hands and holding them in between us. The
contact soothes me, just like it always does, and when I look up at him,
I think he can read my emotions written all over my face. "There were
plenty of other options. I wouldn't expect you to choose me over
everyone else."

"But I would've."

The words leave me before I can stop them. Aiden inhales sharply,
as if he's just as surprised I said them as I am. We stare at each other,
the craziness of our situation forgotten, as if we're the only two people
in the world. There is still so much I want to say to him, so many questions I haven't asked.

"Not to interrupt this touching moment," Queen Amaryllis walks
back over to our side of the room, "But now that I know who is
helping her, I need to go to my people."

"No," I reply, turning to face her. "You have one more question left
to answer."

"Which is?"

"The Oracle said my father was much closer than I anticipated and then she dumped me right near Liam's house, smack dab in the middle of your court. So, tell me, Your Highness, where is my father?"

◈

LIAM JERKS AT MY WORDS BEFORE SPINNING TO FACE HIS AUNT. SHE doesn't speak at first, standing up straighter, as if she needs to appear more queenly around me.

"Do you know where Maddie's father is?" Liam asks, a note of anger coming into his voice. He's full on in protective mode now, and I wouldn't blame him if he used some of the queen's magic on her. I didn't realize this before, but while the Oracle is fae, she's an older, wiser version of the queen in front of me. If she truly wanted to mess with me and mine, she would sprinkle pieces of truth into her lies.

"Do you or do you not have Maddie's dad?"

I've never seen Liam this angry before, and if he wasn't on my side, I would be terrified. He's fae through and through, and until this very moment, I didn't realize just how much he's been holding himself back.

"Yes."

One word, and it's like a nuclear explosion has gone off inside of me. But then, before I can think of it, I'm moving, my battle magic at my fingertips. I slam right into Liam, my hands on his chest, as I force him to look at me.

"Liam! Don't!" The fae glances down at me and there is so much power in that one look, it takes so much out of me not to cower. But I keep my gaze steady, willing him to calm down. My magic sparks at my hands, the pressure of his own beating against my palms. But he doesn't unleash it.

Closing his eyes, he takes a few steadying breaths, and his magic retreats to sit right under the surface. My own follows suit, calming in sections. When Liam opens his eyes again, they're the regular kind, green ones that I love.

"I'm sorry, Mads," he whispers, and that's when it clicks. It's not just that she's been keeping my dad a secret. It's that it's my dad. Somehow, Liam feels responsible. Without a thought, I throw my hands around his middle, holding him to me. His own entwine around my body, as he ducks his head into my shoulder.

"This isn't your fault."

"But I—"

"You didn't fail me." I know exactly what he's going to say because it's what I've been saying this whole time. I've blamed myself for every decision I've made, for every spell that's gone awry. But now, I'm finding out that I've been a puppet from day one. I can only control the decisions I make, and I've made my choice to be a better version than they think I am.

Stepping back, I face the queen. Aiden is beside her, ready to pounce if she makes one wrong move, and when I meet his eye, he gives me a firm nod. He's got my back. As usual.

When I finally look at the queen, I find surprise in her eyes. She glances between Liam and me as if she's never seen either one of us before.

"Your friendship, it is...different."

"You can say that again." I narrow my eyes, my own hatred for what she's done rising up inside me. There's a slight pressure on my hand and then Liam's fingers entwine with me, as if it's his turn to keep me in place. I give it a grateful squeeze, as I stare down the queen.

"It is not what you think, Madison Hawthorne."

"Then you better explain it to me."

She does that long slow study of me that I'm really starting to hate, before she replies.

"He is no prisoner of mine, any more than you are."

"I don't understand."

"We saved him from the Ancients and kept him as such while he conducted research for us. A deal for a deal."

That's when it comes together for me. My dad, the smartest man I know, would never be so reckless or unprotected that he would disappear. But he would, if he didn't have a choice. That's why we thought he was kidnapped. But I guess we were half right.

"He made a bargain."

"He did."

❧ 2 2 ❧

I honestly don't know what to do with that information. A bargain is an unbreakable bond, even for someone as powerful as an Ancient. In truth, Queen Amaryllis has kept my father safe. Maybe safer than he would've been if he stayed out there on his own.

"When can he contact his family?" I ask, because that has to be the reason he's been gone. It's probably the terms of the contract. The queen inclines her head, solidifying my suspicions.

"When he has found a way to cast the spell." That stops a lot of questions I have, and I zero on just one.

"What spell?"

"Unfortunately, I am not at liberty to discuss the matter with you. I am incapable."

Stupid fae and their stupid rules.

A loud crash sounds from somewhere close by, making the walls shake once more. The sound makes me jump, and I get another slight squeeze of comfort from Liam. Glancing at him, I realize our time is up.

"Then, I guess that's that. Unless you can tell me where he is exactly."

"I cannot."

Seriously, can't I catch a break? Shaking my head, I look at Liam.

"Better get her out of here before the bind breaks," I say, and he nods in response. I love the understanding between us. He doesn't have to question every move I make.

"Is there anything you can tell us?" Aiden calls out as Liam and the queen move toward the back door. He's stayed quiet through most of the exchange, giving me the opportunity to lead. But I can see the alpha in him wanting to protect, and he's ready to do so at a drop of a hat.

"I can tell you that this is about to get much worse," Queen Amaryllis says, looking each of us in the eye. "Everything until now was just one big lesson. Now, you are entering the test."

She doesn't say anything else, leaving Aiden and I alone in the room. He moves toward me carefully, as if unsure of his welcome. True, we haven't talked since he bolted from the room when Natalie was making no sense. But I'm not holding that against him. A plan is formulating in my mind, and I need his help to execute it.

"What are you thinking, Duchess?"

I guess he knows me well enough to know I'm scheming.

"I'm thinking my father has to be close by. And I want to go and see if I can find him. She didn't say anything about it being against the bargain, did she?"

"No." Aiden grins, looking a little proud of me. "She most certainly did not."

His complete trust in me, and willingness to go along, makes my heart expand two sizes. I know we need to talk, and we will. But right now, first things first.

After we check in with the rest of my friends, Aiden and I prepare to leave. Liam is at the back door, a bit restless himself.

"Are you sure I can't come with you?" he asks.

"You're needed here," I reply, giving his upper arm a quick squeeze. "If the queen is to be believed, your wards aren't going to stay up much longer. You need to hold the fort here while Aiden and I sneak over to the castle."

He nods, clearly not pleased with the situation. But he knows I'm right. Jade isn't happy either. But if we're to have a safe haven, we need to make sure Liam's house is standing when we return. And my friends understand that. They'll do what it takes.

"Stay safe, cupcake," Liam calls as Aiden and I step out of the house.

"You too, cupcake," I reply. Liam stands in the doorway, watching us as Aiden and I run toward the woods.

"I'm never going to understand the cupcake thing," the alpha comments once we're in the forest.

"That's okay, it's a Liam and me thing."

Aiden makes a noise, and I'm not sure if it's a grunt or a growl. He's come to appreciate Liam in the last few weeks, of that I am sure. But no one but Liam and me need to understand our inside jokes. I'm okay with that.

We continue through the forest as quietly as we can. Well, Aiden is a pro at that. I'm the one who has to keep watching where I step. The sounds of the battle echoes all around us. It's as if the leaves themselves amplify the noise. We haven't run into anyone yet, but it's inevitable. As far as we know, the woods are crawling with the Ancient's minions now. It takes us about twenty minutes to get close to the castle with Aiden weaving in and out of a straight path, to keep our scent confused.

"Duchess." Aiden's voice reaches toward me as he looks over his shoulder at me. We've been quiet for a while, and his voice jerks me out of my thoughts. "Are you okay?"

I understand what he's asking, and the simple care in that one question almost breaks every wall I have erected. Because in that room, when the queen said my father is with her, a lot of emotions assaulted me at once. It was only my focus on Liam and preventing World War three that stopped me from losing it. But Aiden can see it anyway. There's genuine concern in his voice and that makes my mind go to the conversation we haven't had yet.

"I would be better if we talked about what Natalie said."

"IT'S HARD TO EXPLAIN," HE SAYS AS WE FIND A PLACE TO CROUCH down at, with visibility of the castle. There are a few trolls roaming around, as if they too set up a perimeter outside the walls. I'm not seeing anyone in a physical battle at the moment, but the sound of it is still all around us.

"Try."

He studies me with those gorgeous eyes of his, and I think I've never been looked at quite like this. There is promise and want there. My heart is too full and too fragile to guess at the meaning behind that look, but I still hope. I still want. But for now, I wait.

"Natalie...she thinks we're true mates," he finally utters, but it seems like it's almost painful for him to say. I furrow my brow because I don't really know what that means. "Actually, they all do."

"What is it?"

"It's a story passed down through generations. It speaks of a pair of leaders, an alpha and his or her mate who are true mates, a bond that transcends magic itself. In a hundred generations, we haven't had one. It's always been just a fairytale. Until now."

"You think that's what we are?"

I can't imagine what I feel for him to just be some magical prophecy or spell. It's so real, so powerful, it can't just be a fulfillment of an old story. But maybe that's all I am to him, and he's been fighting it because he doesn't want it to be true.

"True mates..." I swallow against the lump growing in my throat. "They have to stay together? Rule together?"

"Yes. The pull between them is unbreakable."

"Okay."

What else am I supposed to say to that? I want to get up and walk away, but I can't exactly do that when we're crouching down in the middle of a war zone. The smart thing to do would've been to wait to have this conversation until later. But I'm not smart when it comes to Aiden, that has already been established.

"Maddie." His voice reaches toward me, only a name on his lips, but I feel it all over my body. "It's not some magical prison. It's called a true mate because the relationship is a genuine connection that grows, and when the connection is acknowledged, only then does it bind magically."

I'm completely helpless against the pull I feel toward him, and so once again I'm looking at him as he looks at me. I let the words he spoke wash over me, but it's still too surreal for me to comprehend. I can't actually imagine him choosing me over Natalie. I can't see myself being enough for him. Not after everything I've done.

"And if the connection is not acknowledged?"

"Then, the two can go on living their separate lives. But never truly finding home. Not like they would together."

I can't seem to look away from his intense gaze, and if I'm being honest, I don't want to. All I want to do is close the distance between us and lose myself in his kiss. It's like he hears my inner thoughts because his eyes flash with desire, and he doesn't bother to mask it.

"I heard you, Duchess. That day in my room. You promised me you'd tell me when I was awake. And you haven't. Did you change your mind?"

Suddenly, I can't force enough air into my lungs. He heard me. My measly confession that wasn't a confession at all. Just the ramblings of a girl too far into a guy that she can't have. I thought it didn't work, I thought he wouldn't be able to hear me.

"It doesn't matter." He recoils as if I've slapped him. But maybe that's for the best. He still has a duty, and I'm still not the one he's promised to. It's why I've had to keep my distance. Though, even that tastes like a lie now.

"If you think it doesn't, do you want to hear what I have to say anyway?"

It seems that Aiden is done keeping things inside. There's determination in his gaze, now mixed with that same desire I glimpsed earlier.

"I don't want you to say anything you will regret," I manage, my voice soft because it's taking everything in me not to cry. Aiden pauses briefly, as if shocked by my words, before he scoots closer. Our faces are inches apart now, and he reaches over to cradle the side of my face with his hand. The contact is feather soft, and it sends my heart into overdrive.

"I could never regret saying that I love you," he whispers.

My eyes fly up, tears running down my cheeks instantly. He may not have shouted the words from a rooftop, but it still feels like it's echoing all around me. I want to say it back, but suddenly I can't make my mouth work. But he's not done anyway.

"You told me I make your see yourself in a better light. You do the same to me. You push me to be the best version of myself, and you are always there to have my back. Every battle we've fought, every one we are yet to fight, I will always be there. I ran because I didn't want to push you into anything you weren't feeling. But I'll regret it for the rest of my days if I don't say this now.

"I fell in love with you quietly, as the first drops of a summer rain on a long hot night. And now, you are my thunderstorm and there is nothing I want more than to stand in the storm with you. You've never needed me to save you. But I will always be here to back you up. You're it, Duchess. There is no hiding from that."

We're both breathing heavily, as if we've just fought off a hundred Ancients, and I can't look away from him even if I tried. His words are everything I've wanted to hear and everything I thought I never would. I want him to understand just how much he means to me, but I still can't find the words. Swallowing my tears, I try anyway.

"I don't have pretty words or speeches, Aiden," I begin, pushing all my love into my eyes. "But I know that I love you. And that..." He doesn't wait for me to finish but closes the distance between us, his lips on mine. He tastes like sunshine and magic, even better than the last time. There's no hesitation this time because we're two entities coming together, like we always should've been. I could spend a lifetime kissing him, and it wouldn't be enough. It doesn't matter that I'm young, or that we may die tomorrow, this is the surest I've ever been of anything. He and I. We're meant to be.

❦ 23 ❦

When we finally pull away, I realize how foolish it is for us to be so lost in each other in the middle of a battle. We could've been surrounded, and we wouldn't have even known. But I think it was time to say what needed to be said because there is no guarantee we're coming out of this intact. I don't want to be a Debby Downer, but it's the simple truth of the matter.

"Aiden—"

"I know." He gives me a quick kiss on the forehead before placing his own against it. "We find your dad, get the school back to our realm, and then we'll talk about it."

There's really nothing I can do but grin. He gets me. Plain and simple.

With that said, we both peek over the rocks we've been hiding behind, giving the place another quick study. The trolls are still making their circles around the grounds, and I wonder if there's someone else nearby, watching from above.

"Does it look like they've breached the castle grounds?" I ask, trying to see a hole or something to indicate the Ancients have been able to get in.

"I don't think so." Aiden's sight is much better than mine. "At least not from this side. What do you want to do?"

"Do you remember when you came and got me? I think we can get in the same way."

Aiden nods, still looking down at the trolls patrolling.

"Are we in the right place?" I realize that I actually don't know. Aiden got me out last time. I didn't pay much attention.

"I think we're a little bit north. Come on." He reaches for my hand, taking it in his as he pulls me after him. I smile at the gesture, pleased with how easily my hand fits in his. But then again, we've always fit perfectly together. However, true mates or not, I'm still not sure what all of this means for us. I guess that's part of the conversation we're going to have later.

After a five-or-seven-minute walk, we arrive at the wall bordering the garden. There are only two trolls patrolling here, but I have to say, they're not looking that great. There's something off about them.

"Aiden, do you see how they move?" I point as we find a place between the trees so we can observe them. "Should they be doing that?"

The shifter watches the trolls for a few seconds before shaking his head.

"There is something off about them, but I'm not sure what. It's like they're in a trance, maybe?"

"Could they be?" I realize that while the trolls have attacked us in the past, I never expected them to be on the Ancients side. They're usually just a little more barbaric than other creatures. Not purely evil.

"It's possible. We don't actually know what powers the Ancients have. They've surprised us more than once."

This is true. Since none of us has any actual information on who or what the Ancients are, we're learning as we go. I think a part of me is always expecting them to be some mythological creature, but in truth, they're just like us. The Oracle looks like any other fae. Beautiful and deadly. Yet, she's been around since magic began. Could I have predicted that? I don't think I could've. Not even with all the information we know now.

"Maddie." Aiden pulls my attention back to him. "They're moving to the other side. Let's go now."

Without hesitation, I follow his lead as we race toward the wall.

Just as we're about to reach it, I call on my magic, giving the area a quick sweep to make sure we're not running into anything unusual. The only thing I feel is the same barrier magic that Liam has around his house.

"Can you get through?"

Thankfully, I think I can. Sometimes spells are impossible to do quickly. Sometimes quickly is the only way to go. The whole way here I was thinking of the way to get through without ripping a hole in the entire thing. I've only come up with one solution.

> *"A witch and a shifter,*
> *Jumped over the wall.*
> *Leaving no surprises,*
> *Keeping safe, them all."*

Aiden gives me a questioning look, but I only shrug. It isn't my best work, but it should do the job. I feel the story spell casting magic rising up in me.

"It's the best I got," I say before I'm swept into his arms on the run. Suppressing a yelp, I hold on tightly, and then we're flying. The barrier opens up in front of us and then we're through. Aiden lands softly to his feet, keeping me pressed against him. I glance up to watch the barrier shut back up, a smile on my lips.

"That wasn't so bad," I comment, pulling back as Aiden places me on my feet. However, the moment I'm on solid ground, a wave of dizziness overcomes me, and I stumble against him.

"Duchess?"

"I'm okay," I say, placing a hand against my head. Every time I think I've gotten a better handle on this magic, I get hit again. Liam won't be happy with me, and Aiden doesn't seem to be either.

"I'm okay," I repeat, this time adding a note of determination to my voice. Aiden doesn't look convinced, but he also doesn't argue. We don't have time for that. The queen knows I'm here, of that I have no doubt. Taking another cleansing breath, I focus my mind on my father. I don't have a location spell in place, but I do have my magic, and I call on it to find my dad. The trust my friends seem to have in me, I finally have in my magic.

"Let's get a move on." This time, I'm the one taking Aiden's hand and pulling him toward the door to the castle. However, halfway there, I freeze.

"What is it?"

"There's something..." I trail off, giving our surroundings a quick study. There seems to be a hum all around me, and I glance at Aiden to see if he hears it.

"What?"

"You don't hear that?"

"No."

If a shifter doesn't hear it, then it's meant only for me. Without hesitation, I focus my complete attention on the noise. Spinning in a slow circle, I look for the source, for some indication this isn't just in my head. A part of me wonders if it's the residual effect of the story spell casting, but then I see it. Tugging on Aiden's hand, I move toward a small opening between the vines in what seems to be a large gazebo. The noise intensifies the closer I get.

"You really don't hear it?"

"I don't." But he doesn't stop me from moving toward the opening. Once we're there, the noise is louder than before, like a lightbulb that's about to burst, and it seems to be coming from this area. Tentatively, I reach my hand out through the opening. But when I do, it seems to disappear on the other side.

"Maddie, let me." He steps before me, but when he touches the space in the doorway, it zaps him back.

"I think this one is only for me," I reply, not exactly sure how I know it, but it sounds true the moment I say it.

"Are you sure about this?"

"I don't think we have a choice."

I give his hand one quick squeeze before I turn toward the opening.

"Keep an eye out," I say right before I step through the door.

THERE'S A POP IN MY EARS, AS IF I'VE JUST COME UP FROM BEING underwater, and then I'm through. Instantly, I know exactly where I am. It's a forest that's I've seen too many times out of my window. And then, there it is. The window itself and a small door right in the corner of it. Without hesitation, I walk toward it and pull it open with no resistance. Stepping inside, I stare at the secret library I've spent countless hours in. A place that's only remembered by Aiden and me.

It looks exactly the same, but different somehow. As if the colors in my library are a little muted. A carbon copy of the place that rises in front of me. The sound of a book closing snaps me out of my awe, and I step farther into the room, glancing to the side.

"Dad!" I yell, and the man sitting at the table jumps at my voice, twisting around. He looks exactly the same, and the grin that splits his face brings tears to my eyes. Then I'm running toward him, and he catches me just as I start full on ugly crying.

He holds me tighter than ever before, as I cry myself out like I'm five years old again, and I've just scraped my knee on the sidewalk.

"My smart, brave, beautiful girl. I knew you'd find me." He keeps mumbling into my hair, running his hand up and down my back. Pulling back, I study his face, just as worn and tired as I feel. But there are no signs of torture, or malnourishment. He seems exactly like I remember him.

"Daddy, what happened to you? Why are you in this place? What is this place?" I can't stop looking at him, afraid he'll disappear if I do. He leads me to a chair, holding my hand tightly in one of his as he uses the other to wipe away my tears.

"First of all, are you okay?"

"I am now. I have so many questions."

"I'm sure you do. You were always eager to learn."

"Is this really you?" I blurt out, because I know better than to trust fae and their tricks. Even more so now than before.

"It's really me." He runs his hand over my hair, in a way he always does, and I try to reel in the tears. "What is one way you can see through an illusion?"

Grinning, I sit up straighter. This is how Dad has always been. Instead of just giving me the answers, he makes me think of them on my own. He's always said that a mind actually retains a lot more information than we think. So, a lot of questions we already have the answers to.

"You can't ask an illusion a question that only you know the answer to. It gets confused."

My dad smiles, giving me an encouraging nod. I think back to my childhood, to the many experiences we've shared, and one memory pops into place.

"What is the name of my favorite tree...to climb?"

Dad chuckles at the question but doesn't hesitate with his answer.

"Cherry blossom tree. A tree you should not be climbing."

"But why do I love it so much?"

"Because you feel like you're in another world among the blossoms."

The tears escape again as I reach over to hug him. I was only five when I climbed a cherry tree and Dad explained to me how dangerous it was for the tree because they are more fragile than others. But I wanted to be a princess of flowers and thought I was amazing to be surrounded by them.

"What happened to you?" I ask, pulling back once more. Dad wipes at my tears before diving into an explanation.

"You know I've been looking for a way to defeat the Ancients, and I started getting close to a particular spell. They found out about it because they don't just have magical minions all over the world. There are people hungry for power who will sell us out for a good price."

My mind briefly shifts to what Aiden said months ago. We're so quick to blame the Ancients for all the evil in the world, but there are others who are just as bad.

"Queen Amaryllis came to my aide."

"You mean she tricked you into a bargain."

"I knew what I was doing, Maddie," Dad replies, shaking his head. "I wish I had more time to craft a more careful set of parameters, but it was either Queen Amaryllis or the Ancients. I made my choice between the lesser of two evils."

I knew that decision all too well. I feel like this is exactly where I've been tethering this whole time.

"So, you've been here this whole time? And where is here exactly? Are we even still in Faery?"

"We are. And were not. The library is a birthright of our bloodline. This is the spell I found, the doorway to this place."

"But Dad, I've been in this library before."

"What do you mean?"

"I mean, this library has an entrance under Thunderbird Academy. Look." I stand, moving to one of the stacks of books on the table. "These human history books go here," I point to a wall on the other side of the room before turning to the other. "And here, there's a table with a scuff mark all across the top." I move some books out of the way, and there it is.

Dad stands, walking over to stand beside me.

"No one knows of it, except for me. And Aiden. But I kind of think that's because we're true mates, but I'm not sure what that means exactly. Anyway, it only shows up for me. And no one else can know about it."

"Hold on a minute, Maddie. True mates? Aiden?"

"Ah, yeah. I guess you've missed a lot."

"I'll say."

"Well, let me give you a quick rundown."

❧ 24 ❧

After I finish speaking, Dad sits quietly for a full minute, mulling over everything. I don't interrupt, giving him the time he needs to process. I did kind of just dumped my last six months of adventures on him. Truly, I didn't even realize how much has happened until I needed to share all of it with him.

"I can't believe this, Maddie," he finally says, looking up at me. "I never imagined anyone in our family would have story spell casting. It's so rare."

"Dad, I don't...I don't want it," I say honestly, speaking what I've been keeping inside all this time. "All I keep doing is messing up. And it drains me. Liam said it could destroy me. Is it wrong that I don't want it?"

"No, honey," my dad replies, squeezing my hand reassuringly. "Your emotions are what they are. But I can tell you that story spell casting isn't something that's just passed down. It's a type of magic that chooses you when it believes you are powerful enough to wield it."

"I don't understand."

"Everything you've been through, honey, those have been the building blocks of who you are meant to become. That's life summarized in the simplest of terms."

Dad leans forward, as if making sure I'm paying attention. But I'm already holding onto every word.

"You are a daughter of a witch and a Watcher. Not only that, you are a Hawthorne, one of the most powerful lineages in magic. But neither one of those matter unless the magic chooses you. You think that you've messed up,"

I nod, and my dad smiles.

"Which is perfectly normal. Don't you think I've messed up a thousand times in my lifetime? I'll make another thousand mistakes before it's over. But that just makes us human. We are both of this world and of magic. And magic, it plays by its own set of rules."

"So, it chose me, but what do I do with it? I can't seem to write a spell that fixes it all."

"It's not only about a spell, honey." He smiles, leaning back in his chair. "It's about your heart. Who healed your friends from sickness?"

"I don't know," I reply, still confused about that whole situation. I thought maybe the Oracle did, now that we know she's been the puppet master behind the whole thing.

"But you do."

"Me? You think I did?"

"I don't have to think. I know."

"But how?"

"What you did in the water, letting go and letting Aiden in, it opened up your heart to its full potential. And the magic saw that and rewarded you for it."

"You don't mean..."

"I do. I don't know this boy, but he is your perfect half. In our circle, we call them soulmates."

My mind instantly goes to my sisters and the men they found in their lives. The change it made to their magic and the people they've become because of their relationships. The story I found in the library was an answer, I just didn't think I deserved it.

"You don't think I'm too young for that kind of connection?"

"Honey, there is no such thing as an age limit for meeting your other half. I'm not saying you're to marry this boy right now. But you can allow your relationship to blossom. Trust yourself, and trust him to know what it means for both of you."

I let that sink in, the hope and excitement blossoming in my heart. Maybe I have been hesitant to trust myself when it comes to Aiden. Even after telling him I loved him, there are so many other obstacles we are to overcome. But if I am to trust myself and him, I think it's possible.

"I see it in you, Maddie," Dad comments, pulling me out of my thoughts, "The more accepting you are, the stronger your magic grows. It will only hurt you if you don't trust it fully."

Just then, a noise comes from the outside. Not quite the boom we heard in Liam's house but close.

"Now you have to go." He grabs his notebook, scribbling something down and tearing the page.

"What? No! I'm not leaving you."

Dad stands, tugging me toward the door I walked in through. I try to pull him to a stop, but he doesn't budge.

"You have to go. I am safe here as long as you do what must be done."

"I don't understand."

He places a piece of paper in my hand before pushing me out the door.

"I thought I had to find the perfect witch without realizing she's my own daughter. The spell is yours to make your own. When you win, I will be free."

"Dad!"

The door shuts and I grab the handle, trying to pry it open. Screaming his name, I pound on the door, but it won't move. Rushing over to the window, I look through it and at him standing on the other side.

"I love you," he mouths, and the tears are once again streaming down my face. Then, I hear my name being called, and I twist toward the doorway to the garden. Aiden is in trouble. I can feel it in my bones.

"I'll make you proud, Daddy," I say, turning back to the window. "I love you."

Then, tucking the paper into the pocket of my jeans, I race for the doorway.

❦

WHEN I BURST THROUGH ON THE OTHER SIDE, THE GARDEN IS IN chaos. Fae are in every corner, fighting. Trolls, winged creatures I've never seen before, along with magic wielders that look like humans have infiltrated the grounds. My eyes scan for Aiden just as a winged creature attacks. I duck automatically, coming back up with battle magic at my fingertips. Sending a blast at the creature, I push it back but only barely. Whatever this thing is, it's more powerful than I anticipated. Some have claws for hands, other have tentacles. They're a mesh of different creatures all rolled into one. The only thing they do have in common are the wings. Which gives them an advantage.

"Maddie!"

Aiden's voice comes from my left and then he's there. He grabs my hand, pulling me out of the way as another creature descends. We roll out of the way, and this time, I call on my water magic, blasting the creature right in the face and keeping the water there. He thrashes around as he tries to get it off, but it's no use. The moment he's down, I let up.

"What are they?" I yell as a troll jumps at me. I grab my sword, pulling it out of its sheath on my back in one quick motion. The troll attacks again, but this time instead of dodging him, I attack. They're quick, aided by their size, but I've been training with Aiden. He's just as quick as they are, and so I'm prepared.

"We need to get out of here," Aiden calls over his shoulder as he reaches for me once again. Sweat drips into my face, and I wipe at it with my other hand, surveying the garden in front of me. The queen's guards seem to be holding their own a little better now, so I turn to Aiden.

"Let's go."

Instead of racing to the wall, Aiden leads us to the castle. Trusting him to know what he's doing, I push myself to keep up. Even in human form, he's much faster than I am. Reaching back, he takes my hand, tucking me beside him. We rush through the hallways, and I only have a moment to notice the carnage around me. Many of the rich fae who've spent their time at the castle are dead. Their playrooms turned into their graves. I glimpse blood and bodies thrown everywhere before we're moving away. My stomach overturns itself, bile threatening to rise, but I push it away. I don't have time to dwell on what I'm seeing.

When we reach the grand entrance, the queen is there. She's holding her own against the creatures trying to get in through the front doors. When she spots us, she beckons with her hand, and Aiden doesn't hesitate to move us toward her.

"I knew you would come to look for him," she says as she sends a big blast of magic at the door before it slams shut. "That will not hold them long. They are much more powerful than I anticipated."

"What are they?"

"Her enhancements. The Oracle has given creatures a boost in magic, her own special breed of soldiers."

"What does she want?"

"Ultimate power of course." The queen gives me a pointed look. "You found him, did you not?"

"I did." Aiden's head whips in my direction, surprised. But I stay focused on the queen. "Why didn't you tell me?"

"The bargain prevented it. Now do what he has instructed. There is a portal in the throne room. It will lead you to Liam's house. Go now."

I open my mouth to thank her but stop at the last moment. She seems to understand anyway, a smirk forming on her lips.

"I knew who you were when I saw you, Madison Hawthorne. She has come, and you must fight. Now, go!"

Aiden doesn't hesitate. He takes my hand once more, racing to the throne room. The portal is there, already shimmering in the empty space, waiting for us to go through. More shouting comes from behind us, but we don't stop until we run right through the shimmer.

Landing on the other side, hands still entwined, we come face to face with my friends.

"Maddie!" Jade rushes to me, throwing her arms around me. Immediately, I see that they look out of breath, as if they too have been fighting.

"What's going on?" Aiden asks as he looks around the room.

"They're almost through the barriers," Ben replies, his voice absent of any of the humor he usually carries with him. Owen stands beside him in quiet determination. Natalie is pacing, looking angry at the world.

"These wards won't let us out either!" she snaps, glaring at Liam.

"The wards are keeping you safe. So, a thank you should be in order," he replies, matching her tone. Her death stare doesn't seem to have any effect on him, but she tires anyway. "What happened out there?"

"The Oracle is here," I say, receiving a few gasps from around the room. Noel has been the quietest through all this, and when I look at him, I can see he's scared. Walking over to him, I don't reach out. Just stand beside him and wait for him to make the move. When he finally meets my eye, I read every emotion there. "We'll get through this."

"Will we?" Noel asks, and I hear it in his voice. The doubt, the uncertainty. I can't really be making these promises, and I won't lie to my friends.

"We will try our best," I say, and for a moment Noel looks surprised, but then he nods.

"Thank you for not lying to me."

Jade comes over to stand beside him and takes his hand, and I see him instantly relax. They're good together, I knew that much. But to see it, it makes my heart happy. Now, I just need to make sure I get them out of this. That's when I realize I haven't looked at the paper Dad gave me. Pulling it out, I give the words a quick scan. So simple, yet so powerful.

Looking up, I see that my friends are watching me, as if waiting for me to come up with a plan. Meeting Aiden's eyes, I find complete trust there. Somehow, he has given me this position of leadership, even though as an alpha, he could take it. No questions asked. But this is something only I can do, and as he walks to stand beside me, I realize what that is.

"I know you're scared," I begin as Aiden reaches for my hand and entwines our fingers together. His pack doesn't miss the small movement, because even though he's done it before, there's a difference in the way he holds it now. Ben and Owen exchange a glance before their full attention is on me. The intensity in their gaze speaks volumes. Natalie doesn't look as displeased as I thought she would either. Jade is beaming at me, which is very unnatural in our current situation. Liam and Noel don't look even remotely surprised. But all of their focus is on me now. So, I take a deep breath and continue.

"I have a spell, but to execute it, I have to be on campus. Which is mostly overrun by these creatures by now. Headmaster Marković is...possessed would be the best word, by the Oracle's magic. That means the academy is not safe. But we have no choice but to try and get in anyway. I know it's asking a lot of you. We've been training for this all year, but none of us actually expected the Ancients to break through the walls and become a personal threat to us. At least, I didn't.

"I know we can't stop all of them. The Ancients are too powerful and there are too many. But we can stop the ones here and now. I can't do that alone. Every time I try to fix things on my own, I keep messing them up. Because this isn't just about me. We are all chosen to protect our birthright. We are witches and shifters and fae who have a responsibly to our magic. *This* is our responsibility. This is what we have to do in order to keep our families safe. I'm not backing down." Aiden gives me a scorching look, pride shining in those gorgeous eyes of his. "If you can't fight, I understand. But I ask you to trust me. With all of us, we can do this. I know it."

"We're here, Maddie. We're with you," Aiden says, and I watch as every single person in the room nods their head. My heart swells with love for these people. For my people.

"What do we do?"

I study the faces in the room, the family I have become part of at the Thunderbird Academy, and I know there is only one answer to that question.

"We go to war."

‹§ 25 §›

The fighting is so loud outside, I'm afraid they'll come through those doors any minute.

"Your barriers are stronger than the queens?" I ask, and Liam gives me a quick smile.

"No, she put some of her magic into them before she left."

All this time I thought Queen Amaryllis was the bad guy, and she ended up being the good guy. I guess it's true when they say not everything is what it seems.

"Can you portal us to the school?" But even before I finish asking the question, Liam is shaking his head.

"The Oracle is feeding off the magic. She'll either prevent the portal or be right on the other side of it. Either way, it doesn't look good for us."

"That means we have to go through," I say, turning to face the front doors. It's not an ideal way of doing this, but we don't have a choice. Aiden walks back over to stand beside me. He was conferring with the pack. Since they are so much better at strategy, I'm open to every idea. I told him as much.

"We have to scatter," he says, and it's what I've been afraid of. I'm not exactly excited to send my friends out there by themselves. "Maddie, it's the only way. If we push all together, we won't make it far. We might get stuck, surrounded somewhere."

"You're talking about a diversion," Noel comments.

"I am." Aiden looks down at me, determination fueling his words. "We can do this. It's dangerous, but if we play our cards right, we will get through faster."

"So, what's the plan then?" Jade asks, her magic already at her fingertips. I have to admit. My friends are pretty powerful.

"One shifter, one non-shifter. We leave the house at the same time, then separate when we get close to the edge of the barrier. Ben, you go with Noel. Owen goes with Liam. Nat, you go with Jade."

The two girls eye each other immediately, and I glance at Aiden as he pairs people up. There's a strategy in that as well, so I'll have to ask him about it later. If we get out of it alive. Surprisingly, I'm not worried about Jade. I know Natalie won't allow her pride to do anything but her best when it comes to protecting Jade. But I can feel Liam's eyes on me.

He doesn't want me out of his sight, of that I am sure. The bond we've created between us makes me want to keep him where I can see him as well. But it's smarter this way, and we both know it. I think he's going to protest anyway, but he doesn't. An understanding passes between us, a promise without words that we will do our best to get through this in one piece.

"Okay, then let's do this."

As a group, we move toward the front entrance. Exchanging a few looks, I force my mind to memorize my friends as they are right now. There are no guarantees in life. I remember thinking that when I started this school year. How silly that day seems now. The worries that I experienced back then were nothing in comparison to where we are today. But just like my dad said, every experience is a building block to who we are meant to become. There are no goodbyes exchanged between us. We know we've been trained for this, and now, we get to prove ourselves.

After one last look at my friends, Liam opens the door, and we run out. The scene that greets us is much worse than I anticipated. The creatures are right at the barrier, clawing to get in. There are at least two dozen of them, pure hatred coming off them as they gnash their teeth.

However, we don't pause. We run toward them and then, at the last moment, we separate. There's a loud screech made by a dozen creatures, and then they give chase. I pull on my water magic, feeling it rush over my body.

Aiden and I burst through the herd, my magic making a tunnel as the water pushes the creatures to the side. It only lasts a moment, but it's long enough for us to get to the woods. I think we're ahead enough when something yanks me from behind.

I slam into a tree, dropping to all fours, my sword flying out of my hands. Aiden shouts my name as I shake my head to clear it. When I look up, a winged creature is upon me. We slam into the ground, the creature's saliva dripping onto my skin as his claws dig into my upper arms. I'm completely pinned down by the sheer weight of the monster. I hear Aiden yelling, but when I glance to the side, I see him battling two creatures of his own. One of them manages to draw blood, and my heart stops at the sight.

The creature above raises one claw to swipe at me, but I use that as momentum, slamming my free hand, now full of magic, into its chest. The impact and the emotion behind it, sends the creature flying, and the next thing I know, he's pierced through the heart on one of the branches. Grabbing my sword, I jump to my feet, racing toward Aiden. He's holding his own against the two, and when I get there, I dispose of one from the back. Aiden finishes the other before reaching for my hand.

The sound of more of them coming follows us as we race toward the school. When we finally reach the outskirts of the academy, my heart drops. The place is nearly unrecognizable. The building itself looks like it's been through a bombing, and there are students and faculty fighting on the lawn.

"Where do you need to go?" Aiden asks, his eyes scanning the area, looking for his pack.

"The greenhouse," I announce, receiving a quick nod.

"Our best bet is just head straight in." It's what I thought as well. "Ready?"

"Yes."

We take off once again, but this time, we don't get any farther. Suddenly, Headmaster Marković is there, blocking our path. Aiden and I halt, as the headmaster smiles.

"It's about time."

❧

"HEADMASTER MARKOVIĆ," I BEGIN, KEEPING MY VOICE CALM. "I know you're under a spell. But you can fight it."

"Why would I want to?" He chuckles, and the laugh is so unnatural, it causes goosebumps to break out over my skin. He looks wrong somehow. Maybe like he hasn't eaten or drank anything in days. His clothes are dirtier than I've ever seen them, and there's a crazy look in his eyes.

I let go of Aiden's hand and begin moving slowly around the headmaster. There's no way to know how juiced up he is on the Ancient's magic. Technically, he could blow us all out of the water here. Keeping his attention on me, I continue to circle while Aiden reads my mind and moves behind him.

"This isn't you, Headmaster Marković," I say, trying to keep him focused. "You're our teacher. My mentor. Look at what has happened to your school. You can't—"

"You can try to distract me all you want." Headmaster Marković interrupts me, sick amusement shining in his eyes. "But you are no match for her. No matter how much you pretend to be all perfect and powerful."

"When have I ever pretended to be—"

"Since the moment you came into the school. Little Miss Hawthorne. Has to show off her magic."

His speech is getting more frantic the longer he speaks. It's like it's revving him up for something, but what, I can't even begin to guess. I don't think I want to. Suddenly, a sword appears in his hand, taking me by surprise.

"I think we should battle it out the old-fashioned way." He grins, spit dripping down his chin. But Aiden is now directly behind him, and he doesn't hesitate to pounce. At the last moment, Headmaster turns, slamming the sword right into Aiden's stomach.

"No!"

The scream rips out of me, and I stumble toward Aiden as Headmaster yanks the sword out. Aiden drops to his knees, holding a hand over the slash in his torso as blood flows out.

"Aiden, no. No." I'm unable to utter any other words as I land hard on my knees beside him. The headmaster stands over us, laughing his diabolical laugh.

"You're going to be okay. You are," I mutter over and over, placing my hand over the gaping wound. The blood stains my hands red, my tears blinding me for a moment.

"Tsk, tsk, Miss Hawthorne," Headmaster says, twisting his sword around as he looks down at us. "It's not nice to lie."

I ignore him just long enough to meet Aiden's eyes. My magic and my love for him rushes to the surface, the power of it burning in my veins.

"Shift," I command, and something comes over Aiden's eyes right then. He jerks in my arms as his body begins to morph. I feel more than see the headmaster move toward me, and I'm ready for him. Spinning around, I bring my sword up as he swings his down. The impact jerks my body, but I keep hold. Pushing back, I rise to my feet, my magic begging to be set free.

"I have always respected you," I say, keeping my sword firmly against his. "But I will not let you destroy everything I love."

With those words, I push my magic though my arms and into my sword. I'm not even sure how I'm doing it, I just know I'm acting on instinct. Headmaster Marković stumbles back, pushed by my magic. Moving toward him, I swing my sword faster and faster as the headmaster tries to block me move for move. My body doesn't feel tired for some reason. It feels like it can go for days. I don't slow down, and I don't let up. Headmaster is holding his own, but I can see the uncertainty in his eyes the faster I move. Magic pours out of me in waves, and I don't hold anything back. I'm not running from this power, not anymore.

Our swords cling together, echoing in the space around us. Others are fighting all over the school, the screams of pain and shouts of triumph molding together. My feet are sure on the grass as we do the dance. Headmaster Marković is knowledgeable in combat, but I have a little more determination on my side. Even so, when he swipes at me, I'm a second too late, and he makes a clean cut across my upper right arm. The pain is instantaneous, and even though the blood sprays everywhere, I don't stop my advance.

"You can't win," Headmaster Marković spits out as I deliver another blow to his sword.

"Maybe, maybe not." I grunt though the pain. "But I'm going to try."

One more thrust, and I catch his side. The feeling of my sword going into his body is a lot less strange than I thought it would be. When I yank it out, blood begins to flow out of the wound. He drops to his back, and I send a blast of magic at him, knocking him out by cutting off his breathing with a few well-placed water puddles. When he's out, I finally move away.

Turning, I see Ben is near Aiden now, who has shifted but is not moving. I rush toward them, but then Liam is there.

"Go!" He points toward the school, stopping me in my attempt to reach Aiden. "We'll protect him. Go."

Anger rises up in me, and I want to push Liam out of the way. But it's not him who's making me feel these emotions.

"You stay safe too," I call before I pivot and run for the greenhouse.

❧ 26 ❧

Rushing through the now broken doors of the greenhouse, I only have a second to take in the absolute destruction in front of me before I am hit with a blast of magic. The impact sends me flying against a table, breaking it from the impact.

Rolling to my side, I look up to see the Oracle standing at the inside entrance of the greenhouse. Gone is her college senior look. Her dress is bright purple, the color associated with royalty. Her hair is no longer short but flows down her back in stylish curls.

"Welcome to the party, little witch."

Staggering, I push myself to my feet, using what's left of the table for leverage. It's not like I'm surprised to see her. I just thought she'd be somewhere that's not on the front lines of the war she created.

"Do I keep calling you the Oracle, or do you have a name?" I spit some of the blood out, keeping my eyes on her. She smiles that unnerving smile of hers as she sashays farther into the room.

"I've been called many names through the ages," she begins, examining her nails as if she doesn't have a care in the world. "Some you haven't even heard of."

"So, give me one I have heard." It's difficult to breathe, but I'm managing somehow. With the amount of times I've been thrown around today, I'm a little surprised I'm still standing.

"Hmm, I suppose Abonde will do."

For a moment, I think I have her. The name is vaguely familiar, and I'm sure I've learned of it in history classes. Fae attribute a lot of power to one's true name. But then I realize it doesn't matter. She may have told me her name, but she is beyond the rules of fae.

"You've heard of me, haven't you?"

"Should I have?"

That doesn't sit well with her. She sends another blast of magic at me, picking me right off my feet and then slamming me back to the ground.

"I could do this all day."

"You need a hobby."

"I had a hobby!" She's suddenly in my face, her mask of indifference slipping long enough for me to see pure hate. "It was my favorite pastime, moving house to house to collect the offerings left for me. I am owed hundreds of sacrifices, and yet, this world barely remembers who I am."

"I heard there was another one like you." I probably shouldn't be goading her, but I can't help it. "She was mad too, and now she's just sleeping."

The next wave of magic sends me straight into one of the glass displays, and when I drop to the floor, the shards dig into my skin. I scream because I can't help it, and the witch smiles.

"Do you know who my favorite pets were? Don't worry I'll tell you." She walks over to a table before gently pulling herself to sit on top of it, legs crossed. She could be having a friendly conversation with someone the way she looks so relaxed. "It used to be that the third born child was obligated to travel with me on nights I collected my bounty. Sometimes covens overlooked third born children but not I. I knew the power they had brewing right under their skin. I feasted on their magic, just like I feasted on the offerings."

And just like that, with a simple explanation, I understand why she's been playing this game with me. She may not even know just how powerful I am. To her, I'm a third-born witch.

My cuts are bleeding all over as I get to my feet once again. She hasn't moved from her perch, watching me carefully. She's monologuing now, the need to hear her amazing plan out loud overpowering any logic.

"You were so easy to manipulate," she says, flipping her hair over her left shoulder. "You knew nothing about us or what we are capable of. A few rumors here and there, and your precious shifter came running to look for answers. And you followed, no questions asked. The bargain, that was too easy. I didn't even have to give anything away. You did all the work for me."

"Why?" I dare ask, "Why go through all that trouble?"

"I guess it doesn't really matter if I tell you," she says, hopping off the table and walking toward me. "Your school is a powerful conduit, and with a bit of tweaking from your lovely headmaster, it's now collecting magic for me. The greatest offering of all. After I drain your blood magic, there will be enough in the conduit for me to absorb. With that kind of a power, I can stand up to any and all of the filth rising up from their slumber."

"Not a fan of your family, are we?"

"You have no idea," she says, flipping her hair once again. "But it doesn't matter now. I will be powerful enough to stand up to any and all of them. Then they'll see what I'm made of."

"What?" My blood continues to drip down my arm, but all my focus is on her. The pain is just a dull reminder that I'm still alive, that I still have a chance. "An Ancient in need of borrowing magic from a bunch of high schoolers?"

This time, the wave of magic picks me right off my feet and carries me a good ten feet before I slam into the ground. My head spins from the impact, my vision blurry. But as I struggle to my knees, I realize I did what I needed to do. I'm right over the area where the library sits. It's right under my feet.

THE ORACLE, OR ABONDE, ADVANCES TOWARD ME WITH COMPLETE hatred in her eyes. It's a tale as old as time. She wasn't good enough for her family, so she took the matters into her own hands. The anger around her is almost thick enough to touch. Abonde grabs my hair, yanking my head back.

"You think your witty digs and sarcasm can save you? You're not as powerful as everyone thinks you are. You're just a teenage girl who hasn't found her place in the world." She drops my hair, pushing my head forward, and I think she's about to stomp on me, but she doesn't. She paces away, all pretense of that calm and indifferent Oracle completely gone. These are her true colors, and she's not that far off from being a confused teenager herself.

"What I know," I say, keeping to my knees, but still calling on my magic slowly. "Is that you're the one without a place in this world."

The scream of rage that rips out of her shatters my eardrums. Slapping my hands over my ears, I try to hold on to my magic as she advances on me.

"Stupid, stupid witch. You know nothing." She screams right into my face. But I do know something. She's finally crossed right into the area I wanted her in. I grab her upper arms, completely surprising her as I raise myself up to look at her.

"There is a little girl,
Longing for home.
But all she does,
Is ruin it all.

Her magic is weak,
Her temper is frayed.
She's tired and lonely,
Powerless and afraid."

"No!" Abonde begins screaming and tries to yank her body away, but I have a magical grip on her, and I'm not letting go. "Shut up!"

Her magic tries to battle my own, but I'm not alone. The words flow from my lips, as natural as saying good morning to my family.

"She had a plan,
But her plan has failed.
She had a reason,
But that's all been derailed.

She's never going to rise,
She won't win this war.
She's going to lose it all,
And go to sleep for a thousand years more."

THE LAST TWO LINES HAVE TO BE YELLED OVER THE GROWING MAGIC cyclone around us. The wind blows, carrying with it fire, earth, and water. Abonde thrashes under my fingertips, blasting her magic at me every second. But I still don't let go. I push my own magic into her, taking over her being from inside out. I feel the power flowing through me. Every doubt I've ever had evaporates with the knowledge that this is who I am. I am a Hawthorne. I am in love. And I am a strong witch with generations of magic on her side.

Just as suddenly as the wind comes, it disappears, and Abonde drops straight to the floor. Then, before I can move, the ground opens up, swallowing her whole. Just like that, she's gone. Dropping to all fours, I try to find my breath, but I can barely keep myself from passing out. The sound of the battle ceases. The quiet is abrupt after so much noise. Honestly, I have no idea how much time has gone by since this all began, but it feels like years.

Giving in to my exhaustion, I lay down on the floor, not caring about the possibility of another attack, or the fact that I'm still bleeding all over. She's gone, and with it, all of my strength. All I want is to be home again, surrounded by my family, walking the streets of

Hawthorne. I want the school to find its rightful place once more, away from Faery.

When I close my eyes, the final thought in my mind is that I hope I get to see cherry blossoms again.

$\mathscr{X}$ 2 7 $\mathscr{X}$

The first thing I notice is a tight grip around my hand. Forcing my eyes to open, I'm momentarily blinded by the light. When I grunt my discomfort, something blocks the light momentarily, and when I look, I see that it's my sister Harper.

"Holy moly, it's about time," she says before she's on top of me, hugging me to her. I realize I'm in bed, bandages over my whole body. I'm sore all over, and thirsty. Very thirsty.

"Here," Bri says, pushing Harper away and handing me a cup of water. With Harper's help, I sit up and take the offered cup gratefully.

"Where am I? And how long was I out?" I ask between sips before I realize that my sisters are here. "Wait, you're here! How is that possible?"

"It's possible because you got everyone home." The voice comes from the doorway and then my dad steps in. He comes right over, sitting down carefully on the bed.

"I don't understand. The last thing I remember was fighting Abonde."

"That's who that was?" Bri asks, and I see a little excitement on her face. "Sorry, she's pretty iconic. I've studied so many of her spells. I never thought she would be real."

"Well, she is. And she's a very angsty teenager." I settle into my bed, and Harper rushes over to place a pillow or two at my back. I smile thanks, and she returns it.

"How long was I out?"

"About two weeks."

"What?"

Dad pats my hand before giving it a reassuring squeeze.

"Your spells drained you. That was two too many for you to handle at once."

"I only did the casting you instructed." Dad smiles at that, as I remember what he wrote on the paper. It was simple three-part plan. Get her to the area over the library. Spill a little blood to activate the spell Dad already had in place on his library. Then, say the spell straight from the heart. No preparation. Just a simple story spell casting done on the spot.

"It worked, right?" I ask because I have to make sure.

"It did," Dad replies, giving me another one of his signature smiles. "The blood worked as connection between my library and yours. I was able to bind her to the spot until you worked your magic."

"And then you got out."

"I did."

"Are you going to explain the library thing to me?"

"It's not that complicated. It's a place bound just to us, to your family. I found it when I cast a spell looking for answers. You found it because your magic called upon it. It'll be there again when you need it."

That makes sense. I guess. My mind is still muddled on the details, but I'm missing a very important part of this whole thing.

"What did you say about casting more than one spell?"

"I think you subconsciously story spell casted the academy back to i's original place," Dad replies, shocking me into silence. I honestly have no idea what to say to that. "When it came back, it was restored to i's original glory as well. No holes in the walls."

"What about Aiden?" I ask, sitting up a little too fast, as memories start rushing back. My sisters exchange a look, and I can't tell if it's a good one or a bad one. "Dad?"

"He's okay." He gives my sisters a quick reprimanding grunt. "If you hadn't ordered him to shift, he may not have been."

"Ordered?"

"That was your first spell of the day. Apparently, you used your alpha voice, and he had no choice but to shift."

Nothing is making sense anymore. I'm not the alpha, he is. I didn't cast any spells. I don't think I can handle any more information. I just need one last thing.

"Are my friends okay?"

"They were beat up pretty bad, but they're healing nicely."

"Okay, that's good," I say, and then I'm closing my eyes once more, the feeling of calmness coming over me. The door opens, and I think I see Krista walk in before I'm lost to my dreamless sleep.

❧

THE NEXT TIME I WAKE UP, THERE'S ONLY ONE OTHER PERSON IN the room.

"Mama," I whisper and then she's taking my hand, squeezing it in both of hers.

"Hello, my sweet girl," she says, and just her voice soothes whatever worries I had left over in my mind. "I am so proud of you."

"I've missed you, Mama."

"I've missed you too."

Then, my eyes close, and I'm drifting again.

❧

WHEN I OPEN MY EYES, IT'S DARK OUTSIDE AND EVERYTHING SEEMS quiet. I glance to my right and find Aiden sleeping in a chair. Just the sight of him raises my spirits, and I turn over and go back to sleep.

❧

WHISPERS REACH ME THROUGH THE SLUMBER, AND I FORCE MY EYES to open. Aiden is there, shutting the door behind someone I can't see.

"Duchess." He's at my bedside instantly, as if he felt me wake up. "How are you?"

"Better knowing you're here."

"Where else would I be?" He picks up my hand, kissing my knuckles gently. I tug on my hand before scooting over in bed, and he seems to read my mind. Climbing in, he takes me in his arms, holding me close to his chest.

"Did we really win?" I ask, settling myself against him, as if this is where I'm made to be.

"We did. Ben and Liam got the worst of it, trying to fight off the packs of creatures away from me and the greenhouse, but they're fully recovered," he hurries on to add, and my heartbeat slows once more.

"Why am I not healing as fast?"

"The healers think the spells drained your magic, making you nearly as human as anyone out there in the world. You have to heal more like them as it replenishes."

It's the guess I would've made if my mind was working a little better.

"I don't remember any spells besides the sleeping one. They said I alpha commanded you?"

Aiden chuckles, holding me a little closer to his body.

"You did. It's something true mates can do. Even if you're not a shifter."

"Interesting. It could come in handy." I trace random patterns against his chest as he chuckles again before sobering up.

"I thought I lost you, Duchess," he whispers against my hair, and I feel a shudder that goes over his body. "For a moment there, I couldn't feel you anymore, and I didn't know if I'd survive."

"Hey," I sit up, leaning on my elbow so I can look into his face. My fingertips trace over his strong profile, a small smile blossoming on my face. "I'm not going anywhere."

"Is that a promise?"

"It most certainly is."

❧ 28 ❧

"Are you coming or what?" Jade calls out as she grabs her jacket and does a little spin in front of the mirror by the door. I tear my gaze away from the vanity that I've been staring into for way too long and nod. A quick glance at the table, and I smile at the cherry blossom branch magically blooming near my bed. Aiden gives the best gifts. It helps that he knows a certain fae with an affinity to Spring. "You look amazing. Let's go!"

She pulls me out of our room and down the hall, entwining her arm through the crook of my elbow. Ever since we returned to school, she's been staying a little closer than before, but I don't mind. I think we both realize how precious every moment is now. There's nothing that compares to a good girl friend, and I will never again take mine for granted. I was finally able to contact Kate. She's staying safe with her parents, and I'm happy for her. But I'm also happy that Jade was here through all of this.

We race down the stairs and toward the back of the school, passing a bunch of students still milling around the halls. A few call out a greeting, and I wave in return. Although the evil headmaster dropped my name in the announcements and made everyone mad at me for a while, everything else that transpired has seemed to sway the student body back into my favor. Especially after Headmaster Marković made a public announcement and an apology. He blames himself for taking the elixir without consideration, but I know sick people do crazy things. Whether they're magical or not. So, I don't hold it against him. And I no longer hold things against myself as well.

When we reach the back field, bleachers have been set up along both sides of it for spectators. I see Vera sitting with her hawk shifters and give her a little wave that she returns. We haven't been as close since everything happened. I don't think we ever will be. A part of me wonders if she will always associate our friend group with Christie and her betrayal. But maybe it's good Vera finally feels better being around her own kind. After all, I finally found my people too.

Noel and Owen make room as Jade and I reach the bleachers.

"I thought you were playing." I look at Owen as he shrugs.

"Didn't feel like it."

The always quiet shifter is definitely different from the rest of his pack, but I find his presence comforting. Especially since Ben is an overactive puppy, and Natalie is mean. Even though she's been the biggest supporter of Aiden and me. It's what they were arguing about the day they were healed. He was so afraid that what he and I had was only a prophecy, he wanted to protect me if I didn't feel the same. Natalie pushed him anyway.

The rest of the pack have been nice to me, but I'm not making any lasting connections yet. It'll take a while. Noel and Jade start talking immediately, while she tucks herself against her boyfriend. I smile at them before I scan the crowd for mine. It's not hard to find him. His own eyes have already gravitated toward me and he grins.

"You guys are so sweet it's sickening," Liam announces as he plops himself in the seat beside me. Surprised, it takes me but a moment to throw my arms around him.

"I didn't think you were coming."

"Well, Auntie has decided to give me a little more leeway with the portals."

Ever since the battle for the academy, as the kids began calling it, Liam has been working with Queen Amaryllis. She's become a bit more open to council, and I guess that means something good came out of this for Faery too. They lost a lot of their people when the creatures attacked. We lost a few students and faculty too. It could've been worse. So, I try to remain thankful, even as my heart hurts for those families.

"You're still not coming back to school?" I ask, tucking my hand around his arm.

"I think I'm better served at home. At least for the time being."

As sad as that makes me, I know he's right. The Ancients are part of our world now. There is not one perfect spell that can send them all back to their slumber. But we can take them, one at a time. My parents will continue searching for answers. And so will I. Thunderbird Academy is once again spelled, and is the safest place, with student coming to find refuge within her. It's strange to think how much our lives have changed in such a short period of time. Now, even almost two months later, we are still feeling the aftershocks. But we're not giving up. We're living our lives to the fullest.

Just then, the whistle blows, so I turn my attention back to the field. A referee takes centerfield, his eyes on the crowd, his voice amplified by magic.

"Everyone knows the rules of the game. The field has been nullified of all magic. This is a human game and will be played as such."

"Whose idea again was it to play football?" Natalie asks, taking a seat on the bleachers in front of us.

"Bored people?" I reply, shrugging. She throws me a quick smile over her shoulder, before she realizes what she's done and turns back to the field. Aiden and Ben are both playing, and they take their positions grinning.

"If they get hurt," I comment, "I refuse to heal them."

Aiden raises his head as if he heard me, a devilish smile on his face. A moment passes between us, an electric current full of promise and love. I may be a high schooler, but I know a good thing when I see it. As I glance around at my friends, I'm determined to hold on to it. No matter what.

<<<<>>>

MADDIE'S LIST OF OLD SLANG
WORDS/PHRASES

Abercrombie - a "know-it-all"

All wet - "no good"

Debby Downer - someone who is constantly making others feel bad or dampening the mood of a group with negative comments

Flabbergasted - surprise greatly; astonish

Take the rap - taking responsibility for someone else's crime

Trip for biscuits - a task that yields nothing.

Source: paper-dragon.com, first hand experience

WANT MORE FROM THE WORLD
OF HAWTHORNE?

Get the complete series in one boxset:
Faerie Destiny

Or read the books individually here:

Shadow of the Fae
Blood of the Fae
Revenge of the Fae

Wanted by all of Faerie...hunted by a mysterious fae prince.

I was ready for a quiet and normal high school senior year. But then, I read something I wasn't supposed to and now every illusion I had about my magic is shattered.

Something in my blood allows me to read spells thought to be lost long ago. It's a power the courts of Faery will fight over...with me as collateral damage.

If I'm found, my life is over. Which is how I end up on the run.

When the breathtakingly beautiful and arrogant Fae finds me, I'm prepared for him to drag me kicking and screaming back to the Faerie Realm.

He doesn't. He decides to help. Or so he claims...

Gorgeous and deadly. A dangerous combination. And my only chance at survival.

If I don't outwit the fae and learn to control my magic, I will lose my life. And all those I love will perish with me.

Featuring a fierce heroine, a broody prince, enemies-to-lovers slow burn romance, and a magical adventure, Faerie Destiny is a thrilling young adult paranormal romance series by USA Today bestselling author Valia Lind!

Faerie Destiny Box Set includes all three full length novels, plus a prequel novella: Marked by Fae, Shadow of the Fae, Blood of the Fae, and Revenge of the Fae!

CLICK HERE to start reading!

NOTE FROM THE AUTHOR

Thank you for reading my book! If you have enjoyed it, please consider leaving a review. Reviews are like gold to authors and are a huge help!

They help authors get more visibility, and help readers make a decision!

And, if you'd like to stay up to date with all of my shenanigans, sign up for my newsletter today!

CLICK HERE TO SIGN UP!

Thank you!

ABOUT THE AUTHOR

USA Today bestselling author. Photographer. Artist. Born and raised in St. Petersburg, Russia, Valia Lind has always had a love for the written word. She wrote her first published book on the bathroom floor of her dormitory, while procrastinating to study for her college classes. Upon graduation, she has moved her writing to more respectable places, and has found her voice in Young Adult and cozy mysteries.

Sign up to receive updates, behind the scenes, & more!
CLICK HERE

ALSO BY VALIA LIND

The Skazka Fairy Tales

The Scarlet Rose (A Beauty and the Beast Retelling)

The Golden Slipper (A Cinderella Retelling) - coming Autumn 2022!

The Skazka Chronicles

Hardcover Omnibus - 4 books in one

Remembering Majyk (The Skazka Chronicles, #1)

Majyk Reborn (The Skazka Chronicles, #2)

The Faithful Soldier (The Skazka Chronicles, #2.5)

Majyk Reclaimed (The Skazka Chronicles, #3)

Crooked Windows Inn Cozy Mysteries

Once Upon a Witch #1

Two Can Witch the Game #2

Witch's First Zombie - FREE short story

Third Witch's the Charm #3

Witches Four the Win #4 - coming Spring 2022!

Blackwood Supernatural Prison Series

Witch Condemned (#1)

Witch Unchained (#2)

Witch Awakened (#3)

Witch Ascendant (#4)

Hawthorne Chronicles - Each season can be read as standalone!

Season Three

The Complete trilogy Boxset

Shadow of the Fae (#1)

Blood of the Fae (#2)

Revenge of the Fae (#3)

Season Two

Of Water and Moonlight (Thunderbird Academy, #1)

Of Destiny and Illusions (Thunderbird Academy, #2)

Of Storms and Triumphs (Thunderbird Academy, #3)

Season One

Guardian Witch (Hawthorne Chronicles, #1)

Witch's Fire (Hawthorne Chronicles, #2)

Witch's Heart (Hawthorne Chronicles, #3)

Tempest Witch (Hawthorne Chronicles, #4)

The Complete Season One Box Set

Havenwood Falls (PNR standalone)

Predestined

The Titanium Trilogy

Pieces of Revenge (Titanium, #1)

Scarred by Vengeance (Titanium, #2)

Ruined in Retribution (Titanium, #3)

Complete Box Set

Falling Duology - YA contemporary romance

Falling by Design

Edge of Falling

www.ingramcontent.com/pod-product-compliance
Lightning Source LLC
Chambersburg PA
CBHW060809120726
47909CB00006B/1840